Prai...
#1 *New York*... ...ing author

STEPHANIE LAURENS

"The last in the trilogy is trademark Laurens, featuring a fast-paced romance, a spunky heroine, and a very male hero, who can nevertheless be brought down by one small woman. Cynster fans will cheer as love wins the day."
Romantic Times on *The Capture of the Earl of Glencrae*

"Laurens's writing shines…"
Publishers Weekly

"Regency setting is brilliantly detailed and the romance heated and passionate."
BookPage

"Sinfully sexy and deliciously irresistible."
Booklist

A frisson of awareness streaked down her spine.

She froze. She hadn't heard anything, but she'd just proved that it was easy to move silently through the house, even without trying. And her senses, previously focused on the hall below, were belatedly screaming that someone a great deal larger than she was standing directly behind her.

Her breath caught, strangled; her lungs seized. Senses flaring, she forced herself to turn *slowly* . . .

Her gaze, level, landed on an exquisitely tied ivory silk cravat.

Roscoe watched the woman's large eyes, already wide, widen even further, then she jerked her gaze up to his face.

He didn't smile. "Can I help you, Miss . . . ?"

By Stephanie Laurens

THE LADY RISKS ALL

The Black Cobra Quartet

THE UNTAMED BRIDE • THE ELUSIVE BRIDE
THE BRAZEN BRIDE • THE RECKLESS BRIDE

The Bastion Club Novels

THE LADY CHOSEN • A GENTLEMAN'S HONOR
A LADY OF HIS OWN • A FINE PASSION
TO DISTRACTION • BEYOND SEDUCTION
THE EDGE OF DESIRE • MASTERED BY LOVE
CAPTAIN JACK'S WOMAN *(prequel)*

The Cynster Novels

DEVIL'S BRIDE
A RAKE'S VOW • SCANDAL'S BRIDE
A ROGUE'S PROPOSAL • A SECRET LOVE
ALL ABOUT LOVE • ALL ABOUT PASSION
THE PROMISE IN A KISS • ON A WILD NIGHT
ON A WICKED DAWN • THE PERFECT LOVER
THE IDEAL BRIDE • THE TRUTH ABOUT LOVE
WHAT PRICE LOVE? • THE TASTE OF INNOCENCE
WHERE THE HEART LEADS • TEMPTATION AND SURRENDER

The Cynster Sisters Trilogy

VISCOUNT BRECKENRIDGE TO THE RESCUE
IN PURSUIT OF ELIZA CYNSTER
THE CAPTURE OF THE EARL OF GLENCRAE

STEPHANIE LAURENS

The Lady Risks All

AVON

An Imprint of HarperCollinsPublishers

AVON BOOKS
An Imprint of HarperCollins*Publishers*
10 East 53rd Street
New York, New York 10022-5299

The
Lady
Risks
All

Prologue

Lord Julian Roscoe Neville Delbraith, second son of the Duke of Ridgware, was a wastrel. Indeed, profligate beyond belief, he gave the term new meaning. Tall, dark-haired, and dangerously handsome, he prowled the ton with the lazy grace of a well-bred panther whose appetites were perennially sated, as, indeed, he ensured they were. He was considered by the gentlemen to be a capital sort, one with whom many wished to claim acquaintance, while the ladies appreciated his ineffable elegance, his expertise on the dance floor, his ready charm, and his occasionally exercised rapier wit. His attire, naturally, was invariably exquisite, and his horses turned Corinthians green. Wine, women, and gaming, in reverse order, were his principal occupations, which surprised no one; the Delbraiths had a long and venerable history of spawning males with an addiction to wagering. It ran in the blood.

That said, Lucasta, Lord Julian's mother, acknowledged Savior of the Delbraiths in the recent generation, was credited with having been sufficiently strong in her handling of Marcus, Julian's father, to have preserved the family fortunes. Marcus would have liked to have gambled his income away, but Lucasta had put her foot down and vetoed it. Adamantly. More, her firstborn son, George, was the first Delbraith in generations uncounted to have escaped the family curse.

Some felt that Lucasta's sterling efforts with Marcus and George had left her with insufficient reserves to effect a similar transformation with Julian, while others considered Julian's headstrong will beyond even his mother's ability to rein in, even had she been free to concentrate solely on him. In society's eyes, Julian was the epitome of the archetypal male Delbraith.

Yet to society and the family, Julian's enthusiastic embracing of the Delbraith curse mattered not at all. George was the heir.

Large, solid, quiet, and rather stuffily reserved, unlike his younger brother, George appeared to have no vices at all. While Julian could be counted on to be flippant, irreverent, and entertaining, George stood with his hands behind his back and said as little as he could. In short, George was boring, but that, too, wasn't a concern, because, after all, George was *safe*.

Consequently, when, on Marcus's death, George succeeded to the title, the family and society smiled. They continued to smile when George contracted an eminently suitable marriage with Caroline, daughter of the Earl of Kirkcombe, a sensible young lady well-regarded within the ton.

Caroline, following her mother-in-law's lead, considered George a paragon, at least with respect to his lack of susceptibility to the family curse. That she found him significantly less of a paragon in more private arenas she kept very much to herself; outwardly, she championed George at every turn, and society nodded approvingly. Unsurprisingly therefore, Caroline had no time for the rakishly attractive, outrageously dissolute Julian; her attitude made it clear that she regarded him as a potentially corrupting influence, one she wished to keep well distanced from her husband, herself, and the child she was soon carrying.

Not at all insensitive, Julian bowed to his sister-in-law's unspoken wishes; she, after all, was his brother's duchess. His visits to the family estate, Ridgware, in Staffordshire, previously quite frequent when he would dutifully call on his mother and then stay to play with his three much younger sisters, grew further apart, eventually dwindling to rare. The great house's staff, who saw far more than anyone supposed, counted that a real shame, but no one paid their opinion any heed.

Then Caroline's baby was born and proved to be a son. Christened Henry George Neville Delbraith, the boy bore all the physical hallmarks of a true Delbraith. Viewing said signs with due concern, Caroline swore that, come hell or high water, her son would never be touched by the Delbraith curse.

On the morning of the christening, Julian arrived at the church, sat with his mother and sisters, then under Caroline's baleful eye, feeling very much like the wicked witch of the fables, he passed his entirely innocuous christening gift to his mother to convey to his nephew, and immediately the service was concluded, shook his brother's hand, civilly wished his sister-in-law and the bundle held tightly— protectively—in her arms well, and drove himself back to London.

Subsequently, Julian only called on his mother and sisters when Caroline, and preferably baby Henry, too, were not— at least at that moment—under the same roof. If George was about, Julian would look in on him, but with such dissimilar characters and the weight of the title on George's shoulders, the brothers had never had all that much in common; a comment, a shared observation, and they parted, amicably, but distantly.

Meanwhile Julian filled his life with his customary round of gambling and dissipation; cards, dice, horse racing—

anything racing—he was always willing to gauge the odds and sport his blunt accordingly. Dalliance, with Cyprians initially, but increasingly with bored matrons of his own class, filled whatever time he had to spare. His reputation as a wine connoisseur continued, but no one could recall ever seeing him in his cups. Then again, it was widely acknowledged that being three sheets to the wind while wagering large sums was never a winning proposition, and everyone knew Julian took his worship at the altar of his family's curse very seriously.

And the years rolled on.

Through those years, if any had requested enlightenment as to Lord Julian Delbraith's financial state from anyone in the ton, the answer would have been that Lord Julian was certain to be one step away from point-non-plus. From falling into the River Tick and very likely drowning. To all seasoned observers it was inconceivable that anyone could maintain such a profligate lifestyle, and wager so consistently and so extravagantly, without outrunning the constable. Gamblers always lost, if not immediately, then ultimately; everyone knew that.

Caroline, Duchess of Ridgware, certainly subscribed to that view. More, she believed her feckless brother-in-law was draining the family coffers, but whenever she attempted to raise the issue with her husband, George scowled and told her she was mistaken. When, driven by the need to protect her son's inheritance, she pressed, George's lips tightened and he coldly and categorically assured her that Julian received only the modest quarterly stipend due to him under their father's will and nothing more—that Julian had never requested further funds from the estate, not even from George personally. Caroline didn't believe it, but faced with her husband's uncharacteristic flash of temper she had to accept his word and retreat.

In actual fact, only two people knew the truth about Lord Julian's financial position—his gentlemen's gentleman, Rundle, and Jordan Draper, the son of the family's man of business. At Julian's request Jordan had assumed the handling of Julian's financial affairs, thus separating them from his brother's ducal holdings. Only those two knew that Julian was one of the Delbraiths who cropped up every third or so generation. He was one of the Delbraiths who won. He didn't win every bet, but over any period of time he always came out ahead. Not since he had, at the age of five, first discovered the joys of wagering had he ever ended a week a true loser; some weeks he only gained a farthing, but overall, he never, ever, lost money.

It fascinated Jordan Draper that no one had ever questioned why it was that a family as old as the Delbraiths, cursed with such a ruinous compulsion, had never run themselves or their estates into the ground. Through his association with Julian, Jordan knew the answer. Grandfather, father, son— over the three generations, one male at least would have the winning touch. Of course, that no longer mattered as, thanks to Lucasta and her influence on Marcus and subsequently George, the family was no longer hostage to the curse. The curse had been defeated . . . but in administering Julian's accounts and investments, Jordan had to wonder if, all in all, the family truly was better off.

Consequently, Julian's life, along with his extravagant lifestyle, rolled on largely uneventfully. He was well aware of the ton's view of him; the knowledge reinforced his natural cynicism and made him inwardly smile.

Until late one night in 1811, a knock fell on the street door of his lodgings in Duke Street.

It was November, and the weather had turned bleak. Few of the ton were still in town, which explained why Julian was sitting by his fire, his feet propped on a stool and an open book in one hand. At the knock, he'd raised his head; hearing Rundle's footsteps pass the parlor on the way to the front door, he waited, vaguely wondering—

"My lord!" Rundle burst into the room without knocking, not his usual practice. "It's Higginbotham from Ridgware."

Looking past Rundle at the senior groom from his

brother's estate, taking in the man's disheveled appearance and grave face, Julian straightened. "My mother?"

Higginbotham blinked, then shook his head. "No, m'lord. It's your brother."

"George?" Julian couldn't imagine why George would have sent Higginbotham racing to town to summon him, the wastrel younger brother. "What's he want?"

Higginbotham looked like he'd swallowed his tongue, but then he shook his head again. "His Grace don't want anything. He put a pistol to his head and pulled the trigger. He's dead. We think you'd better come."

Julian drove like the devil and reached Ridgware midmorning. Leaving his phaeton in the stable yard, he crossed to the house, entering via the side door. A pall had fallen over the mansion; the silence was oppressive. His footsteps echoed as he walked onto the tiles of the front hall. For a moment he stood silently, at a loss. Higginbotham had known nothing of what had driven George to such a rash and irreversible act. To an act so out of character.

To an act so *inexplicable.*

A sound down one corridor had Julian turning.

From the shadows, an older man in a fastidiously neat dark suit emerged. "Thank you for coming so promptly, my lord."

Lips tight, Julian nodded. "Draper." This was Draper senior, his brother's man of business, Jordan's father. The Draper offices were in Derby, much nearer than London. Julian searched Draper's face. "Do you have any idea why George . . . I still can't believe it . . . why he took his life?"

Sober and solemn, Draper nodded; he looked pale, worn down—significantly more aged than Julian remembered him. "Sadly, my lord, I do. That's why I was relieved the staff had taken it upon themselves to send for you. This is a bad business, and we'll need decisions made quickly if we're to protect the family."

"Protect . . . ?" Julian frowned. "I don't understand."

"I know." Draper waved down the corridor. "If you will come to the office, I'll endeavor to explain."

Julian hesitated. "My mother?"

"Prostrated by the shock, as is the duchess, but the doctor was here yesterday and both were sedated. I'm told they might wake in a few hours."

"My sisters? And Henry? Good God, the poor boy's the duke now."

"Indeed, but the staff have the young people well in hand, and I fear . . ." Draper broke off and rubbed his forehead. "I fear our discussion won't wait, my lord. In such a situation, time is of the essence."

Draper was a solid man, a steady, unruffleable, conscientious man, which was one reason Julian had chosen his son as his own man of affairs. Growing even more puzzled— more alarmed—Julian nodded. "Very well." He gestured. "Lead on."

Following Draper down the corridor, he asked, "When did it happen?"

"Yesterday morning, my lord. The staff heard the shot at eleven o'clock, I believe. They had to break down the library door, but of course there was nothing they could do."

Julian had had time to think during the long hours of the drive. "How many others know of George's death?"

"At the moment, my lord, I believe the knowledge is restricted to the indoor staff, the stable staff, and the family. And the doctor and myself, of course."

"So we have a chance of concealing the suicide." His first thought was for his sisters, his mother, for Henry, and even for his sister-in-law; a suicide in the family, whatever the reason, cast a long social shadow.

Draper hesitated before saying, "Possibly." He didn't sound at all certain.

Julian followed Draper into the estate office.

Draper waved him to the chair behind the desk. "It will make it easier for me to show you the accounts."

"Accounts?" Lowering himself into the chair, Julian frowned. "Why do I need to see the accounts?"

Lifting a heavy ledger from a shelf, Draper turned and met his gaze. "I regret to inform you, my lord, that your brother wasn't, as was generally supposed, immune to the Delbraith curse."

"Hell's *bells*!" Julian speared the fingers of both hands through his hair and stared at the evidence of George's addiction. In the past half hour, Draper had laid ledger after ledger before him, driving home one very simple fact.

George had succeeded where all Delbraiths before him had failed. He'd run the estate into the ground, then had compounded the damage by mortgaging every last asset to the hilt.

Lowering his hands, Julian sat back. "All right." His mind was whirling, juggling figures and sums, chances and possibilities. He now understood why Draper had wanted him there. "Tot up the sum. All of it. And send for Jordan—tell him to bring all my current accounts."

"Yes, my lord." Draper hesitated, then admitted, "I took it upon myself to send for Jordan earlier—he should arrive within the hour."

Julian raised his gaze to the older man's face. "That was strangely presumptuous of you." He said it without heat, more as a question.

Draper met his gaze. "I apologize, my lord, but I've known you and your brother since you were infants. I knew the family could count on your help, and, as I've said, we—"

"Don't have time." Julian grimaced, then nodded curtly. "Very well." He pushed back his chair. "I'm going up to see my sisters. Send for me when Jordan arrives."

He found Millicent, Cassandra, and Edwina in the small upstairs parlor they used as their own. They'd been informed that George had died, but they had been told nothing else. However, having heard the shot and witnessed the resulting furor, they were more than capable of putting two and two together.

"He killed himself, didn't he?" Millicent, fourteen years old and bidding fair to becoming another Lucasta, sat sideways along the window seat, knees to her chest, and cut straight to the heart of the matter.

Having exchanged kisses and longer-and-tighter-than-usual hugs with all three, Julian sat on the cushion beyond Millicent's toes and hesitated, wondering what he could spare them, whether he should . . .

Cassie, eleven, snorted. "Just *tell* us—you know we'll get it out of the staff if you don't."

Julian sighed and complied, keeping an eye on Edwina, just ten, to make sure nothing he said was too much of a shock.

"But . . . why?" Millicent frowned. "It's a thoroughly horrible thing to do—he must have had a reason."

This was the tricky part. "I understand from Draper that George had begun gambling. It seems the curse had caught up with him, and rather than risk the estate and his family, George . . . well, he put a stop to it."

Julian hoped they would swallow the white lie.

All three frowned, considering, then Cassie humphed. "That sounds like George. So stuffy that he couldn't bear asking you for help." Cassie turned her gray eyes on Julian. "You've been living with the curse all your life and it's never hurt you—and you've never hurt the estate or the family, either."

He managed a weak smile. "Sadly, George wasn't me."

"No." Millie swung her legs down and briefly clasped his arm. "You're made of much sterner stuff. But what about the taint? Of suicide, I mean?"

"You don't need to worry about that. The doctor left a note saying that in the circumstances he would suggest we put it about that George died suddenly and unexpectedly of apoplexy."

The three thought for a moment, then Edwina said, "Well,

then, I suppose what we need to do next is get some mourning clothes so we can see George off in proper style."

Millie grimaced. "True. He might have been an idiot, but he was our noble idiot and he sacrificed himself for us, so we should at least do him proud in the matter of his funeral."

From the corner of his eye, Julian spotted a gig, driven by Jordan Draper, come bowling up the drive.

"We should go and talk to Mama," Cassie said. "Discussing clothes might cheer her up, or at least take her mind off the manner of George's passing." She looked at Julian. "Have you seen her yet?"

"No. Not yet." He paused, then said, "Why don't you three go and distract her, and tell her I'm here, and that I'll be up to speak with her as soon as I can?" He rose along with the girls. "I have to go and sort things out with Draper, just to get everything squared away. Tell Mama I'll come up as soon as I've finished."

His sisters nodded and hugged him again, then they all quit the parlor. Parting from the girls in the corridor, Julian surreptitiously sighed with relief; that had gone better than he'd hoped.

He spent the next hours with the Drapers, father and son, then they were joined by Minchinbury, the family solicitor. The office was crowded with all four of them in it, but no one suggested they take their discussions into a less secure and well-shielded room.

Minchinbury confirmed that George's will named Julian as sole executor, and also joint guardian of three-year-old Henry. In regard to the latter, Julian merely nodded and set that problem aside for later; one hellish scenario at a time.

"There's no way around it," Jordan eventually concluded. "No matter how we structure payments, even if we liquidate every saleable unentailed asset and devote the entirety of the estate income to said payments, the outgoings still far exceed the duke's ability to pay."

While they'd been going over the horrendous figures, a

plan had taken shape in Julian's mind. It was beyond outrageous, but outrageous was something he did well. Across the desk, he met Jordan's eyes. "Factor in my funds—all of them. Liquidate my assets, all of them, and add them in, too—reduce the capital owed. Leave me . . ." He considered, then said, "Ten thousand in cash. Assume an ongoing income through me of . . ." That took a little longer to calculate, but eventually he named a sum.

Draper and Minchinbury looked startled, but Jordan only grimaced, jotted down the figures, and started reworking the complex web of mortgage and loan repayments again.

While he did, Draper and Minchinbury traded looks . . . and slowly worked out Julian's direction. It was Minchinbury who, faintly shocked, finally looked at Julian. "My lord . . . what are you planning?"

Julian held up a finger and patiently waited while Jordan did his sums.

Eventually, Jordan blew out a breath. "We're close. Just a whisker in it." He looked at Julian. "You could pull it off."

Julian hadn't needed to explain to Jordan what he was thinking of doing; Jordan had worked for him for long enough to guess what he might, and could, do, but he was grateful for the younger man's unequivocal support. "You've included the running of this house and the estate in general, the usual payments to my mother, the girls, and the duchess, and left the girls' portions intact?"

"Well, the girls' portions are already long gone," Jordan said, "but that will return them to their previous amounts by the time each of them reach sixteen. I've also included an escalating amount for Henry in the years to come, starting from his fifth birthday."

"Good man." Julian paused to gather his arguments, then transferred his gaze to Draper and Minchinbury. "What I'm proposing to do, gentlemen, is this."

He told them his plan, the whole of it; if he was to succeed in saving the Delbraiths—family, title, and estate—he needed them on his side. At first, they were shocked, then aghast as the full ramifications of what he was proposing came clear in their minds, but finally, like Jordan, they, too, accepted that, when it came to it, he had no other choice.

George had taken the easy way out and left Julian to rescue the Delbraiths.

His interview with his mother was difficult, not least because Lucasta was inclined to blame herself for George's disgrace.

Seated in an armchair angled before the wide window in her sitting room, a still handsome woman with graying hair pulled back from a grief-stricken face, she clenched a damp handkerchief in one fist. "I should have seen it! I can't *believe* I missed the signs."

Contrary to general assumptions, Julian got along well with his mother; they were much alike when it came to will. They'd long ago reached an accommodation; Lucasta didn't try to push him, and he didn't push back.

Standing gazing out over the rolling lawns to the trees of the home wood, he sighed. "Mama, if *I* didn't see anything, there wasn't anything to be seen. He was . . . excellent at hiding it."

"He deceived us. He *betrayed* us." After a moment, in a quieter voice, Lucasta asked, "For how long?"

Julian hesitated, but he knew better than to try to lie to her. Turning, he said, "According to Draper, since he started at Eton, but initially the amounts were small enough not to alert Papa or you. Only after he inherited did he start wagering larger sums."

Helplessly, Lucasta shook her head. "You never heard any whisper?"

"No." Which said a great deal about what establishments George had frequented. Any socially accepted hell, and Julian would have heard of it, so George had slid into the underworld to sate his addiction.

Slowly, Lucasta drew in a deep breath, then exhaled and raised her chin. "What's done is done. We'll do as Doctor

Melrose suggested—George died of an apoplexy. We'll bury him with all due circumstance. And then"—she looked at Julian—"we'll pick up the pieces and rebuild." She paused, eyes narrowing on him. "So." She heaved a tight sigh. "Given George blew out his brains rather than face the consequences, tell me—how bad is it?"

He didn't try to soften the news—pointless where she was concerned. His mother had always been fierce in defense of her family; she would detect any prevarication and, terrier-like, drag the truth from him. So he drew up another armchair, sat and told her all, and when the shock, unsurprisingly, held her stunned and silent, he smoothly continued, "I've spoken with the Drapers, both of them, and with Minchinbury, and worked out a plan. It's desperate, but for us these are desperate times. They've agreed that it's our only possible way forward—we've canvassed every other course, and none will get us through this except what I propose."

She looked him in the eye. "I'm not going to like your plan, am I?"

"No, but it is the only plan we have." He proceeded to tell her the whole of it.

She heard him out in silence.

Then they argued.

That he'd expected; he held to his guns and eventually, bit by bit, inch by inch, she backed down.

Except, to his surprise, over one aspect, and on that she wouldn't budge, wouldn't shift, would not concede.

"I have lost one son—I will not lose you, too. *No!*" She held up a hand. "I appreciate that to be successful your plan makes open association impossible, *but*"—she fixed her eyes on his—"you will continue to visit this house, to visit me and your sisters. They are my daughters and are as capable of keeping your secrets as I am. You will *not* cut yourself off from us—and I assure you we will not let you go." Her eyes filled. "That, my dear, is something you cannot ask of us. If your plan is to succeed, you will need to factor that in."

He hadn't expected such a vehement reaction. Searching her face, knowing her adamantine will, he reconsidered, then nodded. "Very well. But my visits will be, for want of a better word, furtive."

"Secret." She nodded. "You know the staff will do anything for you, so that won't be a problem."

"The girls . . ." He grimaced. "I'll leave it to you to tell them—you'll know better than I how to put it, and I don't have time for the inevitable arguments and explanations. Jordan and I must leave for London as soon as possible. If we're to paper over the gaping holes George has left in the family's financial façade, we need to act immediately."

Lucasta's eyes searched his face, then she quietly asked, "And Caroline? I'll explain to her if you wish."

Lips thinning, he shook his head. "No—I'll speak with her. She's Henry's other guardian. She and I are going to have to find a way to work together, for Henry's sake if nothing else."

He rose.

Lucasta rose, too, gripped his arm, and stretched up to plant a kiss on his cheek. "Go, my dear. I know you must."

She released him and turned away, but not before he saw a tear slide down her cheek.

His interview with his sister-in-law set the seal on a long and horrendous day.

As he approached her suite, he saw Draper and Minchinbury emerge from Caroline's sitting room. They closed the door behind them and came along the gallery. When he and the pair met, they all halted.

Minchinbury spoke. "I've explained the terms of the will to the duchess. She understands that you are sole executor and also her son's co-guardian, and comprehends the rights that are yours by virtue of those facts."

Julian felt his lips twist. "And how did she take that news?"

Minchinbury grimaced. "Not well, but she had to be told. At least she now knows and understands the situation."

"We also informed her of the financial straits the late duke left behind." Draper's lips primmed. "I explained that, contrary to her long-held belief, you have never drained any undue resources from the estate, and that the current situation has arisen entirely through the late duke's depredations. We did not, of course, venture to explain your plan, although we did allude to the fact that you had one, and that, given the situation, we believe it is the only route by which the family, and indeed the dukedom, can be saved from financial devastation."

Julian looked from one to the other. "Let me see if I understand this correctly—you've left the duchess knowing that whatever I propose, she must agree if she wishes to save herself and her son from ruin?"

Both men thought, then both nodded. "We"—Minchinbury flicked a glance at Draper—"have been privy to the duchess's view of you, my lord, and considered it our duty to clarify matters for Her Grace so that your words should fall on more fertile soil."

Draper nodded. "Least we could do to assist you with your plan."

Julian inclined his head. "Thank you, gentlemen. I appreciate your assistance."

Both bowed and stepped back. Minchinbury said, "If you need any assistance subsequently, my lord, please know you have only to ask."

Julian nodded and continued along the corridor. Reaching Caroline's sitting room, he didn't pause to let himself think but tapped on the door. Hearing a muffled "Come," he turned the knob and entered.

Caroline was standing with her back to the window, her arms wrapped tightly about her. Inclining his head, Julian closed the door, then walked toward her. "My condolences. I would it were otherwise, but we have to talk." Halting a yard away, he met her blue eyes. "Minchinbury and Draper told me they'd explained the situation. Is there anything about it you don't understand?" He kept his tone even, uninflected and distantly polite.

Her face stripped of all masks, Caroline stared up at him; he could see the emotions, the questions, the rage, roiling behind her eyes. In the end, she rasped out one word, hoarse and ragged. "*Why?*"

Julian shook his head. "He couldn't help himself."

"But—" She broke off, then waved a hand and looked away. "I can't . . ." She hauled in a breath and, lifting her head, continued without looking at him. "I'm still finding it hard to . . . accept that, for all these years, while I've been imagining you the villain, it was him all along."

Julian frowned. "You suspected?"

"Not him." She laughed harshly. "Never him. But some of my jewelry—it's paste, not real. Even some of what used to be real is now paste." She glanced at Julian. "I thought he'd used the jewels to pay your debts, perhaps thinking that I would never notice the difference in the stones, and that in his mind that was better than drawing from the estate—" Her breath hitched and she swung away. "Oh, you needn't tell me—I can't believe how stupid I've been."

He didn't have time for hysterics, even of this sort. "Caroline—if I'm to avert financial catastrophe, I need to act quickly."

She cast him a bitter glance. "According to Minchinbury and Draper, I have no choice but to allow you to do whatever you wish, not if I want to continue to live here in comfort with Henry, or for my son to have any kind of future at all."

This was the downside of the older men's well-intentioned interference. "In that, they're correct, but what they didn't make clear was that for my plan to succeed, you, too, need to play a part. And for that, you need to know what the plan is."

Caroline considered him for a long moment, then settled on her feet facing him, arms tightly folded, and nodded. "All right. Tell me your plan."

She didn't sit, much less invite him to. So he stood and told her his plan.

When he'd finished, she stared all but openmouthed at him.

After a minute ticked by, he baldly asked, "Well? Will you do your part? Play the role you obviously have to play to carry the fiction off?"

She blinked, stared again. "I . . . don't understand."

His temper was getting the better of him. "It's a simple enough question. Will you—"

"No, not that. I . . ." She lowered her arms and drew a huge breath. She paused for a second, then, her gaze on his face, said, "You're proposing to sacrifice yourself. *Why*? That's what I don't understand—what I don't trust. If I accept this plan of yours and actively support it, I'll be placing myself, and even more my son and his future, in utterly insurmountable debt to you."

He thought, then nodded. "True."

She laughed, a broken, discordant sound, and turned away.

"Caroline." By main force, he kept his tone even, calm. "Are you really proposing to let your pride dictate your actions even now, and to reject my help?"

She glanced at him, met his eyes.

A distant, high-pitched shriek reached him—a sound of happiness, not despair. Glancing through the window, he saw his sisters and Henry come out of the wood. They'd been for a walk and were returning, Millie and Cassie swinging a delighted Henry between them. He was only three; the reality of his father's death hadn't yet touched him. Two footmen and a nursemaid followed behind, talking quietly while they watched over the foursome.

Julian looked at Caroline. He was much taller; she couldn't see what he could.

Although tempted to grasp her arm and haul her across, he beckoned to her and stepped closer to the window. "You want to know why I'm doing this?" When she joined him, he pointed at the group below. "That's why. None of the four down there—hell, none of the seven—have done anything to deserve the future they will have if I don't act to fix this. And there is only one way."

He watched her watching her son and let that sink in.

After a moment, she moistened her lips and more quietly asked, "No other way?"

He hesitated, then said, "The Delbraith curse got the family into this. It's only right that the Delbraith curse get us out of it again."

"But at what cost?"

"Regardless of the cost. And, ultimately, that's my decision to make, not yours."

She continued watching for a moment more, then her features firmed and she nodded. "All right. I agree. I'll do whatever I have to to . . . shore up the situation."

One hurdle down. He drew breath, metaphorically girded his loins, and approached the next, the even higher and more thorny one. "Speaking of the curse, I have one stipulation which is entirely nonnegotiable. In return for acting as I must to save the family—yourself and Henry included—you will ensure that Henry knows the truth about his father's death, that it's never hidden from him."

"*What*?" Caroline swung to face him. "You can't be serious! He's a baby—"

"Not now, obviously. I mean as soon as he's old enough to know—to ask. Because he will. I don't want you hiding the curse from him." He held her gaze. "I'm not doing what I'm about to do only to have you encourage him to think he's immune to the curse and so throw everything away the instant he reaches his majority." She opened her mouth. Julian pointed a finger at her nose and spoke first. "What's more, when I come to visit, as his guardian I'll expect to meet him, to talk with him. You can be present if you wish, but I will speak with him."

Caroline's face set. "No. I won't have you—"

"Caroline." The steel in his voice cut her off. He held her

gaze and ruthlessly stated, "Neither you nor Mama saw the curse in George. Try to 'protect' Henry, and you'll make the same mistake Mama made with George. The curse will still bite, but he'll hide it. If he does, you won't see it. I will because I know what to look for—and I assure you that with Henry, I'll be watching." He searched her eyes. "Understand this—the curse is real. It's an inherited disease—if Henry gets help, the right help, it can be managed. Pretend it's not there and it will eat him alive, just as it did George."

"And what about you?" Caroline produced a credible sneer. "Is your addiction so well managed then?"

He was silent for a moment, then said, "As things stand, my addiction is what's going to stand between you and Henry and the poorhouse. Think about that before you dismiss my use of it. Also as things stand, I'm the only one living who has personal experience of the curse—who knows what Henry will face as he grows, who knows the tricks of dealing with the compulsion." He paused for a moment, his eyes locked with hers, then more quietly said, "I know this is hard for you to accept, but as matters stand, I am Henry's only hope for a future, both financially and personally."

Until he'd said the words, he hadn't realized how true they were—how much responsibility he was taking on.

Not that it mattered; in this he had no choice.

When Caroline said nothing, simply chewed her lower lip and looked shaken and lost, he stepped back and turned to the door. With his hand on the knob, he paused, then glanced back at her. "Don't risk your son, Caroline—if you want to keep him safe, you'll do exactly as I've said."

She swung to face the window and didn't reply.

Julian opened the door and left.

Half an hour later, having bid good-bye to his sisters and his small nephew, Julian tooled his phaeton down the long drive, then whipped up his horses and headed for London.

In the small hours of the morning, he drew rein outside the stables near his lodgings. Handing over the ribbons to a sleepy stable lad, Julian walked slowly out into the street.

Sinking his hands into his greatcoat pockets, through the quiet darkness, he strolled toward Duke Street, and finally allowed himself to think of what he was about to do, something he'd refused to dwell on during the long journey; the activity smacked too much of a dying man's last thoughts.

Reaching his lodgings, he climbed the steps, put his key to the lock, and opened the door.

Stepping inside, he shut the door.

And his life as Lord Julian Delbraith was, quite simply, no more.

Chapter One

October 1823, twelve years later
London

Miranda Clifford halted in the deep shadows cast by a stand of trees and watched her younger brother, Roderick, stride across a manicured lawn toward a massive mansion glowing pearly white in the moonlight.

About her, stretching away to either side, the thick bushes and mature trees of established gardens enfolded the house in a lush embrace. The breeze was a mere whisper, a soughing sigh stirring the tiny tendrils of hair that had come loose from her chignon to drift over her nape.

Silent and still, her gaze fixed on Roderick, she watched as he reached a shallow terrace and without hesitation strode up the three steps and went straight to a glass-paned door. Opening the door, Roderick stepped inside, closing the door behind him.

"Damn and *blast*!" Miranda stared at the door. This was far worse than she'd thought.

She'd first realized Roderick was secretly slipping out of

the house at night three weeks ago. She'd told herself that unannounced and unmentioned nighttime excursions were only to be expected in a twenty-three-year-old gentleman, but she'd spent the last twenty-three years protecting Roderick; denying such long-ingrained instincts was difficult. Sufficiently so that she'd made a pact with herself—she would follow him one night, just far enough to assure herself that wherever he was going, whatever he was doing, he wasn't putting himself at risk in any way.

It wasn't that she didn't trust him; her plan was purely to reassure herself. She would learn just enough to appease her instinctive anxiety, then she'd go home and Roderick would never know.

Ten minutes ago, she'd followed him down the darkened stairs of the house they shared with their aunt in Claverton Street, Pimlico; the hands of the long case clock on the landing had put the time at twenty minutes short of eleven o'clock. She'd trailed Roderick through the morning room, across the side lawn, and out of the garden gate into the alley. Clutching her reticule and her new fashionable short cape close, she'd hugged the shadows along the alley walls, and like a shadow herself had flitted in his wake, puzzled when he'd stuck to the alleyways, until, to her considerable surprise, five minutes' brisk walking from their own garden gate, he'd stopped at another gate set in a high stone wall.

He'd opened the gate and gone in. She'd hesitated for only an instant before following.

She hadn't known whose rear garden she was creeping through, not at first, but once she'd seen the house, once she'd been able to take in its size and magnificence, and most especially that telltale color . . . "What the devil is he doing visiting Neville Roscoe's house?"

The question needed only to be asked to be answered. Neville Roscoe was the most celebrated—as in infamous and notorious—denizen of the neighborhood. He was London's acknowledged gambling king, the owner of a vast array of hells, dens, and clubs catering to the wealthy, the affluent, the aristocratic; gambling was one of society's favorite vices, and Roscoe was, by all accounts, a past master at supplying exactly the right drug to sate society's craving.

Roscoe was known to be immensely wealthy and also to wield significant power, both in his own arena and in murkier spheres. He wasn't, however, considered a criminal. Instead, he inhabited a nebulous strata between society and the underworld; he could rub shoulders with dukes one day, crime lords the next, and yet remain free of both worlds.

Speaking generally, Roscoe was an enigma, and very much a law unto himself.

He'd already been living in the huge white mansion on Chichester Street, overlooking the treed expanse of Dolphin Square to the Thames beyond, when Roderick had bought the house in Claverton Street, just around the corner, a year ago. Miranda had heard all about the neighborhood's most famous citizen within days of taking up residence.

She hadn't, however, as yet set eyes on him, but she had no ambition to do so.

"Wretched man." She wasn't sure if she was speaking of Roderick or Roscoe; that Roderick might wish to chance his hand at gambling wasn't such a surprise, but . . . her lips thinned. "He can't afford to become involved with Roscoe."

It wasn't that Roderick couldn't afford to gamble; even at Roscoe's level, he most definitely could. But his wealth derived from trade, and as she and he had been taught all their lives, that meant that, far more than others born more acceptably, they had to cling, rigidly and beyond question, to respectability.

Seeing Roderick walk into Roscoe's house had instantly evoked the specter of their elder sister, Rosalind. The three of them had been orphaned as children; with Miranda and Roderick, Rosalind had grown up in the care of their aunts. Rosalind had been subjected to the same lectures on respectability, the same unbending strictures, but when she'd reached sixteen, Rosalind had rebelled. She'd run off with gypsies, only to return two years later, diseased and dying.

Rosalind had died tragically, just like their mother, who had eloped with their father, the son of a mill owner.

Every time anyone in their family stepped off the path of rigid respectability, disaster and death followed. Miranda didn't want Roderick to die young, much less tragically; returning home and leaving him to his fate wasn't in any way an acceptable option.

Keeping to the shadows, she circled the lawn, making for the house and that glass-paned door. Her mind threw up images of what she might find inside—a private gambling party or . . . an orgy? From all she'd heard, she might stumble into either. Women were invariably a part of Roscoe's entertainments; his clubs were renowned for their large female staffs.

"With luck, I'll pass, at least for long enough." She was old enough, looked experienced enough. Reaching the terrace, she glanced down at the lilac twill walking dress she wore under her cape. It was hardly evening wear but was elegant enough to establish her class. Regardless, she wasn't about to retreat. She didn't intend remaining for longer than it took to find Roderick and catch his eye; that would be enough to shock him to his senses, after which he would walk her home.

Crossing the terrace, she opened the door and stepped inside. A corridor wreathed in dark shadows stretched before her. Quietly shutting the door, she registered the oddity of the pervasive silence, of the dark, unlit rooms. Even from the other side of the lawn, where the entire back of the house had been visible, she hadn't noticed any lighted windows, any sign of a party, no matter how refined. Halting, she let her senses stretch.

The ground on which the house stood sloped sharply down to Chichester Street, leaving the rear garden elevated. The floor she'd entered on was in fact the first, not the ground floor, which fronted the street. Presumably the party, the gathering, whatever it was, was being held in a reception room on the ground floor. She strained her ears for some sound to show her the way, but heard nothing.

Puzzled, she started along the corridor. Roderick must have gone that way; other than the occasional room to either side, all silent, their doors shut with no light showing beneath, there was nowhere else to go. She followed the corridor toward the front of the house, step by step growing more aware of an omnipresent sense of quality and solidity. The house wasn't old. Roscoe had had it built for him, which presumably explained the workmanship she sensed more than saw; there was an understated elegance in every line, complemented by luxurious finishes and furnishings. She didn't have time to stop and peer, but the paintings on the walls, each perfectly framed, looked to be originals, and not by any back alley artist, either.

She wondered if the solidity of the house explained the lack of noise. That, and the furnishings; the runner on which she was walking was so thick she couldn't hear her own footsteps.

The corridor opened into a wide semicircular space, a gallery of sorts circling the well of the main stairs. Pausing inside the corridor's mouth, she peeked right, then left. Three other corridors gave onto the gallery, but silence prevailed. No lamps were burning, either, the space lit only by weak moonlight washing through a domed skylight high above and a large window directly opposite; through the latter she could see the tops of the trees in Dolphin Square and the distant shimmer of moonlight on the river.

Directly ahead, in front of the large window, lay the head of the wide staircase that swept elegantly down.

Drawing in a breath, she raised her head, walked calmly toward the stairs, and finally heard the rumble of male voices. Those speaking were somewhere on the ground floor, but deeper in the house, still some way away.

The clacking of hooves on the cobbles outside drew her to the window. Looking out and down, she saw a gentleman,

fashionably dressed and hatted, alight from a hackney. The
man carried a silver-headed cane. He paid off the jarvey,
then walked toward the front door of the mansion, a little
further along the façade from where she stood.

She didn't recognize the man, but his style, the way he
moved, suggested he belonged to the upper echelons of the
ton.

A bell pealed within the house. Almost immediately the
measured tread of a butler's footsteps crossed the tiles in the
front hall below. She debated going to the head of the stairs
and looking down, but the risk of being seen was too great;
she stayed where she was and listened.

"Good evening, my lord."

"Good evening, Rundle." The visitor stepped inside; the
door shut. "I fear I'm late. Are the others here?"

"Yes, my lord, but the master has yet to join the gathering."

"Excellent." Rustlings reached her as the visitor divested
himself of his overcoat, gloves, hat, and cane. "I won't have
missed anything, then."

"Indeed not, my lord."

"The library, as usual?"

"Yes, my lord."

"No need to bestir yourself, Rundle—I know the way."

"Thank you, my lord."

Two pairs of footsteps strode away from the hall, going in
different directions. She hurried to the head of the stairs; she
was too late to see which way each man went, but a door at
the hall's rear was still swinging. The butler must have gone
that way, which meant the visitor's footsteps were the ones
fading down the corridor leading away from one corner of
the hall. The library and the "gathering" lay in that direction.

Drawing in a breath, she reached for the stair rail—

A frisson of awareness streaked down her spine.

She froze. She hadn't heard anything, but she'd just proved
that it was easy to move silently through the house, even
without trying. And her senses, previously focused on the

hall below, were belatedly screaming that someone a great deal larger than she was standing directly behind her.

Her breath caught, strangled; her lungs seized. Senses flaring, she forced herself to turn *slowly* . . .

Her gaze, level, landed on an exquisitely tied ivory silk cravat.

Roscoe watched the woman's large eyes, already wide, widen even further, then she jerked her gaze up to his face.

He didn't smile. "Can I help you, Miss . . . ?"

She didn't immediately reply, but he didn't make the mistake of thinking her mind paralyzed by shock; swift calculation showed in those wide eyes as she debated her response. Fine-boned, graceful, and quintessentially feminine though she might be, he was accustomed to sizing up people with a glance and didn't need to look further than the refined strength in her face, echoed in her upright carriage and the gliding stride he'd glimpsed when he'd first seen her crossing the gallery, to guess what manner of lady she was.

Determined, resolute, and, at least when it came to those things she believed in, unbending.

Consequently, he was unsurprised when she drew in a tight breath, straightened to her full, significantly taller than the average height, and haughtily stated, "My name is Miss Clifford."

The information very nearly made him blink.

Her gaze drifted from his face, skating over his shoulders and chest to land on the ledger he carried in one hand. A frown crimped her finely arched brows. "And you are?"

Her tone made it clear she thought him some lowly secretary. Despite his intentions, his lips quirked. "I'm the owner of this establishment."

Apparently, that news was more of a shock than discovering him at her back. She stared, patently stunned and making no effort to hide it. "*You're* Roscoe?"

He could imagine the speculation she'd heard; an inner devil prompted him to further confound her. He bowed, imbuing the gesture with all the grace he'd once exercised daily. Straightening, he drawled, "I would welcome you to my humble abode, Miss Clifford, only I have to wonder why you're here."

"*Humble* abode?" Her voice was husky, the tone a low contralto. Her gaze flashed to the three paintings hanging on the walls between the corridors—two Gainsboroughs and a Reynolds—then shifted to the large Gobelin tapestry on the wall behind him. "For a gambling king, sir, you have remarkable taste."

Interesting that she'd noticed, but he didn't distract that easily. "Indeed. But that doesn't answer my question."

Miranda was frantically assessing a different question: how to get out of this without a whisper of scandal. While most of her mind wrestled with that problem, the rest was thoroughly distracted; she hadn't had any mental image of Roscoe, but not in her wildest dreams would she have imagined him as he was. As he stood before her.

He was tall, significantly taller than she was, but his shoulders, chest, and long, muscled limbs were in perfect proportion, creating an elegance of form that simply took her breath away. His attire, too, wasn't what she would have associated with a gambling king; in a superbly tailored dark coat over pristine ivory linen, with that gorgeously tied cravat, a subdued blue, gray, and black striped waistcoat with simple black buttons, and plain black trousers, he could give any ton exquisite points and he would still come out ahead.

As for the way he moved, and that drawl . . . quite what manner of man he was she wasn't sure, but a single glance into that chiseled face, at those well-set dark eyes steadily regarding her, at his patriarchal nose and sharply cut jaw, was enough to assure her that he wasn't manageable. More, that he was dangerous, on multiple levels and in complex ways.

The man who stood before her was a conundrum.

She had no experience dealing with such as he, but following her instincts had got her into this—perhaps they'd get her out. Tipping her chin higher, she held to her hauteur. "I'm here to rescue my brother."

One dark brow slowly arched. "Rescue?"

Undefined warning shaded the word. She ignored it. "Precisely. You cannot be so distanced from the polite world not to know that association with a man of your . . . propensities would be ruinous for my brother, should such an association become widely known."

No reaction showed in the hard planes of his face. An instant ticked by, then he said, "My propensities?"

She refused to be intimidated. "Your business. Your activities." She glanced at the front hall, then looked at him. "I'm unsure what form of entertainment you and your patrons are indulging in tonight, but if you would be so good as to let Mr. Clifford know that I am here and require his escort home, you will not be troubled by either him or me again."

Far from showing any inclination to accede to her request, he regarded her steadily, his dark eyes—she couldn't tell what color they were, but she didn't think they were black—studying her eyes, her face. His expression was unreadable, utterly uninterpretable.

"Tell me, Miss Clifford," he eventually said, his deep drawl almost a purr, "just what forms of entertainment do you imagine I provide for my . . . close acquaintances in the privacy of my home?"

Yes, she was in the wrong venturing into his house like this, but she'd be damned if she allowed a gambling king to patronize her. "I have no idea, and less interest, but the two that leapt to mind when I realized that Roderick was coming here were a private gambling party, or else an orgy. Regardless, I believe attending will not be in my brother's best interests, just as I know that associating with you will definitely not be to his advantage."

His heavy lids flickered, fleetingly screening his eyes. "Are you accusing me of corrupting your brother, Miss Clifford?"

She refused to quake at his quietly steely tone. "Are you?"

"No." But she wasn't the first lady to view him as a corrupter of innocents; perhaps that long-ago echo was why Roscoe felt compelled to prove her wrong. To open her eyes to her misjudgment of him, to make her acknowledge it, and apologize, now, tonight.

He wasn't normally so sensitive; some part of his mind found it strange that she, a lady he hadn't previously met, had so quickly got under his skin sufficiently to needle him in such a very private spot. A spot he was surprised to discover still tender. Regardless . . .

"I suggest, Miss Clifford, that you come with me." Stepping back, he waved her to the corridor leading off the far end of the gallery.

She viewed the corridor with open suspicion. "Why? I can just as well wait here until you send Roderick to me."

"Ah, but I have no intention of embarrassing your brother in such a way." He started strolling toward the corridor.

Three strides, and she huffed out a breath and came after him. "Where are we going?"

"To a place from where you can watch our proceedings without any of my guests being aware of it."

"No!" She halted.

When he didn't stop walking, she hurried to catch up, then tipped up her chin and breathlessly amended, "That is, there's no need for me to see—"

"Oh, but there is." He kept his expression utterly impassive, but inside he was smiling.

Reaching a door set in the paneled wall, his hand on the knob, he halted and faced her. "You would have to possess a remarkably peculiar view of such things to imagine I would host an orgy in my library."

She blinked. "I would?"

"Trust me—I hold no orgies in my library. So the worst you're going to see is eight men gambling, although in fact it won't even be that." He met her gaze, open challenge in his eyes. "You followed your brother here intent on discovering what he was about—are you going to turn tail and run at this point, or are you brave enough to face the truth?"

He was enjoying himself, and despite his best efforts some glimmer must have shown. Her eyes slowly narrowed, then, lips firming, she nodded. "Very well. Show me."

Opening the door, he waved her in.

Head high, she stepped over the threshold. He followed her into the first-floor gallery that circled the library proper, on the ground floor.

She clung to the shadows by the book-lined walls, staring down at the seven gentlemen seated about the central table. Ledgers and notebooks at the ready, they were waiting for him to open the meeting, meanwhile trading the usual social conversation gentlemen of their ilk used to pass the time.

The gallery was thickly carpeted, allowing Miss Clifford and him to move without attracting attention. Lifting a large armchair, he set it down by the gallery railing and waved her to it.

She hesitated, then crept forward and sat. He waited while she settled her cape and set her reticule in her lap, then, standing behind the chair, he leaned over her and whispered by her ear, "Unless you stand up, they won't see you. Unless you make a loud noise, they won't hear you. You, however, can see, and you'll be able to hear every word said about that table."

Ruthlessly suppressing the intense, unprecedented, and unnerving sensations that deep voice murmuring in her ear, his breath stirring the tiny tendrils of hair dangling about her nape, evoked, Miranda tuned her ears to the conversations about the table and discovered he was right. The gallery was perfectly positioned acoustically; she could easily make out all that was said, even though the men were speaking relatively quietly.

Roscoe was still hovering over her—close, too close; his warmth, his strength, his scent—everything about his nearness made her senses seize. Her lungs felt so tight she could barely breathe; with an effort, she managed a nod.

Satisfied, he started to draw back, paused, then returned, lowering his head to murmur, again maddeningly in her ear, "Incidentally, we call ourselves the Philanthropy Guild."

She blinked.

Before she'd fully processed his words, he'd slipped back to the door and left.

Roscoe joined his fellow Guild members around the library table, apologized for keeping them waiting, then opened the meeting and fought to keep his mind on the business he and the other seven had gathered to discuss.

Their organization was straightforward. They ran charitable projects, with each member having oversight of one project at a time and reporting to the group on progress at each meeting. Normally they met once a month, but lately they'd been evaluating and embarking on several new projects—Roderick's, given he'd only recently joined the group, and two others replacing completed projects—so had stepped up the frequency of their meetings.

Each project was financed through a fund administered by a finicky, dour solicitor. Each of them contributed however much they wished, but the minimum contribution of five thousand pounds a year kept the membership exclusive.

Ro Gerrard, Viscount Gerrard, had been the first real member. Ro might have made an excellent gambler, but his heart had never been in it. However, the same incisive mind that would have proved an advantage juggling odds was even better at gauging risks and potential outcomes of more human-based investments. Venturing into the arena of philanthropic endeavors, Ro had stumbled across Roscoe, and, after getting over his surprise, had—as Ro was wont to do—asked questions, and offered suggestions, and persisted until Roscoe had agreed that joining forces was a sensible move.

From that small beginning, the Guild had grown.

"The young women at the academy seem to be responding well to Mrs. Canterbury's methods of instruction."

Sebastian Trantor, relatively recently recruited after he'd married Ro's sister-in-law, continued with his assessment of progress at a Guild-funded school in Lincoln that taught selected female orphans the necessary skills to become ladies' secretaries.

Roderick followed with the latest information on the project he was assessing—a small bailiff-run school in Battersea. It was a straightforward proposal, one the other members felt would help Roderick cut his teeth. "I'm not yet entirely satisfied with some of the suppliers the school wishes to continue to use. I believe we should hold firm to our principle of not allowing firms owned by relatives of those running the establishment to be engaged—not unless they are the only supplier available."

"Hear, hear," Max Gillard said. "We instituted that rule early on, and it's saved us—or rather our blunt—countless times."

Roderick nodded. "I'll tell Hendricks, the head bailiff."

"If I were you," Roscoe said, "I'd also have a quiet word in Father . . . is it O'Leary's? . . . ear. He's on the school board, and while he might not feel the prohibition is necessary"—with a cynical smile, Roscoe looked around the table—"telling him that our considerable experience will not allow the Guild to invest in any project that doesn't adhere to such rules will almost certainly be sufficient to ensure he sways all the other board members. No need for you to waste time trying to argue them around when he can do it for you."

"I second that," Hugh Bentley put in. He met Roderick's eyes. "It's not simply a matter of getting them to do things our way—the trick is to leave them feeling that it was their wisdom behind it."

Roderick grinned, nodded, and jotted a note in his journal.

The reporting continued around the table, with Roscoe briefly detailing the progress of his own current project—an endeavor to teach young boys from the dockside slums enough to allow them to become apprentices in the nearby shipyards; the Guild already worked with the shipyard owners to oversee the training and subsequent placement of the apprentices into paying jobs.

As Hugh—Lord Hugh Bentley, the Duke of Raythorne's second and rather more brilliant son—took center stage, Roscoe sat back and wondered what his uninvited and dis- approving guest in the gallery was making of the meeting.

Of the eight men about the table, seven—Ro, Sebas- tian, Marvin Grayle, Edward Bremworth, Hugh, Max, and Roscoe himself—were scions of noble houses. The only ex- ception was Roderick. While nobility of birth wasn't a crite- rion for membership in the Guild, the simple fact was that, other than in exceptional cases such as Roderick's, most of the money available for charitable works lay in the hands of the aristocracy.

Considering their secret observer, Roscoe wondered if she was squirming yet. He hadn't known Roderick hadn't told his family about joining the Guild, but given his sister's overbearing protectiveness—given Roderick was twenty- three and in sole charge of his considerable fortune—it was understandable that Roderick had wanted to do something entirely on his own. A declaration of independence, as it were.

Despite the fifteen years and the lifetime of experience that separated Roderick and him, Roscoe could nevertheless appreciate that.

His mind returning to the hoity Miss Clifford, he won- dered if she would.

Miranda sat through the meeting in absolute silence.

The men's voices reached her clearly, their every word sinking her deeper into a quagmire of embarrassment heavily tinged with mortification.

But how could she have known?

Even before Roscoe had appeared in the library to take his chair at the head of the table, she'd picked up allusions to the social status of the other men. They knew each other well enough to refer to each other by name rather than title, but while trading jocular remarks several had called one of the others "lord" and in one case "viscount."

Alerted, she'd looked more closely at their features, all of which confirmed the likelihood of their belonging to the aristocracy, including, once she saw him in better light, Roscoe himself. There could be very little doubt that features like his derived from noble progenitors, but in his case said ancestors had presumably engaged on the wrong side of the blanket.

Regardless, that face . . . held her attention effortlessly. While she heard the various reports and absorbed the implications, her gaze remained, not on whoever was speaking, but on Roscoe. At no point did he glance up at the gallery, leaving her free to indulge her now rampant curiosity and study—examine—him.

It wasn't every day she got the chance to so closely scrutinize any male, let alone one of his caliber. One who embodied the devilish attraction she'd spent all her life being warned, in dire terms, against.

He wasn't prettily handsome; he was too old for that, and there was a touch of harshness, of sharply edged hardness, in the sculpted planes of his face. His finely shaped lips often held a cynical twist, while his heavy lidded dark eyes—she still wasn't sure what color they were—combined with his frequently impassive expression, hinted at world-weariness and distance.

If his face, with its suggestion of veiled strength and reclusive personality, intrigued, his body fascinated. She'd been impressed enough in the gallery, but being able to measure him against other men left her even more appreciative of his height, his long-limbed grace.

He moved in a manner that transfixed her senses. He leaned back in his chair, listening to one of the others speak, and she drank in the pose, one that spoke of a male in his prime who was utterly at ease in his large, powerful body.

Only when the meeting broke up and he rose and, with the others, left the library—still without glancing her way—did she blink free of the spell and finally turn her mind to other things.

The instant she did, the import of all she'd heard rushed into the forefront of her mind.

No matter how she viewed things, what she'd learned through the meeting made it abundantly clear that in suggesting that Roscoe was corrupting Roderick, she'd transgressed. Badly. She would have to apologize.

Sincerely.

Roscoe might be a noble bastard, might be London's gambling king, but beneath his hard, aloof, and powerful exterior lay a thinking and caring man. A man who deserved her applause, not her censure.

He might not be a gentleman, but clearly he was accepted by others within the pale, and as long as Roderick's association with him remained discreet, no matter from what angle she viewed the situation she couldn't see any valid reason to interfere. Roderick would come to no direct harm through interacting with Roscoe in his role as chairman of the Philanthropy Guild. Indeed, Roderick most likely would learn a thing or two from London's gambling king—a conclusion that was faintly discombobulating.

Stranger situations no doubt existed, but she couldn't offhand think of one.

A part of her—the more craven part—wanted to leave the gallery and, while Roscoe was engaged with seeing his guests out, slip out through the rear garden and hurry home . . . but no. She'd come into his house and insulted him, but he'd allowed her to watch the meeting and through it learn what she'd needed to know about Roderick's new venture.

Rather than being anxious about her brother, she was now rather proud of him.

And that—the slaying of her anxiety and her improved appreciation of Roderick—lay at Roscoe's door, so like any considerate guest, she sat and waited for him to return and show her out.

Five minutes later, the door opened. Her disconcerting host halted in the doorway, filling it, and looked at her.

Drawing in a determined breath, she rose and faced him. Raising her head, she met his gaze levelly. "My apologies, Mr. Roscoe. Clearly I was laboring under several misapprehensions with respect to both yourself and my brother. I must thank you for allowing me to learn the truth."

Roscoe didn't blink, but he was surprised. In his experience, ladies with strong opinions—and Miss Clifford struck him as very much that sort—didn't readily change their views. Yet scrutinizing her expression, and her lovely hazel eyes, he detected nothing other than absolute sincerity.

Roderick's sister, it seemed, was one of those rare strong women strong enough to admit to being wrong.

Releasing the doorknob, he inclined his head. "Apology accepted." He'd anticipated spending half an hour goading her, eventually dragging a grudging apology from her; she'd taken the wind from his sails, but he could hardly admit to feeling deflated. "And most who know me call me Roscoe."

Why he'd added that he wasn't sure, yet it seemed appropriate. Stepping back, he waved her to join him. "Come— I'll walk you home."

She'd started forward but now stopped and met his gaze. "Thank you, but that won't be necessary. As I daresay you know, we live just around the corner."

He couldn't keep his lips from curving. "Yes, I do know. However, Miss Clifford, it appears you're harboring yet another misapprehension—a gentleman like me would never allow a lady to walk home alone, whether at night or during the day."

Miranda studied his face; the set of his lips—that suggestion of a smile—was subtly taunting. She'd apologized, and he'd accepted, but he wasn't yet finished rescripting her view of him.

Replaying his words, she searched for some way to acceptably decline, but what could she say? I'm not that much of a lady?

Accepting the inevitable, she inclined her head and went forward to join him in the corridor.

Side by side, they walked back to the gallery. The lamps had been lit; in the soft light, she paused to look more closely at one of the paintings. She pressed her lips tight but couldn't hold back her question. "Is this . . . ?" She waved at the canvas.

"An original? Yes. One of his better works, I feel."

She glanced at him; he'd halted at the top of the stairs, waiting with unruffled patience for her. "I'm tempted to make some comment about the wages of sin, but that would be another misapprehension, wouldn't it?"

He smiled. A genuine, utterly heart-stopping smile, it warmed her in places she hadn't thought could be warmed. But "Yes, it would" was all he said.

She glanced at the other two paintings, then at the tapestry, then, having delayed the inevitable for as long as she could, joined him.

They went down the stairs; she'd wondered if he would lead her through the rear gardens or go via the streets, but she wasn't about to argue his choice. Despite the risk of being seen with him—and given it was so late, in such a quiet neighborhood that wasn't so great—at this time of night, she would much prefer the open streets to the narrow alleys.

His butler was hovering in the front hall. Tall, gray-haired, and stately, and so well-trained that he evinced not the slightest sign of surprise at the appearance of a lady who, as far as he knew, hadn't been admitted to the house, the butler bowed, then at Roscoe's request went to fetch his coat. She used the moment to look around the hall, drinking in the elegant paneling and the three large landscapes adorning the walls.

The butler returned bearing a stylish overcoat. As Roscoe shrugged into it, then settled the sleeves, she allowed herself to glance at him again. Lowering his head, he looked at her, and in the stronger light cast by the lamp on the hall's central table she finally saw his eyes well enough to make out their hue.

Dark, sapphire blue.

It was an arresting shade, jewel-toned and vibrant. As for his hair, fashionably cut, the thick locks layered over his well-shaped head, she suspected it was a deep sable brown that appeared black in most lights.

The butler had moved to the door. At Roscoe's glance, he opened it.

With what she now realized was innate grace, Roscoe waved her through. As she descended the shallow front steps, he told the butler, "I'm walking the lady home. I should be back inside half an hour."

"Indeed, sir—I'll let Rawlins know."

Pausing on the pavement, she turned as Roscoe joined her. Polite custom dictated that she shouldn't ask, but . . . "Rawlins?"

Roscoe met her gaze briefly, then waved, and they stepped out in unison. "One of my bodyguards. At least one of them is on duty at any time, and they get anxious if I disappear without warning."

"I see." She paced beside him. He didn't offer his arm, for which she was grateful; refusing it would have been awkward, but she would have done so nevertheless. Accepting his support would have signaled a degree of acquaintance that could never be. Helpfully, the street was, as she'd hoped, deserted. The dense shadows beneath the trees in the square spilled across the opposite pavement, but the moon shone unimpeded along their side of the street, lighting their way. "As you appreciate your bodyguards' concerns, I hope you will also understand my motives in following Roderick to your house."

Roscoe hesitated, then murmured, "As a matter of fact, I do." None better; he knew to what lengths protective instincts could drive a man, and, presumably, a woman, too. He waited, knowing what would come next.

It took her several minutes to find the words, but eventually she tipped her chin a fraction higher and said, "I know I have no right to ask this of you, but if you could see your way to not mentioning my presence tonight to Roderick, I would appreciate your discretion."

"I hadn't intended to."

Without looking at him, she inclined her head. "Thank you."

He waited a few seconds to let her relief sink in before saying, "I am, however, curious as to why you think Roderick, at twenty-three as levelheaded a gentleman as any I've met, still needs protecting."

Glancing at her, he saw a frown take over her fine features. "That . . . isn't all that easy to explain."

The intersection of Chichester and Claverton streets was still some yards away. "We have a few minutes, at least."

After a moment, she exhaled. "If you must know, we were orphaned very young. The three of us—our older sister, Roderick, and I—were brought up by two aunts, our mother's elder sisters. In light of our background, we must, understandably, always behave with the utmost respectability, but"—she gestured—"young boys will be boys, so it fell to my sister and me to . . . shield Roderick."

"So you've been protecting him for what? Twenty years?"

"More than that. Hence it's become an ingrained habit." They turned the corner and she added, "One I'm clearly going to have to break."

He wished her luck with that; long-standing protective habits weren't easy to mute, let alone eradicate.

They were nearing the house he knew was Roderick's. As they approached the mouth of the alley that ran alongside the gardens, she slowed. "I prefer to use the garden gate."

She diverted down the alley. Without comment, he followed.

The garden gate lay midway down the property. Miranda halted before it, lifted the latch, pushed the solid wooden gate open, then paused and looked at Roscoe. "Thank you for your escort."

In the faint light, she saw his lips twist cynically. "Even if it was, in your eyes, unnecessary?"

She regarded him, then said, "It was the gentlemanly thing to do." She dipped her head. "Good night."

"Good night, Miss Clifford."

Turning, she stepped through the gate—and tripped on the low stone step.

Steely fingers gripped her elbow.

Sensation—unnerving and intense—shot up her arm.

He held her up, steadied her.

Straightening, she gulped in a breath, struggled to steady her senses. Her heart was thudding. A second passed, then she forced herself to look at him, now much closer, a superbly masculine rock by her side—suddenly so much more *real,* and infinitely more dangerous.

"Thank you. Again." She forced the words out, grateful that her voice sounded passably even.

He looked down at her, dark eyes searching her face, then, his own expression impassive, utterly unreadable, he released his grip on her elbow . . . slowly, as if, finger by finger, he had to force himself to let go.

Then he stepped back into the alley, briefly—almost curtly—nodded. "Good night, Miss Clifford."

She managed to draw a freer breath. Nodded back as she reached for the gate. "Thank you . . . Roscoe—and good night."

She shut the solid panel, stood staring at it as her thudding pulse slowed.

As the unprecedented wave of sensation slowly ebbed.

Hauling in a long breath, she lifted her head, turned, and walked toward the house.

Roscoe stood for a full minute inwardly frowning at the closed garden gate, then swung away and continued down the alley, taking the shortcut back to his house.

Miss Clifford—he didn't know her first name, but it would be in his file on Roderick if he cared to look—was . . . different from the usual, run-of-the-mill lady.

Different in exactly what way he wasn't sure. Sinking his hands into his pockets, he pondered the point as he strolled unhurriedly home.

Admittedly, she was older than the usual ton miss; he didn't know her age, but she was older than Roderick, he judged by at least five years. Twenty-eight years old seemed about right, and would in part account for her strength—the sort of inner strength a man of his experience recognized instantly. Yet despite that strength, she'd seemed . . . off-balance, uncertain.

Not quite sure of herself in a rather strange way.

That moment when courtesy of the garden step and her trip he'd touched her flared in his mind. It had been a long time since he'd felt such a jolt of sensual awareness, if he ever had; it had been amazingly intense. That she'd felt it, too, wasn't in question; he'd seen the truth in her wide eyes, her parted lips, had heard it in her suddenly shallower breathing.

Regardless, any thought of further exploring the possibilities suggested by that moment of stark attraction was, he judged, doomed. Unless he missed his guess, Miss Clifford had shut the gate, and in so doing had shut him permanently out of her life.

"In light of our background, we must, understandably, always behave with the utmost respectability."

Contrary to her expectation, he didn't understand why she thought that, but if she was rigidly wedded to respectability, then the very last man she would be interested in developing any degree of acquaintance with was London's gambling king.

He walked on for several minutes, then, lips twisting cynically, he looked ahead and increased his pace. The reality of his life lay waiting.

* * *

Miranda dallied in the cool of the gardens until her violently jarred senses had settled back into their customary quiescent, if not somnolent, state. She'd never felt such a spark—had never before felt alive in such a way. She didn't want to think what that meant. From the first her instincts had warned that Roscoe was dangerous; clearly they hadn't been wrong. She was beyond sure she didn't need such a distraction in her life—anywhere near her respectable life.

Finally setting the episode aside as a never-to-be-repeated experience, she crossed to the side terrace and entered the house through the morning room French doors. The morning room was largely her domain; going to the escritoire, she set her reticule on the desk, then swung her cape off her shoulders and draped it over the back of the chair.

Her thoughts circled back to Roderick's project and the work of the Philanthropy Guild. Crossing to the door, she opened it; through the dense shadows of the downstairs hall she walked to the stairs and started climbing.

A pale-robed figure loomed out of the shadows on the landing.

Miranda very nearly squeaked. Swallowing her shock—it seemed to be a night for shocks of all kinds—her hand at her throat, she fought to catch her breath. "Aunt—you frightened me."

"Indeed, miss—and you frighten me." Gladys glared at her, then gestured with her cane. "Where have you been, heh? Coming inside at such an hour—how many times have you heard me say—"

"I was merely walking in the gardens. Roderick had gone out—you know I can't sleep until he gets home, so I was wasting time until he did."

Gladys humphed. "He came in a good half hour ago—he's probably already snoring."

"Yes, I know—I got distracted." By London's gambling king.

"You need to be more careful, my girl." Gladys ponderously turned and started to heave her considerable bulk back up the stairs. "Never forget you can't afford even a whisper of improper behavior."

Following, Miranda let her aunt's well-rehearsed admonitions flow over her; she'd heard the litany so many times the words were engraved on her soul.

Gladys halted at the top of the stairs, forcing Miranda to halt lower down. Turning her head, Gladys bent a sharp look down at Miranda and delivered her invariable culminating exhortation. "You don't want to end like your mother and your sister, do you?"

Stifling a sigh, Miranda dutifully replied, "No, Aunt. I don't."

Gladys humphed again, then waddled on to her room. "Roderick's a wealthy gentleman—society won't bat an eye over him coming in late. But you, girl—just one false step and your reputation will be shredded. Never forget—respectability is all."

On that ringing note, Gladys stomped through the open door to her room and shut it.

Suddenly feeling claustrophobic, Miranda dragged in a breath, let it out on a sigh, then continued down the corridor, and into her room at its end.

Closing the door, she paused, all but palpably feeling the restraints of her aunt's doctrine of inviolate respectability cinching around her.

Weighing her down. Hemming her in.

Trapping her. Smothering her.

While she'd been focused on saving Roderick, through her interaction with Roscoe and the walk back to the house, that feeling of being smothered, of being restricted and restrained—of being, as the Bard had put it, "cabined, cribbed, confined"—had weakened, eased.

Grimacing, she walked to her dressing table and started getting ready for bed. Tonight had been a momentary escape. A fleeting few hours in a different world, one that operated under different license.

But this was her real life, where she had to guard against

putting so much as a toe wrong, where if she was ever to have a life of her own she had to, at all times and in all ways, adhere without the slightest deviation to propriety's dictates.

Courtesy of those few hours of freedom, the returning weight of society's expectations felt heavier than ever, a millstone around her neck. One that, according to her aunts, she especially could never escape.

Not if she expected to have more of a life than her ill-fated mother and sister.

Gown and chemise doffed, her nightgown donned, she lifted the covers and slid into bed. Turning on her side, she gazed at the window—at the moonlit night outside.

"Sometimes, I wonder." Her voice was so low she barely heard the words. "They might have died, but at least for a few years they were happy."

After a moment, she settled her cheek on the pillow, closed her eyes, and sank into slumber within her prescribed world—the one in which respectability ruled.

Chapter Two

Miranda next came face-to-face with her aunt over the breakfast table the following morning.

Iron-gray hair scraped back in a tight bun, her heavy figure concealed beneath multiple layers of fluttering draperies, already engaged with reading her correspondence, Gladys merely hmmed when Miranda greeted her.

Sitting and thanking Hughes, their butler, for the fresh pot of tea he set before her, Miranda busied herself with pouring a cup, then helped herself to toast, waiting for Gladys to make some reference to their midnight meeting on the stairs, but as the minutes ticked past in blessed silence it seemed Gladys's correspondents had succeed in diverting her mind. Grateful for the reprieve, Miranda did nothing to draw her aunt's attention.

As usual, Roderick had already broken his fast and gone out riding. She crunched, sipped, and pondered the revelations of the evening, in particular Roscoe's assertion that her brother had grown to be a steady young man, and the implication that Roderick therefore no longer needed her protection.

"Well, miss!"

She glanced at Gladys. Pince-nez perched on the end of her long nose, her aunt was holding a letter almost at arm's length as she perused it.

"It seems that Mr. Wraxby still has you in his sights. He writes that he'll be visiting town next week and will look to call on us." Lowering the letter, Gladys focused sharp brown eyes on Miranda. "So you still have a chance there. Mr. Wraxby is everything and more Corrine and I might have hoped for you."

Corrine had been Gladys's elder sister; spinsters both, and bitterly resentful of what they'd termed their younger sister Georgiana's irresponsible love-match, the pair had nevertheless assumed responsibility for Georgiana's three children when Georgiana and her regrettable husband, Frederick Clifford, a well-educated mill owner's son, had perished in a boating accident twenty-three years ago.

If anything, Corrine had been even more adamant than Gladys that Georgiana's children had to consistently and devoutly worship at the altar of respectability in order to minimize the taint of that most deplorable of stigmas, Trade. The daughters of Sir Augustus Cuthbert, Baronet, as minor gentry, and determined to cling to every vestige of social advantage that station might confer, Corrine and Gladys had never allowed their wards to forget that they forever remained just one small step away from social ostracism.

When they'd all resided in the country, at Oakgrove Manor in Cheshire—the house and estate Roderick had inherited from Frederick, purchased with the despised fortune Frederick had inherited from his mill owner father—Miranda hadn't found the social restrictions imposed by their aunts either remarkable or onerous. Having lived under her aunts' thumbs from the age of six, their view of the world had been all she'd known.

But the years had passed, and on Corrine's death two years ago, with Miranda still unwed and with suitors thin on the ground, Gladys had agreed that they—Roderick and Miranda with Gladys as chaperon—should spend a few years in London, assessing the marital opportunities there, for Roderick as well as Miranda.

Roderick had bought the Claverton Street house, and a year ago they'd moved to Pimlico, only on the fringes of the expanding metropolis, but the quieter area had found favor with Gladys.

Miranda wondered if anyone had ever mentioned to her aunt that the neighborhood was also the home of London's most notorious gambling lord. . . .

"Miranda! Pay attention!"

She blinked, dispelling the image of a chiseled face with dark eyes and a sardonic expression. "I'm sorry, Aunt. Wraxby, you said?"

"Indeed." Gladys's eyes were hard chips of cloudy onyx. "You'd do well to reflect on the fact that after so foolishly rejecting the Honorable Mr. Jeffers, you've never had another offer. If you ever want a household of your own, you'd do well to keep your mind on the task of landing Mr. Wraxby. Put yourself out to be everything he's looking for in a wife, and the signs are that he might well offer for you."

"Indeed, Aunt." Miranda looked down at her plate. "I daresay you're right."

Jeffers. Despite the passage of time, the name still shook her. Depressed her. The memory opened a deep well of bruised emotions, of lasting, lingering, deadening self-doubt.

Lionel Jeffers had been a Cheshire gentleman, rather older than the usual suitor, but that had only made his attentiveness toward her twenty-year-old self seem more special. She'd been swept off her feet, and had for a short time lived in hope that she would find the sort of happiness her mother and sister had aspired to, until a kind matron had told her the truth. Jeffers wasn't interested in her, only in her fortune.

Bad enough, but when, shattered and dismayed, she'd told her aunts, they'd blinked at her uncomprehendingly. They'd known the basis of Jeffers's interest, and of the existence of his long-standing and very expensive mistress, all along.

Recollection of the railings and recriminations that had followed her rejection of Jeffers still held the power to make her shudder.

Roscoe would be about the same age Jeffers had been . . . but she wasn't twenty anymore.

Hauling her mind from the distraction—from the face and the body that had, last night, invaded her dreams—she forced her mind to the here and now. "Next week . . . I'll make sure the house will be presentable, and I'll warn Cook that we'll be entertaining and wish to show our best."

"Do that," Gladys forcefully replied. She ran critical eyes over Miranda. "At least now it's cooler, your gowns have long sleeves. Wraxby seemed taken aback when he last visited and your summer gowns showed too much skin. I'm quite sure that was one of the aspects that made him hesitate. Make sure this time that you give him no reason to question your respectability."

"Yes, Aunt." Miranda pushed back from the table and rose. "I must speak with Mrs. Flannery."

Gladys dismissed her with a wave.

Heading to the morning room for her daily meeting with the housekeeper, Miranda bludgeoned her brain into providing an image of Wraxby—a forty-something-year-old widower who lived in Suffolk, and who had spotted her in Bond Street and subsequently sought her out. She studied her mental picture of that stultifyingly reserved gentleman . . .

She'd known Wraxby for nearly a year, Roscoe for just one evening.

Yet Wraxby had never appeared in her dreams.

"Gelman is waiting downstairs and, as requested, he's brought Jennifer Edger with him."

Seated in the admiral's chair behind the massive desk in his study, Roscoe glanced up from the ledger he was perusing—the monthly accounts from the Pall Mall Club, which Gelman managed for him—and arched a cynical brow at Jordan Draper.

Brown-haired, brown-eyed, garbed in a brown suit deliberately designed to make him appear innocuous, Jordan, returning from checking downstairs, crossed to the desk and took his customary seat on Roscoe's right.

"And how are they getting along?" Roscoe inquired. "Any hints of acrimony? Of Jenny wanting to slit Gelman's throat, or vice versa?"

Jordan grinned. "Actually, no. Your lecture last month appears to have borne fruit."

Roscoe snorted. "We'll see." He returned his gaze to the columns of figures. After a moment, admitted, "Regardless of whether they kill each other or not, the club's doing well."

"Yes." Jordan leaned forward, pointing to a series of subtotals and explaining his projections for the coming months.

Roscoe listened and learned; he might have the world's best head for figuring odds, but he remained eternally grateful that Jordan had, years ago, consented to leave his father's country-based practice and throw his lot in with him. Over the last twelve years, while he'd grown and developed his now massive empire of clubs, dens, and hells, Jordan had stood, quiet and self-effacing, by his side—and made sure every last farthing was accounted for.

Even now, while he thought in multiples of thousands of pounds, Jordan was likely to chase a shilling.

In the matter of building his gambling empire, and in the even more difficult and ongoing challenge of managing what was in essence a massive enterprise built of myriad small units, they'd become a near invincible team. There was no one he trusted more than Jordan Draper.

After studying the accounts for another five minutes, he sat back. "Let's have them up." He looked at the footman standing beside the distant door. "Fetch Mr. Gelman and Miss Edger, Tomkins."

The footman—rather larger and distinctly heavier than

the general run of fashionable footmen—nodded and left on his errand.

He was back within minutes, ushering in a tall, aesthetic-looking man who, by his attire and manner, would easily pass for a gentleman, and a woman of middle height with lush black hair and strikingly pale skin, neatly turned out in a dark blue gown.

Both male and female paused some yards from the desk and inclined their heads. "Sir," they said in unison.

Roscoe studied their faces, their eyes, then, slowly straightening from his elegant slouch, waved to the chairs before the desk. "Please be seated."

His initial impression was that, as Jordan had said, the pair had buried their differences, but, given the root cause of those differences, he felt it prudent to reserve judgment. Jenny Edger was unquestionably the best piquet player he had on his books, other than himself. As such, she was best employed in the Pall Mall establishment, his club closest to the houses of the older aristocrats, who still preferred that particular game and were happy to wager large amounts on every point.

Jenny was an asset he intended to exploit to the full, but Gelman, who otherwise managed the subtleties of running the Pall Mall Club to his and Jordan's complete satisfaction, had taken what, on the surface, appeared to be an instant and unreasoning dislike to Jenny, matched in virulence only by her apparently equally instant dislike of him.

Roscoe's own assessment was that the pair should just sleep with each other and get it over with—or at least move on to whatever the next stage in their relationship might be—but meanwhile each too often provided the spark for the other's tinder. Both were otherwise levelheaded and pragmatic, but put them together and drama and fireworks inevitably ensued. Last month, after being alerted to a near disaster on the floor of the club, Roscoe had called the pair before him and given them both a vicious dressing down.

By insisting on continuing to see them both together—

holding them both responsible for the profitability of the club, which in fact was the case—he hoped to make each of them more aware of the other's importance to him, as well as underscoring that their continuing employment hinged on them both performing to his satisfaction.

The meeting went well; by its end he was hopeful that the pair had at least accepted that they had to work together.

Satisfied for the moment, as Tomkins ushered Gelman and Jenny out, he turned to Jordan. "Who's next?"

"The Tower." Having closed and removed the ledgers of the Pall Mall Club, Jordan opened another set, laying them on the desk. "I think we need to take a closer look at the faro table. I'm not sure, but I think there's something not quite right there."

That was the sort of thing Roscoe would know; just by looking at the figures he could tell whether the variation in take was within reasonable limits, or . . .

Two minutes of looking and he grunted. "You're right. Clapham's the manager—is he here?"

"Yes. He's waiting."

"Good. Let's have him up so we can ask him who he's let loose on his faro table this month."

The rest of the day proved very much a case of business as usual. Of the four reviews he conducted—two clubs, one den, and one hell—the Pall Mall meeting was the least troublesome. He sent two of his men back with Clapham to the Tower Club to deal with the crooked faro dealer—to explain his transgressions and see him off the premises. The Tower had its own security staff, but his men were of a different caliber—the sort to instill fear into those who sought to cheat without resorting to violence. He himself had taught them the knack of intimidation by suggestion, a skill he'd been forced to perfect through his early years in the business.

The den, in Soho, a recent acquisition, was having difficulties coming up to scratch in the matter of adhering to his standards of play; he had from his first foray into managing gambling establishments instituted a policy of no cheating, no card sharps, no weighted dice. In all his establishments, the house played fair—one of the principal reasons gamblers of all stripes flocked to his doors. His ironclad rule, backed by an inflexible will and an iron fist where necessary, had at first been regarded as a ridiculously naive ploy . . . until the results had started to show.

Ten years later, those few others who owned gambling establishments in London knew that to compete with his premises, they had to provide the same uncompromising guarantee . . . which very few could.

After due deliberation, he sent the den's manager off with a flea in his ear, then called in one of his gambling specialists, an unprepossessing little man who could spot a cheat with remarkable and unerring accuracy. After dispatching Bowen to monitor the den for the next week, he spent half an hour with Jordan working out limits the exceeding of which would instantly trigger another, more urgent, review. Between Jordan's financial vetting and Bowen's practical vetting, Roscoe felt confident that if the den did not swiftly rectify its problems, he would be in a position to do so.

The problem at the hell, off the Strand, was more disturbing, but more easily dealt with. Two female staff leaving from the back of the building in the early hours had been attacked. They'd managed to scream and guards from the hell had come to their rescue. Roscoe consulted with his bodyguards, Mudd and Rawlins, then dispatched them to hire additional men to monitor the alleys surrounding the hell sufficiently to ensure the female staff were safely away every night.

Very early in his career, he'd realized that women were far better dealers and bankers; a very large percentage of those who ran his tables were female. As he reiterated to the hell's manager, keeping his female staff safe and happy to work was critical to generating income; to drive the point home to the manager, his male staff, and the females concerned,

Roscoe arranged to have several of the large, well-trained men he kept on retainer step in for a time to oversee the new recruits.

By late afternoon, his desk was clear.

Jordan gathered up the ledgers, saluted, and left.

Roscoe waved Tomkins in in Jordan's wake, then slouched back in his chair, stretched out his legs, and relaxed.

His mind wandered . . . throwing up an image of a face far less striking than Jenny Edger's, yet infinitely more riveting. Large hazel eyes under finely arched brown brows, a straight, no-nonsense nose, a mouth a trifle too large yet with lips luscious and full, pale, flawless, peaches and cream skin, brown hair glinting honey and gold, and a firm yet feminine chin, all set in an expression that held too much seriousness, too much . . . unrelenting sobriety.

Why he should feel that he had no idea, but his instincts were rarely wrong.

Why he was sitting there thinking about Roderick's sister was an even greater mystery.

Banishing the image, shaking free of the compulsive spell—the impulse to learn more about something he didn't understand—he sat up and opened the center drawer of the desk.

Extracting the latest missives from his family, one from his mother, the other from his sister-in-law, both delivered that morning, he briefly debated, then opened the packet from Caroline. After reading her brief note, he unfolded the enclosed report from Eton. Reading that made him smile.

Setting those sheets aside, he opened the slimmer missive from his mother, one of her usual brisk communications bringing him up to date with his sisters and their offspring. This one informed him that his sisters would be descending on Ridgware in a week's time to spend several days planning Edwina's wedding. The youngest of his sisters, Edwina was the last to wed. Despite the unstated yet underlying suggestion that his input would be welcome should he be able to visit, he couldn't imagine that the five females who would be closeted at Ridgware would need any help from him.

He'd attended Millicent's and Cassandra's weddings by slipping inside the church at the last minute, remaining out of sight, then sliding out again before the bride and groom had even turned to come back up the aisle. If matters had been otherwise, he would have led both girls down the aisle . . . Henry, a mere boy, had had to stand in for him.

And that had hurt.

More than he'd expected.

Now Edwina was about to marry, and he wouldn't be able to lend her his arm down the aisle, either.

Staring at the letter, imaging his little sister walking down the aisle—experiencing in a visceral way the irretrievable passage of time, of years gone that he could never have back, of opportunities passed up that would not come again—his mind slid in a direction he rarely allowed it to take, to dwell on his regrets.

On the dreams he had, so long ago, set aside.

At the time with little thought, with little real appreciation of what he was sacrificing. That hadn't seemed important at the time. Now . . .

Twelve years on, his frame of reference had shifted.

He was thirty-eight and could see no hope of ever achieving the one goal that, underneath all else, solid and real but unrecognized until recently, encompassed his ultimate desire.

Family had been his lodestone, the pivot about which his life had swung . . . but the family he'd given up so much for was fragmenting. The girls would soon all be married, with husbands and children, families of their own. His mother was aging, and Henry, although currently still dependent on him, would be grown and his own man all too soon.

And he . . . would be left with no one.

No family to care for, no one to look out for.

He was too cynically clear-sighted not to know that his

role—his one true purpose in life—had always been to protect others. That was who he was.

So who would he be, and what would he do, when he had no one?

The blankness in his mind cleared, and he saw again the face that had proved so riveting last night.

He wondered why his mind made the connection . . . then recalled that he'd told her Roderick no longer needed her to watch over him.

His lips twisted; the advice had been sound. He knew all about sacrificing, and then having to let go.

A moment passed, then he sat up, set his mother's letter back on the desk. Determinedly shaking off his melancholy mood, he reached for a pen and settled to write to his sister-in-law, reassuring her that Henry's performance at Eton was perfectly acceptable—indeed, to be expected. Anything more and he would have been concerned that his nephew wasn't learning all that he should.

Imagining Caroline reading that, he grinned.

"These pigs' trotters in calf's-foot jelly are excellent." Gladys looked at Miranda, seated at the foot of the table. "We should have them when Mr. Wraxby comes to dine. I'm sure he'll appreciate them."

Miranda nodded. "I'll speak with Mrs. Flannery in the morning to make sure Cook gets more in." On Corrine's death, she'd assumed control of the household; it gave her something to do, something to accomplish. Glancing at Roderick, seated in the large carver at the table's head, she added, "We don't yet know when—or even if—Mr. Wraxby will be able to dine, but he wrote to Aunt Gladys that he'll be in town next week and will look to call on us."

Roderick arched a brow. He made no comment, but she read his thought clearly in his expression: Wraxby wrote to *Gladys*?

She looked down at her plate. Roderick thought Wraxby a cold fish and no suitable suitor for her, but Roderick, with his light brown hair, clean-cut features, and significant fortune, wasn't the one facing a lonely old age.

The thought of Roderick's sizeable fortune brought her discovery of what he was planning to do with at least some of it back into her mind. In the drawing room earlier she'd had a few minutes alone with him before Gladys had joined them, but she hadn't yet made up her mind whether to broach the subject. If she did, how would she explain how she'd learned of his private endeavor?

As Roscoe had implied, Roderick had grown to be no callow youth, no dissolute profligate, but a quiet, steady, and able gentleman. He'd thought things through and had decided to do good, and in joining the Philanthropy Guild he was on the right path.

He'd found the Guild, and the support of its members, on his own.

There was no avoiding the obvious conclusion: in this, Roderick didn't need her help.

By the time Hughes ferried in the trifle, Roderick's favorite dessert, she'd decided that the time had come to step back and let her little brother have the privacy he was owed.

"Pigs' trotters." Mrs. Flannery made a note on her list. "Now, as for luncheon today, I was thinking of a light bisque to begin with, and then perhaps . . ."

Miranda sat at her escritoire in the morning room and, with Mrs. Flannery in a chair nearby, worked through the menus for the day. They'd already settled sundry other matters, including the purchase of new linens and moving the tweeny's day off.

"Now, for dinner, Mr. Roderick told Hughes he wouldn't be dining in, so as it's just you and Miss Cuthbert, miss, I was thinking we could . . ."

Miranda nodded but barely heard a word of what followed. Roderick had told Hughes, but she'd passed Roderick in the corridor earlier and he hadn't said a word to her.

"So, miss, do you think that'll do?"

Blinking back to the moment, she found Mrs. Flannery looking at her inquiringly. "Yes. I'm sure that will be ample." She paused, then asked, "Is there anything else we need to discuss?"

"No, miss. I think that's it for this morning." Mrs. Flannery rose. "I'll leave you to your work, and I'll get on with mine."

She found a smile for the housekeeper, but it faded before Mrs. Flannery had quit the room.

Roderick had always told her . . . well, until recently.

Until he'd stepped into adulthood and taken charge of his own life.

As he should.

As she'd always hoped he would.

But now he had . . .

She shook her head irritably and told herself she would simply have to get used to not being Roderick's keeper anymore.

She kept herself busy for the next two days, filling her time with all the minor household tasks she often let slide. She focused on her role as de facto lady of the house and filled it to the very best of her ability . . .

Until the afternoon she found herself walking the garden, shears in hand, deadheading the numerous rosebushes dotted about the beds. The gardener, digging at the back of one bed, eyed her anxiously, as if worrying that her sudden burst of activity might presage a cutting back of his duties.

Reaching a large bush of faded roses, she halted.

What was she doing?

Trying to convince herself that she had some real role, that running Roderick's house wasn't a temporary occupation, one she'd have to hand over to his bride when he married?

The realization rocked her. She could manage this household to the top of her bent, yet it never would be hers.

Just as Roderick, and managing his life, no longer fell to her.

Neither Roderick, nor his household, could provide her with an ongoing purpose, could give long-term meaning to her life.

She stared at the withered roses, one question, strident and unavoidable, in her mind.

What am I going to do?

With the rest of her life.

After dinner two evenings later, Miranda started up the stairs, intending to fetch the novel she'd been reading and sit with Gladys in the drawing room, when she heard Roderick's footsteps striding along the upper corridor, then he swung onto the stairs and came hurrying down. Smiling, she stopped on the landing and drew back to let him pass.

Dressed for the evening, polished and precise, he grinned but didn't slow. "I'm off for the evening." With a wave, he continued down the lower flight. "I'll see you in the morning."

She remained on the landing, staring after him. Reaching the ground floor, he strode toward the front hall. She heard voices, Hughes and Roderick speaking, then the front door opened. A moment later, it shut.

If she asked . . . would Hughes know where Roderick had gone?

Not that she would ask.

It was, patently, no longer any of her business, no concern of hers.

Her time as Roderick's carer and protector—as his big sister—was over.

"So what now?"

The whisper echoed softly in the stairwell.

Turning, she resumed her climb.

As advised, Wraxby called the following afternoon. He'd visited three times earlier in the year but had retreated to his estate in Suffolk over the summer to oversee his three sons during the months they were out of school.

"Now they're once more at Rugby, and as I had to venture to London to attend to business, I felt I should not pass up the chance to renew our acquaintance, Miss Clifford." Wraxby bowed over Miranda's hand.

He'd already paid his respects to Gladys, ensconced in an armchair flanking the drawing room fireplace and watching their interaction like a predatory owl. Roderick wasn't at home; Miranda hadn't seen him yet that day, but she was determinedly *not* keeping track of his whereabouts.

"We're delighted to receive you again, sir." Retrieving her hand, she waved Wraxby to the sofa, then sat at the opposite end. "Will you be remaining in town for long?"

"A day or two." Wraxby fussily settled his coattails. His attire was always rigidly precise, not fashionable so much as finicky.

The conversation that followed—a set of stilted statements from Wraxby with which Gladys invariably agreed—left Miranda questioning what her lot would be if he made an offer and she accepted, and he no longer felt the need to put himself out to be entertaining.

Inwardly sighing, she told herself to give him a chance—to give herself a chance to discover if, via him, she might find a life of her own to live.

Difficult with Gladys there, encouraging him to remain strictly within the unchallenging social parameters Gladys deemed suitable for the drawing room.

Somewhat to Miranda's surprise—perhaps noting her silence and that his entire conversation was with Gladys and not her—Wraxby himself took the initiative. "Perhaps, Miss Clifford, you would do me the honor of walking with me in the nearby square? I drove in along the river and noticed the new tea gardens at the end of the street. Have you sampled their service?"

"Not as yet." She rose. "But I would be happy to walk with you, and perhaps we might both determine their quality."

"Excellent."

After taking his leave of Gladys, assuring her aunt that he would take all due care of Miranda, Wraxby joined her in the front hall. He waited in silence while a maid fetched her coat, bonnet, and gloves. After donning them, she turned, expecting him to offer his arm. Instead, he waved her to precede him.

Their walk to Dolphin Square via Chichester Street retraced the route she'd walked nearly a week ago with Roscoe. Wraxby paced alongside her and made innocuous comments about the quietness and quality of the neighborhood; glancing briefly at the huge white mansion that dominated the other side of Chichester Street, she bit her lip against a wayward urge to point the house out and tell him who lived there.

However, his guaranteed response—centering on how she had learned who lived there, and why she felt that an appropriate subject to mention—wasn't one she wished to invite.

Leading the way under the trees of the park, feeling the cooler shadows engulf her, she looked down the long, sloping expanse to the low stone wall that edged the lane along the river. Forcing her mind from the distracting memory of a starkly, darkly elegant face made suddenly more potent by the proximity of his house, she steered her errant thoughts to the many questions she had concerning Wraxby. He was strolling beside her, his pace slowed to match hers, his head up, his gaze fixed ahead. She glanced at him. "You said you drove along the river—was it a pleasant journey?"

Did he have any appreciation of the finer things in life? Given the paintings on his walls, Roscoe certainly did. Watching Wraxby, she saw a slight frown cloud his features.

"I took that route to avoid the congestion on the other roads. It was faster, certainly."

She kept her reaction from her face; one couldn't have everything. "You've said little about your house. Is it situated pleasantly?"

"Well enough." After a moment, as if realizing that was

an unsatisfactory answer, he added, "Others have told me that it's an attractive property. Certainly Maude, my first wife, thought it comfortable."

Comfortable. Well, that was better than the opposite. Further questions on the house's surroundings and the neighborhood in general elicited little more. It wasn't, she judged, that Wraxby was being deliberately unhelpful but that he was naturally reticent. And perhaps unobservant.

And possessed very little conversational flair.

Against that, he seemed as honest as he was stultifyingly correct.

She could understand that, with his first wooing long behind him, he was rusty and perhaps diffident over putting himself forward in the customary ways, yet that left her with no notion of why his interest, however lukewarm, had fixed on her. Casting her mind over all she'd thus far learned of him . . . "You mentioned your sons. How old are they?"

"Eleven, twelve, and thirteen years old."

"That young?" She'd been under the impression they were older. "I see." She might just be starting to.

They strolled on in silence, a light breeze strengthening as they neared the river.

They reached the tea gardens on the riverbank. Wraxby conducted her to a round table affording a generous view over the wide gray ribbon of the river. Once their orders were delivered and the serving girl withdrew, he cleared his throat. "Miss Clifford, let me be plain. I am, as I believe is apparent, looking about me for a second wife. One of my reasons for doing so is that I find myself unsuited to the gentler side of rearing my sons."

Once started, he continued to elucidate and explain his view of their potential association. She sipped the excellent tea and paid attention. She listened as he described . . . the position he had vacant, and why he thought she might be a suitable candidate to fill it.

Her qualifications included her age, her pleasant, conventional, and unexceptional appearance, and her apparent lack of interest in what he termed the more reckless side of social life. Her portion was mentioned in the sense that its size, apparently divulged by Gladys, reassured him that they were social and capital equals, which she took to mean that the funds would ensure that in marrying her he could not be said to be marrying beneath him. He belonged to the same social stratum as the Cuthberts; as was the case with her aunt, social appearances were paramount.

As for his vacant position, it became clear that it could be adequately and comprehensively described as that of a glorified nursemaid. That said, given his position and hers, there was nothing to take exception to in his suggestion. His vision of a potential union wasn't one society would consider unworthy of a lady like her.

To her great relief, having communicated his thoughts, he made no move to press her for either opinion or decision. Indeed, she got the impression that he viewed a period of protracted social meetings as an essential caution. So as they strolled, again in silence, back to the house, she was free to ponder all he'd told her . . . and to wonder if fulfilling the role of a glorified nursemaid was all she, and her life, were worth.

Muting her sisterly concerns was proving no simple task, but to her relief Roderick joined Gladys and herself at the dinner table that evening.

The instant they were all seated, Gladys fixed Roderick with a commanding eye. "Mr. Wraxby called this afternoon and went walking with your sister. When they returned, I invited him to dine tomorrow evening and he accepted. I expect you to be present—it won't do for Mr. Wraxby to get the impression that you consider his interest in your sister of no account."

Because she was watching, Miranda saw the sudden blankness that overtook Roderick's normally relaxed expression as he hid his reaction to the peremptory demand, but an instant later his features eased and he inclined his head. "Yes, of course. I'll be here." He glanced at her, met her gaze, and, his light brown eyes smiling reassuringly, arched a brow.

He'd be there to support her; she smiled to herself as much as at him, and gave her attention to her plate.

Later, after dallying to speak with Hughes about dinner the following evening, she was walking to the drawing room when Roderick came clattering down the stairs.

He flashed her a grin. "I'm going out for a few hours."

She paused beside him in the front hall. He thrust a journal he'd been carrying into her hands, then reached for his overcoat. While he shrugged into the coat, she studied the book . . . identical to the ones Roscoe and several other members of the Philanthropy Guild had used.

Coat settled, Roderick reached for the book. She smiled and handed it back. "Enjoy yourself," she said, and meant it.

"I will!" He was already heading out of the door. Without looking back, he waved, then leapt off the porch and strode up the garden path.

Leaving Hughes to shut the door, smiling still, she headed for the drawing room.

She wasn't smiling when, the following evening, the clocks in the house chimed seven times and there was still no sign of Roderick.

"Where *is* he?" Agitation mounting, she threw up her hands and rose to tug the bellpull. She'd put off asking after him, holding to her new tack of not keeping track, but this was getting serious.

"Mr. Wraxby will be here any minute." Gladys wasn't any happier than Miranda was over Roderick's absence, but Gladys was less concerned. "Stop fussing! He's doubtless just late getting home."

The drawing room door opened. Miranda swung to face Hughes as he entered. "Has Mr. Roderick come in?"

Hughes looked faintly uncomfortable. "No, miss."

Frowning, she cast her mind back over the day, then surrendered to her instincts and asked, "When did you or any of the staff last see him?"

Faintly converted to definitely; Hughes came as close to a grimace as a well-trained butler could. "Not since last night, miss. You were there when he went out of the front door."

Her knees felt suddenly weak; carefully she moved to her right and sank onto the sofa. "Are you saying he hasn't been home since then?"

Hughes's expression blanked; he stared at the wall above her head. "Yes, miss. The maids said his bed wasn't slept in. As far as we know, he didn't come home last night."

"This is the first I've heard . . ." One glance at Gladys's face confirmed that her aunt had had no more idea than she. Miranda looked back at Hughes. "Why didn't anyone think to mention that my brother has disappeared?"

Color seeped into Hughes's cheeks. "We—that is, the staff—well, we assumed the master had some reason . . . some interest, as it were, that had induced him to spend the night elsewhere."

Miranda's jaw dropped. *Dalliance*? They thought . . . "No." She heard herself, heard the denial in her tone, remembered that Roderick was twenty-three . . . chin firming, she shook her head. "He assured us he would be here."

Gladys snorted. "Men! They're all the same, especially at that age. No doubt he's been out carousing in one fashion or another and has forgotten entirely about our guest."

"He wouldn't!" Miranda would have said more, but the rap of the front door knocker cut her off.

"That'll be Mr. Wraxby." Gladys waved at Hughes. "Go and let him in—and when Mr. Roderick arrives, tell him we expect him to join us no matter what state his head is in." Gladys humphed. "Serve him right." As Hughes left, she turned her agatey gaze on Miranda. "And you, girl, will stop wringing your hands, put on a smiling face, and set your mind to entertaining Mr. Wraxby. Don't forget"—Gladys leaned closer and lowered her voice—"situated as you are, you can't afford to put off the only worthy suitor to have come your way in years."

Faced with no alternative, Miranda hauled in a breath and rose as Wraxby entered. Plastering on a smile, she held out her hand. "Welcome, sir. I hope we see you well."

They dallied longer in the drawing room than was customary, but Roderick didn't appear. For Miranda, focused on listening for sounds of an arrival—sounds that never came—the conversation went in one ear and out of the other. In the end, she was forced to apologize for Roderick, saying that he'd been delayed but might yet arrive in time to join them. Without actually saying so, she managed to convey that Roderick had sent word to that effect.

Wraxby merely inclined his head, then gave Gladys his arm into the dining room.

The meal passed uneventfully, but the conversation around the table was more stilted than usual, even for Wraxby. Constantly reminded of Roderick's disappearance by the empty carver at the table's head, Miranda had to battle to maintain even a thin veneer of attentiveness. Gladys commenced the meal with a show of dismissive bravado, but by the time dessert was served even she had started to fall prey to anxious silence.

The hour that followed their return to the drawing room was the most stressful Miranda had ever endured. She couldn't imagine Wraxby hadn't realized that something was amiss, but when he eventually rose to make his farewells and she went with him into the hall to see him out, he gave no indication that their distraction had impinged on his consciousness.

Apparently Wraxby was utterly impervious to anything that didn't directly affect him.

Any inclination she might have felt toward confiding in him, perhaps seeking his advice, died. Telling Wraxby anything wouldn't help, and letting him guess might be even worse. Thanks to his overweening self-absorption, they had escaped having to deal with that complication.

Bowing over her hand, Wraxby straightened, accepted his hat from Hughes, then met her gaze. "I must return to Suffolk, but I expect to be in town in a few weeks' time. Can I hope that you will still be in residence and willing to receive me?"

She forced a smile. "Of course, sir. You will always be welcome. We have no plans to quit the capital just yet."

"Excellent." Donning his hat, Wraxby inclined his head. "I bid you a good night, Miss Clifford."

She held her smile until the door closed behind him, then it fell from her face like water. Turning, she strode back into the drawing room. "We have to summon the constables."

"*What*?" Shocked, Gladys goggled at her. Then, "No!"

Halting, Miranda stared at her. "What do you mean, no? Roderick's *disappeared*—something's happened to him. We have to notify the authorities—"

"Absolutely not!" Her jaw setting belligerently, Gladys narrowed her eyes. "I will *not* have you creating a furor. Notify the authorities, indeed! And what will that get us? Talk! Gossip! Scandal! And what do you imagine those authorities are going to do, heh? How will they find your brother? They *won't*—they'll send constables here to badger us, and otherwise just wait for him to come home, but meanwhile you'll have set the gossipmongers' tongues wagging. And all to no purpose!"

Gathering her shawl, Gladys hauled herself to her feet and met Miranda's disbelieving gaze. "You listen to me, girl." Gladys spoke with the truculent authority she'd wielded for the past twenty and more years. "I absolutely *forbid* you to speak a word of this to the authorities. They can't help us. No one can. The only thing we can do is wait for your brother to find his way home." Pushing past Miranda, Gladys waddled toward the door. "That, and pray that he has the sense to get himself back here without undue fuss."

Undue fuss. Miranda watched her aunt stump out of the room. Stood and stared at the empty doorway long after Gladys had gone.

"They can't help us. No one can."
For all Miranda knew, the first statement was true.
The second, she felt sure, was not.

"Good evening." Miranda held her head high and met Roscoe's butler's gaze. "My name is Miss Clifford—I'm Mr. Roderick Clifford's sister. I would like to speak with your master on a matter of some urgency."

Despite the hour, despite everything, the butler opened the door wide and stepped back. "Of course, miss. Please come in."

Stepping over the threshold, she walked forward to halt before the central table. The tall, ornate Venetian glass lamp upon it was lit, but set low.

Having closed the door, the butler turned and bowed. "If you will wait here, miss, I will apprise the master of your arrival."

"Thank you." Drawing a breath into lungs already tight, she tried to keep her mind from dwelling on what she was doing. Gladys's prohibition had left her no choice; she needed help to find Roderick, effective help, and she felt certain that if he chose to assist them, Roscoe could provide that.

Undoing the ties of her cloak, she swung the garment off, half folded it and laid it on the table. She was still wearing her dinner gown—a modest, round-necked, long-sleeved gown of very pale brown watered silk.

The butler—Rundle, that was his name—had retreated down the same corridor she'd seen used to access the library.

Within a minute, he returned. "If you would come this way, miss."

She followed him down the corridor, noting the rich oak paneling on the walls, and the vibrant paintings of horses and hounds judiciously spaced down the corridor's length. Ornate double doors stood at the end of the passage; the butler opened one and held it, allowing her to walk into the section of the library she hadn't before seen, the area beneath the wider part of the gallery.

It was a sumptuous setting; pausing just inside the door, sensing it silently close behind her, she drank in the beauty, the sybaritic comfort. In the center of the wall at this end of the long room, a massive fire blazed in a huge hearth, throwing flickering golden light over the ornate stone mantel and sending warmth washing out into the cavernous room. A large jewel-toned rug covered the flagstone floor, and four large armchairs in rich brown leather sat angled before the blaze. Oak side tables stood beside each chair. Matching sideboards flanked the fireplace, and were themselves flanked by floor-to-gallery bookshelves that spread from there to circle the room.

Paintings of similar quality to those elsewhere in the house hung over the mantel and above the sideboards. Several strategically placed lamps shed a steady glow over the scene.

Despite the visual distraction, her eyes locked on the man who, long legs uncrossing, gracefully rose from the depths of the armchair on the far side of the hearth. As before, he was immaculately dressed, this time in a superbly tailored black coat, blue-and-black striped waistcoat, and dark trousers. A book held loosely in one long-fingered hand, eyes narrowing on her face, Neville Roscoe studied her for an instant, then, his expression inscrutable, he waved her to a chair. "Welcome once more to my humble abode, Miss Clifford. You perceive me agog to learn what could possibly be so urgent as to bring you to my door."

Stiffly, brittlely, she inclined her head. "I must thank you for agreeing to see me, sir."

He looked at her, one long, incisive look from those dark sapphire eyes, then he gestured impatiently for her to come forward. "Cut line, Miss Clifford. What the devil's happened?"

As if freed by his demand, able again to draw air into her lungs, she walked forward, sank into the chair facing his, and simply said, "Roderick's disappeared."

Still standing, he looked down at her, then laid aside his

book and sat. She half expected him to respond dismissively. Instead, his gaze on her face, he asked, "When was he last seen?"

"Yesterday evening. I spoke with him as he was leaving the house—I thought he was coming here for one of your Guild meetings."

"He was. He did. He left here with the others at the end of the meeting."

She leaned forward. "Did you see which way he went?"

Roscoe thought back. "He didn't go upstairs—he went via the street. I heard him call a farewell to Gerrard, who left at the same time. Gerrard had a carriage waiting and departed in the opposite direction." He refocused on Miranda Clifford's face; he'd been sufficiently curious to look in Roderick's file for her name. "He left here a little after twelve o'clock. Are you sure he didn't reenter the house, then leave again later?"

"No one saw him . . ." She paused, then drew breath and went on, "And I checked before I came. The clothes he was wearing aren't in his room, and the book . . ." She raised her gaze to his face. "The journal he brought here—if he took it with him when he left, then that's not in his room, either."

Roscoe kept his expression impassive. "He had the journal when he left . . . so it appears he was taken between this house and his."

"Could someone have been after the book? Was there anything of value in it?"

"He used it to jot down questions to ask of the board of the school he was assessing for funding." Roscoe considered any possible link, then shook his head. "No—besides, if anyone had been after the journal, they would have taken it and left Roderick in the street." Rising, he crossed to the bellpull. "As they didn't, he was the target."

Rundle appeared in response to the summons.

"Tell Mudd and Rawlins I need them immediately."

"Yes, sir." Rundle departed, significantly more swiftly; if

Roscoe wanted his bodyguards at this hour, then something major was afoot.

Roscoe returned to his chair but didn't sit, his mind already considering the first moves in his plan to locate Roderick.

Miranda Clifford looked up at him. "I don't know how such things are done, but as you know, we're wealthy, so of course we'll pay for yours and your men's help."

He refocused on her face. Saw very clearly the anxiety eating at her. "Don't insult me or my men. We'll search for Roderick, find him, and get him back because he's a friend and an ally—and believe me, Miss Clifford, I am very well known in this town for keeping my allies safe."

She stiffened; her chin rose. Her eyes met his as her lips firmed, but then she thought better of whatever she'd been about to say, and inclined her head stiffly. "Thank you."

He only had a second to savor the small victory—and his success in diverting her, if only for a few seconds; heavy footsteps in the corridor heralded the arrival of his two closest and most trusted men.

They tapped, and at his command, entered. Both were of above average height, heavyset, with hamlike fists and close-cropped heads. Both had noses that had been broken at some point, but despite the signs of their rough pasts, they were neatly dressed in somber suits, and both were quick-witted and intelligent.

And both would be carrying several knives concealed about their persons.

Rawlins closed the door, then joined Mudd a few yards before it, facing Roscoe—awaiting their orders. From where they stood, they couldn't see Miranda Clifford, but, of course, that meant she couldn't see them. Smoothly she rose and turned to stand alongside him, facing Mudd and Rawlins.

Both men blinked, but then shifted their gazes back to his face. Prepared to pretend they hadn't seen Miss Clifford. If matters hadn't been so serious, he would have smiled;

he'd trained them well. As it was . . . "This is Miss Clifford. She's just informed me that Mr. Clifford, her brother, did not return home after leaving here last night."

Mudd frowned. "He left after the meeting—I saw him walk away up the street."

"Did you see anyone else?" Miranda asked. "Anything else?"

Mudd glanced at her, shook his large head. "No, miss. Wasn't anyone else about, far as I could see."

"But there might have been someone under the trees in the square," Roscoe said, not so much a statement as an instruction to his men.

They understood. Rawlins nodded. "Aye—could well have been. You want us to go and check?"

Roscoe glanced at the clock on the mantelshelf. "It's almost twelve o'clock. The same time of night. Send all the men out—I want the area combed. Chichester Street, the square, and Claverton Street in particular. You know the Clifford house?"

"Big one, two up from the corner on the right, just past the first alley," Rawlins replied.

Roscoe nodded. "That's the one. Search for the next two hours. Speak with anyone you see—jarveys, coachmen—anyone at all. Even at this time of night, the chances are that someone saw something."

They went, closing the door behind them.

Roscoe glanced at the woman beside him, presently chewing her full lower lip. "If there's anything to be found, any trail at all, my men will find it."

She met his eyes. "And then what?"

"And then we'll follow it, find Roderick, and bring him back." He meant every word and let her see that he did, watched the realization sink home. Watched her earlier franticness—the fear and anxiety that had driven her to his door—recede a step further. From the first word she'd uttered, he'd known she was strung as tight as a piano wire; he'd done what he could to ease the tension and had allowed her to remain and hear him give his orders in the hope it would ease her further.

It had, but she was already starting to think ahead—to move on to the next stage of worry.

"Come." He remembered just in time not to reach for her arm, and instead waved her to the door. "I'll see you home." He sensed, more than saw, her draw breath to protest, and with greater asperity added, "And, Miranda Clifford, you should know better than to argue."

Miranda blinked at his use of her name, but if she didn't want him taking her arm and triggering those violent sensations again, she had to move; he all but herded her to the door, and then it was simply easier to give in and walk beside him.

He swiped up her cloak and held it for her, shrugged on his own overcoat while she tied the ribbons and put up the hood, then, forestalling the butler, he opened the door and followed her through.

They set off walking unhurriedly along the pavement. There were as yet no streetlights in this neighborhood, but the moon shed enough light for her to make out the shapes of men moving under the trees in the square. There seemed to be quite a few. She tipped her head in that direction. "Are they all your men?"

He glanced that way briefly, then faced forward again. "Most are mine, but a few have other allegiances. Tonight, however, those others might just prove useful to me." After a moment, he added, "To our cause."

She realized he'd given no guarantees about sharing whatever he learned. "I'll want to know anything you learn about Roderick."

"Naturally. I promise to send word of anything I hear."

That promise had come far too glibly, but . . . "Thank you." She would have to think it through—think of how to ensure he told her what he learned sooner rather than later. Later, when it was all over, whatever it proved to be.

They turned into Claverton Street and she saw several

more figures moving through the shadows. A man was talking to a jarvey further along the street.

As if she'd voiced the question forming in her mind, Roscoe murmured, "Most jarvies have certain routes, certain areas they service, especially this far out of the city. Even if they'd just been driving past, they might have seen something."

He glanced down at her; she felt his gaze on the side of her face. "We only need one clue—the rest will follow."

She nodded and turned down the alley.

Roscoe halted, watched her walk into the shadows, then followed.

He caught up with her before she reached the garden gate. "Humor me—why this gate rather than the front one?"

Reaching the gate, she halted, then looked at him. "Because of my aunt. She didn't want me to tell anyone about Roderick's disappearance—I wanted to go to the authorities, but she forbade it."

He frowned.

Before he could think of how to word his next question, she went on, "She's too afraid of creating a scandal—that people will point us out, and that will sink us socially. She's probably right, but I couldn't let that rule me, at least not totally, not in this case." Even in the poor light, he saw her jaw firm. "Not when Roderick's life might be at stake."

She glanced at him again, through the shadows met his eyes. "Of course she's as worried as I am, and she probably knows I've gone out to seek help of some kind, but if I come in through the garden gate and into the house via the side door, she can pretend that I've just been walking the gardens, as I sometimes do."

He would have asked more, but now wasn't the time. Instead, he gave her what he knew would help her most. "Try to get some sleep. I know that won't be easy, but remind yourself that you'll be more help to Roderick tomorrow if you're well rested and not living on your nerves." He stepped back with a nod. "I'll send word as soon as I have any real information."

She hesitated, but then inclined her head and opened the gate. "Once again, thank you. Roderick and I are in your debt."

This time, when she stepped in through the gate, she glanced down and took care not to trip.

A pity, a part of him thought.

He remained where he was as, with one last glance back, she gently shut the gate.

After a moment, he turned and, as he had a week before, walked home via the alleys. They held no terrors for him. Although he called Mudd and Rawlins his bodyguards, he was, truth be told, infinitely more dangerous than either of them.

He'd had to be—had had to learn to be—to survive as Neville Roscoe.

As he walked, he thought of Miranda Clifford. Considered the strange fact that he was fascinated by her, with the conundrum that was her—fearless on the one hand, uncertain on the other.

Given her aunt's apparent obsession with avoiding scandal, while he hadn't yet probed why the aunt thought the news of Roderick being kidnapped would create a scandal of the sort to sink the family socially, he suspected he now knew the cause of Miranda's uncertainty, her lack of confidence over how to act.

What he hadn't expected, hadn't foreseen, was the quality of her strength, of her adherence to her convictions. She'd walked away from all safety and come to him because Roderick was in danger.

That took commitment, resolve, and passion. Passionate devotion of a sort he understood, that called to him on such a visceral level he couldn't—wouldn't be able to—easily turn from it.

If there was one thing the past twelve years had taught

him, it was not to bother trying to fool himself. He wanted, possibly needed, to learn a lot more about Miranda Clifford.

And finding Roderick, and rescuing him, would unquestionably be the fastest route to her soul.

Chapter Three

The following morning, cradling a cup of coffee Rundle had provided, Roscoe sat behind his study desk and surveyed the documents Jordan had left laid out across the polished surface. The day's business; Jordan was presently in his own office but would return shortly to begin.

Sipping his coffee, he was about to shift his mind from the happenings of the night and focus on the matters before him when a light tap was followed by Rundle looking in.

He arched his brows.

"Miss Clifford has called, sir." *And has asked to see you* didn't need to be said.

He should have expected it.

He hesitated; he had work to do . . . but he wasn't going to turn her away. He inwardly sighed. "Show her up." His study was on the first floor overlooking the rear gardens. "Wait." Sitting up, he drained his coffee; he was going to need his wits about him. He held out the empty cup. "Take this."

Rundle came forward and did, then departed.

Two minutes later, Rundle returned and held the door for Miranda Clifford, today modestly gowned in pale olive green twill, her brown hair severely restrained in a lustrous chignon at the back of her head. As he rose and came out from behind the desk to greet her, Roscoe wondered whether she knew that, on a woman with a body and face like hers, deliberately modest gowns and severely restrained hair tended to fire rather than defuse male imaginations, tended to incite rather than douse male interest and intent.

Regardless, that her preferred style definitely worked that way on him wasn't something he intended to mention.

As he neared, she met his gaze. "Mr. Roscoe—"

"Just Roscoe, remember?" Despite the years, he still found it easier to answer to the name without any title.

Lips firming, she raised her chin a fraction. "Roscoe, then. I hope you'll excuse the early hour, but—" She frowned when he reached for her gloved hand, but she surrendered it and watched while he bowed over it.

"Good morning, Miss Clifford." Straightening, inwardly pleased by the tinge of color that bloomed in her cheeks— why throwing her off-balance delighted him he had no idea—he waved her to the two sofas facing each other before the fireplace at the far end of the room. "Please, sit, and I'll tell you what we've learned thus far."

She glanced at him, a hint of disapproval in her eyes, then walked to one of the sofas. "I was going to apologize for disturbing you at such an early hour. I'm well aware it's scandalously early to be calling on anyone."

"It's not that early for someone in my line of business." He followed and sat on the other sofa. "And as I'm sure you're prepared to remind me should I protest, if I'd wanted to ensure you didn't visit, I could have sent a note to your house, detailing my findings."

"So you have learned something?"

Seeing the leap of anxiety in her eyes, hearing it in her voice, he stopped playing. "One of the men in the park saw Roderick leave this house, but toward the end of Chichester Street, Roderick was accosted by two men. He collapsed and was carried to a coach." Her eyes widened. His expression impassive, he went on, "My men are currently trying to trace the coach. As yet they've had no luck, but they now have something definite to search for."

The faint frown that signified she was trying to reconcile something about him with her preconceptions was in her eyes again. "Forgive me for being blunt, but while I'm exceedingly grateful for it, you appear to be exerting considerable effort on my brother's behalf. You mentioned your business—won't those who deal with you see your distraction as a weakness?"

"No—quite the opposite. I mentioned last night that I'm known to protect my allies. To those with whom I deal, Roderick qualifies as an ally, and if I failed to act, indeed, if I fail to succeed in, at the very least, bringing those who took him to justice, then my power will be seen to be . . . not as great as those business associates currently believe." He held her gaze. "That would not serve me and my interests well. So you may dismiss any notion that searching for Roderick will in any way disadvantage me. In addition, this is widely held to be my territory, and the underworld in general knows to give it a wide berth. My men even more than I consider Roderick's kidnapping akin to an enemy incursion on home soil, and they are keen to respond appropriately."

He saw no reason to mention that the helpful watcher in the square had been a minion of Gallagher, a major underworld figure. The watcher, along with his master, had imagined the long-running surveillance had been undetected, a misconception now dispelled; Roscoe had known of Gallagher's man from the first, and having nothing he considered worth hiding from Gallagher, who specialized in selling information about criminal activities, he had elected to leave the man in place. He'd had a vague thought, even then, of just such an incident as Roderick's kidnapping.

He added, "I've had men watching your house since the early hours in case anyone appeared to deliver a note, but other than the mail and the news sheets, nothing's arrived. As you haven't mentioned it, I assume no ransom demand arrived in the mail."

Miranda blinked at him. Ransom? "No." Perhaps she should have stayed at home, but . . . she frowned. "Is it likely such a demand will arrive now—two days after Roderick was taken?"

Roscoe's face gave nothing away. "No—or rather, it's less likely with each passing day. If ransom were behind this, I would have expected you to have received a demand yesterday morning."

"No demand. No communication of any kind." She studied his face, wondered if she should take issue over him having men watching Roderick's house . . . decided she couldn't be that hypocritical. "Thank you for mounting a watch."

"If anyone turns up, my men have orders to alert me, and follow them." He paused, then said, "Rest assured, Miss Clifford, when I hear anything further, I will send word."

His tone signaled that the conversation, and their audience, was at an end, but she made no move to rise, as he was clearly waiting for her to do.

As she'd come to expect, he waited, watching her.

She drew in a determined, if too shallow, breath, boldly held his gaze, and brazenly asked, "Is there any reason I can't stay and wait for news here?"

She'd succeeded in surprising him enough for it to show. She hurried to say, "Yes, I'm aware that's a shocking thing to ask, but . . ." She raised both hands, palms up. "If I go home and wait there, I'll do nothing but pace and drive myself demented with imagining . . . while if I'm here, then at least I'll *know* that no trace has yet been found, that nothing has yet been learned of Roderick's fate."

Specifically, she would know that he hadn't received news of her brother and acted on it before sending word to her. It wasn't that she doubted his assurance; he would send word, but when? She suspected the answer was when he felt it appropriate, or when it suited him. And, she judged, he was perfectly capable of sending her word that Roderick had been sighted and he'd gone to rescue her brother, without telling her where.

She was starting to get a much clearer notion of what sort of man Neville Roscoe was. Although her insights and suspicions did not in the least fit the image widely held of London's infamous gambling king, his words and actions were consistently confirming that her evolving view was closer to the reality than society's image.

That being so, she saw no value in arguing over when he would inform her, opting instead to describe the anxiety she would be subject to if she went home rather than remained where she was, keeping company with him.

Roscoe searched her eyes, her face . . . put himself in her place, and accepted that she wasn't exaggerating how affected she would be.

He'd rather she wasn't there, a potent distraction, but . . . although he had several matters to attend to with Jordan, there was nothing sensitive, no discussion during which she couldn't remain on the sofa, at a good distance from his desk. He could suggest she go to his library, but he suspected that wouldn't serve her any better than Roderick's drawing room. "I fear you'll be atrociously bored."

Her expression eased. She patted the rather large reticule she held in her lap. "I've brought a novel. I'll sit quietly and read. I won't keep you from your business—you won't even know I'm here."

He managed not to snort disbelievingly—revealingly. "Very well." He rose. "If you'll excuse me, I must return to my work."

Her gaze rose, remaining on his face. "Thank you."

If he'd wondered why he'd acquiesced to such an indubitably outrageous plea, the answer was there in her wide hazel eyes, in the green and gold gratitude he drank in like fine wine. With an inclination of his head, he turned and walked back to his desk. Settling behind it, he had to exert considerable effort to force his mind to the matters awaiting his attention, but finally, after a glance down the room showed her with her head bowed, a book open in her lap, he managed it.

Ten minutes later, Jordan tapped on the door and came in. Somewhat gratefully, Roscoe let business claim him.

Two hours later, the door to the study opened. Jordan had returned to his own office to put into action the various decisions they'd reached; assuming he'd returned with some question, Roscoe looked up—to see Rundle carrying in . . . a tea tray.

With an abbreviated bow his way, Rundle carried the tray to Roscoe's uninvited guest. He watched as she looked up, then smiled and thanked Rundle as he set the tray on the low table between the sofas.

Then she glanced Roscoe's way, a clear question in her face.

He shook his head. "No, thank you. No tea for me." Then a delicious smell reached him. He hesitated, then pushed away from his desk. "I will, however, have a biscuit."

Lounging once again on the sofa opposite her, he took three biscuits from the plate on the tray and—pretending not to notice the approving look Rundle, retreating, bent on him—asked about the book she was reading. It proved to be one of the redoubtable Miss Austen's works, but the equally redoubtable Miss Clifford admitted to liking biographies as well.

After discovering they had both read a certain military history and shared much the same views on the recent actions in India, he took himself back to his work and left her to resume her reading.

Not, however, for long. A tap on the door and Rawlins entered. Without preamble he said, "Mrs. Selwidge is here. She's had trouble, it seems."

He was aware of Miranda at the far end of the room but didn't hesitate. "Show her up."

He debated asking Miranda to leave, or shifting the meeting to his library, but . . . this was who he was.

Rawlins opened the door and ushered in a tall woman in her early thirties, respectably, even conservatively dressed, but experience had etched a certain hardness in her face, in her eyes.

Even after all these years, he still had to fight the instinctive urge to rise; Amelia Selwidge wasn't a lady and would have been surprised if he had. He waved her to one of the chairs before his desk. "Rawlins said you'd had trouble. What happened?"

Amelia had worked for him for long enough to know she didn't need to beat about any bush. "Lord Treloar. The younger one."

"That would be . . ." Eyes narrowing, he cast his mind over the relevant family tree. "Christopher?"

Amelia nodded. "Definitely thinks he's descended from God, an' all. I've spoken to him twice before, but he refuses to listen—or rather refuses to believe my girls aren't the type to want a roll in the hay, not with the likes of him, at any rate. Last night, he propositioned two of them again. When the first—Cindy—reported it to me, I put our George on to following Treloar, quiet like. Just as well. Half an hour later, he started in on Jane—you'll remember her, slip of a thing, but she's a damn fine baccarat dealer—and when she said no a second time, Treloar went to strike her. Didn't manage it only because George was on him by then. We threw Treloar out, but he'll be back sure as some eggs are rotten."

"Trust me, he won't be back." He glanced at Rawlins, then looked again at Amelia. "Was he drunk?"

"Not even a little bit tipsy. We follow your rules to the letter—halfway drunk and they're shown the door. Most go, too, but Treloar wasn't even drinking. Nasty piece of work, he is."

He nodded. "You can stop worrying about Treloar. Tell Cindy and Jane—and yes, I recall both of them—that I seriously doubt they'll set eyes on Treloar again, but if they do, if he approaches them in the club or out of it, they're to report it to you or George immediately." He scanned the lines in Amelia Selwidge's face. "And that goes for you, as well. Any trouble from that quarter again and I want to hear of it. But otherwise, as of this moment, Lord Treloar is banned." He smiled grimly. "From all my establishments."

"All?" A slow smile broke across Amelia's face as she realized the implications of such a sentence. "Heh! That's going to put a wrinkle in his lordship's evenings when he won't be able to join his friends about your tables."

"Indeed." Roscoe reached for a pen. "Who knows? It might even teach him some manners."

After entirely unnecessarily thanking him, Amelia, clearly much relieved, departed; only as she walked back to the door did she notice Miranda Clifford, but his guest had her eyes on her book and kept them there.

Rawlins returned after seeing Amelia out. "You want for me to pay his lordship a visit?"

Already writing a letter—more in the nature of an excommunicatory decree—to Christopher, Lord Treloar, Roscoe shook his head. "No—I want you and Mudd with me. Mr. Clifford's disappearance is more urgent, and this letter . . ." He paused and read what he'd written, then, lips curving with dark satisfaction, continued, "Will, I fancy, suffice to take care of Treloar." He signed and blotted the missive, folded it, wrote Treloar's name on the front, then handed the letter to Rawlins. "Jordan will have his lordship's direction. Send one of the other men to deliver this, then explain the situation to Jordan and ask him to send word to all the clubs. Treloar is banned for life—or until I see fit to rescind my decision."

Rawlins grinned. "Yes, sir." Taking the letter, he left, a distinct spring in his step.

The door closed behind Rawlins and silence descended. Roscoe sat in his chair and considered Miranda Clifford's down-bent head. Waited . . .

When she finally glanced sideways up the room at him, he caught her gaze. "I do not permit prostitution, or soliciting for same, to be practiced in my establishments. I have a large number of female staff, but I ensure they make an excellent living at their trade—dealing cards and managing the social aspects of said establishments."

She returned his gaze steadily, then said, "I hadn't really thought of it, but if I had . . . I suspect I would have made the same mistake as all of society and assumed such practices were an integral part of gambling establishments."

"Which shows how much society knows." He hesitated, then said, "My establishments are specifically designed to attract hardened, inveterate gamblers—they're the ones who lose the most money—and the truth is that all hardened gamblers are essentially blind to feminine company while gambling."

Her lips quirked. She looked down. "I can imagine that's true—in my experience, men, all men, tend to focus on only one thing at a time." Settling on the sofa, she raised her book and fixed her gaze on the page.

He studied her for an instant, then, inwardly shaking his head, returned to the letter he'd been writing.

Why he'd felt the need to defend himself—and the women who worked for him—he didn't know, but he had felt not just an impulse but a compulsion to do so.

While he escorted Miranda Clifford downstairs to the smaller dining room, where, Rundle had informed him, luncheon was awaiting them, he wrestled with the realization that, for some reason, her opinion of him and his people mattered.

Given his history, that made little sense; he'd long ago turned his back on the opinion of polite society.

Then again, as he ushered her into the dining parlor and saw the linen cloth on the table, the dishes, silverware, and crystal laid out, it seemed he wasn't the only one trying to show his best face to Roderick's sister.

After settling her in the chair to the right of his carver, he sat, and wondered if his staff's reactions, their insistence on providing the sort of service they considered her due—

morning tea on a tray, luncheon in the dining parlor—had arisen because she was the only lady he had ever permitted inside this house, much less inside his study, his inner sanctum.

That was, he had to admit, excuse enough for their actions. He wasn't entirely sure what had moved him to acquiesce, but he was and doubtless always would be an easy mark for anyone devoted to protecting family.

Miranda looked about her with keen interest, drinking in all she saw. Far from being bored, she'd spent her morning being . . . educated. She hadn't expected to be waited on, to be served morning tea from a Sèvres service, then escorted to a luncheon table so elegantly laid. Nothing jarred; nothing was too ornate or heavy. Or too extravagant.

The food followed a similar principle; a light soup, followed by platters of cold meats and seafood patties, with various vegetable garnishes. Cheeses followed, along with a fruit platter. The wine was light and fruity, too.

On entering the room and sinking into the chair Roscoe had held for her, her gaze had fallen on the wide painting adorning the opposite wall—a Scottish scene complete with stag. It had looked vaguely familiar, so she'd asked him about it, then extended the conversation to the other artwork she'd seen—the paintings on the walls, the busts, figurines, and sculpted bowls placed here and there, the fabulous tapestries.

While they ate, he answered her questions; his eye for art was one subject they both, apparently, felt was safe. Regardless, his answers and the appreciation and knowledge they revealed only underscored her increasingly definite conclusion.

Neville Roscoe, London's gambling king, wasn't who, much less what, society thought him.

"I have to ask." Leaning back in his chair, long fingers idly stroking the stem of his crystal goblet, he fixed her with a direct blue glance. "Won't your aunt be missing you by now?"

"No. I told her at breakfast that I was going out to visit someone I hoped would help me find Roderick."

"From all I've gathered, she would be horrified to learn that you're here, under this particular roof."

Miranda quelled a shudder at the thought of Gladys's reaction. "I daresay she would, but I'm twenty-nine years old and very much my own person—and at this point my first and only aim is to find and rescue Roderick." She considered, then added, "Gladys is, in all probability, frantic with worry as we speak. However, her obsession with avoiding scandal is such that she will not lift a finger to find out where Roderick is, which leaves finding help and rescuing him up to me."

"Speaking of which . . ." Roscoe caught her gaze. "As you've yet to receive any demand, I think we can rule out ransom as a motive. Which leads me to ask if, to your knowledge, Roderick had any enemies."

She thought, after a moment shook her head. "I honestly can't think of anyone with whom he's had even a significant disagreement."

Roscoe inwardly grimaced, unsurprised by her answer. Her brother was quiet, earnest, kind and generous, personable, but not stupid, the sort of person who created very few ripples while walking through the pond of life. But . . . he considered her. "I know a little of Roderick's background— that he was born in Cheshire, at Oakgrove Manor, which he inherited from your father and continues to own. But I need to know more—there might be something in your joint pasts that might connect with this, so give me a potted history."

His reason was real enough, but he also wanted to learn more about her, and it would keep her occupied while they waited for his men to find some sign.

"Well . . . Roderick is the youngest of the three of us— Rosalind, me, then him. We were all born at Oakgrove. Our parents were alive, then, of course, but when Roderick was an infant and I was six, and Rosalind seven, our parents died in a boating accident." She sat back in her chair, her gaze on her plate, then fleetingly arched her brows. "Truth be told,

even I can't remember much of our parents. Our aunts—
Corrine and Gladys Cuthbert—our mother's older unmarried sisters, came to live with us, and—"

He listened, and with a question here, a query there,
teased out a far more detailed history than the one in his file.
A history of Roderick, but equally, indeed even more so, a
history of her.

It took a little probing to make sense of the basis of her aunt's
belief in Miranda's and Roderick's social vulnerability—the
reason they had to live by a rigidly respectable code. He'd
known that Roderick's money, and therefore hers, too, derived from the mills, but they hadn't themselves engaged in
trade, nor had their parents. At least in the circle to which
he'd been born, that absolved them of any implied taint.
Money—as the aristocracy well understood—was money;
where it came from only mattered if the connection was still
fresh enough, as someone had once put it, to be smelled.

That said, in the lower gentry, the circle in which her aunt
moved, the rules might well be different; for all he knew, her
aunt's view might be entirely valid in that sphere.

But as he'd hoped, Miranda's revelations took him further.
Her position in Roderick's life, largely standing between her
brother and her aunts, explained her habit of toeing the line
her aunts had drawn regardless of whether it suited her or
not. It wasn't so much what she said in describing Roderick's
life as the minor asides, and what she didn't say, that told
the tale; especially after her elder sister's sad death, she had,
over and again, bowed to her aunts' dictates in order to keep
the peace, in order to protect Roderick.

By the time they rose from the luncheon table and he
agreed that he could see nothing in all she'd told him to suggest any enemies who might have kidnapped Roderick, he'd
also solved the conundrum she herself posed. The trenchant
respectability she clung to wasn't natural but had been imposed, constantly, over many years, on her.

She had never embraced the doctrine but had accepted

the imposition because that had been the best way to protect Roderick. However, now that clinging to respectability was no longer a viable way to protect Roderick, she'd forsaken that path, stepped away from it, and, even though the move had meant walking into an arena in which she was out of her depth, had come to him for help.

As he climbed the stairs by her side, he wondered where her new path would lead her, whether she would step back to respectability once Roderick was safe, or . . .

Regardless, his compulsion to help her find and rescue her brother had grown even more impossible to defy.

Late that afternoon, when Miranda had set aside her novel and had been standing, restlessly, by the window looking out over his rear gardens for over half an hour, playing havoc with his concentration, a tap fell on the door, then it opened and Mudd looked in.

Mudd saw him, glanced at Miranda, ducked his head in a bobbing bow, then entered. Shutting the door, Mudd faced him—but had to battle the urge to look at her.

"Well?" Setting down his pen, Roscoe put his henchman out of his misery. "What have we found?"

"Located the coach." Mudd seemed relieved to know which of them to address. "Or leastways, we know where it hails from. A jarvey dropping off a fare in Claverton Street saw it roll away—it passed him so he got a good look. He recognized it—swears it belongs to the owner of the Blue Jug, a tavern down by the docks. He—the jarvey—says the owner hires the coach out."

He glanced at the ormolu clock on one corner of his desk; it was after five o'clock. "Best we arrive at the tavern when it's most crowded." He looked at Mudd. "Tell Rawlins the three of us will leave at half past seven. We'll take one of the carriages."

"Yessir." Mudd grinned, turned, nodded politely to Miranda, and went out, closing the door behind him.

Rising, he walked down the room to where Miranda stood, frowning. "I'll go and question the owner and see what he can tell us."

Her head snapped up; she stared at him. "I'm coming, too."

He felt his face set. "No. You're not. I—"

"Mr. Roscoe." She straightened to her full height, tipped up her chin. "I—"

"Just Roscoe," he growled.

"Regardless!" Her eyes flashed. "I will not sit tamely—"

"*Miss Clifford.*" He had extensive experience in using his voice to command obedience; he used every ounce of both experience and will to shut her up.

Lips compressing to a thin line, she glared.

He ignored the glare. Only just stopped himself from returning it. "I have allowed you to sit in my house, in my study, all day, and wait so you could hear the news firsthand. That, in case you hadn't noticed, was a boon—something I didn't have to grant but elected to extend to you. However, you cannot expect me to step over the line of what I can in all conscience condone and allow you to accompany me to a dockside tavern. Even were you to agree to remain in my carriage, protected by my coachman, the area is too rough and dangerous for me to countenance taking you into it. To say it's no place for a lady, let alone a respectable one, would be a massive understatement." His impassivity teetered. "Great heavens, woman—even *I* will be taking two bodyguards with me."

She frowned, rebellion still roiling in her eyes.

"Don't make me regret allowing you to stay."

Her lips pressed tight again, holding back whatever rash words she might have uttered.

Deeming that a victory a wise man would seize with all speed, he stepped back and waved to the door. "Come. I'll walk you home." Even as he turned to the door, he sensed her drawing in a breath. "And for the Lord's sake, don't try to tell me that's not necessary!"

They left the house in stiff silence, this time taking the route through the rear gardens and out into the alley.

Irritated, but accepting she would get no further concessions from her erstwhile host, Miranda glanced at the gate as he shut it. "Is that never locked?" When he shook his head, she frowned and started down the alley. "Given the wealth of artworks in your house, many of which would be easy to carry out, aren't you worried about burglars?"

He looked at her until she met his gaze. "I'm Neville Roscoe."

She blinked. "And that's enough?"

He shrugged and faced forward. "Even the most idiotic of burglars is going to find out whose house they plan to burgle, especially a house that looks like mine. Once they learn I own it, they look elsewhere."

"Hmm." He wasn't, in her view, that frightening; from all she'd learned today, the bogeyman Neville Roscoe was largely an illusion created by a man with a subtle mind and a remarkable understanding of human foibles.

But she wasn't short of understanding herself, which was why she hadn't bothered continuing their earlier argument. She allowed him to walk her to Roderick's garden gate, bade him a civil farewell, coolly received his promise to tell her tomorrow of all he learned on the docks tonight, then inclined her head and shut the gate.

She waited until she heard his footsteps fade away down the alley, then snorted, turned, and marched to the house. Reaching the terrace, she opened the door and went into the morning room. Crossing to the escritoire, she plunked her reticule down on the desk, then planted her hands on her hips, glared at the innocuous wall, and told it what she hadn't told him. "If you imagine I'm going to sit quietly by the fire and wait until tomorrow to learn what's happened to Roderick, you, sir, need to think again."

Three hours later, from the darkness inside a hackney drawn up under the heavy shadows of the trees at one corner of

Dolphin Square, Miranda watched a sleek black town carriage turn out of the drive that led to the portico at the side of Roscoe's house. The carriage headed down the street toward the city. With the head of her grandfather's walking cane, she raised the trapdoor in the hackney's roof. "That's the one." She kept her voice unnaturally low, her tone gruff. "Follow, but don't get so close they notice you."

"Aye, sir." With a jingle of harness, the driver set his cab on the trail of the black carriage.

She drew the cloak she'd found in Roderick's armoire closer about her—about the trousers, shirt, cravat, waistcoat, and topcoat she'd borrowed from the same location—and savored the frisson, not of fear but excitement, that shivered through her. She'd never done anything so outrageously risky in all her twenty-nine years . . . and thus far she'd enjoyed every second.

She was quietly amazed by what, given just a few ounces of determination, her mind could come up with. She'd refused to accept being left at home; she'd set her eyes on a goal, and here she was, following Roscoe to his appointment at the dockside tavern.

Forty minutes later she was still clinging to the sense of mild triumph when the hackney finally rocked to a stop.

The driver leaned down so his words reached through the trapdoor. "That's them just ahead, sir. Can't go closer than this without drawing their coachman's attention."

She was already peering ahead through the murk. Sulfurous smog hung low, wreathing the buildings, adding shadows to their dilapidation and rendering the weak, distantly spaced street flares even more ineffectual. The area was every bit as insalubrious as Roscoe had intimated, but his carriage stood in the lane, more or less blocking it, solid, respectable, and reassuring. They'd drawn up just in time to see Roscoe and his men stride into the tavern, a low building slumped between two taller ones, none of which looked sound.

"Wait here." Opening the hackney door, she climbed

down—to slippery, uneven cobbles. She gave thanks she'd worn her riding boots. Quietly shutting the door, keeping her head tipped down, she walked unhurriedly toward the tavern, using the cane as if she needed it. She'd wound her hair high and tight, and anchored the mass beneath a flat-brimmed hat, her face further shadowed by the hood of the cloak she'd pulled up over the hat.

Her leather riding gloves covered her hands. As she neared the tavern, she prayed she'd covered everything that would advertise her gender.

Barely pausing to draw breath, she opened the tavern door and went in.

The atmosphere inside was even murkier than outside, but here the fug derived from a poorly drawing fire and from numerous smelly pipes various denizens were puffing. She didn't make the mistake of standing and staring but immediately turned and claimed the single chair at a small table mere feet from the door. It was the perfect spot, tucked aside, not well lit, and close to an exit. Propping her cane against the table, she sat, leaned her elbows on the scarred surface, linked her fingers and hunched forward so her gloved hands obscured the lower half of her face, and only then allowed herself to, from the shadows of her hood, scan the room.

Roscoe wasn't hard to find. He was leaning on the long counter that faced the door and talking to the balding man behind it. Mudd and Rawlins had taken chairs at a table further into the room from where they could see the door and keep an eye on their master's back at the same time, but both were presently watching Roscoe; she'd entered quietly enough that they hadn't noticed.

She stared at Roscoe's back, stared even more at the bar-keep's face, at his lips as, while polishing a glass, he answered Roscoe's questions.

"Damn!" she whispered. She couldn't hear or see well enough to guess what the barkeep was saying.

Movement to one side caught her eye; a barmaid was going from table to table taking orders, but the girl had halted and was watching Roscoe. That suited Miranda; she had no idea what to order to remain true to her disguise.

A swift glance around showed that most, if not all, of the tavern's patrons were watching Roscoe; even those chatting were keeping a wary eye on him. Everyone knew when he straightened from the bar and turned. His gaze swept the tavern; she kept her head down and held her breath as his gaze swept over her. She breathed again when that searching gaze didn't stop, didn't halt and return to her, but instead moved on to . . . glancing out from beneath the edge of her hood, she saw him push away from the bar and stroll to where a much older man sat in a shallow booth along the other side of the tavern.

Roscoe drew up a chair, set it down at the old man's table, and sat.

She swallowed another muttered imprecation; he was now closer, but still facing away from her, and he and the old man were speaking too quietly for her to hear . . . and she couldn't risk shifting nearer. Her ingenuity had got her this far, but she could see no way of furthering her aim.

Roscoe forced his mind from the cloaked figure hunched over the table by the door. He'd learned long ago never to let his temper rule him, yet in that instant when he'd sensed her—when he'd known that, somehow, she was there—and then he'd turned and seen her, his control had teetered on the very brink of failing.

It had taken every ounce of his vaunted self-control to focus instead on the old man the barkeep had said was the tavern's owner, to push away from the bar and, ignoring her, pretending his senses hadn't locked on her, walk across and engage the old man.

The owner was a gnarly old coot, but he hadn't lived as long as he had by being dim-witted. Beady eyes searching Roscoe's face, the old man asked, "What's it to you who hired me coach?"

"Sadly, it appears they didn't mention that they intended to kidnap an associate of mine. I have reason to believe that my associate's life now hangs in the balance, so"—Roscoe let his lips curve—"here I am, asking politely for information on who used your coach."

The old man read the expression in his eyes. "Heard tell of you, even down here. If'n those two wanted me to keep their business secret, they should've paid me more, now shouldn't they?"

"Indeed, they should have."

"Aye, well, as they didn't, and here you are, askin' politely, then I can tell you it was two heavyweights, call theirselves Kempsey and Dole, strictly work-for-hire, who had me coach out that night. Hired it, and the driver, too."

"Any idea who they're working for or what their current project is?"

The old man shook his head. "No idea who they're in with—they don't usually hang 'round these parts—but I'd assumed it were burglary or kidnapping, given they wanted the coach, but o'course I didn't ask. All I know is the coach was back in the stables the next morning, and I heard tell Millet—he's me driver—was sleeping in, happy enough with his outing."

Roscoe considered, then asked, "What can you tell me about Kempsey and Dole themselves? Anything you've heard might be useful."

The old man shrugged. "Like I said, they're not generally 'round here, but I've heard they'll work for anyone who can meet their price."

Roscoe read between the man's lines. "So there's very little they won't do?"

"That's what I've heard."

"All right." Roscoe straightened. "Where can I find Millet?"

After extracting the driver's likely location, Roscoe rose, nodded to the old man, then turned and headed for the tavern door. Nearing it, he slowed, then smoothly diverted to grasp the elbow of the cloaked "man" seated at the last table, effortlessly drew her to her feet, and, swiping up the cane that had rested against the table, thrust her before him out of the door.

Emerging into the cramped lane, still gripping her arm, he propelled her several yards deeper into the shadows away from the tavern door, then, jaw clenching, swung her to face him, locked his eyes with hers—wide and already kindling with fury—and snarled, "What the devil are you doing here?"

"Learning what's happened to my brother!" She didn't exactly snarl back, but she certainly didn't cower—more like snapped. Her face set in mutinous lines, she twisted her arm, fighting his hold. "Let go!"

Lips compressing, he did—reluctantly. Some part of him felt better pleased and much calmer when he had a firm grip on her.

She glared and rubbed her elbow.

The implication of the action cut through his temper and undermined it. Not that he was about to apologize.

Inwardly sighing, he closed his eyes, pinched the bridge of his nose to help him focus, then opened his eyes. "How did you get here?"

Miranda heard the resigned tenor of his tone; struggling to dampen the surge of sensation sizzling and singeing her nerves, she grudgingly replied, "That hackney." She tipped her head toward the carriage, stationary in the shadows. "He's waiting to take me back."

Roscoe frowned. "How did you get him to wait? They rarely will, not in this area."

"I paid him an extra guinea and promised him another if he waited."

Roscoe turned as Mudd came up. "Give the jarvey two guineas and tell him he won't be needed more tonight."

She took heart at the words. As Mudd, after one quick look at her, trudged over to the hackney, she asked, "So what did you learn?"

Roscoe glanced down at her. As Rawlins, faintly stunned to see her, joined them, he said, "Your brother was kidnapped by two men called Kempsey and Dole. They're hired thugs. So far I've no idea who hired them, but I know where the coach driver lives. He might have more information."

Mudd had returned in time to hear most of that. "So are we going to go and have a word with this driver, then?"

She looked up into Roscoe's shadowed face and waited.

Roscoe studied her features, even shaded by the hood far too feminine to ever be mistaken for a man's. Instinctively he weighed the odds, ranked his options, but in this case one course was imperative; they needed to get on Roderick's trail as soon as possible. "Yes." He glanced at Mudd and Rawlins. "Ride up top—tell Cummins we want Ryder Lane in Clerkenwell."

Taking her arm more gently than before, he turned and led her to his carriage. Mudd opened the door on his way to speak with Cummins, the coachman. Roscoe caught the swinging door, held it while she gathered her cloak and the cane, then steadied her as she climbed inside. Releasing her, he followed her up and in, and with commendable restraint quietly shut the door.

Miranda hung back in the shadows of the fetid runnel that was Ryder Lane and listened as Roscoe questioned the coach driver, Millet.

From her position against the opposite wall, with Mudd's shoulders partly screening her from the doorway where Millet, a pasty-faced little man with thinning hair, stood facing the three large men on his stoop, she watched Roscoe impress on the hapless coach driver why answering his questions quickly and honestly would be in Millet's own best interests.

Until then she hadn't seen even a hint of anything frightening in Roscoe, but in the tiny lane, everything about him—his stance, his voice, his every movement—projected a lethal menace that made her shiver.

It made Millet quake. "Yessir." Wringing his hands, he bobbed. "I understand—I do."

"Excellent. So, Kempsey and Dole—the men who hired the coach and you to drive it—where did you pick them up?"

"They was waiting at the Blue Jug, at the stables out back, when I arrived. They helped me put the horses to, then had me drive all the way to Pimlico."

"You pulled up where?"

"End of Chichester Street, it was. Past the square and where it meets the next street—Claverton, that'd be."

"So you halted there. Then what? Tell me what happened, everything you saw and heard."

"The pair o'em—Kempsey and Dole—they didn't talk much. Once I pulled up, they climbed down, told me to wait just there and not move, and then they sloped off. I thought at first they'd gone under the trees in the square, but later—when they lugged the baggage, whatever it was, to the coach—they came from the other side of the street, so p'rhaps they hid in one of the doorways along there."

"Most likely. What was the baggage they put into the coach?"

Millet looked nervous. "The truth, guv'nor, is I can't be sure."

"Why not?"

"Well, it were dark, for a start—no street flares along there. All I could see was they were lugging something—looked like a lumpy rug rolled up—with one o'em at each end. Seemed heavyish, but not so they was straining under the weight." Millet paused, as if reviewing a memory. "Dole put his end down, opened the coach door, then Dole picked up his end again and backed up and into the coach and Kempsey followed."

"So their baggage could have been a man wrapped in a cloak or blanket?"

Millet nodded warily. "Aye—could've been."

"Very well. What happened next? Where did you take them?"

"That was the strangest bit. I'd assumed I'd be driving 'em back to town, but no—Kempsey sent me north. They had me drive 'em up Paddington way to a lane where they had another coach waiting."

"Another coach?"

"Aye—it were a traveling coach, see? Just a local lad watching it for 'em—no driver or groom. They sent the lad packing, then they moved the baggage from my coach to the other one, then they sent me off with the rest of m' pay."

Roscoe paused, then asked, "Any idea which way they went?"

"I didn't stick 'round to see, but the coach was facing northwest-ish. Away from the city."

"You know coaches and horses—tell me what you can about this other coach."

Millet scrunched up his face. "Couldn't see much—there weren't any lights—but I'd say it was just an ordinary, average, run-of-the-mill traveler, not new, much the same age as the one from the Blue Jug. No great shakes, most likely another hire. As for the horses, they was jobbers, sure as eggs. Slow plodders, I'd say. . . ." Millet paused, then went on, "Just remembered why I was so sure they were heading out of town—there were bags in the boot. I spotted 'em as I was turning my rig around."

Roscoe searched Millet's unprepossessing face. "Very well." He held Millet's gaze for an instant, then nodded. "Good night, Millet."

Millet all but sagged with relief.

Roscoe turned away; reaching for Miranda's arm, he drew her with him as he strode back up the lane.

"Do you have any idea who might want Roderick dead?" Sitting facing Miranda in his town carriage as it rocked through the city on the way back to Pimlico, Roscoe scanned her features in the faint light cast by the coach's interior lamps. He'd drawn the curtains over the windows and lit the lamps so he could better question her. Leaning forward, his elbows on his thighs, he watched her wrack her brain.

But, as before, she shook her head. "No. I can't think of anyone." She met his gaze. "Perhaps this *is* about ransom—"

"No. Quite aside from the lack of a ransom demand, moving Roderick out of London makes very little sense in terms of holding him to ransom."

"But *has* he been taken out of London? Are you sure we can trust Millet's reading of Kempsey and Dole's intentions?"

He replayed the interview with Millet, then grimly said, "In general, I wouldn't trust Millet about anything, but he had no reason to invent what he told us, and everything he reported was exactly what a man in his line of business would notice—the age and type of coach, the horses, and the luggage in the boot."

Glancing at the window, away from her and the worry in her eyes, he let his mind range over all they'd thus far learned, gauging the possibilities . . . on an exasperated sigh, he sat back. Across the carriage, he met her eyes. "None of this adds up. We're missing something."

She frowned. "What do you mean?"

"I mean that if someone wanted Roderick dead, then dead is dead, and if killing him had been what Kempsey and Dole had been paid to do, then we should have found his body on the pavement in Chichester Street."

Miranda sucked in a breath, then let it out with, "But as we didn't?"

"As we haven't found a body yet, then . . ." Roscoe frowned. "I don't know. The facts don't fit with ransom, but they don't fit a simple killing, either. Moving him out of London . . . I can't see what would have prompted them to that."

She seized on the implication. "But as they did move him, that suggests he's still alive, doesn't it?" She fixed her gaze on his face. "Why would they move an already dead body?"

He considered, then nodded. "You're right—they

wouldn't. Or at least, I can't see any reason hired killers like Kempsey and Dole would bother. The river was there at the end of the street. So . . . at the moment we have no reason to imagine that Roderick isn't still alive."

After a moment, he said, "One classic question—who profits from Roderick's death?"

When she glanced at him, he arched a brow. She frowned. "As far as I'm aware— and as I am twenty-nine and in charge of my own fortune I know the terms of my parents' wills—if Roderick dies, *I'm* the only one who stands to gain."

He nodded grimly. "That's what I thought. So no clues there."

A minute ticked past. She felt as if her brain was only slowly absorbing the full implications of all they'd learned . . . she looked at Roscoe. "What about Kempsey and Dole? Can we learn more about them?"

His gaze distant, he nodded. "That's our next step."

She waited, but he didn't say more, and a few minutes later the carriage slowed, then turned. Fine gravel crunched under the wheels; seconds later, the carriage halted.

Roscoe opened the door and climbed out, then turned to assist Miranda, in her male attire but with the scandalous sight concealed by her cloak, down to the flags in the portico of his house.

Mudd and Rawlins dropped down from the carriage's roof.

He turned to them. "Go and tell Gallagher I want a meeting. He can choose where, but it has to be in the open."

"Yes, sir."

He nodded at the carriage. "You may as well take it—just make sure you bring it back."

Mudd and Rawlins grinned. They opened the carriage door, calling the direction to Cummins on the box, laughed at Cummins's predictably dour reply, then climbed quickly in.

Drawing Miranda into the shadows beneath the portico, Roscoe waited while Cummins drove the carriage forward and around the turning circle, then past them and back into the street.

"Who is Gallagher?" she asked.

"Someone you really don't want to know." He glanced at her, then waved down the drive to where marble steps led up to the rear gardens. "Come along, Miss Clifford—regardless of your attire, I'll walk you home."

Chapter Four

Miranda arrived at Roscoe's house even earlier the next morning, but from Rundle's smile she got the distinct impression that she'd been expected.

Anticipated.

Rundle showed her upstairs to the study, announced her, and left, closing the door behind him.

Roscoe, seated behind the desk and sipping from a mug as he looked over various documents and letters, glanced up as she neared.

His gaze fixed, arrested, on her, as if he hadn't seen a lilac walking dress before, then he blinked and focused his dark blue gaze on her face. "I have a meeting scheduled with Gallagher at eleven o'clock."

"Where?" Setting her reticule down on a side table, she remained standing. Slanting sunlight struck red glints from his richly dark hair.

"The museum. The main hall."

The notion of the museum hosting meetings of underworld figures was rather eye-opening . . . she smiled. "Excellent! So I can attend, too."

"Yes, and no." His gaze skated down her figure again. "Gallagher doesn't need to know you exist. He doesn't even need to know it's Roderick who's been taken. No sane person ever gives Gallagher information of that sort. One can have no certainty what such information might subsequently be used for." He met her eyes. "So you can attend the meeting, but—"

"I'll need to be disguised again."

"Yes." He sat back in his chair, regarding her in what she now realized was a measuring way. "But not as a male. You'll need bonnet, veil, gloves—things to cover as much of you as possible. I'll have a maid and footman of mine go with you—you'll travel to the museum with them in one of my town carriages." He met her eyes. "Be back here at ten-thirty. We'll leave then."

With that, he returned his gaze to his papers.

She was not one of his men. She stood where she was, looking down on his dark head.

Eventually, he sighed, looked up at her, and arched a weary brow.

She smiled. "Thank you."

With that, she whirled, swiped up her reticule, walked back to the door, and let herself out.

Roscoe watched the door close. When he was sure she was gone, he shook his head. "What the hell am I doing?"

No answer came.

With another shake of his head, he hauled his attention back to his desk, to the work he wanted to finish before she returned to distract him.

Superbly disguised in her mourning weeds from when her aunt Corrine had passed on, Miranda stood in the museum's great hall, her veiled gaze fixed on a large painting of a crucifixion, and waited for the meeting to begin.

She even had a black-lace-edged handkerchief clutched in one hand.

The maid Roscoe had provided, also soberly dressed,

stood a pace behind her, carrying her black shawl. Her footman, a strapping young man, suitably handsome, stood idle but attentive beside the maid.

Roscoe had told her which painting to stand near; now she was in position, she was growing impatient, but the large clock on the wall above the entrance showed that it still wanted a few minutes to eleven o'clock.

She was about to shift her gaze back to the painting when the entrance doors swung open, held open by two men to admit a third—a massive mountain of a man who, gripping two walking canes, one in each hand, shuffled his bulk, plainly garbed in a brown suit, into the hall. Halting inside the doors, the huge man glanced about; his face was a mass of fleshy jowls and puffy cheeks from which small beady eyes surveyed the world.

Sighting the bench facing the painting before which she stood angled, the massive man grunted and heaved himself toward it.

Gallagher. From behind the screen of her veil, she watched him reach the bench, then, with his henchmen hovering, lower himself onto it. With a wave, he dismissed his men; they retreated to stand by the walls, one to either side, keeping watch over their master.

Although the great hall wasn't crowded, it wasn't deserted, either. Aside from herself and her attendants, there were several other couples and small groups strolling and admiring the works on display, while a steady stream of patrons crossed the hall on their way to other rooms.

Before she had time to grow impatient again, Roscoe arrived. Striding into the hall with Mudd and Rawlins behind him, he paused, saw Gallagher, turned his head and spoke to Mudd and Rawlins, then walked unhurriedly to the bench. Without looking at or acknowledging Gallagher in any way, Roscoe sat on the bench, a few feet distant; leaning forward, resting his forearms on his thighs, he looked at the painting.

Behind her veil, she sighed, then crossed to the other side

of the painting, head tilting as if studying the work. The new position gave her a clearer view of Gallagher's face.

His beady eyes flicked sideways to Roscoe. "So what can I do for you on this fine morning?"

Roscoe's impassive expression didn't change. "I'm sure the man you had watching my house has reported that two thugs, Kempsey and Dole, snatched an acquaintance of mine off the street near my house, which he'd just left. As I'm sure you can imagine, I'm unhappy about having my hospitality tainted by such an occurrence."

Gallagher kept his gaze fixed on the painting. "Understandable."

"Indeed. I want to know everything about Kempsey and Dole, and most importantly I want to know who hired them."

"Not why?"

"Why would be nice, but in this case, once I know who, the why should be apparent."

"Hmm." Gallagher paused, then in quite a different tone asked, "How's my great-nephew doing?"

"Well. You were right—he has a good head for figures and is quick to learn. If he keeps his eyes on the path and doesn't stray, I expect he'll be climbing several rungs shortly."

"Good to know." Gallagher's tone became more brisk. "As for Kempsey and Dole, they're not locals. Word is they hail from Birmingham, but they've been operating out of the Hood and Gable tavern in Mile End for the last several years, strictly for hire. My sources say they're good at their business. Never had cause to use them myself, but that's what I've heard."

"Any notion who hired them?"

"I only know it wasn't one of *us*."

It was Roscoe's turn to cast Gallagher a sideways glance. "You're sure?"

"Like you said, I heard that it'd happened. Seemed downright reckless, shall we say. Sure as the sun rising you were going to come asking, so I asked first. None of the usual suspects hereabouts know anything about it, but Quirk—

his lads sometimes use the Hood and Gable—let me know that a couple of his lads had seen Kempsey and Dole take a packet from some man. Looked like a deal had been struck, which is why his lads thought to mention it to Quirky. Naturally, Quirky asked after who the man doing the hiring was, but he was a stranger and entirely forgettable—brown hair, middling to tall, average otherwise, clothes not new, even a trifle shabby. Seems he sported a slashing scar down one cheek, but with all the men back from the wars, in terms of identification a scarred face isn't what it used to be."

"Sadly not." After a moment, Roscoe said, "So it's likely Kempsey and Dole are working for some man indistinguishable from untold others, and unconnected with any of the major operators."

"Aye. And the only other tidbit I've got that might help is that Kempsey and Dole often use a coach from the stables behind the Hood and Gable. Seems they've currently got the coach out, along with the regular horses. Dole usually drives. The coach isn't notable in any way, but the horses—one's a dun with a pale mane and the other's a muddy gray."

Roscoe straightened. "That will help. What about Kempsey and Dole themselves?"

"Heavyset, the pair of them, but Kempsey's the real bruiser. Dole's a trifle taller and quicker on his feet. Kempsey's the leader, the talker. Dole follows and keeps his tongue between his teeth. Kempsey's got short brown hair, going salt-and-pepper. Dole has longer, dark brown hair and has a cauliflower ear. Both dress plain but neat enough, and speak with an accent, Birmingham-way, most like."

Roscoe committed the sketchy descriptions to memory. "One last thing. Do they carry pistols?"

"Not generally. Both favor knives, or their fists or blunt weapons." Gallagher paused, then added, "They're that sort of thug."

Escorted by his people back to Roscoe's house, then shown into the dining parlor where the previous day they'd lunched,

Miranda paced and wondered where the devil Roscoe was, and, more importantly, what he was doing. She'd remained in the great hall with her attendants, ostensibly viewing further paintings, while Roscoe, followed by the much slower Gallagher, had left the building; only then had she quit the scene.

Finally the door opened and Roscoe entered. Facing him, she halted. "So what now?"

Closing the door, he met her gaze. "Now, we eat." Waving to the table, he strolled around it to hold her chair. "And then I'll see you home."

She sat, settled, restrained her impatience enough to let him sit in the carver to her left before asking, "But what about following Kempsey and Dole? What about Roderick?"

"I've sent men to hunt down that coach, or more specifically those horses." He flicked out his napkin, glanced up as Rundle arrived with a platter of sliced meats. "No matter who's paying them, those two won't be silly enough to travel via the posting houses. They won't change horses—they'll roll slowly along and stop whenever they need to rest their mismatched pair."

She used the minutes while Rundle served them to cogitate further. When the butler withdrew, she glanced at Roscoe, took in his entirely uninformative expression. But of course he had some plan. "Once you've located Kempsey and Dole—and hopefully that will mean Roderick as well— what then?"

Roscoe chewed, swallowed, and kept his gaze on his plate. "Once I learn where they're heading, I'll go after them and bring Roderick back." *Assuming Roderick is still alive.*

A second passed. "Do you think he's still alive?"

He inwardly sighed, then looked at her. "I think it's likely. I can't fathom what's going on here—if they'd killed him, that coach would be back in the stables, but my men have already confirmed it's not. So . . ." He ate another mouthful, then offered, "The next most likely option is that they're taking him somewhere, possibly to deliver to someone, presumably whoever hired them." He glanced at her, at the concentration in her face as she, too, ate; he felt irrationally pleased that she was at least eating. "I take it you've as yet had no revelation over who might be behind this?"

She shook her head. "I have no idea."

"Nor I. Regardless, what we now know suggests that if we move quickly to follow Kempsey and Dole, we'll have a reasonable chance of getting Roderick back alive."

She sipped the water she'd had Rundle pour for her instead of the headier wine. "So once you know where they are, you'll send some of your henchmen to deal with them and get Roderick back."

A statement that was in fact a question.

"No. I'll go myself."

She looked at him, met his gaze. "You will?" When he nodded, she frowned. "But I've seen you're constantly busy—"

"Miss Clifford." Briefly he compressed his lips. "Why am I bothering?" The question was rhetorical; he went on, "Miranda—I may have described Roderick as an acquaintance to Gallagher, but I view your brother as a friend. He's put his trust in me and followed my lead philanthropically, and I will do for him what I would for any friend—I'll go after him myself, not leave his rescue to my men, no matter how trusted and able said men might be."

She searched his eyes, then inclined her head. "Thank you."

She returned her attention to her plate.

He followed her lead, wondering . . .

"I'll go with you, of course."

He inwardly sighed. "No. You won't."

"We're not having that argument again, are we?"

He shook his head. "You're not coming with me."

She shot him a narrow-eyed glance, one he pretended not to notice. "You do realize"—her tone was even, the soul of reasonableness shining through—"that I will follow you regardless, on my own if need be, and, of course, I'm much more likely to get into difficulties, into danger, while traveling on my own than if I travel with you."

Setting down his knife and fork, he tossed his napkin down by his plate, then turned to her. "There's no reason for you to further involve yourself—"

"Actually, there's several." Waving a fork to emphasize, she stated, "I'm Roderick's sister—his nearest kin. If he's badly injured, matters will go much more smoothly if I'm there to speak for him."

He pressed his lips together; that, unfortunately, was unarguable, and a possibility.

"More, if he's injured, it will be infinitely easier for him if I'm there—what if he's taken a knock on the head and doesn't recognize you?" Lowering the fork, she looked down at her plate, then set her cutlery down. "And furthermore, I can't just sit here, safe in London, and wait. I'll go mad with worry."

About you both. Miranda kept that little snippet to herself. Folding her napkin, she laid it alongside her plate and turned to face him.

Apparently recognizing that trying to argue her points would be futile, he was frowning. "I can't see how—"

"It's simple." He wasn't the only one who could plan, and she'd had plenty of time to think since leaving the museum. "We travel openly together, with me in my weeds." She waved a hand at her dull black gown. "I'll be a widow traveling to attend some relative's sickbed, and you'll be a friend of the family escorting me thither. That's a perfectly acceptable scenario, and it will also provide *you* with an excellent disguise. When we find Kempsey and Dole, there'll be no reason for them to be suspicious of you. It's vital to give you a plausible reason for being there, otherwise you'll put them on alert simply by appearing.

"*And*, of course, a lady can always have a bad day and feel too ill to travel, so if we need to dally nearby to spirit Roderick out of Kempsey and Dole's clutches, we won't need to invent anything else to excuse us lingering in the vicinity."

She paused, then added, "I also know how to care for injuries, at least minor ones." Raising her gaze, she met his and stated categorically, "My plan will work perfectly well."

Roscoe let his frown grow blacker. "I can just as well take Mudd and Rawlins—"

"No, you can't. Gallagher said Kempsey and Dole were good at their business, which means that immediately they clap eyes on Mudd and Rawlins, they'll recognize them for what they are—someone's henchmen."

"They prefer the term *bodyguards.*"

"Indeed. Men who guard someone powerful enough to need and pay for them, and who will very likely do violence at that someone's behest." She nodded. "Precisely." She held his gaze. "If you go with Mudd and Rawlins, or on your own, you'll stand out from the populace, no matter how you dress, and Kempsey and Dole will spot you and see you for the threat you are." She broke off, caught her breath, then, her gaze now distant, her expression sober, said, "Who knows? If they sense a threat, they might even kill Roderick so he can't be a witness against them."

There was nothing he could advance against that.

She refocused on him, her expression even more resolute. More stubborn. "We need to present an unthreatening appearance, one that will allow us to find Kempsey and Dole, to approach closely enough to rescue Roderick, and then be able to care for and protect him if he's hurt."

He inwardly sighed. "Miranda, it's not going to take just a day. What do you imagine—"

She demolished every argument he advanced. No matter which way he tacked to get around "her plan," to get around her, she blocked him, and argued, and the more she did, the more her plan seemed the only viable course.

He even tried to prick her temper, but she realized, narrowed her eyes, and glared, then, with supreme disdain, if not contempt, ignored the jibe.

Finally, he was reduced to invoking an authority that, had it been at all possible, he would rather have not. "What about your aunt? What's she going to say about you traveling alone with me?" When she didn't immediately respond, he pressed his advantage. "Does she even know you're here? That you're spending your days with me, under my scandalous roof?"

She met his eyes, then coolly stated, "No, my aunt doesn't know I'm here. However, if given the choice, she would prefer *not* to know, rather than for me not to be here. That might sound convoluted, but Gladys is now just as worried about Roderick as I am. She knows that, wherever I am, I'm doing everything I can to find him and bring him home. If we have to follow Kempsey and Dole into the country, as seems likely, then of course I'll tell her, but only that I'm going after Roderick with the friend who's been helping me trace him, and that I must go. That's all there is to it, and that's all I'll tell her. And while she might wring her hands, she won't forbid it or stand in my way."

He absorbed the unwavering, rock-solid resolution in her eyes, took in the rigid, unbending stubbornness investing her chin and the set of her lips . . . she'd become more definite, more confident, much more her own woman since that first night she'd walked into his house.

He was powerful enough to say no and enforce it, and quash her emerging confidence.

He couldn't do it, couldn't bring himself to push her back into the cage of inexperience and uncertainty from which, it seemed, she was escaping, pulled to it, drawn to it, by her need to rescue Roderick.

Heaven knew, he knew all about the transformative power of a protective instinct called to action; he was in no way the same man he'd been twelve years ago, and the man he was now was so much more than the man he had been.

But . . .

He'd held her gaze throughout, and she'd held his, waiting.

He grunted noncommittally, then growled, "We'll see. Before we can institute any course of action, we have to find some trace of Kempsey and Dole and their mismatched nags."

He'd half expected her to smile triumphantly, but she merely inclined her head and agreed, with no further fuss, to allow him to escort her home.

Given it was broad daylight, Miranda found herself seated beside Roscoe in one of his town carriages as it rattled the short distance down Chichester Street, up Claverton Street, then down the alley beside her brother's house. When the carriage halted alongside the gate, Roscoe opened the door, stepped out, then handed her down.

She felt the disconcerting frisson when his fingers clasped hers, but she'd expected it and had steeled herself against the effect; it wasn't nearly as bad as the incidents the previous evening when, again and again, he had without warning gripped her elbow or her arm. Once safely on the flags of the alley, she slid her fingers from his grasp and congratulated herself on concealing the unsettling reaction. "Thank you."

She faced him and said nothing more, simply waited.

He returned her gaze. Seconds ticked past, then he grudgingly yielded. "I'll send word the instant I hear."

Approvingly, she inclined her head, let him open the gate for her, then carefully stepped through. Catching the gate, she turned to close it. Stepping back, he saluted her; she smiled and shut the gate. She paused and heard the carriage door shut, then the wheels rattled away.

Turning, she made her way slowly through the garden, thinking over all she'd learned. Not just about Roderick, and Roscoe, but even more about herself. That fear for Roderick would dictate and drive her actions came as no surprise. What did surprise her was what she'd done and achieved, how she'd behaved and responded.

She hadn't hesitated to argue with Roscoe, to insist and demand that he allow her to claim her due role in Roderick's rescue. She hadn't felt reticent over pushing her view of how that rescue would best be accomplished. All in all, over the last two days she was proud of what she'd accomplished . . . and felt somehow freer, clearer, more certain of herself, more definite in her own mind about a self she didn't entirely recognize.

As she walked toward the house, she tried to pin the elusive feeling down, to bring it into sharper focus. Reaching the terrace, she crossed it, opened the door, and stepped into the morning room.

Gladys sat on the sofa facing the windows. "There you are! About time! Where have you been?" Gladys leaned forward, peering at her face. "Have you heard anything about Roderick?"

The fear in her voice made it clear that the last question was Gladys's principal concern. Miranda used the minute it took to set down her reticule and shawl, and reach up and pull the pins from her black hat, removing it and the veil she'd left pushed back, to decide what to say. Facing Gladys, she opted for brevity. "Roderick was kidnapped on his way home that night. Two men bundled him into a coach and drove off—we haven't yet learned where they've taken him, and we have no idea why."

Gladys paled. For a long moment, gaze fixed on Miranda's face, she grappled with the bald facts. Eventually, lips primming tight, her aunt sat back. "'We' who? Who have you been with? And where?"

"'We' means me and the friend of Roderick's who's helping me search for him. I've been at Roderick's friend's house—it's not far away." She'd told Roscoe the truth; Gladys was as distressed as she was over Roderick's disappearance, but also felt helpless, and therefore panicky, and that left her aunt caught on the horns of a dilemma. Gladys wanted Miranda to find Roderick, wanted him rescued and restored to his home safe and sound, but the specter of a scandal, as always, loomed large in Gladys's mind.

For herself, in the matter of rescuing Roderick, scandal had lost its bite. *Being ruined. Rescuing her baby brother.* Against the latter, the former didn't even register in the scales.

Perhaps that was why she no longer felt constrained by the strictures she'd lived under for so long.

Gladys shifted restlessly, then held out a hand. "Here— help me up. I'm going to sit in the drawing room."

Taking Gladys's arm, Miranda helped her aunt to her feet. Shaking off Miranda's support, Gladys used her cane to stump slowly to the door. She almost always sat in the drawing room, embroidering or reading—just in case someone should call. Few did, but Gladys set great store by appearances and on being ready to give the right impression.

Reaching the door, Gladys opened it, then looked back at Miranda. "I'm not going to ask and you're not going to tell, but mark my words, miss, you need to watch that no matter what you do you don't step over any line. You can't afford to ruin your chances with Wraxby—he's likely the last chance you'll get to leave Roderick's roof, so beware. Gentlemen like Mr. Wraxby have very strong views on what constitutes proper behavior for a lady."

She raised her brows and spoke in a tone she couldn't remember using before. "That may well be, Aunt, but if Mr. Wraxby is so lacking in proper feeling that he can't accept that I will do whatever I must to rescue Roderick . . ." *Then Wraxby isn't the man for me.* She heard the words in her head but drew breath and substituted, "Then we'll just have to ensure that he never learns of Roderick's rescue, and as he's conveniently returned to Suffolk, we don't need to worry about him at this juncture."

Declaring that she wouldn't marry Wraxby if that was his attitude would only throw Gladys into a different sort of flap and precipitate a long and difficult argument that neither Miranda nor Gladys needed.

Gladys's narrowed, agatey eyes held her gaze, then her aunt humphed and turned away.

Listening to Gladys's heavy footsteps recede, Miranda waited, expecting to start thinking about her aunt, about the household, the menus, the this and that—the myriad small demands of her life within the house. Instead, while she sensed all those issues hovering, waiting to trap her and drag her back into her daily net of busywork, they no longer held sufficient power to trap and hold her.

Collecting her reticule and shawl, she went into the hall and climbed the stairs. In her room, she tugged the bellpull and dispatched a maid to find her traveling bag, then started sorting through her wardrobe, selecting the clothes she would take on her adventure to rescue her brother, assembling all she would need while traveling with Roscoe once he learned where Kempsey and Dole had taken Roderick.

She was cinching the bag's strap when she realized that she *expected* to hear from Roscoe, at the very latest by the next day. Her confidence in his abilities had grown to be that complete—along with her faith that, when he learned that vital piece of information, he would indeed tell her.

Chapter Five

"I can't believe I'm doing this." Roscoe grumbled the words to himself, but he didn't care if his companion heard them.

"That makes two of us." Her tone made it clear her view of their present situation was the opposite of his.

Seated beside him on the box seat of his curricle, alert and upright with a dark cloak over her mourning gown and her face screened by the black veil attached to her bonnet, from the moment he'd flicked the reins and driven them out from beneath the portico of his house, she'd been absorbed with everything about them, her eyes behind the veil attentively scanning the busy streets.

He wouldn't have been surprised if she'd been sunk in her own thoughts, dragged down by worry and concern for her brother. He didn't doubt that the worry and concern were there, beneath her glib veneer, but he could appreciate the philosophy of making the most of any moment.

He'd driven north and west, out along the Oxford Road, following the trail of the battered old coach with its mismatched nags that Kempsey and Dole had bundled Roderick into.

When he'd dispatched a note to her at eight o'clock that morning, despite her resolution of the previous day he hadn't been sure she would still wish to accompany him. Wiser heads might have prevailed. She might have come to her respectability-loving senses and recognized the unwisdom, the potential for social disaster.

She hadn't replied to his note.

She'd arrived on his doorstep, cloaked and veiled, with a traveling bag at her half-booted feet.

If anything, her resolution had vulcanized; he hadn't even attempted to remonstrate further. That said, while he could accept that she might not regret their venture, he wasn't sure he wouldn't come to regret his leniency in allowing her to be his accomplice. He'd had to argue with Mudd, Rawlins, Rundle, and even Jordan, none of whom could understand what had driven him to accede to her request.

He knew what it was; he just couldn't put it into words or explain it to anyone. "How's your aunt taking this? What did you tell her about this trip?"

"I explained that you—Roderick's friend—had found his trail, and we, you and I, had to follow it and rescue him."

"And she didn't protest?"

Miranda glanced at him. "I've explained my aunt's equivocal position, and I'm twenty-nine years old—I've been able to make my own decisions for some years." Not that she had, but she was making up for that now. "While I might acquiesce to Gladys's wishes in most things, in this"—she shrugged—"I didn't ask her permission, and she didn't attempt to dissuade me."

She'd acted decisively, and it had felt *good*. Good to make up her own mind and act on her own judgment. Good to step beyond her aunts' confining strictures and instead follow her own instincts and principles.

Leaning forward, she peered through her veil. "The village ahead looks larger than any we've seen to this point."

"Uxbridge. We'll stop there and check that our quarry did, indeed, pass this way."

* * *

Several hours later, they halted for lunch at High Wycombe. Roscoe handed her down in the yard of the Five Bells.

"Thank you." While he dealt with the ostlers, she resettled her gown, then glanced up to find him offering his arm. She hesitated for only a second before placing her fingers on his sleeve; better that than having him take her arm.

Nevertheless, as she walked beside him up the shallow steps to the inn's front porch and into the foyer, she was distracted by the feel of steely muscle beneath his sleeve, by a compulsion to sink her fingertips more firmly into said muscle and *feel*.

Subtle warmth spread through her; she was glad of her veil.

They halted before a counter at the rear of the foyer. Roscoe arranged for a private parlor and gave orders for their meal, then glanced at her.

Reaching up and putting back her veil, she smiled wearily at the innkeeper. "We're following two men my family hired to escort a gentleman, my cousin, north. We were supposed to leave London all together, but we were delayed and they went ahead. It must have been three days ago that they passed this way. I wondered if you or your people had seen them."

At Uxbridge, they'd discovered that if she, in her weeds, asked for information, she elicited sympathy and more ready, less restrained answers, and often active help.

The innkeeper shook his head. "I'm sorry, ma'am—I don't recall such a group stopping here. But I'll ask around and see what I can learn."

"Thank you." With a grateful smile, she lowered her veil, then let Roscoe escort her in the innkeeper's wake into the parlor. They'd agreed to treat each other as two friends would, calling each other by first name, avoiding the possible complication of him referring to her as *miss* rather than *Mrs.* For their purposes, her being taken for a widow worked best.

Once the meal was served and the staff had retreated, leaving them alone, Roscoe said, "If there's no word to be had here, when we've finished eating I'll go and ask at the stables down the road, and at that tavern on the edge of town."

"We know they came through Uxbridge, and we found sightings along this road past every crossroads since, so they must have passed this way." Her concern for Roderick dampened her appetite, but she forced herself to eat; she would be no good to her brother if she fainted.

"Given the time they left London, and when they went through Uxbridge, I would have expected them to stop for the night somewhere along this stretch. They weren't being pursued. They're using slow horses and haven't changed them, so there's no reason I can see for them to have driven through the night." Roscoe paused to eat another mouthful, then added, "We don't have any idea where they're heading—we need to keep that in mind."

She nodded. "We don't want to overshoot and miss them turning off the highway somewhere." After a moment, she said, "I still can't see why they've taken him out of London at all."

Roscoe grimaced. "Neither can I."

They were assaying a cheese platter when a timid tap on the door heralded a young maid. Hands clasped tightly before her, the maid bobbed and breathlessly said, "If you please, ma'am, Figgs"—she tipped her head toward the foyer—"said as you was asking after two men with a gentleman, a few nights back?"

Miranda smiled encouragingly. "Yes, that's right. Do you know anything of them?"

"No saying it was the ones you're after, but m'sister works at the tavern down the way, and we walk from home together of a morning. It'd be . . ." The girl scrunched up her face in concentration. "Three mornings back. Two big men were carrying a younger man looked to be a gentleman from the tavern and loading him into their coach. Tam, m'sister, told me later that they'd arrived in the wee hours and stayed over, then set off again, which was when we saw them."

Miranda let gratitude infuse her smile. "Thank you."

"Indeed." Roscoe held out a coin. When the girl, blushing and bobbing, took it, he asked, "Do you know which road they took when they left? We're assuming they went straight on to Oxford, but it's possible they may have taken a roundabout route."

"No—they went straight on, sir. I'm sure 'cause the coach passed me just as I reached here. They had a horse with a pale mane, so I knew it was them."

Roscoe held out a second coin, to the girl's round-eyed wonder. "One last question—you said the two men were carrying the gentleman. Carrying how?"

"Well"—the girl glanced at Miranda, then looked at Roscoe—"one had his shoulders, the other his legs. One of the gentleman's feet was all bandaged up like, and he seemed unconscious. All limp, he was." The girl glanced again at Miranda, read the shock she couldn't hide. The girl started to wring her hands. "I'm sorry, ma'am, I thought you'd known."

Miranda hauled in a breath. "No, no." She waved a calming hand and managed to find a weak smile. "Thank you for telling us—that's exactly what we wanted to know."

Roscoe rose and ushered the girl to the door, distracting her from Miranda's agitation. "Indeed. We knew the gentleman was injured, but we didn't know how he was faring. You've been a great help to us."

Clutching the largesse he'd bestowed, the girl bobbed and scurried away. Closing the door, he turned to see Miranda pushing away her plate.

She looked up and met his eyes. "We should get on."

He studied her for a moment, then nodded. "Just remember—he's alive."

They stopped after every crossroads and inquired, but their quarry had, apparently, rolled steadily on toward Oxford.

They found the hedge tavern on the outskirts of the town where Kempsey and Dole had stopped for a bite to eat early in the afternoon three days before.

Returning to the curricle where Miranda had waited, Roscoe climbed up, took the reins, released the brake, and set the horses in motion. "Kempsey and Dole went in. No one saw the man in the coach, but Dole took some water out to him."

Armed with the information that Roderick was injured and very likely unconscious, he could now ask for information as effectively as she; just her presence, all in black, on his box seat was enough to gain all the sympathy and help needed to trace her injured "cousin."

With the spires of Oxford rising before them, he said, "We need to start thinking like them. If they reached Oxford as early as it appears they did . . ."

She stirred. "They would have driven through it, not stopped in the town itself."

"Exactly. We're coming into the town from the east. There are several—three, I think—roads leading south."

"But why would they come this far north only to head south again?"

"Indeed. So I propose finding us a decent hotel in the north or west of the town, and while you see what you can learn there, I'll drive on along the road west, and the roads—there are two, I think—to the north, and see if I can pick up their trail." He glanced at her, saw the frown on her face.

"Perhaps," she said, "it would be better if I went with you."

He pretended to consider it, then grimaced. "Given the type of establishment they're using, it's easier for me to investigate alone." Much easier; having her near meant half his mind was focused on watching over her.

"I suppose that's true." She sighed. "Very well." She gestured ahead. "Let's get on into Oxford and find a place to stay."

* * *

They rattled into the university town in the late afternoon. The pavements were busy with students and dons, and a, to him, familiar bustle.

"It's term-time," he said when Miranda commented on the crowds. It had been decades since he'd last spent any time there; he doubted anyone would recognize him, but . . . "Oakgrove Manor's in Cheshire. I assume you and your neighbors pass through Oxford on your way to the capital."

"Usually, yes."

"So it's possible someone here or passing through might recognize you."

He heard her grimace in her voice. "Yes."

"So we'll avoid the major hotels. One of the less frequented establishments will suit us better."

They found a quiet, family-run hotel tucked off the Woodstock road. After hiring two rooms and a private parlor, Roscoe departed to search for their quarry's trail, leaving Miranda to oversee the disposition of their bags and to order dinner.

Her disguise and their tale of him being a family friend escorting her, a widow, to some family gathering stood her in good stead; she detected no suspicion or disapproval in either the female innkeeper or her staff. Warm water was quickly delivered to her room; after washing off the dust, she descended to the parlor. Before she'd had time to start worrying, a maid popped in to ask if she required tea and scones to revive her. Deciding she did, she spent the following half an hour doing her best to divert her mind with some excellent scones, clotted cream, and delicious raspberry jam.

Sadly, the distraction didn't last.

As the light started to fade, she paced before the window, stopping now and then to peer out into the gathering gloom. Roderick was injured, severely enough to be rendered unconscious. She hadn't expected that, hadn't, truth be told, allowed herself to imagine just how Kempsey and Dole had subdued her brother. Roderick wasn't particularly large, but neither was he small or slight, and he'd been in rude health when he'd last left the house . . .

With a mental curse, she hauled her mind from dwelling on his current condition. Find him first, rescue him second, worry about caring for him once she had him back.

The parlor door opened and she whirled.

Roscoe walked in.

"Thank heavens!" Rapidly scanning his face, she waited impatiently while he closed the door. "Did you trace them?"

Halting by the table in the room's center, Roscoe read the desperate eagerness in her eyes, her almost fevered need to hear something encouraging. "It was as we guessed. They drove on through the town, then stopped at a tiny inn in Kidlington."

She frowned. "They're heading north."

"I suspect," he said, "that they're going—or rather, have gone—to Birmingham. If you recall, Gallagher said they hail from there."

"Yes, I remember." Her frown deepened. "Why would they take Roderick there—to their home, as it were?"

"I agree it seems, if not senseless, then certainly not part of any obvious and expected plan."

Her gaze returned to his face, her expression sober. "Did you learn anything of Roderick's injuries?"

He hesitated, but the anxiety in her eyes forced his hand. "When they carried him into the inn, he was unconscious, and he was unconscious again when they carried him out. However, he wasn't unconscious for much of the time he was there—the inn's staff heard Kempsey and Dole speaking to him, but they didn't hear Roderick reply." He debated, then drew breath and said, "I think they broke his foot deliberately. It's an effective way of incapacitating a man without doing any long-lasting or life-threatening damage. The pain is significant and can render a man unconscious easily enough. And with a broken foot, they don't need to worry about him escaping."

She'd already paled, so he didn't add that he doubted Roderick's foot was his only injury; he would own himself surprised if Roderick hadn't been coshed first. With the pain from his foot plus a tender head, another tap on the skull would be enough to render him unconscious whenever it was necessary to move him past strangers—such as inn staff—to whom he might otherwise appeal for help. In private, they would gag him, which was why the inn staff at Kidlington hadn't heard Roderick—"the sick young gentleman"—speak.

"One point to bear in mind," he said, "is that the only reason Kempsey and Dole would have for breaking Roderick's foot is that they intend to keep him alive. They aren't planning on killing him, at least not soon."

She stared, shocked but nevertheless taking in his words. Some of her welling desperation eased, but her anxiety remained. "They weren't intending to kill him when they seized him, but for how long do they plan on holding him? And *why*?"

Unanswerable questions. He was saved from having to respond by the innkeeper and her daughters, who arrived to set the table and then serve them a simple but excellent dinner.

Over the meal, his partner in pursuit remained captive to her imagination and the anxiety it spawned. He attempted several conversational gambits, but none succeeded in breaking the hold of her worry.

The sight of her overcome by dire thoughts pricked and prodded at him. Made him restless in a discomfiting and unfamiliar way.

Until finally, with the meal at an end, he pushed back his chair and rose. "Come on. Get your cloak. Let's go for a stroll."

She was surprised, but she fell in with his plan, doubtless imagining he had some purpose in mind.

Which he did.

Her hand resting feather-light on his arm, they walked

into the town. It wasn't far to the hall he'd noticed when they'd driven through earlier; when he drew her to join the queue of well-dressed patrons, interspersed with students and dons, waiting to pay for admission, she blinked at him. "A concert?"

"There's nothing we can do about Roderick tonight. I thought we could both use the distraction."

She read the playbill posted beside the door, then glanced at him. "Handel?"

He paid at the little window, then took her arm and steered her into the foyer. "I'm partial to Handel."

She humphed disbelievingly. He smiled.

He sat riveted through the performance, sparing only the occasional glance to confirm that she was riveted, too. The choir excelled with a selection from the maestro's secular oratorios, with a few arias for contrast; the quality of the accompanying small orchestra suggested it was drawn from the university's music school.

At the end of the performance, when the resounding applause had died and they joined the wave of patrons flowing out of the doors and finally found their way onto the street, it was to discover night had long ago fallen, and that the music was powerful enough, memorable enough to follow them, filling their minds as they walked back to the inn.

Soothed on multiple planes, he nevertheless kept his eyes peeled as they walked through the darkened streets. Oxford was safer than London, but they were on its poorly lit fringes.

Slowly drifting back to earth, with the music only gradually relinquishing its grip on her, Miranda realized that her lips were curved, a glow of simple pleasure gently coursing through her. Her concern for Roderick was still there, but held in abeyance; as Roscoe had said, there was nothing they could do to help her poor brother tonight.

Instead, he'd set out to distract her. For the past two hours her mind had been held hostage by the music, a respite from her thoughts, her compulsive cares. He might have enjoyed the interlude, too, but the impulse to bring her to the concert hall hadn't sprung from self-interest.

Most of the audience had come from deeper in the town; strolling along the Woodstock road, she and he were now alone, the night peaceful and still about them.

Roscoe halted at the corner where they needed to cross the street. He paused, looking ahead, his features etched by the light from the last lamp they'd passed, some yards behind them.

She studied the face of London's gambling king, the long, chiseled planes, the strong lines of nose and lips, the sculpted jaw, broad brow, and heavy lidded eyes.

A face others saw as hard and unyielding, but one she'd learned hid a bone-deep kindness.

Yielding to impulse, using the hand resting on his arm for balance, she stretched up to brush a kiss—a simple, unadorned, thank-you caress—across his cheek.

Just as he turned his head her way.

Their lips met.

Touched, brushed.

They both froze. For an instant, for a fraction of a heartbeat.

Lids lowered, her gaze had locked on his lips. His gaze was on her face.

Then he moved. She moved.

And their lips touched again.

This time they clung.

Hers softened; his firmed.

And the connection became real.

Transformed, aching and sweet, into an exchange so delicate, so unrehearsed and unintended, its very fragility fascinated and lured.

With no plan, no intent, no purpose, the mutual pressure of their lips, so tantalizingly novel, spun out and stopped time . . . letting sensation flare and wash through her.

She forgot what she was doing. Forgot where they were, why they were there.

For seconds, minutes, however long, the touch of his lips on hers imprinted, the gentlest of brands, on her senses.

For those minutes, nothing else mattered. Nothing else had ever captured her like this, had ever been this exquisitely enthralling.

Roscoe's head slowly spun. Giddy. Him. And all from just the touch of her lips.

He wanted more. His muscles tensed, well-honed instincts rearing, ready to direct, to take charge and orchestrate . . .

What was he doing?

His mind reengaged with a rush, a mental slap.

Abruptly, he raised his head, shattering the delicate, evocatively innocent caress.

Stunned, he stared into her shadowed face—tried to see the siren who had captured him so easily. She had to be there . . . somewhere.

Miranda Clifford blinked lustrous eyes wide and stared back.

Even in the poor light he saw color flood her cheeks.

Then she stepped back.

Putting distance between them.

He hadn't even taken her into his arms, but he had to fight a sudden urge to reach out and haul her back.

She swung away, faced the street. "I'm *sorry*." The words reached him on an agonized whisper. She dragged her cloak more tightly about her. "I only meant to . . . thank you." Without glancing at him, stiffly she inclined her head his way. "It won't happen again."

Why not?

He bit his tongue, banished the errant thought. She was right—she was a lady and he was London's gambling king. There could never be anything between them; better they both kept that in mind.

No matter their impulses.

But what could he say? What, that wouldn't be an outright lie?

Accepting there were no glib words he could utter to ease her, he went to offer his arm, realized the futility, and converted the gesture into a wave. "Come—we should get back."

Head rising, she nodded. Still without looking at him, she stepped out, and he fell in beside her.

Chapter Six

They were, Roscoe discovered, both excellent at dissembling. Regardless, as he and Miranda traveled at a good clip up the road to Birmingham, awareness sat, an all but tangible phantom, between them.

On reaching the hotel the previous night, they'd retreated to their rooms with barely a mumbled "Good night." This morning she'd emerged and had joined him in the parlor for breakfast; no matter how hard he'd looked, he hadn't detected the slightest sign that she even remembered what had passed between them.

Except that she'd reverted to treating him with rigid correctness; he hadn't realized how much she—and he, too—had relaxed in each other's company. Now, however, they were once more London's gambling king and a lady wedded to respectability, with nothing in common beyond their mutual desire to rescue her brother—a simple, straightforward connection with no overtones or undertones of any complicating attraction.

He wondered if they'd be strong enough to hold to that line until they found Roderick and returned to London.

Last night, alone in his room, he'd had time to think—about that kiss, about what it had revealed. He'd been attracted to Miranda Clifford from the instant he'd set eyes on her in the upstairs foyer of his house, her face and figure lit only by diffuse moonlight. But he was accustomed to feeling such physical tugs and, on learning her identity along with her purpose in coming to his house, had dismissed it with little further thought.

Then she'd returned and asked for his help, a plea of a sort he was constitutionally incapable of refusing; he knew his own weakness on that score. But he couldn't claim to have been unaware of the particular edge to his interest in her, an edge further honed by increasing fascination.

He'd never been a monk; his thirty-eight years encompassed ample experience of the opposite sex, from the Cyprians of his wild youth to the bored matrons of the ton seeking relief from the ennui of their marriages, who, over the last decade, had been his principal source of incidental bedmates. Since becoming Roscoe, he hadn't kept a mistress—a dangerous proposition, for him as well as the lady—but he certainly hadn't retreated from that aspect of life.

Experience had, from the first, told him that his attraction to Miranda Clifford was reciprocated.

The same experience had warned that far from embracing, let alone encouraging, that mutual attraction, she found it unsettling, something she wished to ignore.

Despite his wolf's clothing, he was a gentleman born; he'd done his best to oblige her and ignore it, too.

Until last night.

Neither of them had meant it to happen, but it had.

That reality sat between them, large as life, as the wheels rattled and they rolled on up the road.

Eventually Birmingham rose before them, a haphazard conglomeration of buildings old and new. He was familiar with the town; it was the closest to Ridgware, although he usually traveled to the estate by a more direct route.

Miranda looked about her with increasing dismay as Roscoe drove into Birmingham. The town had grown significantly since she'd last visited; finding Roderick in such a teeming city would be a harder task than she'd supposed.

As they approached the town's center, she glanced at Roscoe. "What now?" Other than the simple courtesies, they'd barely exchanged three words through the day.

"Now we take rooms in one of the smaller hotels, then I'll go out and make inquiries."

"But if this is where Kempsey and Dole call home, they won't be using taverns and inns."

"No, but we need to confirm that they have, in fact, remained here, rather than simply passed through on their way to, for example, Liverpool."

She was tempted to ask why he'd thought of Liverpool—the port from which many vessels left for the Americas—but decided she'd leave exploring that until it became more than hypothetical. She had to keep focused.

They'd inquired after her "sick cousin and his companions" at numerous small inns and taverns along the way. At the last, on the outskirts of Birmingham, they'd learned that the battered coach with its odd pair of horses had driven into the town. The possibility—like Roscoe, she would put it no higher—that Roderick lay somewhere within reach left her equal parts excited, reassured, and apprehensive, but it definitely spurred her on.

And helped keep her from dwelling on the man beside her and that wholly unexpected, eye-openingly magical moment they'd shared on an Oxford street.

She'd told herself she had to regret it, that scintillating moment, yet she couldn't quite force herself to be that hypocritical, even in her own mind, so she'd decided that ignoring it, wiping it from her conscious memory and denying it any scope to influence her behavior, was the wise, sensible, and respectable course. But all that had accomplished was to make her even more tense, as if she was constantly battling herself, her true inclinations . . .

Realizing her mind had once more drifted, she ruthlessly hauled it back on track. And realized he was glancing at her, puzzled.

He'd asked her something.

She blushed. "I'm sorry. I was woolgathering. What did you say?"

Woolgathering. Viewing the color in her cheeks, Roscoe could guess about what. Looking forward, he clenched his jaw against any unwise retort, reminded himself of the line to which wisdom dictated they both should hold, and after a moment managed to reply in a halfway reasonable tone, "I wanted to know if, as at Oxford, we should be wary of any neighbors from Cheshire who might be passing through."

She grimaced. "We should. Most travel to London via other routes, but enough come through Birmingham for us to need to be on guard."

"So we can't use the major hotels." He wasn't keen on using the larger hotels either; the years might have aged him, but there were those in Birmingham who would still recognize him as the man he no longer was. His family didn't need any unexpected sightings of a scion society hadn't seen for twelve years. "Luckily, the town has several smaller establishments."

He drove to a minor hotel with a tiny yard and rooms overlooking nothing more exciting than narrow streets and alleys. Catering to professional men traveling on business, the hotel nevertheless boasted several suites. After being shown around one, its sitting room and the two bedrooms on either side overlooking the rear alley, he left Miranda in the suite and descended to finalize the arrangements. After seeing their bags carried up the stairs by a footman, he walked out of the hotel and set off to learn what he could of Kempsey, Dole, and Roderick's whereabouts.

He returned sooner than he'd expected. After barely an hour of wandering into taverns and chatting innocuously about mismatched carriage horses, the instincts honed by his years in London had started flickering.

He'd used Kempsey's name only once, his description twice, and Dole's name only once, all at different places, yet he'd caught enough arrested glances to grow wary; he might want to know where Kempsey, Dole, and Roderick were, but he didn't want to attract attention, especially not that of Kempsey and Dole.

Accepting the outcome as confirmation that Gallagher had heard aright and Kempsey and Dole were indeed Birmingham born and bred, he'd stopped asking questions and, even though he hadn't spotted anyone following him, had taken a roundabout route back to the hotel.

Climbing the main stairs, he paused on the landing on the first floor and, looking down into the narrow foyer, waited. After five minutes had elapsed and no one had sidled in to inquire about the gentleman who had just entered, he continued on to the second floor, and their suite.

Opening the door, he walked in.

Standing at the table between the two long windows, Miranda glanced up from some packages she was unwrapping. Hands stilling, her gaze searched his face. "What did you learn?"

Shutting the door, he shook his head. "I had to stop asking. My queries were attracting too much attention." Shrugging off his greatcoat, he laid it over a chair.

She straightened. "If we can't ask, how will we learn?"

"We have other options." He crossed the room to her. "The Philanthropy Guild funds a large project here. Through that I have contacts who'll be happy to help, and who are likely to be more successful than I. They're locals, so information on other locals will be easier for them to get."

Halting by the table, he studied the contents of various brown-paper-wrapped parcels. Bandages, ointments, gauze, a small pair of scissors, a set of small splints, several pills and powders. "Where did you get these?"

Miranda might not know him well, but she recognized

the import of his too-quiet, too-even tone. However, having no idea why on earth he would disapprove, she ignored it. "From the apothecary's a few streets away. If Roderick's foot is broken and he's in pain—and he may well be fevered by now, too—then I'll need these to tend him once we rescue him. The sooner he gets help the better, and as we have no idea if there'll be a doctor close—"

"You went out alone—you walked to the apothecary's shop, and back, alone?"

She frowned. "Yes. I asked the clerk downstairs and—"

"Since when did walking the streets in a large city alone become acceptable practice for a respectable lady?"

She stiffened, straightened. "It was the middle of the afternoon and it was only a short distance—"

"How far away it was isn't the point."

Roscoe watched her hazel eyes ignite.

The carapace of rigid restraint behind which she'd retreated cracked and fell away, and she asked with heated intensity, "Then what *is* your point?"

Jaw set, he held her gaze and implacably stated the obvious. "You should have waited for me."

Her eyes flew wide in wholly spurious shock. "Good gracious! If you imagine I'm going to ask your permission to fetch bandages for my injured brother, you can think again. Or is it that you believe me too weak to carry these parcels?" A haughty wave at the items on the table. "Or, no—wait. I have it. You believe that I'm too witless to know what to buy!"

"*None* of those things." The sheer weight of reined temper in his voice should have made her back down; any of his men would have.

Instead, she leaned closer, her eyes boring into his. "Then *what*?"

The belligerent, stubborn, imperious demand rang in his ears. Eyes locked with hers, equally furious, he dragged in a breath, grimly held onto his temper. "*Miss* Clifford."

Her eyes widened again. "What happened to Miranda?"

She jabbed a finger at him. "You were quick enough to use my name when it suited you."

His jaw felt as if it would crack. "Miranda, then. I—"

"For your information"—she tipped her chin higher—"I am not a child who needs to be watched over. I'm twenty-nine years old, I've managed a household for years, and I'm perfectly capable of walking several hundred yards in broad daylight without getting lost, or accosted, or whatever it is you're imagining!"

She was a twenty-nine-year-old lady whose posture and glide evoked visions of a goddess, who dressed beyond conservatively yet succeeded in drawing male eyes wherever she went, but she lived too distanced from the wider world to have any notion of such visceral attraction.

Leashing his temper was what he needed to do; why it had escaped him, why the notion of her being potentially exposed to danger when he hadn't been close enough to aid her had succeeded in so provoking it . . . eyes still locked with hers, he drew in a deep breath. Felt his temper quiver like a hound about to pounce. "It would," he said, his tone deadly, low, precise, "have been better all around if you had waited until I returned—"

She threw her hands in the air. "I had no *idea* when you would come back!" Narrowing her eyes on his, she demanded, "And better for whom?"

His temper erupted. "*Me,* if you must know!"

She flung her arms wide. "*Why?*"

Involuntarily, he stepped closer.

Head tipping back, she held her ground, her adamantine gaze locked with his.

They stood toe to toe, temper to temper, will to steely will—while he battled the urge to sweep her into his arms and answer her question.

The heat of their tempers, and something else, licked like flames over them both.

This wasn't wise. The effort it took to haul his impulses in and lash them down, then ease one small step back, away from the precipice on which they'd both stood teetering, left him inwardly trembling.

She blinked, seemed to realize only then how close to real danger she'd stood.

Breathing in enough to have her breasts rising, she edged back a step, too.

That made it easier for him to swing away, to swipe up his greatcoat, then stalk to the door before which his traveling bag sat. Bending, he hefted the bag, and with his hand on the doorknob glanced back. "What time's dinner?"

She met his gaze levelly. "I arranged it for seven o'clock, in the dining room downstairs."

"I'll meet you here just before." Not a question. Pushing the door open, he walked through.

Miranda watched the door close with careful precision.

She stared at the uninformative panels for a full minute, then, her heart still racing, lips firming, she turned back to sorting her supplies.

Nine o'clock the following morning saw her, garbed in her black mourning gown but without her hat and veil, standing beside Roscoe on the pavement outside a large church. A sign declared the massive edifice to be St. Philip's, including St. Egbert's Home for Boys. "The Philanthropy Guild supports the boys' home?"

Starting up the steps, Roscoe glanced sideways to ensure she was following. "It was one of our first projects." His first project, long before the Guild had been born. "And we don't just support it. The Guild is the principal benefactor."

Pushing open one of the heavy church doors, he held it for her. When she paused in the foyer, he waved down the nave. "There's a corridor off the transept."

He would have preferred not to have brought her with him, risking her learning more than he wished, but the thought of leaving her to spend her day alone, at liberty to wander wherever she took it into her head to go, had occurred only to be dismissed; the potential for calamity was too great.

Opening the door at the end of the transept, he stepped into the inner courtyard onto which the main building of St. Egbert's faced. The clang of the school bell echoed off the stone façades; boys ranging in age from six years old to youths of fourteen were still racing across the cobbles, plunging into the various buildings in which their classes were held.

Waving toward the main entrance, he led Miranda on. "Reverend Nightingale's in charge. With luck, he'll be in and able to see us."

The matron, Mrs. Swag, was hurrying across the front foyer; spotting him, her face creased in a wide smile. She bobbed, declared that Father Nightingale would be delighted to see them, and volunteered the information that the good reverend would be found in his study.

Roscoe let his rusty charm color his smile. "I know the way."

"Of course you do, sir." Mrs. Swag beamed. "I'd better get along." With nods to them both, she hurried on.

Aware of Miranda's gaze on his face, he took her arm as if to guide her, in reality to distract her. It worked; she allowed him to lead her down the long corridor to the study without posing further questions. After knocking and being bidden to enter, he opened the door, released her and waved her through, then followed.

Ensconced behind an ancient desk supporting a small mountain of papers, Reverend Nightingale glanced up. His eyes widened as they alighted on Miranda; setting down his pen, he rose, then he saw Roscoe and a broad smile lit his face. "Ah, my son—welcome. Welcome!" Shifting his bright blue gaze to Miranda, Nightingale beamed even more. "And to what do we owe this pleasure?"

After shaking hands, Roscoe performed the introductions, adding, "Miss Clifford and I are searching for her brother, Mr. Roderick Clifford. He's a fellow member of the Guild and was kidnapped by two men while returning home after a recent Guild meeting."

"Great heavens!" Nightingale looked from his face to Miranda's, then waved them to the chairs before the desk. "But please, sit and tell me how I and St. Egbert's can help."

Roscoe explained about Kempsey and Dole, how he and Miranda had traced the pair to Birmingham, their home territory, and how he as an outsider couldn't easily ascertain their whereabouts. "I know some of the lads here hail from similar areas as Kempsey and Dole. While I would normally hesitate to ask such a thing of youngsters, the truth is they could slip back and chat to their old friends and acquaintances and learn what I—or indeed anyone in authority—could not, namely whether Kempsey and Dole, and the sick and injured gentleman they have with them, are here, still in town, or if they've moved on, and if so, in which direction."

Brow creased, Nightingale was nodding. "I see your point, and while I couldn't, in all conscience, *order* the boys to help—and I know that's not what you're asking me to do—I agree that we should put the matter to them and ask if they're willing to do what they can." He glanced at Miranda. "I take it that finding Mr. Clifford is urgent?"

Her anxiety was so transparent that she hardly needed to say, "We believe so, sir."

"If the boys agree to assist," Roscoe said, "with your permission I'll speak to them first, to stress that I don't want any of them pressing their questions to the point of drawing attention." He met Nightingale's gaze. "I don't doubt their abilities or their enthusiasm, but we want no heroics."

"Indeed not." Steepling his fingers, Nightingale retreated into thought.

Roscoe glanced at Miranda and found her gaze, every bit as pensive as Nightingale's, studying him.

"I believe," Nightingale said, "that I know just the lads to assist you." Waving them to remain where they were, he rose. "I'll ask one of the tutors to fetch them, and we can lay the matter before them and see what they think."

Ten minutes later, after the boys had been summoned from their classes to the common room and addressed by

Nightingale, then by Roscoe, it was apparent that all twelve were thrilled to be asked to assist the orphanage's major patron—Miranda had heard enough to realize that Roscoe himself, Guild aside, was that—in such an exciting and adventurous way.

She was reassured by Roscoe's lecture, by the weight of his will and the restrictions he imposed on the boys, including that they shouldn't go "scouting" alone but remain in pairs at all times.

When he finished detailing exactly what they needed to know—stressing he wanted that and no more—Nightingale stepped forward and released the boys to their hunting, adding, "And remember, we want you back here by three o'clock at the latest, even if you've discovered nothing at all."

Roscoe reinforced the edict with a look.

The boys nodded, grinned, saluted, and streamed out of the room.

"Well!" Nightingale turned to Miranda and Roscoe. "Why don't I have the housekeeper bring us some tea, and over it I can bring you up to date with our achievements here?"

Roscoe nodded. "Thank you. As I'm here, if you have the time, I would appreciate a report."

Miranda graciously accepted the offer of tea, and they repaired to the study.

The tea arrived, brought by a brisk housekeeper. Suitably supplied, Nightingale talked of his charges, reporting on their number, their achievements, and the orphanage's board's plans for the immediate future. Roscoe listened, his attention focused, his questions incisive and insightful.

Miranda sat back in her chair, sipped, and watched and learned. Her worry over Roderick was a living thing, roiling and surging inside her, but her curiosity over Roscoe was strong enough to distract her so that she could await the boys' return with some semblance of patience.

Even while listening to Nightingale's report, Roscoe was acutely aware of his silent companion, seated a little further back from the desk on his right. He suspected she'd eased her chair back deliberately so she wasn't in his sight as he focused on Nightingale. So she would watch and listen without intruding, without him being conscious of it and therefore guarding his tongue.

He continued to guard his tongue and stood ready to guard Nightingale's, too, if necessary. He'd first encountered the good reverend when he'd been in his late teens; a hellion from one of the local aristocratic families, he and his friends had occasionally stopped in Birmingham to carouse . . . Nightingale, then much younger, too, had stepped in to try and halt a fistfight between the well-heeled interlopers and a bunch of local lads.

In the end, Roscoe had felt compelled to cease his own contribution to the melee to help the—in those days—unworldly and severely outclassed reverend.

That had been the start of an unusual acquaintance; it had been through Nightingale and his supporters that he, wealthy enough even in his pre-Roscoe years to have been wondering what to do with all his winnings, had first been exposed to philanthropic ideals.

Although they'd never discussed it, and Nightingale had never questioned his conversion to Roscoe, Nightingale nevertheless knew who he really was. Which family he belonged to, and what his real name was.

Roscoe saw no reason to allow Miranda Clifford access to that highly scandalous fact.

Luckily, Nightingale seemed to have no difficulty remembering he was now Roscoe. As their discussion wound down, Roscoe glanced at Miranda. She'd returned her cup to the tray. His and Nightingale's closing comments had failed to hold her interest; he could almost see her anxiety rising like a tide to reclaim her.

He returned his gaze to Nightingale. "We've taken up a considerable amount of your morning, for which you have our sincere thanks, but we should leave you to your duties." He rose, glanced at Miranda. "Perhaps we might walk in the grounds until the boys return."

"Indeed, indeed!" Nightingale rose as Miranda came to her feet. "Please feel free to wander where you wish. We have no secrets here, and, frankly, your visit won't go unremarked—both boys and staff will see the sincerity of your interest regardless of the reason that brought you here. And that does help."

Walking them to the door, Nightingale continued, "I would be honored if you would join me for luncheon at the high table in the refectory—it will do the boys no harm to have to exercise their manners, and I suspect our intrepid questioners won't return until the afternoon."

They accepted with thanks, then, as Nightingale closed the study door behind them, Miranda turned to Roscoe. "So where can we stroll?"

He waved her down the corridor and fell into step beside her. "There are gardens, quite pleasant, on the other side of the church. They're used to train the boys who show interest in becoming gardeners."

"If I understood Reverend Nightingale correctly, the program here is structured to give the boys an occupation, rather than just an education."

"That's the board's aim."

"One you—and the Guild—clearly support."

"None of us in the Guild can see the point of teaching such boys their letters and numbers and nothing else. There's precious few jobs they might get with their reading and writing skills, and most don't have an aptitude for such work anyway. The few who do can usually be found positions as clerks, printers' apprentices, or the like, but the majority need something else."

They reached a door and he held it open; they stepped outside onto a narrow path edging a slope of lawn, dotted here and there with mature trees interspersed with beds of herbaceous perennials, as well as beds of annuals now past their prime.

"For the older boys, their days are divided between lessons in the mornings and occupational teachings or apprenticing in the afternoons. Most seem to thrive on the regimen—the tutors report that it's easier to get them to pay attention to their lessons through the morning when they know they'll be escaping to other activities after lunch."

Strolling down the path, Miranda surveyed the neat state of the lawns and beds. "Are all the Guild projects of a similar flavor? Focused on teaching young people the basics and getting them into trades? I recall that the project Roderick was looking into was a bailiff-run school, and there was mention of a Mrs. Canterbury's Academy in Lincoln."

Pacing alongside her, he considered, then said, "Most of the Guild's current projects do, in fact, involve teaching less fortunate youngsters with the aim of helping them get jobs, but that wasn't by any deliberate intent. It's more a result of, over recent times, such projects having been assessed by the group as most worthy—as the most productive use of our funds."

"From what I heard that night, you put considerable effort into not just your assessments but also into subsequent oversight of the projects." She glanced at him. "Was it you who started the Guild?"

He hesitated, then lifted one shoulder. "I'd already got involved in a few projects when Ro Gerrard learned of it and sought me out, asked my opinion. He's . . . tenacious when he sets his mind to something. The Guild was more his idea than mine."

"But you're the senior member, as it were." She glanced at his face. "At that meeting, the others certainly treated you that way."

"They could manage just as well without me, but . . . I do have more resources in certain areas than they do."

She inclined her head. Sensing his resistance to being the focus of her questions, she let the subject fall.

They strolled in the gardens until a bell summoned them to the refectory and lunch with Reverend Nightingale and his staff. Although separated from Roscoe along the high table, Miranda found herself engaged and entertained—

well enough to hold her rising anxiety over Roderick at bay.

Her brother rarely left her thoughts, but as there was, literally, nothing she could do, she reined in her concerns and chatted with the music tutor and the art master.

After lunch, Roscoe was approached by the games master; after speaking with the man, he glanced her way.

In company with the orphanage's nurse, to whom she'd just been introduced, Miranda joined him. "I thought I might visit the infirmary."

He nodded and smiled at the nurse. "In that case, I'll be out on the east lawn with some of the boys. I'll come and fetch you if the other lads return."

They parted, and she accompanied the nurse, a short, bustling, unflaggingly cheerful woman, to the well-appointed infirmary at the end of one wing. After having been shown around its facilities, Miranda asked, "Are you called on to tend many injuries?"

"Lots of cuts, grazes, skinned knees, and even black eyes, but with more than fifty lads running amok, there's always a few broken bones and the like."

"Ah—I'd wondered." She paused, then went on, "As Reverend Nightingale mentioned, we're searching for my brother. We've heard that his foot's been injured, most likely broken."

"Ooh, ouch." The nurse grimaced. "That'll be painful. Has he had it set, do you know?"

Miranda fought to block a mental image of just how bad Roderick's foot might be, how much it was likely to be hurting him. "We believe he's had no medical attention. I wonder . . . could you tell me what would be most helpful to do to make him more comfortable until we can get him to a doctor?"

She spent the next hour being instructed in how to initially administer to a patient with a broken foot.

Later, concern over Roderick's injury dominating her mind, Miranda followed the nurse's directions downstairs and around to the door giving onto the east lawn.

Emerging onto a path that edged what was in reality a playing field, she saw a group of boys scattered about the sward, all intent on . . . the man who stood in the center of the lawn bent over a bat before a wicket at one end of a cricket pitch.

His coat off, in shirt and waistcoat, he was facing away from her, watching a boy run up to bowl a ball down the pitch. The ball flew fast, but Roscoe raised the bat and, the muscles in his back fluidly flexing, swatted the ball away across the lawn. With a yell, three boys went charging after it.

Laughing, Roscoe ran down the pitch to the other end, touched the tip of the bat to the ground, then came racing back to the nearer end.

He hadn't seen her; when he turned to face the bowler again, she glided across the lawn into the deep shadows beneath an old oak.

For the next half hour, curiosity piqued, she watched him and the boys, watched how he interacted with them and wondered how, where, and when London's gambling king had not just learned to play cricket but had also gained the ease he demonstrably possessed in dealing with children. From the youngest, about seven, to the oldest on the field, possibly twelve, they were all his; it wasn't hard to see why the games master, hanging back on the fringes of the field, had invited him to spend time with his charges.

Recalling all she'd seen of him in London, combining that with what she was seeing here, it was obvious he was a leader—one born to the role, who instinctively knew how to draw others to him, knew how, regardless of age, to inspire and command them while lightly holding their loyalty in his hands.

Despite being much older, all his men viewed him in much the same way as the boys.

Exactly when Roscoe realized Miranda was there, watching, he couldn't have said; the knowledge of her presence simply appeared in his brain, the touch of her gaze recognizable even at a distance. It took several carefully disguised scans of the area to spot her, but once he had . . . something within him calmed.

Regardless, he wasn't all that comfortable with how much he was revealing—all she was seeing—of him, yet he couldn't find it in him to curtail his time with the boys. But then a young lad came pelting out of the building to summon him and Miranda to Nightingale's study.

After handing over the bat and complimenting his opponents, he retrieved his coat and, shrugging back into it, strode across to where she stood. Settling his sleeves, he met her gaze. "The lads we sent searching have returned, and apparently they have news."

They regathered in the common room. Some of the lads had targeted the Kempseys, others the Doles. All they'd gleaned from the relatively tight-lipped Kempseys was that "their Jack, him as now lived in Lunnon" had been back but had left Birmingham again.

However, from a cousin who lived on the same cramped street as the Doles, one pair of boys had learned that Herbert Dole had stopped by to see his mother several days ago. He'd been driving a coach with mismatched nags and had offered the cousin a copper to look out for the coach and horses while Dole visited with his mother. Several hours later, Kempsey had arrived, and Dole had paid off the cousin— who had loitered near enough to hear Kempsey and Dole argue about the best route to take to Lichfield, to a cottage there.

"M'cousin said they said they were going to take some gentleman there." Perched on a bench, bright-eyed, the ten-year-old orphan swung his legs, pleased as punch to be the bearer of the best tidings. "Kempsey told Dole the cottage belonged to Kempsey's cousin, but was empty on account of the cousin being in jail. Kempsey said it was the perfect place for them. After that, they climbed up and drove off."

A few questions established the time of the encounter as four days before.

Roscoe praised all twelve lads; with Nightingale's permission he rewarded each with a shilling, and gave the boy whose cousin had been so useful another shilling to convey to said cousin.

With the boys dismissed, Roscoe glanced at Miranda and saw the banked anxiety in her eyes. He thanked Nightingale, and they left St. Egbert's.

But as they passed through the church, she halted. When he glanced her way, she met his gaze. "If you don't mind, I would like to spend just a moment"—she waved at the pews—"here."

He nodded, followed her into a pew, and sat a foot away.

She bowed her head in prayer.

He looked down the nave at the altar—and said a silent prayer of his own. The cousin who had held the horses for several hours hadn't mentioned either movement, or any sound, from inside the coach.

From Roderick.

That didn't bode well for his young friend's state.

When they reached the hotel, Miranda fell to pacing.

Roscoe watched her. The reserve she'd maintained throughout the day, the screen behind which she'd largely successfully hidden her emotions, was fracturing. Agitation fell from her in waves.

After several moments, he moved to one of the armchairs and sat. Wondered what he could say, what he could do to distract her.

She flung him a glance. "There's nothing we can do tonight, is there?"

He shook his head. "Lichfield is too far away—by the time we reach there, night will be falling. Not a good time even to reconnoiter, so regardless we would have to wait until tomorrow. And finding somewhere to stay out there, somewhere we could be sure our presence wouldn't be communicated to Kempsey and Dole, might well be impossible. We might end up driving back into Birmingham to spend the night."

She pulled a face. "No point." Looking down, she paced on.

The restless, reckless energy in her stride, her overflowing frustration, communicated itself very effectively to him. Eventually, he could stand it no longer. He rose. When she glanced his way, he said, "I suggest we dine early, then we can retire early and set off at first light."

She nodded. "Yes, that would be best."

"I'll make the arrangements." Walking to the door, he opened it, and with a last glance back at her, left her pacing.

An irritating, irrational sense of failure over not being able to ease her agitation, her frustration—her fear—continued to eat at him through the four-course meal, then followed him up the stairs and into the suite's sitting room.

He'd hoped she would retire, retreat to her room and her bed, so he could retreat to his, but no. She marched to the track she was well on her way to wearing in the carpet and fell to pacing once more, back and forth before the twin windows and the table between.

Back and forth; forth and back.

Halting inside the suite's door, he stood silently watching her.

A small sound escaped her; when next she swung around, she'd raised her fist, pressed her knuckle to her lips.

Enough.

He stalked forward and, facing her, blocked her path. For an instant he thought she might try to mow him down, but at the last second she came to a quivering halt with no more than six inches between her bodice and his coat.

Raising her head, she frowned at him. "What?"

He looked into hazel eyes awash with anxiety, provoked by nebulous, imagined fears. She was held captive by those lurking terrors. He had to break their hold. "What can I do to distract you?"

She blinked, then her eyes, her whole expression, cleared. "This." Like a drowning man reaching for a lifeline, she lifted one hand, cupped his nape, stretched up, set her lips to his, and kissed him.

He froze.

The pressure of her lips wavered, suddenly unsure.

His restraint collapsed; instinct took over. One hand cupped her face, tipped her lips to his, and he kissed her back.

Holding her steady, he returned the caress, extended it.

She was right; this would distract her. *This* was possibly the only thing that could, the only interaction sufficiently powerful to cut through her worry and fear, and for however many minutes focus her mind on something else.

On something pleasurable.

So he gave her what she wanted and kissed her again; as before, he found it easy, so easy to dive into the exchange, to feed her demand and satisfy his own, that prowling hunger that rose through him, evoked, provoked by her need.

Her lips were a delight, lush and luscious, pliant and captivating; savoring them, exploring the delectable curves, was a bounty he gladly claimed.

Wits whirling, Miranda clung to the fascinating exchange, to the promise, the allure—to him. She dropped all pretense; *this* was what she needed, what she craved. What she longed to explore.

This side of life. This side of her.

Only with him had she ever even sensed it—ever seen or felt it enough to be sure of its existence, let alone explore it. Just this, with him, was enough to grow intrigued enough to yearn to discover what it was to be with a man.

He, with this, opened the door to a novel landscape, one to which, for her, only he held the key. With no other man had she ever experienced that telltale frisson, the tug on her senses, that ineluctable focus of awareness.

His lips moved on hers with persuasive command. On a suppressed shudder—of excitement, of sharp anticipation—she parted her lips, shivered to her soul when his tongue cruised the curves, then dipped within. And stroked.

He supped. There was no other word for it; a gentle but inexorable drinking in, an exploration laced with a subtle claiming.

Then he angled his head over hers, snared her senses, and drew them deeper.

Into an exchange that evoked heat, and desire, and a burgeoning more primitive wanting.

To her senses he was all dark heat, masculine strength, and male hardness; she kissed him back, gave him back caress for caress, driven by a swelling compulsion.

And he returned the pleasure.

For uncounted moments the kiss spun on, driven first by him, then by her. Eventually by them both, by the heated mating of their mouths, the hot mingling of their breaths, the evocative, provocative tangling of their tongues.

She was dimly aware of his arm sliding about her waist, of him drawing her closer . . . a flash of sensation, a flush of warmth cascading through her as her curves met his muscled heat. The blatant strength of him surrounded her, reassured and comforted in some strange way, but also held a wordless promise. A primal one some equally instinctive part of her understood.

Through the hand that had fallen to grip his upper arm she could feel the steel in him, feel the increasing tension that even to her untutored senses spoke of rising desire. Of reined passion.

She sank against him, into him, lured by his heat. His arms tightened, gathering her closer still; the hard ridge of his erection pressed against the soft swell of her stomach.

And some never before recognized part of her sang.

He wanted her.

And she wanted him.

She yearned to know more, all, everything her twenty-nine-year-old self had thought forever denied her.

With no other man had she ever felt like this, would she ever feel like this—emboldened and sure, and so wanting.

And if wishing to hold her worries over Roderick at bay added another dimension to her rising desperation . . . did that matter?

Leaning into his embrace, she raised both hands, framed his face, and held him anchored as she kissed him—as she poured every last ounce of her newfound yearning into issuing a demand, a command . . . a blatant invitation.

He read it, understood it. She felt the leap of his pulse, sensed the flash of tension that turned his body to iron. He kissed her back, hard, with his own far more flagrant, more explicit demand. Accepting her invitation, he devoured her mouth and sent her senses soaring—

Abruptly, he reined back.

On a gasp, he broke the kiss and raised his head.

Heart pounding, senses reeling, she stared, stunned, into his shadowed face. He still held her in his arms, locked against him from breast to knees. His back was to the lamplight, his features unreadable, but the sound of his breathing was sharp, harsh, a mirror of her own breathless, giddy state, itself a counterpoint to the rapid cadence of her pulse.

"No." The word was weak, distant; she wasn't sure if he was speaking to himself or her. Then his jaw firmed, along with his tone. "We can't go any further."

Her wits were disconnected, distracted with need, her thoughts in utter disarray. "Why not?"

His dark eyes fixed on hers. After a moment, he said, "Because I won't take advantage of you, and that's what it would be."

She wanted him and he wanted her. Pressed against him, she couldn't doubt the latter, and she was perfectly certain about the former. She wanted to go forward and learn more. "I can't see why—"

He opened his arms and stepped back, briefly steadied her, then released her and turned away. "I'm no cad."

She frowned. "I didn't imagine you were."

"And what sort of man sets out to rescue a friend and seduces his sister along the way?"

"This has nothing to do with Roderick." She lifted her chin. "This is about *me*." She was somewhat stunned to realize that was true.

Roscoe glanced at her, took in her challenging stance, her aggravated gaze. Absorbing the sincerity in her tone, he reconsidered for all of a second, but. . . . he inclined his head. "That only makes our position clearer. You are who you are, and I am who I am. There is, therefore, no sense in taking this interaction any further."

He was as certain of that as he was of his real name.

This couldn't lead anywhere. Anywhere he wanted to go.

He didn't want to argue the point. He turned away, toward the door to his room.

"Wait." Uncertainty and faint disbelief echoed in her voice.

Heaving an inward sigh, he turned back, arched a brow.

Spine poker-straight, she met his eyes. "You're *rejecting* my invitation, which you quite clearly understood?"

Lips firming, he held her gaze, let a moment tick by, then stated, "I'm not rejecting *you*. I'm refusing to be such a cad as to take advantage of you, no matter your offer." Refusing to become more deeply ensnared by a woman who didn't fit into his world any more than he fitted into hers.

He saw a pale reflection of the frustration he felt flare in her eyes. Her jaw tightened, her diction tart as she bit off the words, "That wasn't any senseless offer. It was a deliberate invitation—I know what I'm doing."

"Indeed?" He studied her face. "So tell me"—he trapped her eyes, her stormy green-gold gaze—"*why* do you want me in your bed?"

Miranda ached to open her mouth and trump his challenge with a blisteringly irrefutable answer, but her wits refused to provide one. *Why*? Why did he think? Why was he asking? What did he expect her to say?

More to the point, what answer would he accept as appropriate, as right? As sufficient to come together again, rather than part?

A minute ticked by as she mentally scrambled. In vain; if he'd searched for a way to bring home to her just how much of a novice she was in this sphere, he couldn't have done better.

The fraught silence stretched . . .

Lips thinning even more, he nodded. "Just so." There was a bleakness in his eyes, his voice, she hadn't seen before, but before she could focus on it, he swung away and walked toward his room. "And now, if you'll excuse me, I intend to get some sleep."

She stared at the back of his shoulders, at their rigid line. Immovable, rocklike, adamant; he'd made up his mind— why, she had no clue, but he wasn't about to waver.

Embarrassment and anger geysered; heat flooded her cheeks. She'd taken her first-ever leap off the respectable path, and where had it landed her? Frustration roiled; she hadn't even been able to get that right, even though she'd been sure he'd wanted her, had desired her, as much as she had him.

Pausing with his hand on the doorknob, he glanced back, met her gaze, then arched a cynical, world-weary brow.

Her temper erupted. Flinging her hands in the air, she gave vent to her frustration in a muted scream, swung around, marched to her door, flung it open, stormed through, and slammed it shut behind her.

The sharp sound faded.

Roscoe stared at her door for a full minute, then exhaled. Opening his, he went through and closed it quietly behind him.

He'd done the right thing.

Even though stepping back from her and her blatant invitation had taken significantly more resolution than he'd expected, he'd had to do it. Even though doing so had shaken him on some level he never before had breached, calling a halt to any furthering of their relationship was in his best interests, and hers, too.

He didn't understand the strength of their attraction, but he knew to his bones that he couldn't allow it to lead them into deeper waters.

She should be thanking him, although he doubted she was. Yet. In time, she would. Once they'd rescued Roderick and returned to London, and she saw the foolishness of a respectable lady commencing a liaison with London's gambling king.

The window was uncurtained. He crossed to it and stood looking out at the moon riding the sky above Birmingham's roofs.

He should sleep, but he doubted he could. Not with such a potent mix of frustration, clawing need, and disappointment raging through him. He didn't understand why his reaction to her was so powerful, so complex, so much more compulsive, so much less manageable, but it was.

"So much"—propping one shoulder against the window frame, he fixed his gaze on the night sky—"for an early night."

Chapter Seven

That he didn't fall asleep was the only thing that saved them.

Several hours later, still fully dressed, he'd returned, prowling, restless, and unsettled, to stand before the window in the dark of his room, when scuffing on the cobbles followed by a ripe curse had him peering down into the alley running along the rear of the hotel.

Five heavyset men were jostling their way along the narrow alley, pausing to test every window.

Swallowing a curse of his own, he strode swiftly to the door. Crossing the sitting room, he didn't tap on Miranda's door but opened it and looked in.

She was asleep, lying on her back in the bed, hair spread in thick waves over the pillows. The covers were disarranged, as if she'd been restless, too.

Approaching the bed silently, he pressed a hand over her lips and shook her shoulder.

Her eyes flew wide, but then she saw him and blinked.

Releasing her shoulder, he touched a finger to his lips, then removed his hand from her face. "Kempsey's relatives, or the Doles, or both, have come to pay us a visit." He kept his voice to a murmur. "They're outside in the alley, trying to find a way in. They haven't succeeded yet, but they will. You need to get up, get dressed, and we need to get out of here."

She'd taken in his grim expression; her eyes widened as what he'd said sank in . . . abruptly, her expression cleared. Sitting up, she glanced around the room, then at him; she was wearing a prim flannel nightgown, but as he'd previously remarked, primness only served to underscore her attractions, at least to him.

"We need to pack and make the beds." Throwing aside the covers, she slipped out on the bed's other side and hurried to grab her bag.

He softly cursed. "We don't have time—"

"We don't have time for anything else!" The look she flung him seared. Plunking her open bag on the stool before the dressing table, she flung combs, brushes, and everything else on the table haphazardly into it. She glanced up, saw him still standing there. "Hurry!" She waved him off. "Pack—and make sure there's nothing left to give us away."

Her plan suddenly crystallized in his brain. Pack, make the beds—make it appear they'd already left. Not a bad plan, but . . . he glanced at her. She'd gone to the armoire and was pulling her dress off a hanger . . . they definitely didn't have time to argue.

He spun on his heel and raced back to his room.

Three minutes later, he returned, bag in hand.

She'd pulled her gown on over her nightgown; her cloak lay over her waiting bag. Dragging the covers back over the bed, she tucked them around the already fluffed pillows. "Where are they, do you know?"

"They couldn't get in at the back—they've gone around to the side."

"There's a side door, isn't there?"

"Yes. We don't have much time."

Straightening, she cast her eye over the bed. "That will have to do."

It looked good enough to him.

She swiped up her cloak, slung it over her shoulders as he picked up her bag. "As long as they don't touch the bed and feel the warmth, they won't know."

"Come on." Carrying both bags, he led the way through the sitting room. Feeling her draw near, he eased the door to the corridor open.

Listened.

No sound disturbed the somnolent stillness.

He stepped into the corridor, waited while she slipped out to stand beside him, then silently shut the door. He waved her toward the stairs. With luck, they'd be able to reach the ground floor and hide in one of the reception rooms.

They reached the head of the stairs.

"Which room?" The harsh whisper funneled up the stairwell.

Their visitors were milling in the front foyer.

He and Miranda backed away from the stairs.

"Second floor, number nine," someone else replied.

Roscoe searched through the gloom for the rear stairs, spotted the swinging door at the far corner of the gallery and nudged her in that direction, then, seizing her hand, drew her along as fast as he dared.

As they neared the swinging door, heavy clomping footsteps reached them—coming up the rear stairs.

They both glanced back at the main stairs. As Roscoe's senses refocused, he heard stealthy footsteps creeping up those, too.

They were trapped.

Miranda plucked at his sleeve. He glanced at her. Lips tight, she tipped her head back along the gallery, then tightened her grip on his hand and tugged him back.

He went, although he hadn't a clue what she intended.

She halted in the gallery opposite the head of the main stairs and pulled an insignificant knob set in the wall. Noiselessly, a panel yawned open. A cupboard? She looked past the panel, then glanced at him, tipped her head within, and slipped inside.

His hand still wrapped around hers, he followed . . . urgently, she tugged him into a narrow space bounded by shelves across the back and along one side, each shelf stacked with folded linens.

The space before the shelves had been designed to fit one person, but there was no other option. He stashed their bags at her feet, then pressed in, fitting his body to hers as he drew the door closed behind him—just as stealthy footsteps crossed the landing below, then started up the last flight.

A creak sounded at the corner of the gallery, the back stairs' door opening.

The cupboard door snicked shut *almost* silently. He told himself the sound would seem louder to them in the enclosed space. Told himself the five men looking for them hadn't heard and wouldn't think to search a cupboard . . . it would be a dreadful place to be found in. He had his knives, but he couldn't reach them. His shoulders barely fitted; he couldn't even raise his arms. By default, he'd slid them about Miranda, was all but wrapped around her, his arms cushioning the edges of the shelves, his back to the door.

She'd grasped his sleeve above one elbow; her hand gripped tighter, fingers sinking into his upper arm. The dark was so complete they were effectively blind, but they could hear each other breathing, were so close they could feel the rise and fall of each other's chests, the warm waft of each other's breaths against their skins. They could feel each other's bodies, muscles, bones, contours, and curves imprinting each on the other in the dark.

The irresistible fragrance of a warm, sleep-tousled female tantalized his senses.

She hadn't had time to put up her hair; a lush, living wave, it rippled over her shoulders, the thick mass so close errant tendrils caught on his stubble and teased. And the scent. If sunshine in the country had a smell, it was that.

He rested his jaw against the soft silk and battled to ignore the press of her full breasts against his chest, the pressure of her sleek thighs against his, the alluring swell of her hips all but cradling his.

Fought to focus on the danger lurking beyond the cupboard door.

Initially she stood stiffly against him, but as the minutes ticked by, increment by increment her muscles eased.

Miranda concentrated on breathing, on steadying her giddy head, on calming her thudding heart. Being this close, held so close, was both a sensual shock and an illicit enticement. Neither was easy to ignore, but despite all, despite his muscled warmth, despite his body's reaction to hers, so utterly obvious given how close they stood, she was aware his attention had fixed beyond the cupboard, that he was listening intently.

She had to do the same. Had to be prepared to react if they were found. Despite her body's response to his nearness, despite her excruciating sensitivity to every aspect of that, first and foremost they were partners in rescuing Roderick, and evading their pursuers was their urgent and immediate aim.

Drawing a deeper breath, she held it and, dragging her mind from its sensual obsession, forced her senses beyond the cupboard door.

Two heavy men had passed their hiding place, coming from the rear stairs and heading toward their suite, presumably joining those who had crept up the main stairs.

Minutes passed; nothing more than faint, muted sounds reached them from the direction of their suite. Then footsteps reemerged, congregating about the head of the stairs.

"Damn it—where the devil are they?"

The words were uttered in a rasping whisper, but in the silence of the nighttime hotel they reached into the cupboard clearly enough.

"They must've skipped. Weren't no clothes, nothing left behind."

"P'raps they guessed we'd come a-looking for 'em?"

A dissatisfied grunt.

A moment ticked by, then, "Whatever the reason, they ain't here now—no sense us hanging around. Let's go."

Footsteps started down the stairs.

"What about Jack and Herb?" someone asked.

"We'll go out tomorrow after work and warn 'em the gent and lady was asking around, but it's not as if, whoever they are, they're any great threat—nothing Jack and our Herb can't handle."

A stair creaked, then the sounds of retreat slowly faded.

A minute later, she squeezed Roscoe's arm—a wordless question.

His chin against her hair, he shook his head but didn't otherwise move. "Wait," he breathed. "We can't be sure we're safe yet."

Despite the sensual torture, he took no chances, waiting for what he judged to be a full twenty minutes before carefully easing open the cupboard door. Silence lay thick throughout the hotel; after the darkness of the cupboard, he could see quite well.

Stepping out from their refuge, he scanned the gallery around the main stairs, then drew a deeper breath and stood aside to allow Miranda to slip out. Once she had, he ducked back in and retrieved their bags. When he stepped clear again, she quietly shut the door.

They walked back to their suite.

Once inside with the door safely shut, he set their bags on the floor. Straightening, he looked at Miranda.

She'd halted in the middle of the room and half turned to look back at him. Moonlight washed in through the uncurtained windows, limning her profile but leaving her features wreathed in shadow.

There was a great deal more space between them now, yet . . .

He wanted her back—back in his arms, her body molded to his.

Holding his position, he tipped his head to her. "That was

quick thinking." His voice was deeper than usual, still affected.

She raised a shoulder. "It was lucky we both fitted."

Her husky tone proved he wasn't the only one affected by that hellish squeeze, not the only one still prey to the associated sensations.

Denying the urge to go closer, he watched as she wavered, swayed, vacillated, then she drew breath, straightened; head rising, she slowly, deliberately, turned and walked toward him. She halted before him, her gaze locking with his. He looked into her eyes. "We should get what sleep we can."

That was what they *should* do.

That was undoubtedly the wise thing to do, but Miranda wasn't feeling wise. She looked into his face, studied the strength imprinted in his features, the hard-edged resistance . . . noted, too, that he hadn't stepped back, hadn't tried to avoid her advance.

The long minutes in the linen store, when she'd been all but engulfed by him, had stripped away something—some last layer of reserve. Where he was concerned, she was no longer willing to toe any line, only to go brazenly forward.

Boldly, she stepped closer; raising one hand, she laid her palm on his chest. Sensed the ripple of reaction, the impulse not to step away but to take her in his arms and draw her nearer, an urge he reined in, yet still he waited.

Waited to see what she would do. What she wanted.

The heat of him, the muscled maleness of him, lapped around her.

She looked at her hand, then drew breath and raised her gaze to his face. Locked her eyes with his. "Earlier, you asked why I wanted you in my bed. I wasn't expecting the question, and I didn't know the answer—quite literally did not know. Now I do."

She studied his eyes, but he said nothing, simply waited, a challenge unvoiced but there nonetheless. The next breath she drew was tighter. "I want you in my bed . . . because I desire you. Because I want you—the man you are—to be my lover."

Through the hand on his chest she felt the impact of her words, sensed his immediate reaction. Yet still he waited, his face unreadable, as it so often was. But she wasn't going to back down, not now she'd made up her mind, not now she'd gone so far. "I've never wanted any man before, so you'll have to excuse my obtuseness, but I understand myself, my reasons. I know what I want, and I know why—and please don't try to tell me that I don't. There can be no question of you taking advantage of me—this is far more a case of me taking advantage of you. Of you, and our situation—the chance, the opportunity."

He said nothing, didn't move, but her eyes had adjusted to the dimness and she saw, sensed, his resistance weakening.

She kept her eyes on his. "I'm only asking for one night—just one night, while we're here, out of our usual world, away from all who know us."

Sliding her palm down his chest, she reached blindly for his hand, found it and boldly, deliberately, twined her fingers with his. "And so I'm asking you again. Inviting you again."

His fingers gripped, then gentled, yet they now held hers.

Her pulse leapt; she stepped back, toward her room. "Come with me." She held his gaze. "Be with me." She took another step back and drew him on.

And he went with her.

Two steps, three.

Roscoe was lost in her luminous eyes, captive to the siren's promise of her body, captured beyond recall. He knew it was foolish, that it was somehow tempting fate, that at some point he—and she, too—would come to regret it, yet he couldn't break her spell, couldn't shatter the moment . . . couldn't bring himself to pull away and deny her.

And himself.

She might know her reasons; he didn't want to think of his.

Her lips curved, goddess-like, at his implied surrender,

then she turned, and he let her tow him across the sitting room to the open door to her room.

In the doorway, she paused. Glancing over her shoulder, she met his eyes. Her features, her hair, silvered by the moonlight, a creature of mystery and shadow, she whispered, "Teach me. Show me."

Then she drew him on.

On to the space by the foot of the bed. There, she halted and turned.

Into his arms, arms that were waiting to hold her, to, if she only knew, claim her. He was no saint; her words, her actions, had left him hard as iron, already aching, needing relief.

Knowing he was on the brink of setting aside all reserve—all questions, hesitations, and reservations—he forced himself to focus on her eyes, to forgo the temptation of her lips long enough to ask, "Are you sure?" A simple question, gravelly and low.

Her expression open, her gaze direct, she replied, "I'm twenty-nine. I may be a virgin, but I'm no ignorant young innocent." Her chin firmed. "I'm sure."

She studied his eyes as if gauging his acceptance, then reached up and with her fingers stroked back a lock of his hair.

Quelling his too-intense reaction to that simple yet devastatingly evocative touch, he still felt compelled—felt even more compelled—to ask, "Are you sure this—your wishes, your wants—isn't simply a reaction to the danger, to the relief of escaping those men?"

He knew it could be so, that at least in part it would be so, that in the aftermath of danger came a compulsion to celebrate life.

Miranda focused on his eyes again, for the first time truly heard the underlying question—the same one he'd asked her several times. She'd answered once, yet he was still unsure . . . something inside her softened, and granted her the patience to evenly say, "I asked you before they arrived. Yes, our escaping them clarified my feelings, but our escape didn't give rise to those feelings, it only made them clearer."

And stronger.

Giving in to those feelings, letting the associated impulses guide her, she raised her arms, pleased she was tall enough to drape them about his neck, then she tilted her head, studied his shadowed face; she wished she could read his dark eyes. "If you want me to beg, I will."

His hands had risen to slide beneath her cloak; at her words, his fingers gripped her waist.

"No. Don't." Roscoe hesitated for the barest instant, then drew her to him and bent his head. "That's entirely unnecessary." And might just tip him over the edge he, somewhat surprisingly, found himself walking.

That he wanted her so much, enough to turn his back on all caution, shook him.

So he sought her lips, covered them with his, and kissed her, then let her kiss him. Let her draw him back into their earlier exchange, let her lead him back into that first arena of simple pleasure.

Then he took the reins, took charge, and did as she'd asked.

He taught her.

Showed her.

Just how much pleasure could flow from a kiss.

How much thrill and delight from a single caress.

He was driven to show her so much more, to plunge into the sea of carnal pleasure with her, but she was a novice so he reined them in, held them both back, and took each step slowly.

He claimed her mouth, steadily, thoroughly; comprehensively snaring her senses, he held them in his hands, at his command, as he shifted focus and, inch by inch, claimed her body.

Every lush curve, the full mounds of her breasts, the graceful arch of her throat, the subtle indentation of her waist above the firm swell of her hips. She was shuddering beneath his hands before he undid the ties of her cloak and let it fall from her shoulders.

He undid her laces and she wordlessly urged him on.

A virgin she might be, but there was nothing hesitant in her commitment; she was open in her appreciation, in her desire, in her wanting.

In her wonder.

That last held him like a crystal cage, one he committed himself to never shatter. Her soft "oh's" of surprised delight and her even softer "ah's" of pleasure created a siren song that held him entranced, effortlessly enraptured.

She wasn't the first virgin he'd bedded, but she was the most engaged, the most bold and, in her own special way, demanding.

Entirely unexpectedly, she made him smile, albeit inwardly.

Entirely unexpectedly, she captured him.

From the moment she'd drawn him into the room, Miranda had consciously set aside all restraint, had given herself permission to simply follow her instincts, wholeheartedly, openly, without guile.

Without any pretense of missish sensibility.

She wanted to learn and he was willing to teach her, and to her mind that gave her license to insist. To insist that, once he'd reduced her to nothing more than the short chemise she'd worn beneath her fine nightgown, that he should reciprocate. When he tried to catch her hands and prevent her from unbuttoning his shirt, she managed to gasp, "I need to know. . . ."

Pressing even closer, using her body in a catlike caress, she made him hiss in a breath and succeeded in distracting him enough to have her way.

The small victory encouraged her.

It spurred her on.

The result was a sensual tussle that landed them both on the bed in a tangle of limbs and a rush of smothered laughter.

Lying on her back, she dragged in a breath, then raised

her head and looked down her body, past her heaving breasts barely concealed by her chemise, looked into his dark sapphire eyes. "Is this how it's supposed to be? I didn't realize . . ."

His eyes, faintly smiling, held hers. "There's no one way. It's different with different people, different circumstances . . ." He looked a trifle surprised, too.

Then he drew himself up the bed and propped on his elbow alongside her. He framed her face with one hand, looked into her eyes, then bent his head and kissed her.

And waltzed her, whirled her, back into heated pleasure.

Into the rising flames that swelled between them, that licked over her skin, and his, and made them burn.

Made them yearn.

She wasn't overly modest; she was tall, had for years been gangly, but her body was now full, womanly, almost lush in its curves. And she was twenty-nine. And she'd made up her mind. She felt only the slightest quake of uncertainty when he finally drew her chemise away, but even as she caught her breath and glanced at him, that flare of self-consciousness was doused, erased by the look on his face.

Hard-edged, every angle finely honed, his features were locked, but his eyes burned. Blue-black fire caressed her curves, and desire thrummed almost tangibly between them. Then he set his hand to her skin, and she shuddered and closed her eyes.

Murmuring reassurances, gravelly and rough, he gentled her through the moments as he showed her, unstintingly patient, unwaveringly attentive, all she wished to see, to experience, to explore.

He showed her, openly, employing no more guile than she, how much her body fascinated him. Obsessed and satisfied him. Then he allowed her to sate her curiosity, to fill her senses with him, with the breadth of his chest, the heavy curves of his shoulders, the taut ridges of his abdomen.

At her insistence, he finally shed his trousers, let her explore the thick rod of his erection. Allowed her to, with sheer wonder, trace the heavy veins, the broad head.

Chest heaving, he finally caught her hands, drew them up and anchored them over her head, then he leaned over her and kissed her—and effortlessly, masterfully, reclaimed the reins.

And devoted himself to her pleasure, to fulfilling her wants and satisfying her needs . . .

Caring.

The word resonated in her mind as, his body tense with a control she could all but touch, he cupped her softest flesh, stroked, explored, learned, traced until she was urgent and wanting, then his long fingers probed, and readied her.

Pleasured her.

Until she was so consumed by urgency her back arched, and with a desperate sound, she sank her nails into his arms.

He swore, soft and low, and shifted over her. With his thighs forced hers wide and settled his hips between. Covered her.

His naked body on hers was a sensual shock and a carnal delight.

The heavy weight, the oh-so-male hardness. Skin to fevered skin, raspy hair abrading sensitive areas rarely touched.

Her breath coming in pants, she writhed, urged, yet he wouldn't let her rush, didn't allow her to race but held her beneath him, kept her with him, forced her to see, to feel . . . to know.

The final intimacy, when it came, when, hot and hard, his body braced over hers, he thrust slowly, deeply, into her, forging his way into her softness, with barely a sting breaching the barrier that marked her a virgin, was so overwhelmingly powerful it made her cry out, made her cling.

Very nearly made her weep.

The sensation of him within her, hard and heavy, so alien, so male, at her core, was so much more than she'd imagined. So much more intense, more intimate.

More cataclysmically real.

Gasping, desperately panting, her wits flown, her senses rioting, she held him, moved with him, and quickly learned the knack, found the rhythm. Slick and hot, he filled her, and she urged him on, receiving and glorying in each powerful thrust, in every scintillating sensation.

When he lowered his head and nudged, she tipped up her face and let him kiss her, let him claim her mouth as together they whirled.

Into a conflagration of need, of greedy, raking passion.

Into a furnace where desire flared, rapacious and hungry, and filled them. Drove them.

Into a whirlpool of searing sensation that swept them up, up, until she shattered on a peak of coruscating pleasure, of ecstasy so sharp it seared her soul.

Even as she fell, she clutched him tighter, harder, desperately held him close.

On a long-drawn groan, unable to hold back, much less find the strength to withdraw as he'd planned, Roscoe thrust deep, and again, then, shuddering as his release claimed him, blinded by ecstasy, held tight within the sumptuous clasp of her body, he followed her over the soaring precipice and into the familiar void.

For uncounted heartbeats they floated, him and her, wracked and limp, wrapped about each other, clinging.

Familiar . . . yet even as he sank beneath the golden waves of aftermath, even as he brushed her hair back from her face, then brushed a last, gentle kiss across her kiss-bruised lips, that part of his mind that still vaguely functioned registered that this, with her, had been something more.

Something else.

Something he'd never before felt.

Chapter Eight

They quit the hotel after an early breakfast and headed out of Birmingham, not along the direct road to Lichfield but by an easterly, roundabout route. They'd agreed that, for the loss of half an hour and a few extra miles, it was preferable to avoid any chance encounter with Kempsey's or Dole's relatives.

From behind her screening veil, Miranda kept a sharp eye out for any pursuit or potential danger, and otherwise spent the minutes dwelling on the events of the previous night.

In detail. At length. Everything she could recall, which, to her surprise, was rather a lot, enough to make her exceedingly glad of her veil. Quite aside from any blush, it hid the silly, dreamy, far-too-revealing smile that curved her lips every time she relaxed her guard.

The truth was she felt energized, buoyed, on top of the world. Her world, at least. Until she'd met Roscoe, until they'd embarked on this unexpected adventure, she'd resigned herself to dying without ever having learned . . . even half of what he'd shown her last night.

She'd always been curious in an academic sort of way over

what it was that so drew women to men. Especially to men like him. Now she'd felt the attraction, had fallen prey to it and had finally succumbed, she might not yet fully understand what it was, but she understood its compulsion.

When she'd woken that morning, he'd already left her room, but the sheets beside her had still held his warmth; he'd slept alongside her through the night. She'd vaguely recalled the feel of him spooning around her, his chest to her back, as she'd fallen into blissfully sated slumber.

She'd risen, washed, dressed, and repacked in a sunny, contented state. When she'd walked out of her room, he'd been coming out of his. Settling his coat sleeves, he'd arched a brow at her; she'd smiled serenely back, and that had been discussion enough for them both.

Subsequently, no awkwardness had arisen between them as they'd turned their minds to the increasingly urgent matter of locating Roderick. Over breakfast they'd studied a map and evaluated their options.

They'd rattled out of Birmingham shortly after eight o'clock. Now, less than two hours later, she consulted the map she held in her lap, then pointed at a conglomeration of roofs not far ahead. "That's Lichfield."

Unfortunately, there were several cottages scattered about the village, some in fields, others tucked into hollows or screened by trees. Given they no longer felt it wise to openly inquire after Kempsey and Dole, they had to, surreptitiously and covertly, check each cottage. Some were housing families and were quickly eliminated; at others they had to watch until they saw who was inside, and if no one was, they had to approach and knock on the door, then peer in to make sure Roderick wasn't there.

It was midafternoon before, having left the curricle pulled into the side of a rutted cart track and crept over a low hill into the cover of a large copse, they finally located their quarry.

"That has to be Dole." Roscoe watched the man with lank, dark hair and an even-from-this-distance pasty complexion who had come out of the rear door of the cottage nestled down slope of the copse. Lean and hungry-looking, moving slowly, the man gathered logs from a pile stacked against the cottage wall.

As the man retreated into the cottage, Miranda, crouched beside Roscoe, safely screened by the thick bushes beneath the trees, sucked in a breath. "He has a cauliflower ear—didn't Gallagher mention that?"

"He did." Roscoe glanced at her. "That settles it. We've found them."

She met his eyes. "Now what?"

He looked back at the cottage. "First we watch and see if Kempsey's in there, too."

Ten minutes later, a large, heavyset man with thinning brown hair and a ruddy face paused on the other side of the small rear window.

"All right." Roscoe shifted to face Miranda. "They're both inside. Most likely Roderick's there, but he'll be lying down, and even if he's not restrained we can't expect him to help us."

Lips compressed, one eye on the cottage, she nodded. "He might well be unconscious."

"I can account for one of them at a time." When she glanced at him, he shook his head. "Don't ask how. But for that to work—to deal with one without alerting the other and allowing them to use Roderick as a hostage—we need to separate them." He glanced at the cottage. "I need to get one of them far enough away so that he won't be able to alert the other."

They both looked down at the cottage.

"I have a better idea," Miranda said.

His instinctive response was no, but after her quick thinking at the hotel the previous night, he had to at least listen. Despite being someone who'd lived a sheltered life, her mind responded quickly and efficiently to problems, analyzing difficulties and coming up with solutions.

"What?" Despite his decision, the word wasn't encouraging.

From the corner of his eye, he saw her lips twitch, but she evenly said, "Instead of luring one of them out so *you* can deal with him—leaving the second man with Roderick and therefore still a threat to him and us—what if *I* lure one of them out of the cottage and down the slope toward the lane, and while I distract him, you slip into the cottage through the back door and deal with the man left inside? Then when the man I distract returns, you'll be waiting and can deal with him."

I shouldn't have listened.

Now that he had, he was left with no choice but to agree that her suggestion was . . . better than anything else he could think of. He couldn't readily describe how that made him feel, but he knew he didn't like it.

"All right." That his agreement was grudging rang in his tone. "But first, how do you plan to lure the man out and distract him?"

She smiled and told him, slaying any hope that she hadn't devised an excellent plan for that, too.

"Yoo-hoo, the cottage! Is anyone there?" Clutching her reticule in one hand, Miranda took a few tentative steps up the rough drive that ran from the lane along the front boundary of the sloping field on which the cottage stood. Halting, she raised a hand to shade her eyes and looked up at the cottage. She'd left off her cloak and put back her veil the better to be identified as the lady she was. That was part of her plan.

Sighing heavily—allowing her shoulders to rise and slump, then sag with weariness—she turned and looked all around as if searching, then, facing the cottage once more, she lifted her black skirts and trudged on. Slowly.

They'd seen a large manor house a mile further along the lane, but it was hidden from the cottage by a hill and a stretch of woodland. Her story was that she was staying at the manor, had gone out walking and, overcome by somber thoughts, lost her way. Something a recently bereaved widow might do.

She'd hailed the cottage loudly enough for anyone inside

to have heard, but if no one appeared, she would go closer and try again—

The cottage door opened. Halting, she looked up, making everything about the movement look hopeful.

Kempsey stepped out. Standing before the door, he peered down at her.

"Oh—I say!" She waved as if to attract his attention. "I've lost my way. Can you help?"

Kempsey studied her for a moment, then spoke over his shoulder, waited for a reply, then a slow smile broke across his face.

She was too far away to examine it, yet she felt certain that smile didn't reach Kempsey's eyes. It was the smile of a rabid mongrel assessing prey.

Kempsey spoke again, then started down the track toward her.

She held her position, smiling vacuously, and didn't so much as bat an eyelash when Roscoe raced across from the boundary of the field on the blind side of the cottage and disappeared behind it; he'd hidden in the hedgerow so he would see one of the men leave to go down to her, but no one in the cottage would see him.

Kempsey, meanwhile, thinking her nothing more than potential prey, having no clue that she was, instead, bait, came lumbering down to join her.

First stage accomplished. By now Roscoe would be inside the cottage, which meant the second stage of their plan was either in progress, or already accomplished, too.

As Kempsey drew nearer and no ruckus erupted from within the cottage, she concluded that stage two was indeed finished with. *Now for stage three.*

She kept her smile in place—the smile of a gentle, sheltered lady who assumed the brute bearing down on her would, of course, assist her.

Kempsey halted in front of her. Beady eyes regarded her and her heavy reticule, then he dipped his close-shaved head. "Missus. What's the problem?"

She fed self-deprecation into her smile. "Well, you see, I'm staying at the manor and I came out for a walk, but . . ." She bent her head, raised her gloved hand as if to wipe a tear from her eye. "I . . . got lost in my thoughts, and now . . ." Raising her head, her expression now bewildered, she waved and glanced around. "I don't know where I am."

Before Kempsey could reply, she sucked in a wheezy breath, clapped her hand to her upper chest, made a choking sound, then wheezed again.

Kempsey stepped nearer as if to catch her if she fell.

"Oh, dear me." Straightening, she waved him off, but graciously. "Thank you, but I believe I'll be all right. That is . . ." She glanced at the cottage. "Perhaps if I could have a glass of water?"

She'd remembered Gallagher's warning that Kempsey was clever, yet he saw what she wanted him to see—someone very much weaker than he, a pigeon ripe for the plucking.

"Yes, of course." Kempsey's smile returned, oilier, wider, and even more predatory. "Let's get you up to the cottage and you can have some water and a sit-down."

He stepped closer, to her side, and she had to clamp down on an instinctive urge to move away. She definitely did not like this man—didn't like him being near her at all. He and his friend had hurt Roderick; if she'd had a weapon, she would have used it on him.

Instead, she smiled artlessly, inwardly steeled herself, and let him take her arm, supposedly to solicitously help her up the sloping track.

Mimicking Gladys's occasional wheezing attacks, she used her supposed weakness to put off any questioning. Kempsey had taken her right arm; she gripped her reticule tightly in her left. It didn't qualify as a weapon, but the body was made of embroidered hessian and she'd had the thought to fill it with rocks. Now she'd seen Kempsey up close, the precaution was laughable—it would take more than a few rocks to dent his thick skull—but gripping the reticule reassured her, illusory though its protection might be.

As they neared the cottage, she strained her ears but heard nothing. This was the part of the plan she had to play extempore. She had to assume Roscoe lay in wait inside the cottage and—

"Hmm-mph!"

The inarticulate sound was followed by the crack of a chair crashing on flags.

Instinctively Kempsey released her and stepped back—then his eyes swung her way, his lip curled in a snarl, and he lunged for her.

She swung her weighted reticule and he wove back, then she whirled and raced for the cottage as if hellhounds were snapping at her heels.

The door swung open.

She glanced back, saw Kempsey, powering after her, glance at the door.

She looked back at the cottage as Roscoe emerged, a pistol in his hand.

Kempsey slid to a halt, then turned tail and fled.

Fast.

Halting, panting, beside Roscoe, Miranda turned to watch Kempsey tear down the slope toward the lane. "He's getting away."

Roscoe wanted to give chase, but he wouldn't leave her alone with Dole, even if the man was tied and gagged, and was now definitely unconscious. "I know." He shook his head, then slid his pistol back into his pocket. "But where can he go?" He waved her into the cottage. "And we need to deal with Roderick."

She stepped over the threshold, paused as her eyes adjusted, then she gasped and rushed across the single room to the pallet at the far end. "Oh, my God! Roderick!" Falling to her knees beside the crude bed, she gently cradled her brother's pallid face. "Roderick?"

Roscoe watched long enough to confirm that not even for his sister's voice was Roderick going to stir, then he bent and grabbed hold of the now thoroughly unconscious Dole.

"Careful," he warned Miranda as he lugged the man and the broken chair he was tied to out of the way. "I think his collarbone's broken as well."

When she didn't fall apart but after a moment lifted the rough blanket to take stock of Roderick's injuries, he went on, "From the aging of his bruises, he fought when they ambushed him in Chichester Street. All the injuries look that old. Both his collarbone and his foot need to be set as soon as possible." He was already considering where they might find an experienced doctor.

She pushed back from the bed and rose. "I'll go and fetch my supplies. We can bind him up well enough to move him." She turned to the back door.

He opened his mouth to tell her to wait until he could go with her—who knew what Kempsey might think to do?—when a distant noise from the front of the cottage had him glancing out of the front window and down toward the lane.

He swore. Virulently.

She didn't seem to register the crudity but went quickly to the window—and saw what he had.

The men who'd come looking for them at the hotel had just arrived. Kempsey had run into their arms, and they were comparing notes.

She swung around, looked at him, then at Roderick. "What now?"

He was already striding to the pallet. "No time to bind him up. We go out of the back door and through the copse to the curricle."

Reaching the bed, he hauled the blanket off Roderick. Taking his friend's good arm, he drew him up, bent, and hoisted him over his shoulder. "Just as well he's unconscious."

Turning, he saw that his quick-witted partner had closed and was barring the cottage's front door. "Good idea."

Dropping the bar into place, she whirled and raced to the back door. Hauling it open, she held it while he angled

Roderick out, then she followed and quietly closed the door behind her.

He headed straight up the steep rise to the copse. As she drew alongside, he caught her eye and tipped his head forward. "Go ahead." Carrying Roderick's dead weight, he was going to be much slower.

Her lips set in a mulish line. "Don't be idiotic. And don't waste breath arguing!"

Clamping his lips shut, he swore mentally instead.

And, of course, fate proved her right. Several branches snagged on Roderick's coat. She quickly pulled them free, but if she hadn't been there . . .

Grim-faced, he slogged on through the copse, then across to where the sheep track they'd followed from the curricle curved over the shoulder of the hill.

Angry voices reached them. Their would-be pursuers had come out of the cottage and were casting about, trying to determine which way they'd gone.

Still hidden by the copse, he paused to resettle Roderick's body over his shoulder. He glanced at Miranda as he set off again. "They're going to see us as we go over the hill. From there, we'll need to run."

She looked at the open stretch of track ahead, then glanced back at the cottage, gradually coming into view as they emerged from the copse, and nodded.

Sure enough, as they rushed along the unscreened section, howls went up from the men milling behind the cottage.

"There they be!" someone entirely unnecessarily shouted.

And the chase was on.

The men came after them, baying like hounds. Roscoe blocked out the sound, intended to instill fear, and concentrated on where he was placing his feet. He couldn't afford to stumble. With Miranda immediately behind, he hurried down the track as fast as he dared.

He needed her ahead of him. Needed to be able to see she was safe.

The instant the curricle came into sight, he called to her. "Run ahead, get in, and untie the reins. Leave the brake on and hold the reins in your hands." He caught her eye as she drew level. "Go!"

He put every ounce of command he possessed into the word.

Her lips compressed—he thought she was going to argue—but then she nodded, lifted her skirts higher and ran ahead.

He forged on as fast as he could, but Roderick was no lightweight. By the time he reached the cart track and had to slow to drop from the raised bank to the rutted surface, the Kempseys and Doles were pounding down the hill hot on his trail.

Landing in the track, jaw clenched, he pushed up and on.

Reaching the curricle, he shrugged Roderick from his shoulder and manhandled him onto the curricle's seat, shoving his limp body against Miranda. Grabbing the reins from her, leaving her to seize and hold Roderick, he pulled out his pistol, turned, took fleeting aim, and put a ball into the earth just in front of their pursuers' feet.

The report and the sudden eruption of earth had the pack backpedaling, scrabbling and falling over each other.

Then they realized, untangled themselves, and came raging on.

By then he'd leapt onto the curricle's seat, wedging Roderick between Miranda's body and his. Dropping the spent pistol to the floor, he released the brake. "Hold on!"

His horses weren't known for their easy manners, and they hadn't had a real run in days. Given their heads, already spooked by the shot, they took off.

The curricle swayed and rocked, hit ruts and bounced, but his carriage-maker was the best in England; the carriage held up under the rough treatment, and with the horses almost bolting, they rocketed along the track, leaving the Kempseys and Doles howling in their wake.

Only when Roscoe finally reached a decently surfaced

lane and deftly turned his horses—the devil beasts—onto the smoother surface did Miranda succeed in swallowing, and dislodging her heart from where it had wedged high in her throat.

As that organ settled into its accustomed place, into beating at its usual pace, the vise about her lungs released and she could finally draw a decent breath. She glanced across Roderick—who she was holding between them, both her hands locked in his coat—at Roscoe. And couldn't think of what to say. *Thank you* didn't come close to expressing her feelings.

She studied his face. His expression looked entirely normal. More or less impassive, relatively unreadable.

As if feeling her gaze, he briefly met her eyes. "Are you all right?"

"Yes. You?"

"No damage." He cast an assessing glance at Roderick, slumped and still very much unconscious between them. "We need to get him to a doctor."

"Yes. But where?" She looked around, trying to gain some clue as to where they were; in the panic of their escape she hadn't paid attention to their direction, so now had no idea.

The countryside about them was verdant and green with low rolling hills and no sign of any town. They were, she thought, heading roughly north, which meant away from Birmingham and, if she recalled aright, into an area where there were no towns, only tiny hamlets. "Do you know where we are?"

"Yes." After a moment, Roscoe went on, "Kempsey and Dole will try to follow us—we have to assume they'll do everything they can to hunt us, and Roderick, down. We need a place where we can get Roderick the treatment he needs, and at the same time be safe from attack."

He knew of such a safe haven. He would have thought the decision to take her and Roderick there would have been fraught, a step he would have found difficult to take, to accept . . . instead, even before he'd realized what he was doing he'd turned into the familiar lanes. "I know where we can go."

She was pushing and tugging Roderick into a more secure position. "Where?"

He didn't answer until, satisfied with her efforts, she looked his way demandingly.

"Somewhere safe." And that, he realized, was the deciding factor. He needed—beyond question or argument or reason needed—somewhere he could be sure *she* was safe. He kept his gaze on his horses. "I'm taking you to a relative's house. It's not far."

"I'm taking you to a relative's house."

Miranda replayed Roscoe's words yet again, faintly stupefied as he tooled the curricle around the wide, circular drive of a massive country house. They'd driven onto the estate via the rear drive; recalling her suspicion that he was the illegitimate scion of some noble house, she'd initially assumed that his relative was, perhaps, a manager at one of the farms. The further he'd driven she'd successively revised her assumption, first to the manager of the Home Farm, then, when they'd approached the huge house's outbuildings, perhaps the coachman or stableman. But he'd continued driving toward the house itself, so she'd amended his relative's status to the butler or housekeeper at the great house itself, but he'd confounded her by taking the loop of the drive that circled one wing of the three-storied Palladian magnificence, and continued on . . . not to the gatehouse, her final possibility, but around the sweep to the gravel forecourt before the imposing front steps.

When he drew his horses to a halt before said steps, she turned to stare uncomprehendingly at him.

Roscoe felt her gaze but didn't meet her eyes, didn't glance her way. Two grooms were already running up, wide—welcoming—grins on their faces.

Stepping out of the curricle, bracing Roderick with one hand, he held up the other—before the grooms could utter their customary welcome. "Jenks, go and tell Cater we have a wounded man. Tell him to send for Doctor Entwhistle immediately, and we'll need a few footmen to carry Mr. Clifford indoors."

"Aye, m'lord." Jenks snapped off a salute and raced up the steps to the front door.

"Here." Roscoe handed the reins to the younger groom. "Hold them steady."

Then he returned his attention to the occupants of the curricle, Roderick still unconscious, Miranda still staring. Disbelievingly.

He met her gaze. "You'll be safe here. Both of you."

She blinked, frowned. "What about you?"

Before he could clarify even that much confusion, people came streaming out of the house. Not just Cater and the footmen, as Roscoe had hoped, although they were in the vanguard; in their wake, an array of skirts came sweeping over the porch to pour down the steps.

"Julian! You're home!"

"How wonderful!"

"We didn't expect you!"

"How long will you be staying?"

"Who are your friends?"

"How badly is the gentleman injured?"

His mother, his three sisters, his sister-in-law, and his nephew—wisely bringing up the rear—gathered around him and the curricle, the females all pulling his head down to kiss his cheek, before lining up to smile delightedly at Miranda, then peer with concern at Roderick.

He remembered, too late, that his mother had written that his sisters were gathering at Ridgware to plan Edwina's wedding. Glancing at Henry, who'd gallantly offered his hand to Miranda to assist her down, he met his nephew's laughing gaze and very nearly groaned. But . . .

By the time he'd managed to rein in his female relatives' understandable curiosity and perform the required minimal introductions, dusk was falling.

Luckily, Roderick's state precluded further socializing. Two footmen lifted him from the curricle with all due care, then carried him indoors. Cater and the housekeeper, Mrs. Viner, had already conferred; under Cater's direction the footmen carried Roderick up the wide stairs to a room in the west wing.

Despite being utterly distracted by being suddenly dropped into the middle of his family, a family she could have had no notion he had, Miranda had managed the requisite greetings with aplomb, and to give them their due, his mother, sisters, and sister-in-law were understanding and supportive when she excused herself and followed her still unconscious brother up the stairs.

Somewhat cravenly, he used Roderick as an excuse to follow at her heels, leaving his family standing in a group in the hall, watching him and Miranda climb the stairs, intrigued and frankly delighted expressions on their faces.

He wasn't sure what had provoked such delight—his unexpected appearance, the anticipation of entertainment and insight into his other life that Miranda and Roderick promised, or something else? Shaking aside the suspicion that all three causes were, in fact, actively contributing, he followed Miranda, who was in turn following the footmen and Roderick, to the large bedchamber a pair of maids and Mrs. Viner had just finished making ready.

"The poor lad." From the opposite side of the four-poster bed, Mrs. Viner helped Miranda direct the footmen in just how to lay their burden down, then, when the footmen retreated, Mrs. Viner helped settle Roderick more comfortably. She tutted. "Collarbone, and his foot, too." She glanced at Miranda. "Doctor Entwhistle'll be here in two shakes—he lives not far away. While we're waiting, if you'd like I can fetch my shears, and we could cut your poor brother out of those clothes and make him more comfortable."

Miranda met the housekeeper's earnest brown eyes. "Thank you. That would help, I suspect."

The motherly woman beamed. "Don't you worry, miss.

I'll fetch my shears and be back in a jiffy. If you need any-thing else"—she pointed to the bellpull hanging by the mantelpiece—"just ring, and someone will be up straight-away."

Shooing the maids out of the room, the housekeeper left. The footmen had already gone, leaving her alone with Roscoe and a still unconscious Roderick. She honestly couldn't say who was the bigger distraction.

Roscoe had halted at the foot of the bed. "In case you didn't catch it, the housekeeper's name is Mrs. Viner."

He shifted, then prowled around the bed toward her. She turned to face him.

Halting before her, he searched her eyes, then his impas-sive mask fractured and his lips twisted ruefully. "I apolo-gize. I'd forgotten my sisters and nephew would be here. Normally this is a much . . . quieter household."

She glanced at the bed, then at the room, thought of all she'd seen—and understood what he'd meant about them being safe. "That doesn't matter."

"I know it's a shock, a lot to absorb and deal with, but . . ." He waited until she looked at him, then captured her gaze. "Will you trust me?"

Always. The word leapt to her mind, and she realized it was the truth. She'd trusted him since their first meeting; over the last days, she'd trusted him implicitly again and again.

She'd taken him as her lover without the slightest concern. Eyes locked with his, she nodded. "Yes. Of course."

"Good." His lips quirked again, more in resignation this time. "I'll do what I can to keep the curious at bay."

With an inclination of his head, he started to turn away.

She reached out and caught his sleeve. When he glanced back, she met his gaze. "Who are you?"

He held her gaze for several moments, then said, "I'm Roscoe. You, more than most, know who, and what, I am."

When she didn't reply, either to accept or further ques-tion, he lifted her hand from his sleeve, lightly squeezed her fingers, then released them and stepped back. She let him go.

But on the point of turning away, he hesitated, then met her eyes again, and quietly said, "In my earlier life, I used to be Lord Julian Delbraith."

She had no idea what he saw in her eyes; she had no idea what she felt.

With a slight nod, he turned and walked to the open doorway; without glancing back, he went out, drawing the door closed behind him.

She stared at the door, her thoughts churning, but to no real effect. Of all the revelations of the past half hour, all incomplete, tantalizing yet still nebulous, only one stood as immutable fact.

London's gambling king, the man she'd taken as her lover, was the legitimate scion of a ducal house.

A tap on the door heralded Mrs. Viner. The housekeeper brandished two pairs of dressmaker's shears and a man's nightshirt. "I found this, although I daresay we'll have to wait until the doctor bandages him up, but we'll manage somehow." Mrs. Viner smiled. "Shall we get started, then?"

Shaking off her lingering, possibly deepening stupefaction, Miranda nodded. "Yes, by all means."

Dealing with Roderick, at least, was something she knew how to do.

Chapter Nine

Doctor Entwhistle proved to be kindly and competent. Miranda felt immeasurably relieved when, after setting and tightly binding Roderick's shoulder and arm, and his foot, the doctor assured her that with due care he expected his patient to recover completely.

"He was lucky—they're both simple breaks. Nevertheless, it will take several months before the bones are fully healed."

She brushed a lock of hair from her brother's brow. "And the fever?"

"That's a symptom, not a cause for concern in and of itself. Now his bones are aligned and healing can commence, the fever should subside." Entwhistle smiled reassuringly. "It may take a few days, but I expect some improvement by tomorrow. I'll call again to check on his progress tomorrow afternoon, but bear in mind that I've dosed him, sleep being the best balm for broken bones. I doubt he'll wake before then, and even when he does, he'll be weak, and you'll need to discourage unnecessary movement or excitement of any kind for the next several days."

She nodded, then asked the most pertinent question. "We live in London. How soon will he be able to travel?"

Lips pursing, Entwhistle considered Roderick, then said, "I'll be able to be more definite after I see him tomorrow, but I doubt he'll be fit enough to manage that distance this side of ten days. I would advise doing all possible not to jar or put much weight on his foot during that time. Even then, he'll need to stay off it and keep his shoulder and arm strapped for several more weeks."

"Thank you. We'll do whatever you recommend."

Following the doctor to the door, she saw him out—into Roscoe's hands; he'd apparently been waiting in the corridor to walk the doctor out.

Returning to the bed, she looked down at Roderick. He was still terribly pale, his brown hair lank, and there were lines bracketing his mouth that hadn't been there when she'd last seen him a week ago. Yet seeing him sleeping . . . relief flooded her, so intense that she closed her eyes and simply let the wave wash through her.

As the emotion receded, she opened her eyes. Looking around, spotting a straight-backed chair by the wall, she went to it, lifted it and set it beside the bed, then sat, took one of Roderick's limp hands in hers, and settled to wait.

She was recalling various other times when she'd kept vigil by Roderick's bedside when the door opened and Roscoe walked in.

As he closed the door, she met his eyes. "Thank you again for all your help."

He shook his head dismissively. "I didn't question Entwhistle. What did he say?"

While she told him, he strolled to the end of the bed, sank his hands in his pockets, leaned a shoulder against the carved post, and studied her brother. Watching him, she concluded, "So it appears we'll be imposing on your . . . sister-in-law's hospitality for the next ten days at least."

She'd couched a subtle question in the statement; she wasn't sure of the relationship, but she'd been introduced to

Lucasta, Dowager Duchess of Ridgware, who was clearly Roscoe's mother, and also to Caroline, who was the present duchess. The lanky youth who bore a striking resemblance to Caroline as well as Lucasta and Roscoe had been introduced as the duke, so . . . she thought she had it right. Caroline, presumably a widow, was presently lady of this ducal sprawl.

Apparently oblivious to her uncertainty, Roscoe merely nodded. "We can use the time to see what we can learn about who hired Kempsey and Dole. It would be best to know that before Roderick returns to town."

She wondered how . . . but she had another issue to address. "We're in your debt—"

"No, you're not." He met her eyes. "At least not monetarily."

"But the doctor—"

"Is the estate's local man. We have him on retainer."

She studied his face, then said, "You're not going to allow me, or Roderick, to pay for this, are you?"

"No." After a moment, his lips curved. "I am, after all, London's gambling king, and as such, one of the wealthiest men in the realm. And, as I believe I mentioned, I consider Roderick an ally and a friend, and I take care of my allies and friends." He paused, then added, "You could consider this, and all else, as merely me shoring up my reputation."

She humphed, but she might as well leave arguing until later, or even leave it to Roderick. As she sat looking up at Roscoe, lounging with his customary grace against the bedpost, she recalled her earlier assumption—that all about him that screamed of an aristocratic lineage had come via the wrong side of the blanket. Observing him here, in this setting, she could only wonder how she could have thought that; there was nothing diluted about him. He was the genuine article, through and through.

But she was still at sea, adrift as to how and why and . . . so many things. And as he seemed disinclined to explain, she was, apparently, going to have to ask. "The others in the

Philanthropy Guild." She waved at him, then around. "Do they know?"

He studied her for a moment, then said, "They don't know, but the older ones might suspect." Pushing away from the bedpost, he drew his hands from his pockets and resettled his coat. "They're all younger than I am by a few years at least, so none of them rubbed shoulders with me as I was before." He met her gaze. "Lord Julian Delbraith disappeared twelve years ago."

Before she could assimilate that, let alone respond, a light tap fell on the door.

Roscoe—Julian, whichever he was while there—turned and went to the door. Opening it, he looked out; she heard female voices. His voice was too low for her to make out his words, but a lady replied. He paused; she could feel his resignation from across the room, then he stepped back and held the door wide.

The dowager swept in, followed by the duchess.

Earlier in the forecourt, Miranda had absorbed no more than fleeting impressions. Now she registered that the dowager, while no longer young, still possessed both physical and mental energy; she was fashionably turned out, her features fine, her steel gray hair becomingly dressed. Strength of character and an indomitable will were etched in the lines of her face and underscored by her posture; Miranda sensed that the dark blue of her eyes was not the only characteristic the dowager had passed on to her son. In contrast, the duchess was both younger and visually less forceful; blond, indisputably elegant even in a plain day gown, there was nevertheless a hint of inner resolve in a face that seemed somehow older than it should have been.

Rising, Miranda started to curtsy, but the dowager waved her up.

"No need for that, dear, not while it's just us." The dowager peered at Roderick. "So how is your brother? What did Entwhistle say?"

Deeming they had a right to know—they were giving her

and Roderick refuge, after all—Miranda told them. Both the dowager and the duchess asked pertinent questions; subsequent comments suggested both had a passing acquaintance with nursing young gentlemen. From the corner of her eye she saw Roscoe hovering by the open door, as if considering escaping . . . but he shut the door and remained where he was, distanced from the gathering about the bed.

Eventually, her report concluded, she drew a deeper breath and focused on the two ladies. "I can't thank you both enough for permitting us to stay, let alone assisting us—"

"Great heavens, dear—of course we would." The dowager smiled with real warmth. "We're only too happy to have a chance to do so."

The duchess smiled warmly, reassuringly, too. "Please believe, Miss Clifford, that we're only too glad to have you to stay." The duchess glanced at Roscoe. "We're delighted that Julian had the sense to bring you here."

Why? Miranda kept her puzzlement from her face, but inwardly she wondered. Both the dowager and duchess struck her as sincere, openly and honestly pleased at her and Roderick's unexpected arrival.

Another tap fell on the door.

"Ah—that will be Nurse." The dowager waved at Roscoe. "Do let her in, dear."

Roscoe obeyed.

The duchess volunteered, "Nurse is very experienced in watching over patients—she'll watch over your brother and take excellent care of him. Meanwhile, what with the distraction, we haven't had a chance to change for dinner, but as it's just us—*en famille*—we've decided we won't bother with the formalities this evening."

"Indeed." The dowager swept up to Miranda and laid gentle fingers on her arm. "And as Entwhistle has dosed your brother so he won't wake until tomorrow, you, my dear, can leave Nurse to manage here and join us at table."

Miranda knew when she was being herded. She looked into the dowager's dark and surprisingly alert eyes, and sensed that the old lady was rarely gainsaid. Like her son, she expected to get her way.

Miranda looked across the room at Roscoe. Hands clasped behind his back, he was looking down; if a man such as he could ever look self-effacing, as if he wished to fade into the paneling, that was how he was looking now.

Curiosity rose, surprisingly intense.

And Roderick was unlikely to wake.

She looked at the dowager, then at the duchess, and inclined her head. "Thank you. I would be pleased to join you for dinner." She glanced at Nurse, who had come in and now stood quietly waiting; a middle-aged woman in a starched white apron over a gray gown, with iron gray hair, strong hands, and a square face, she appeared rather formidable. "Let me explain my brother's condition to Nurse, and then, perhaps"—Julian? Or Roscoe?—"your son could show me the way."

"Excellent." With an approving pat on her arm, the dowager swung to the door. "Come, Caroline—I believe that's the gong sounding now. The others will be wondering where we've got to."

The two ladies departed, charging Roscoe to bring Miss Clifford along directly. Already engaged with Nurse, she didn't hear his reply.

Nurse proved to be every bit as experienced and rock-steady as the duchess had intimated; she asked numerous questions about the injuries before declaring herself sufficiently advised to assume Roderick's care. "I doubt he'll even stir, not after one of doctor's sleeping drafts, but if he shows any signs of waking, I'll send for you immediately."

Having already surmised that while Nurse approved of her concern for Roderick, the woman did not consider Miranda's input or presence as necessary to her brother's recovery, she accepted the olive branch for what it was. "Thank you."

Turning from the bed, she walked to where Roscoe waited. He met her eyes but made no comment. Opening the door, he waved her through, then followed her into the corridor.

She waited while he closed the door. Joining her, he waved her on, and she fell in beside him as he led her through the corridors. After a moment, she murmured, "I would have been perfectly happy with a tray in the room. You could have rescued me, but you didn't."

A moment ticked by, then he replied, his voice low, "I could have, but they're right—you need to eat a proper meal. We haven't had anything since breakfast, and that was early." Through the shadows in the gallery, he met her eyes. "You'll be no help to Roderick if you faint or wilt away."

She humphed and looked ahead. Internally, the house was not as overwhelming as she'd expected; although the furniture and furnishings were beautiful, luxurious and elegant, the overall ambience was of a house in use, a home, not a showcase.

"Besides," Roscoe went on, "you need time to get to know them, at least well enough to be comfortable over the next few weeks." With a wave, he directed her to the head of the main stairs. "And they need time to get to know you. I know they'll do all they can to help you over the coming days."

They started down the stairs. "Your sisters. Do they live here, too?"

"Only Edwina, the youngest. Millicent, the eldest, and Cassie, the middle one, are both married and not normally here. I gather they're visiting to plot and plan Edwina's wedding. She's engaged to one of the Frobishers."

She didn't move in tonnish circles, but she'd heard the name. "One of the adventurers?"

He nodded. His lips quirked upward as they reached the front hall. "I imagine that will suit Edwina to the ground. Frobisher might not know it, but I'd wager she's planning to accompany him on his next expedition."

He led her not to the main dining hall, which, she felt sure, would be cavernous, but to a nice-sized dining parlor, a more intimate room with a table that sat only twelve. It was presently set for eight. The family had gathered before the long windows at the end of the room; they turned as she entered, Roscoe at her shoulder.

The duchess smiled and came forward. "I know you met fleetingly before, but allow me to introduce the rest of the family in greater depth." She proceeded to introduce Millicent and Cassandra—"Cassie, please"—both stylish young matrons, and Edwina, a delightful young lady of twenty-two summers who was clearly thrilled over her upcoming wedding, but, like her sisters, was agog to learn more about Miranda and Roderick. Each sister volunteered a trifle more about themselves—who the elder two had married, and where in the country their respective homes were, what children each had, and that they'd sent their husbands to Scotland for some hunting, along with Frobisher, Edwina's fiancé, in order to congregate and plan Edwina's wedding without distraction.

Extracting Miranda from the sisters, the duchess continued, "My mama-in-law needs no further introduction." The duchess turned to the youth who stood dutifully at her elbow. She smiled and the love of a mother lit her face. "Which leaves me to present my son, Henry, Duke of Ridgware."

Smiling, Miranda curtsied, and was charmed by Henry's smile as he took the hand she offered and very correctly bowed over it. She judged him to be in his midteens, all long limbs and as yet evolving grace, but he made a commendable job of the courtesy.

"A pleasure, Miss Clifford. I look forward to making yours and your brother's acquaintance over the coming days. I take it he's not in any serious straits?"

"Nothing dire, or so your good doctor assured me. Just broken bones." She turned as Henry, mimicking his uncle's elegance, waved her to a chair; preempting Roscoe, he held it for her.

Henry grinned as he settled her. "I get to claim the guest."

She chuckled; she liked Henry. He'd sat her to the left of the great carver at the head of the table. After assisting his grandmother, the dowager, to the chair opposite hers, Henry

claimed the carver, looked down the table, then glanced at
the butler who'd come to stand by his shoulder. "Right then,
Cater. Let's have at it."

Again she found herself hiding a smile; Henry's youthful
insouciance was infectious. Although serious questions remained over Roderick's kidnapping, about who was behind
it and why, in that moment, with relief mingling with curiosity, and a sense of calm security engulfing her, she felt
justified in relaxing and learning what she could of the man
seated alongside her—Neville Roscoe-Lord Julian Delbraith.

His eldest sister, Millicent, sat opposite him, with Cassie
alongside her. The duchess sat in the smaller carver at the
table's foot, and Edwina sat to her right, opposite Cassie and
on Roscoe's other side.

As the first course—a delicious chicken and cucumber soup—was set before them, Millicent asked where in
London Miranda and Roderick lived.

The ensuing discussion wasn't so much an interrogation
as an exchange. For every piece of information they asked of
her, they offered something in return, some snippet that gave
her a smidgen more insight into their own family's mystery.
Into the man of mystery who sat, not exactly silent but subdued, beside her.

At one point, she caught him bestowing a heavily resigned
look on his mother, but the dowager merely smiled in reply.

Throughout the exchange, her biggest challenge lay in remembering to refer to him as your brother, your son, your
brother-in-law, or your uncle, and not call him Roscoe. His
family and the staff never referred to him as Roscoe, but as
Julian, Lord Julian, or your lordship, and she had no idea
how much they knew of his other life in London.

The other oddity that struck her was the family's un-
feigned, quite pointed and open interest in her, Roderick,
their family, and their life in London; it was almost as if
they lived isolated and hadn't had an outside visitor in an
age, but that wasn't true. Enough comments were dropped

about ton events, enough names mentioned, names even she recognized, to confirm that all the ladies, the elders as well as the younger set, were socially active.

Why, then, their avid interest in her and Roderick?

Because they were a part of Roscoe's other life?

By the end of the meal, she found herself as fascinated by the others about the table as they patently were by her. And the largely silent man beside her was the fulcrum about which everyone's interest revolved.

When they all rose, Henry turned to him. "Come and play a round of billiards."

He sent her a subtly questioning look.

For once she found it easy to read. She smiled and waved him off. "I'm going to return to Roderick."

He hesitated, his gaze going past her, then he inclined his head and followed Henry out.

She turned to thank the duchess, but instead that lady, coming up beside her, took her arm.

"Please call me Caroline." The duchess smiled. "And no, you can't slip upstairs before taking tea. That wouldn't do at all. Come to the drawing room, and I'll have them bring in the tray."

Acquiescing, she walked beside Caroline out of the dining room.

"You'll find your things in the room next to your brother's," Caroline said. "We assumed you would want to be close."

"Thank you." Miranda had no difficulty making the words heartfelt. "You've all been very kind."

"Pshaw!" The dowager was walking immediately behind them. "We might be helping, but please don't imagine you owe us anything, my dear. The truth is that you and your brother have given us an opportunity we've all been waiting for for years."

Reaching the drawing room's doorway, Miranda glanced at the dowager and let her puzzlement show.

The dowager beamed and patted her arm. "You've given

us a chance to help Julian. Even if it's oblique, through helping you and your brother, it's the first chance we've ever had to even the scales."

The duchess had paused to ask the butler to bring in the tea tray. The dowager's smile softened, and she waved Miranda on. Walking with her to the twin sofas set facing each other before the fireplace in which a cheery blaze dispelled the gathering chill, the dowager continued, "From what was said earlier, I gather your brother's London house is close by my son's."

"Yes, that's right." Miranda accepted the dowager's waved invitation to sit on one sofa beside her. "It's a few minutes' walk away, around one corner."

"I see. Have you ever been inside my son's house?"

"Twice, but only in the reception rooms, of course."

"Excellent." The dowager's smile turned delighted.

Roscoe's sisters quickly gathered on the sofa opposite while the duchess came to sit elegantly in a wing chair nearby. The dowager glanced at them, then looked at Miranda. "We would all be greatly in your debt if you would describe his house to us—we've never seen it, you see."

She looked at their faces—all eager, but with a deep-seated, underlying need to know. She didn't understand what was going on, but there was something in their faces, in their need, she recognized. That she knew she would feel if she'd ever been separated from Roderick as they, apparently, had been separated from . . . their son, their brother, their brother-in-law.

They all loved him. Absolutely and without reservation. And so they yearned to know, and that yearning had nothing to do with simple curiosity.

Sitting back, Miranda drew breath, then nodded. "Very well." And proceeded to tell them as much as she could of what they desired, and needed, to know.

They kept to their unvoiced bargain; the instant she finished her tea, the ladies released her to return to Roderick.

He hadn't moved. He lay in the bed, quietly breathing, sunk in sleep.

"His fever's fading." Nurse rose from the armchair.

Miranda sighed. "That's a relief. I did wonder if it would turn worse."

"Never fear. It's as the doctor said—your brother's a fine, healthy young man. He might have lost a bit of weight through his ordeal, but what's beneath is strong, hale, and robust. He'll pull through and be as good as new."

Miranda glanced at the older woman. Smiled. "Thank you."

"It's nothing but the truth, miss. Now, if you're going to sit with him for a short while, I'll go down and have my supper."

"Yes, please do." She turned to the chair beside the bed.

Nurse nodded briskly. "I'll be back in half an hour."

The door closed and the room fell silent. Sitting with Roderick's limp hand cradled in hers, Miranda found her mind drifting back to the drawing room, back over the conversation about the dining table, reliving the exchanges, cataloging all she'd heard, all she'd learned. All she'd offered in return.

She'd been careful to walk a fine but definite line. She hadn't felt comfortable revealing anything that Roscoe might deem private; defining that line had been difficult given she knew nothing of his reasons, his motives, didn't know enough to even guess at why Lord Julian Delbraith, scion of the dukedom of Ridgware, had become Neville Roscoe, London's gambling king.

As Respectability's handmaiden, she recognized the danger that transformation posed to his socially prominent family, but that interested her far less than the insight the dowager had let fall.

"It's the first chance we've ever had to even the scales."

Roscoe was helping her and Roderick; he'd come to their aid the instant he'd known they'd needed help, had aided them unstintingly, without reserve, and refused to even consider repayment.

He'd established and led the Philanthropy Guild, an organization devoted to helping those less fortunate—quietly, without any fanfare or desire for recognition.

But, it seemed, even before that, he'd helped his family—and that, too, had apparently been done with a complete and absolute eschewal of any degree of personal recompense.

In helping others, he gave with an all but ruthless selflessness, leaving those he helped with very little opportunity to, as the dowager had put it, balance the scales.

Neville Roscoe–Lord Julian Delbraith—whoever he was, he was an intriguing man.

Passing the long-case clock in the gallery on his way to Roderick's room, Roscoe saw that it was nearly midnight. Too restless to settle, let alone sleep, he'd been in his room when a sleepy footman had brought a summons from Nurse.

He'd been thinking, pondering, warily curious as to why, after all his years of rigid caution, he'd so readily accepted allowing Miranda and Roderick to learn the secret powerful enough to destroy the family he'd spent the past twelve years, indeed most of his adult life, protecting. The real wonder, however, was that he would do it again, and not one iota of regret or fear of an adverse outcome troubled him.

Then again, he'd spent a lifetime gauging odds and knew beyond question that he'd weighed and judged Miranda and Roderick correctly.

Reaching Roderick's room, he opened the door. Nurse came to her feet and beckoned him in. Leaving the door ajar, he approached the bed, his gaze following Nurse's not to Roderick, still lying on his back apparently sound asleep, but to the figure slumped on the side of the bed.

Miranda.

Seated on a straight-backed chair pulled close to the bed, she lay with her head on her outstretched arms, one hand lightly grasping one of Roderick's. She'd let down her hair. The lustrous brown tresses lay like a living veil over her shoulders, screening her face.

"She's been sound asleep for over an hour." Nurse cast him a sharp glance. "Exhausted, I expect."

She hadn't been his nurse; he'd been twelve or so when she'd first come to Ridgware as nurse to Millicent, then the other two girls. Regardless, Nurse—she'd never been known as anything else—knew him well enough. From the disapproval she was radiating, he got the impression she'd expected him to arrive and deal with Miranda without her having to summon him.

"If she stays like that until morning, she'll be sorry." Nurse tipped her head to his right. "Her room's next door. Bed's made up and waiting."

Her suggestion—her order—was clear.

Stifling a whisper of wary warning, he circled the bed. Gently brushing back Miranda's hair, he confirmed she was dead to the world. Disengaging her fingers from Roderick's, he bent and eased her into his arms. One arm beneath her knees, the other around her back, he lifted her so smoothly she didn't stir.

He turned to the door. Nurse was already there. She held the door open, waited while he angled his burden through, then slipped past, down the corridor, and opened the door to the next bedchamber.

Carrying Miranda in, he walked to the bed; as Nurse had said, it was made up and ready for use, the coverlet already turned down. Walking to the side of the bed, he leaned across and gently laid Miranda down.

He heard the snick of the door latch. Glancing at the door, he confirmed that Nurse had left, presumably to return to Roderick.

Leaving him to deal with Roderick's sister. Alone.

Inwardly shaking his head—he couldn't understand how the two of them being lovers, lovers for just one night, was somehow so obvious—he set about unlacing her half boots. Her being exhausted was hardly a surprise; the previous night had been a long one, what with the visitation by the Kempseys and Doles, followed by the understandably but nevertheless unexpectedly heightened sexual engagement, followed by their early morning departure and the long day searching for the cottage and Roderick, capped by their difficult rescue, their escape from the howling hordes, and subsequent rattling race through the countryside. To Ridgware.

Arriving there had been yet another shock for her, but she'd weathered it with a clear-eyed calm for which he was truly grateful. She'd accepted what he'd told her, what he'd revealed and what he hadn't, and had gone forward with that and had managed.

Setting her half boots aside, he hesitated, then stripped off her hose. She had delicately formed, nicely arched feet; his hands lingered, palms caressing her soles as he drew the silk stockings away. Laying both aside, he considered the tightly laced mourning gown, as uncomfortable a creation as he'd ever beheld. Surrendering to the compulsion that wasn't going to let him turn around and walk away, he eased her over and started on the laces.

He'd undone the laces and the buttons of the bodice and was drawing the sleeves down her arms when she stirred. He froze, wondering if he ought to place a hand over her lips in case she screamed, but then her lids rose; she saw him, appeared to instantly recognize him, then she blinked and looked around.

"Oh." She tried to struggle up to her elbows, but with his hands on her arms, he held her down. She frowned at him. "Roderick. I have—"

"He's sound asleep. I would say dead to the world, but you might get the wrong impression." Moonlight streamed in through the windows to either side of the bed; in the weak light he searched her face, saw the reality of her exhaustion. "Your brother's doing the right thing and resting—you need to do the same."

A mulish look he was coming to know well invested her features.

He responded by taking the tack he should have from the first—the one most likely to persuade her. "You won't be any use to Roderick tomorrow, when he wakes and needs you there, if you're weaving on your feet."

Her lips had parted, presumably to protest, but his words gave her pause. Her frown deepened.

He moved to clinch his victory, minor though it was. "Nurse said she'd come and fetch you if Roderick wakes, and she's experienced and reliable, so there's no reason you shouldn't rest. Aside from all else, you'll need to spell her in the morning, so she can rest then."

"Hmm." Miranda's frown started to lift. He renewed his tugging on her sleeves, and she huffed out a small breath, relaxed, and let him draw the sleeves off her hands and the gown down to her waist.

Lying back on the pillows, she sank both hands in the material bunched at her hips and pushed, wriggled, and helped him strip the gown off. But her gaze had shifted to his face; as he shook out the gown and tossed it over a nearby chair, he could feel her studying his features through the dimness.

"What time is it?"

As if some cosmic authority had heard her, the clocks throughout the house started to chime; as the distant bongs faded, she widened her eyes at him. "Midnight?"

He nodded. He should go. She was in her bed, comfortable enough. He should turn and walk from the room.

Her gaze had drifted down over his clothes. "You haven't changed." Her gaze rising, her eyes found his. She tilted her head; curiosity, an honest interest, colored her expression. "Why were you still awake?"

Because after last night, after the fraught events of the day, some errant part of me didn't want to sleep alone in my bed, away from you.

Sinking his hands in his pockets, he shrugged. "I was . . . restless. After the day we've had, that was only to be expected." He half turned to the door.

"Don't go." When he looked back at her, she held out one hand. "Please. Stay."

Inwardly vacillating, he remained rooted to the spot.

She came up on one elbow yet still kept one hand extended toward him. "I feel it, too, but I didn't know if . . . but now you're here and I'm awake, and . . ." Eyes on his, she turned her extended hand palm up. "Why not stay?"

Why not, indeed? She lay there clad only in her filmy chemise, the moonlight silvering her lush curves, and siren-like asked her question. A question to which he had no good answer, because in that moment, more than anything, he wanted to spend the night, the rest of it, with her.

"Are you sure?"

She fell back on the pillows and sent him a weary mock frown. "How many times am I going to have to remind you that I'm twenty-nine years old and not given to impulsive actions. To reckless starts."

He arched a brow. "And this"—he gestured between them—"isn't impulsive? Isn't reckless?"

She held his gaze for an instant, then shook her head. "No. This, I assure you, is entirely deliberate."

All resistance vanished. Vanquished, vaporized by the look in her eyes, by his own heated response.

He'd taken the fatal steps back to the bed before he'd made any conscious decision—rendering further argument a waste of time.

He shrugged off his coat. She curled her knees beneath her and sinuously rose to kneel on the bed before him. He opened his waistcoat, shrugged that off, too, as she set busy fingers to his cravat. When, after removing the diamond pin, he took over unraveling the complex folds, she shifted her attention to the buttons of his shirt.

She pushed the halves wide as he tossed the cravat away; hands clutching fistfuls of material, she rose on her knees and found his lips with hers, and kissed him.

Lured him into kissing her back, into accepting the bounty she offered and plunging into the honeyed delights of her mouth, into savoring the lush curves of her tempting lips.

She pushed his shirt over his shoulders. Swiftly undoing the cuffs, he let her strip the linen from between them, then, with them both immersed in the increasingly ravenous kiss, he swung around, sat on the edge of the bed, and blindly reached for his boots.

Fluidly shifting with him, high on her knees, she framed his face and kissed him with open ardor, then her hands glided down, tracing the column of his throat, then she spread her hands and by touch devoured his chest.

If he'd expected her to wait and follow his lead . . . but he hadn't. Some part of him was fascinated by her commitment to their engagement, even though as before, during the heat of the previous night, he doubted either of them had any real plan, any script, any clear agenda. What each of them patently did have was wishes and wants, desires and nascent passions that centered on the other, and while he was accustomed to setting the pace, despite her inexperience she—perhaps, as she kept reminding him, because she was twenty-nine—transparently saw no reason not to press her own case.

Her blatant wish to see, to test, to explore. To learn and know.

Miranda was fascinated anew. What it was in him, his mouth, his lips and tongue, his hands and his body, that so called to her she had no idea, only that the tug, the need, was visceral and powerful beyond compulsion.

And after the previous night, she felt even more emboldened. Now she'd been there once and knew their destination, she felt confident in the eventual outcome and thus free to explore the different ways, the other paths to that ultimate goal.

So when she heard his second boot thump on the floor, she saw no reason not to push his shoulders, to use her weight to persuade him to lie back on the bed, his thighs supported but his feet still on the floor.

The instant he complied, she swung one leg over him. Her chemise rode up her thighs, capturing his awareness and distracting him as she settled on her knees, straddling him, and looked down at his chest. Her prize.

She smiled and gave into the urge to stroke, caress, then taste. He sucked in a tight breath when she drew her tongue over one of his nipples; through the inner faces of her thighs, clamped to his sides, she felt the telltale tension infusing his muscles—so evocative and provocative—ratchet higher.

His hands, at her waist, gripped, but he made no move to stop her, to curtail her play, her exploration.

Heat rose to her touch; she could feel it radiating through his skin. She felt powerful, a goddess commanding such a being, evoking his passion, stoking his desire.

She set herself to the task with escalating delight and renewed enthusiasm.

His grip eased; his palms shaped, then slid lower, over the swells of her hips to slip beneath the hem of her chemise and caress the bare curves of her derrière . . .

The heat spread from him to her. The wash of need, of surging passion, rolled through her, spreading beneath her skin, stealing her breath. Her wits had flown long ago.

She bent her head and kissed him—took his mouth as he had hers, then invited him to reciprocate. He did, and his hunger curled her toes.

His hands swept slowly, masterfully, up her body, taking the fine chemise with them. He broke the kiss and, panting, senses expanding, she sat up, raised her arms and let him draw the filmy garment off, away.

She'd intended to lean forward and caress his chest with her breasts, but his hands came between them and he filled his palms with her flesh. His hands closed. Lids falling, she dropped her head back and shuddered.

He held her there, for long moments returning the pleasure, each and every caress she had lavished on him. Until passion was a flame threatening to consume them.

An elemental power that demanded and coerced.

He hauled in a breath, chest swelling, and ground out, "Unbutton my trousers."

She obeyed without thought; thought was far beyond her. Shuffling back until her knees bracketed his hips, she fell on the buttons at his waist, slid them free. Releasing his erection, thick and heavy, fully engorged.

Heaven. She closed her hand around the rigid shaft, stroked, and heard him gasp. Before she could repeat the caress, he caught her wrist, hesitated for a heartbeat, then slowly drew his member free of the tight circle of her fingers.

Capturing both her wrists, he held one in each hand and urged her forward.

She went eagerly, letting him show her . . .

He pressed into her, then released her wrists, gripped her hips and guided her down, down . . . until she'd taken all of him, until, on a primal shudder, she engulfed him in the molten slickness of her body and could feel him high and hard within her.

Then his hips flexed beneath her, thrusting upward. Gripping her hips, he raised her, showed her.

He only had to demonstrate once.

She embraced the new dance with unalloyed delight, with a passionate ardor she could barely contain. Hands braced on his chest, she rode him, experimented and tested and tried. . . .

The climax, when it came, when it roared through her in a geyser of sensation erupting from where they joined, was so shockingly intense that she lost touch with the world.

Knew only the blessed tension, the cataclysmic release, the sheer power of him between her thighs as she came apart in brilliant splendor.

He'd never seen anything like it, had never been treated to such an open display of feminine passion and desire. He was utterly captivated, utterly lost. And he didn't care.

Teeth gritted, he clung to sanity and rode out the torrent of her release, refused to let the powerful contractions of her sheath about his cock pull him under, not yet, not this time.

When, unraveled, she would have slumped, he shifted, rolled, and, rising over her, wedged his hips between her widespread thighs and thrust deeply home once more.

He waited several minutes, thrusting lazily, languidly,

until she caught her breath. Until she opened eyes lustrous with passion and looked up at him. Then she smiled like a well-fed cat, reached a hand to his nape, drew his head down, and fitted her mouth to his.

And flagrantly urged him on.

He waited for no further invitation. He ravaged her mouth and took his fill of her body. Filled her and himself with the pounding pleasure. He held nothing back, with her saw no reason for reticence or restraint.

As she had given, he gave, too.

As she had taken, he seized and claimed.

Pulses thundering, breaths sawing, they clung and raced up passion's peak.

Senses reeling, desire spiraling, they reached for that glorious moment of togetherness. Found it, grasped it, clutched it.

And held tight as the world shattered anew.

As reality splintered and sensation fell away and they flew.

Until ecstasy fractured them, broke them, wracked them, then flung them into the void.

And they fell.

Into the vastness of passionate oblivion, into the glory of aftermath's sea.

Chapter Ten

The next morning, Miranda awoke in a dreadfully rumpled bed with the echo of pleasure still thrumming in her veins.

Spontaneously she smiled, but her smile slowly faded as memory strengthened along with the daylight. Throwing back the covers, she wrapped herself in a robe and rang for warm water. When it arrived, she rushed through her ablutions, dressed, pinned up her hair, then went to check on Roderick.

"Hasn't stirred," Nurse said in answer to her query. "But then we shouldn't expect him to, not until this afternoon, and his fever's all but gone."

Resting her hand on Roderick's forehead, then testing the side of his neck, she confirmed the observation. "That's a huge relief." Straightening, she studied her brother. "Should we change his nightshirt, do you think?"

"Once the doctor has seen him. After that, we'll see how he feels."

"Yes, of course." Roderick would wake, and they'd be able to talk and . . . she would feel so much better. She glanced around; the chair she'd been using had been moved back to the wall. She'd taken one step toward it when a tap fell on the door; it opened to reveal a young lady, blond and blue-eyed, sweet-faced and smiling.

"Good morning, Miss Sarah." Nurse looked at Miranda. "This is Miss Sarah—she's the duchess's cousin."

Sarah turned her smile on Miranda. "Hello." She bobbed a curtsy. "I'm Sarah Morwell—as Nurse says, I'm Caroline's cousin. I'm sorry I missed your arrival yesterday—I was visiting with friends in Derby."

Miranda smiled and inclined her head.

Closing the door, Sarah walked to the foot of the bed. "Caroline mentioned your brother had been injured, and as I've already broken my fast, I offered to watch over him while you and Nurse go down to breakfast."

"Oh." Miranda glanced at the bed. "I'd thought to have a tray up here."

"The dowager thought you might suggest that." Sarah met her gaze. "She said to say she considers it far preferable for you to join her and the others in the breakfast parlor."

Miranda heard the command. She looked back at the bed, at Roderick's still figure.

"He's nowhere near stirring, let alone waking," Nurse said. "And although you might not think it to look at her, Miss Sarah has younger brothers and is sensible enough when she wants to be. She'll watch over him and"—Nurse fixed a commanding look on the younger woman—"she'll ring for us the instant he stirs."

Sarah grinned. "Indeed, Nurse, and thank you for the recommendation."

Nurse humphed and waved Miranda to the door. "Come along, now. It won't do to keep the dowager waiting."

With no viable way to avoid the summons, Miranda acquiesced and allowed Nurse to conduct her to a sunny breakfast parlor on the south side of the huge house. But while the dowager certainly looked pleased to see Miranda when she walked into the room, and waved her to a chair opposite, next to the duchess, and while it was clear from the dowager's first comments that she had, indeed, sent Sarah to relieve Miranda, Miranda quickly realized that it was Roscoe who had put the notion of making sure she ate a proper breakfast into the dowager's head.

He, however, wasn't present.

Correctly interpreting the glance Miranda sent around the table, the duchess volunteered, "Julian and Henry broke their fast early and have gone out riding." She met Miranda's gaze. "Julian is Henry's co-guardian, so we're always pleased when they're both here and Henry gets a chance to spend time with him."

Roscoe's three sisters walked in at that moment and, amid a chorus of good mornings, took seats at the table. The butler and footmen swiftly replenished racks of toast and pots of tea, then the ladies settled to eat and chat.

Miranda had expected a renewed round of questions about Roscoe-Julian, but instead the ladies' queries centered on her and Roderick, on their family and household. She answered such questions as her aunts had trained her, skirting the fact that the family's fortune came directly from trade; she'd been taught from age six never to mention her grandfather Clifford and his mills. Nevertheless, as the minutes rolled past in pleasant conversation, the reality that she—her grandfather's granddaughter—was sitting at the breakfast table in a ducal household being treated very much as an honored guest grew increasingly difficult to reconcile, to fit into her view of the polite world.

Yet the ladies' interest in her and Roderick was patently genuine, and when Miranda attempted once more to thank them for their support, both the duchess and the dowager again assured her that the pleasure was entirely theirs.

Bemused, Miranda shook her head. "I have to confess I'm at sea. Roderick and I have appeared out of nowhere, and regardless of anything our presence is a very real imposition on your household."

The dowager regarded her for a moment, then smiled her

gracious smile. "Yes, there's an imposition of sorts, but it's really very minor compared to what we gain. I realize you find it difficult to comprehend the depth of our gratitude toward you and your brother for being the agents, as it were, that brought Julian home at this point in time, when we're all here to enjoy his company, something we too rarely experience, but, as I mentioned yesterday, through the chance to help you you've also given us an opportunity to, in some small way, balance the scales with my usually stubborn and intractable son."

Her old eyes brimming with patent sincerity, the dowager went on, "And to cap it all, there's really no question that in this season, with so little to divert us, yours and your brother's company is and will be a godsend."

"Hear, hear," came from Millicent, Cassie, and Edwina.

"So, my dear Miranda," the dowager concluded, "you will, I fear, simply have to accept that what you see as an imposition is to us a boon."

After that it was impossible to press her thanks any further, but the feeling that the social ground wasn't quite as she'd expected it to be—and that she didn't really understand how she and Roderick actually fitted in—persisted. In the end, Miranda concluded that she would simply have to deal with any social awkwardness if and when it arose. Clearly any assumption based on her uncertain reading of things would be equally uncertain.

Edwina volunteered to guide her back to Roderick's room. Roscoe's youngest sister was outwardly the sweetest of the three, but in common with her sisters, and her brother, she was quick-witted and assertive; smiling at Edwina's chatter about her wedding, and her current thoughts of an appropriate wedding trip, Miranda recalled Roscoe's somewhat acerbic assessment and had to wonder if Mr. Frobisher, the adventurer, adequately understood the caliber of his future wife.

Reaching Roderick's room, Miranda opened the door and led the way in.

Across the room, Roderick's light hazel eyes, dazed and drowsy, met hers. He'd just taken a sip of water from a glass Sarah was holding. He blinked. "Sis?"

"Thank God!" She swept to the bed and bent to gently— very gently—hug him. "I was down having breakfast. Have you been awake long?"

"No." He patted her arm awkwardly. "Only just opened my eyes."

"I was going to ring," Sarah said, "but he asked for water."

Straightening, Miranda smiled at Sarah. "Yes, of course." She beamed down at Roderick. "I'm just so glad to see you awake."

He grimaced, tried to move his left arm, the one tightly strapped in a sling, and winced. "That may be so, but I'm not at all certain that I want to be awake." He looked down the bed and his face set. "I remember now. They broke my foot, too."

"The doctor said both collarbone and foot will heal as good as new." Drawing the straight-backed chair to the bed's side, Miranda sat. "He'll be here later today to examine you and confirm."

Roderick looked around. "Speaking of which . . . where am I?"

Edwina had drifted to the window. "Julian and Henry are riding into the stables." Turning, she beamed at Roderick. "I know Julian will want to know you've woken up." She looked at Miranda. "I'll go and tell him, shall I?"

Still smiling, Miranda nodded. "Yes, please do."

Roderick's brow furrowed. "Who's Julian?" As Edwina whisked out of the door, Roderick looked at Miranda. "I don't know any Julian." Studying her face, he added, "Do I?"

She took his hand. "It's a trifle complicated."

She'd only just managed to impress on Roderick that Julian—the man who went by that name in that house—was the man they knew in London as Roscoe when the gentleman himself arrived.

Striding into the room, Roscoe's gaze fastened first on her, then shifted to Roderick. Taking in Roderick's sleepy but steady regard, he smiled. "I'm glad to see you awake and compos mentis."

Roderick arched a brow. "I'm awake, but I'm not sure about the rest."

Coming to stand beside her, resting one hand on the back of her chair, Roscoe met Roderick's eyes. "I don't know how much your sister has told you, but what happened is this." Swiftly and concisely he described what had happened, what they'd learned about when, how, and who had kidnapped Roderick, and where he'd been taken. He related the story as consecutive incidents, setting Roderick nodding as his memory came back.

On the other side of the bed, Sarah sat quietly in the armchair, her gaze on Roderick. Twice, she rose and offered him some water; on both occasions, he turned his head and gratefully sipped.

Miranda accepted that Nurse's assessment of Sarah was correct; Sarah wasn't the blond, blue-eyed, sweet young featherbrain her appearance led one to expect.

Reaching the present, with them having sought refuge at Ridgware, a house in which they were assured of being safe, Roscoe finally asked, "Do you have any idea, did you gain any hint at all, as to who hired Kempsey and Dole?"

Roderick nodded. "They mentioned his name a few times when they thought I was unconscious. Kirkwell. That's all I heard that I can be sure of. It might have been John—John Kirkwell." He paused, his gaze drifting to fix, unseeing, on the covers, then he added, speaking as if he was dredging information from a dim and foggy memory, "They—Kempsey and Dole—said they'd sent word to Kirkwell that they had me and were keeping me alive against the rest of the payment . . ."

After several moments of staring at nothing, Roderick swallowed and looked at Roscoe. "The payment from Kirkwell . . . he'd paid them to kill me."

Expression impassive, Roscoe nodded. "We surmised as

much." After a second's pause, he glanced at Miranda, then looked back at Roderick. "Do you know who Kirkwell is?"

Frowning, Roderick shook his head. He looked at Miranda. "You?"

"No." She glanced up and met Roscoe's dark blue eyes. "I've never heard the name before."

Frowning more deeply, Roderick slumped against the pillows.

Roscoe exchanged a glance with her, then spoke to Roderick. "Don't try too hard. It's possible you have no previous connection with Kirkwell." He straightened. "Just rest and I'll see what I can learn. The name gives us a place to start."

Roderick's lips twitched in a wan smile. "Thank you."

Roscoe saluted. He glanced at Miranda, nodded. "I'll look in later."

She watched him go. Turning back, she saw that Roderick's lids had fallen.

Sarah rose, looked at Roderick, then arched a brow at Miranda.

She shook her head—they didn't need to summon Nurse. Sarah subsided into the armchair.

Taking Roderick's hand once more in hers, Miranda settled to watch over him, pleased enough to have Sarah's company.

They sat with Roderick undisturbed through the morning. He'd fallen into a deeper, more natural sleep; listening to his breathing, seeing normal color gradually return to his cheeks, she felt relief transform into more solid confidence.

Her brother was safe again, and would in time be whole again. She spent several minutes sending a prayer of gratitude winging heavenward, and otherwise simply watched him sleep.

Heralded by the fading echoes of the luncheon gong, Nurse arrived, refreshed and ready to take over the watch, and charged by the duchess and the dowager to ensure both Miranda and Sarah went down to the dining parlor.

Neither tried to argue. Nurse assured Miranda, "I'll ring if he wakes and wants you, but otherwise I'll let him sleep, at least until Doctor arrives."

Luncheon was served in the room in which they'd dined the previous night. The ladies congregated about the foot of the table; neither Roscoe nor Henry was present.

"They've gone out to ride around the estate, visiting the tenant farmers." Caroline smiled, fondly wry, and exchanged a glance with the dowager—Lucasta as she'd insisted Miranda call her. "Years ago, I would never have imagined I would be grateful to have Julian teaching Henry about estate management." Caroline met Miranda's eyes. "Which might seem odd, but years ago none of us would have imagined Julian possessed any ability whatever in managing anything."

Miranda blinked. "From what I've seen over the last weeks, I find that . . . not just difficult but impossible to believe." When the others looked at her questioningly, she explained, "He's very business oriented, and he deals with so many people and so many different projects of such varying kinds."

They'd stopped eating; all clearly would have liked to hear more, but that was the limit of what she felt comfortable revealing. She raised a shoulder. "Not that I know all that much of his business affairs, but I have seen that much."

A moment of silent eating ensued, then Lucasta inquired, "Where in the country do you and your brother hail from?"

"Our family home is Oakgrove Manor, near the village of that name. It's in Cheshire, in the Peak District."

"Oakgrove." Lucasta frowned. "I believe I recall . . . it's not that far away, somewhere north of here."

"It's a little south of Macclesfield."

"Ah, yes." Lucasta's expression cleared. "Very pretty country."

More questions followed, circling the subject of her and Roderick's home—the size of the estate, how many rooms, the stables and gardens. The questions weren't impertinent or nosy; they were the sort of questions ladies habitually used to gain a better grasp of a person's social standing. While Miranda could and did answer truthfully, she increasingly felt that by not disclosing the true reality of their situation she was knowingly leading the others astray.

They'd been so openly supportive, so helpful, to thank them with lies, albeit lies of omission . . . no matter how clearly she heard her aunts' voices in her head, warning of the dire consequences of revealing the source of her and Roderick's wealth, she simply couldn't allow the almost-deceit to continue.

Roscoe, she felt sure, knew of her and Roderick's background, but he, quite clearly, had stepped over the line of respectability and resided permanently on the other side.

His family, however, were bluebloods through and through. Regardless of anything, they were the aristocracy, the nobility, and neither she nor Roderick were of their social class.

Laying aside her napkin, she glanced around the table. The others had been distracted by talk of wedding bonnets, but Lucasta noticed her—perhaps sensed her resolve—and quieted her daughters with a wave, then arched a brow at her. "Yes, dear?"

Miranda drew breath. "There's something I should make plain about Roderick and myself. While our mother was the daughter of Sir Augustus Cuthbert, our father was the son of a mill owner. That's where the family's fortune derives from, so . . ." She broke off. Looking down at her plate, she aligned her knife with her fork and more quietly said, "I will understand if you are more agreeable in the future to Roderick and me taking meals in his room."

Silence reigned for half a minute; she was reluctant to look up, to see the change in the others' faces, in their expressions as they realized—

"Well, you might understand, but I, for one, would not."

She jerked her gaze up to meet Lucasta's; it was she who had spoken.

Lucasta arched her brows and went on, "I can't explain, for it's not entirely my story to tell, but believe me when I say, my dear, that you will not find a single person in this family, nor, indeed, in any way connected with it, who would turn their noses up at someone simply because their money hailed from trade, and twice removed at that." As if she found the suggestion absurd, Lucasta snorted and shook her head. "Truth to tell, I cannot imagine any of our peers acting so nonsensically." She met Miranda's eyes, her own gaze sharp. "We are not, still, the rulers of this land, the primary landowners, because we don't have a strong appreciation of the benefits of wealth."

Millicent said, "It's not as if *you're* engaged in trade, is it?"

Edwina shrugged. "I think it far more likely that the ton will turn difficult about the Frobishers. The family may be as old as the hills, but much of their current wealth comes from explorations and ventures associated with that—which is, indeed, trade, albeit it is rather more romantic than a mill."

"Precisely." Caroline nodded across the table at Edwina. "I'm quite sure there will be disparaging mutters on that score, but the solution is to carry it off with a high hand." Caroline looked at Miranda. "As Lucasta intimated, this family in particular got over any negative perceptions of honestly gained wealth some time ago." Her expression softened as she held Miranda's gaze. "I believe I speak for us all when I say that while I appreciate the sensibility behind your revelation, your expectation that that fact will in any way change our view of you and your brother falls quite far from the mark."

Miranda felt . . . disorientated.

"Actually," Lucasta put in, "considering more widely, I cannot think of many major ton families that haven't, at some point, in some fashion, resorted to marrying money from trade, most often at one remove—as, it appears, your mother did." She looked at Miranda, dipped her head. "I acknowledge that we would prefer that the money we married was attached to a long lineage, but in the end, going back through the centuries, when the need was there, lineage was never a deciding factor. The money was. And after all, most of us descend from those who followed William, The Bastard, to these shores."

"And he wasn't called The Bastard for nothing," Cassie chimed in.

"And although that was in the past," Millicent said, "these days more than ever, what with society's increasing acceptance of love matches, and as we all know love pays no attention whatever to social class, then you and Roderick are not all that different from us—we were all born to wealth. While our lineage may be older and on both sides, yours through your mother is old enough, high enough, for you to be entirely welcome within our circles."

"Indeed." Lucasta nodded. "The ton is still the ton, but the gradations within it are blurring with time and changing circumstances." She met Miranda's gaze squarely. "For instance, it takes a great deal of money to run an estate like Ridgware."

From the way they all looked at her—as if willing her to understand—she realized there was some particular message in Lucasta's last statement, hidden within yet conveyed by the otherwise straightforward words.

Lucasta rang and requested tea. It arrived with commendable alacrity. After passing the pot, while the others settled to sipping and discussing wedding details, Miranda sat, sipped, and absorbed all she'd learned.

Despite her aunts' trenchant teachings, she accepted that the others were sincere in not thinking less of her and Roderick because their fortune had originally derived from trade; they were too honest, too open and direct, to doubt. So . . . her aunts had been wrong. Were wrong. Or perhaps in earlier days they had been right, but society had changed and they hadn't known.

Regardless. . . . she drew in a deep breath, then slowly let it out. She felt as if a millstone she'd worn around her neck all her life had slipped free. At least in this company. Whether the laissez-faire attitude of the upper echelons of the ton applied at the lower levels of the gentry, the levels her aunts and gentlemen like Wraxby inhabited, she didn't know, but she would certainly look again, this time with her eyes open.

For all her life, she'd accepted her aunts' view of the precarious nature of her and Roderick's social standing as immutable and unchallengeable fact. But they'd been wrong.

And that changed things, certainly for her, but exactly how and in what way, exactly what new avenues might be available to her that she'd never before this moment contemplated . . . she'd have to feel her way, wait and see, and reassess.

But meanwhile, what had Lucasta meant? That a great estate like Ridgware would require a small fortune to maintain was self-evident. But they'd been discussing the source of funds, hadn't they?

Her mind circled, tempted to connect those questions for which she'd yet to learn the answer. She'd yet to learn why Lord Julian Delbraith had become Neville Roscoe.

One thing she felt sure hadn't changed was society's view of funds raised through a gambling empire such as Roscoe's. All very well for some gentleman to win a fortune at cards, but for a gentleman to own the establishments that were viewed as bleeding other gentlemen of their fortunes . . . no, not acceptable. Money from trade once removed the ton might have come to accept, but money collected professionally, albeit legally, from society's gamblers would, she felt certain, remain forever beyond the pale.

"Miranda?" Caroline leaned forward to catch her eye. "I understand your brother has an interest in charitable projects. I help manage such a project, a local school, and while Julian is here I intend taking him to visit—I wondered if you share your brother's interest and would like to accompany us?"

If they were correct . . . there was no longer anything

preventing her from active involvement in such endeavors; previously she'd imagined her "background" would render her ineligible to be the patroness of anything. Now . . . she nodded. "Thank you. I'd like that." She hesitated, then added, "I've yet to become involved in any charitable works, but it's an area I would like to explore."

As promised, Doctor Entwhistle arrived to reexamine Roderick late that afternoon. Roscoe rode into the stable yard with Henry beside him just as the doctor climbed back into his gig. They exchanged greetings, but Roscoe didn't detain Entwhistle, knowing the doctor would have other patients to see. From Entwhistle's jovial expression, the news about Roderick wasn't bad.

After handing the big gelding he habitually rode at Ridgware over to the grooms, Roscoe strode across the lawns and into the house, Henry beside him, still talking about crops.

Parting from Henry in the front hall, Roscoe paused to speak with Cater, then went quickly up the main stairs and along the corridor to the room Roderick was in.

He tapped on the door, paused for less than a second, then opened it and went in.

Miranda sat in her usual chair, but she'd pushed it back from the bed. Sitting upright, she was smiling at something Roderick, still in the bed but now sitting propped up with pillows, had said.

Glancing his way, Miranda's smile deepened. "The doctor just left. He's confident Roderick will recover fully."

Roscoe nodded. Closing the door, he crossed to stand at the foot of the bed. Roderick's color was almost normal, although the lines about his mouth said he was still experiencing some pain. Roscoe nodded to Roderick. "So what's the detailed prognosis?"

Between them, brother and sister told him.

"So as long as I take care and stay mostly on my back over the next week, Entwhistle thinks I'll be able to hobble around on crutches thereafter, and once I can do that, he

says I should be able to weather the journey to London."
Roderick looked disgusted, but resigned. "I can't say I'm
looking forward to the next week."

"Nevertheless"—Miranda patted Roderick's hand—
"you'll do as the doctor ordered because that's the fastest
way back to, as he phrased it, your customary rude health."

Roderick snorted but didn't argue. To Roscoe's eyes, he
was tiring; no doubt the ordeal of having his injuries exam-
ined had drained him.

Behind him, the door opened. Roscoe glanced around and
saw Sarah come in. She looked first at Roderick and smiled,
then transferred her gaze to him. "You sent for me?"

He nodded. "I wondered if you would sit with Mr. Clifford. I want to discuss a few matters with Miss Clifford, and
as she almost certainly could do with taking the air"—he
looked at Miranda—"I thought we might kill two birds with
one stone."

Miranda met his dark blue eyes. Assuming his invitation
was designed to allow him to speak to her without Roderick
present, she inclined her head. "Thank you. I daresay a walk
will do me good."

A walk with him definitely would; she hadn't seen him
all day. To her surprise, she'd felt the lack, presumably due
to having spent the last several days almost constantly in his
company.

Roderick smiled and extended his free hand to Roscoe. "I
can't thank you enough for getting me out of Kempsey and
Dole's clutches. When I think of what would have happened
if you hadn't . . ."

Roscoe clasped Roderick's hand. "You should thank
your sister." He shot her a look as she rose. "It was she who
alerted me to your disappearance, and without her help, getting you out of Kempsey and Dole's tender care would have
been impossible. I couldn't have done it on my own."

For once, she had no difficulty reading his expression; it
warmed her.

Roderick's smile deepened as he transferred it to her.

"Miranda's always been a rock—she's pulled me out of more scrapes than I can count."

She humphed and patted his uninjured foot. "Rest—you're flagging again."

"Yes, ma'am." Roderick turned his head to smile at Sarah, who'd settled quietly in the armchair, but by the time Miranda reached the door, his lids had fallen once more.

Joining Roscoe in the corridor, she waited while he shut the door, then they walked down the corridor to the gallery. The stairs were at the nearer end, but he waved her on. "We can go this way."

The walls further along the gallery were lined with paintings of . . . she supposed they were his ancestors. When she slowed, openly studying the portraits, he murmured, "Delbraiths have been at Ridgware for centuries."

"So I see." They'd passed numerous early earls, identified by small plaques beneath each painting, then in the seventeenth century, the title changed to duke. As they neared the end of the line of ducal portraits, she slowed even more. Above and below the portraits of each duke were those of family members. She came to the portrait of Marcus, seventh Duke of Ridgware. The smaller portrait immediately below it was of Lucasta. The next and last ducal portrait was of George, the eighth duke.

She stopped. Roscoe halted beside her. After a moment he said, "Henry's father. He died unexpectedly."

Henry's father, Julian's older brother; she wondered at the lack of emotion, positive or negative, in his voice. "No portrait of Henry?"

"They're traditionally done at age twenty-five." He hesitated, then said, "Henry was three years old when he inherited. He's fifteen now, so he has some years yet before he has to weather the torture."

"Did you find it a torture to stand still for so long?" The portrait next to Lucasta's was that of an elegant gentleman. Dark sapphire-blue eyes looked out of the painting; even at twenty-five, he'd possessed the physical allure that, years later, still cloaked him. But the man portrayed was more lighthearted, his smile holding insouciance, irreverence, with a devil-may-care glint in his eyes.

"Standing still was never my forte."

She could see that; barely reined energy radiated from the painted figure. That reckless energy had intensified with the years and coalesced into something more powerful. In more ways than one the man standing beside her was fundamentally more than his younger self. There were subtle but definite physical changes in his face, in the way he wore his hair, in the heavier musculature of chest, shoulders, and thighs. As for the almost effeminate, languid grace investing the figure in the portrait, the grace remained but the languor was long gone.

Faced with the man he was now, she wasn't sure anyone would instantly link him to the man he'd been.

The plaque beneath the painting caught her eye and answered one of the myriad questions circling in her mind. *Lord Julian Roscoe Neville Delbraith.* That was where his alias, Neville Roscoe, came from, and why he preferred to be addressed as Roscoe, that being his second given name, rather than Neville, which she recalled from an earlier portrait was a former duchess's family's name.

Studying the portrait, the face that had grown more austerely masculine with the years, she longed to ask why. Why he'd left this younger man and his life of hedonistic pleasure—something the artist had captured in the luxurious and sensual setting—behind. Why he'd turned his back on that—the epitome of a wealthy young man's aspiration—to become London's gambling king.

She wanted to know, but she couldn't ask. Couldn't pry. If he wished to tell her, he would, but if he deemed it something she didn't need to know, she would have to be content with never knowing.

Roscoe waited beside her with what patience he could

muster. *Stop looking at him, he's dead. Look at me instead—I'm here and he isn't. Not anymore.* The words burned the tip of his tongue, but he swallowed them.

Eventually, she glanced at him. "I don't know what to call you—how to address you. Lord Julian or Roscoe?"

The answer required a little thought. "Dispense with the 'lord,' but here, from you, either will do."

For an instant she held his gaze, then glanced back at the portrait. After a moment, she turned back to him. Brusquely, not bothering to disguise his impatience—his dislike of her studying his former self—he waved her along the gallery. Without another word, she strolled on.

They walked side by side down the stairs at the gallery's end, then he led her through the corridors to the garden hall and out onto the south lawn. She was tall enough, had legs long enough, that he didn't have to adjust his stride much but could amble easily. As they strolled, the peace of the place reached for him, sank into him and eased him.

It always had. Even after so many years, he was unable to comprehend how George had come to risk it all. To lose it all.

The gardens were large; although he had a destination in mind, he saw no reason to rush. Even though he wasn't touching her, having her close somehow soothed him; with no one else around to distract either of them, her nearness felt comfortable, a new, different, yet desirable evolution.

He ambled on without speaking, and she did the same.

And unexpected contentment prevailed.

Miranda was fascinated by the fresh views of the house, and even more by the gardens. The manicured lawns, the gravel paths freshly raked, the beds and borders closer to the house, the shrubberies further back beyond the large trees, with narrow paths disappearing into them. Everywhere she looked, lush order held sway. *"It takes a great deal of money to run an estate like Ridgware."* It wasn't hard to see that it would require a small fortune to keep house and gardens in such pristine state, let alone the rest of the estate. All she'd

seen of it during their drive to the house had been groomed
to the same high standard.

Ridgware was beautiful, and cherished.

Quite aside from the money, it was the care lavished on
the place that made it not just a house but a home, not just
an estate but a living community. A glimpse of a gardener
raking leaves, of a maid tripping down to the woods with a
trug, underscored that what she was viewing wasn't just a
mansion but something more.

And, she suspected, expensive though it might be, it
would be, and was, very much worth it. Certainly to Roscoe
and his family. Family, permanence, continuity; to the older
families, those meant a great deal.

Was this—the money it took to run Ridgware—behind
the transformation of the man walking beside her?

"This way." With a wave, he steered her beneath an arch
and down two stone steps—into a walled rose garden.

"Oh, my!" Even though the season was all but spent, late
blooms still bobbed on the dozens of huge bushes, many
taller than she was and equally wide. "This is glorious."

"*This* is relatively muted. You should see it in high summer
when everything's in bloom." Roscoe followed her down the
central path. "Then you can barely breathe."

Cupping one large pink bloom, she buried her nose in the
scent. "Mmm. So lovely."

He watched her and had to agree.

Finally releasing the bloom, she looked at him. "What
was it you wanted to speak with me about?"

It took a moment to recall his excuse. He waved her
on, down the rose walk, and fell into step alongside her.
"Through Henry I've lodged a complaint against Kempsey
and Dole with the local magistrate—that needed to be done,
a formality that might prove necessary later. I've also set men
on Kempsey and Dole's trail. They may have gone to ground
in Birmingham with their families." Equally, the pair might
be tracking them, hounds on Roderick's scent, but he didn't
see any need to belabor that possibility at this point.

She frowned. "But surely now they've lost Roderick, Kempsey and Dole will draw back. It's this man Kirkwell who was behind the attack—he's the one who, mystifyingly, wants Roderick dead."

"I've sent word to London. My men will see what they can learn about Kirkwell, but there's always the chance that's not his real name." He glanced at her. "I take it you still haven't recalled anyone of that name—an acquaintance of Roderick's, a long-ago suitor of yours?"

"No. I've been wracking my brains, but I can't recall that name at all. Not in any context."

"Which increases the likelihood Kirkwell's not his real name. People are rarely killed by strangers, especially not through an elaborate plot."

"So how can we unmask this villain?"

"The name might be false, but the man is real enough. I've set my men trawling the areas in which Kirkwell was seen— the tavern in which he met Kempsey and Dole and the surrounding streets. Someone must have seen him. Someone should be able to point him out." He glanced at her. "We'll find him." *Preferably before you and Roderick return to London.*

"Thank you." Miranda glanced up and met his eyes. "For everything. Your help rescuing Roderick, your assistance in finding Kirkwell. Neither Roderick nor I could have managed without you."

His eyes held hers, then he inclined his head and faced forward. "It's been some time since I was actively involved in such endeavors." Fleetingly he met her eyes again. "I enjoyed it."

She wasn't sure *enjoyed* was the right word, not for her, but she'd certainly felt very much alive. Quite aside from the excitement of the chase, and the even greater thrill of escape, just being in his company . . . she forced her mind to the question she had to ask. "Will you be remaining at Ridgware for much longer? I imagine your business dealings will draw you back to town." She—and Roderick—

couldn't expect him to remain with them, a guardian of sorts, a friend, a support.

"I have no immediate plans to return to the capital." He paced beside her; she glanced at his face, but, as ever, his expression told her nothing. "I haven't visited for a while, and it's not often all three of my sisters are here at the same time, and Henry, too. A short absence from town won't impinge on my businesses. The people I employ are well able to manage without me for a time."

"I see." The leap of her heart was nonsensical. The effervescent happiness tinged with relief that coursed through her simply from knowing he would remain near might have been uncalled for; it was nevertheless real. "I was hoping to send word to my aunt. Now I have certain and favorable news of Roderick, I should let her know he's well, or at least will be."

"Write a note and I'll have it sent down." Roscoe glanced at her mourning gown, let his gaze slide from the prim neckline to the heavy skirts. "As you and Roderick will be here for a few weeks, you might ask her to pack some clothes— I'll have my men fetch the trunks and send them here."

She dipped her head. "Thank you."

There wasn't anything more he needed to tell her, but he didn't want the interlude to end. A simple pleasure, walking in the old rose garden with her. "Quite aside from spending time with Henry and the others, I'll be using this unexpected visit to catch up with Ridgware, too." He glanced at her, caught her gaze as she glanced at him. "It's not just a large estate—it's made up of many interconnecting elements, many smaller enterprises." Lifting the guard he habitually placed on his tongue, he let himself ramble—set himself to entertain and distract her from the principal reason he was remaining by her side.

The threat to Roderick was far from over. Kempsey and Dole remained a real and local menace, while the mysterious John Kirkwell hovered in the background. Any man who had gone to the extent of hiring Kempsey and Dole wasn't going to simply give up and walk away.

Until all three, Kempsey, Dole, and Kirkwell, had been located and removed, he didn't intend moving far from Miranda or her brother. And remaining near her, in close proximity, was no hardship. None at all—the one thing anchoring him most strongly at Ridgware was, quite simply, her.

Night fell, and with Roderick recovered enough to order all his would-be nurses from his chamber, Miranda found herself restlessly drifting before the uncurtained window in her room. The household had retired; all the others were no doubt seeking their beds, yet she felt too unsettled to sit, let alone sleep.

Together with Roscoe she'd explored more of the gardens, returning to the house as the dressing gong had sounded. Other than her black day gown, she had only one other with her, also black and severe, but at least it was more suitable for evening wear; retreating to her room, she'd changed, then brushed and re-coiled her hair, for some reason eschewing her habitual chignon and instead fashioning the heavy tresses into a plaited bun on the top of her head.

Pleased with the result, feeling acceptably fashionable, she'd gone down to the drawing room and fallen in with the family as if she'd been a longtime acquaintance rather than someone they'd first set eyes on only the evening before. Dinner had passed pleasantly; afterward, once the ritual of the tea trolley had been observed, she and Sarah had come upstairs to relieve Nurse. They'd sat on either side of Roderick's bed and entertained him, but then he'd ordered them out, and she'd carried her candlestick into her room and shut the door.

Halting before the window, she looked out, and in the faint but steady moonlight saw the walls of the rose garden across the lawn.

Ten minutes later, her cloak over her shoulders, she stepped down to the rose garden's paved central walk. The day had been fine; the enclosing walls trapped the lingering warmth along with the heady fragrance of the blooms still nodding on the long, arching canes.

For the past week, she'd been living on her nerves in a state of heightened anticipation and uncertainty. Now she was safe and secure, and Roderick was, too, and Ridgware had enveloped them in its serenity. Hardly surprising she was taking a little time to adjust.

"But," she murmured, starting slowly along the path, "that's not the only thing that's changed."

She had changed. In setting out to rescue Roderick, in appealing to Roscoe for aid, she'd stepped out of her prescribed and rigidly respectable world. She'd done it knowingly, and if the situation were the same, she would do the same again. She didn't regret her decision—quite the opposite—but in acting as she had, something fundamental had shifted inside her, a change she hadn't expected or foreseen.

And then she'd compounded that change and taken Roscoe as her lover.

She didn't regret that either, but that, too, contributed to her present uncertainty, her unsettled state. She was a novice in such matters; she had no real concept of what might come next.

She was the sort of woman who liked to know where she stood. Uncertainty didn't suit her; it ruffled her senses and stretched her nerves. . . .

Three more slow steps, and she realized it wasn't inner uncertainty that was ruffling her senses and affecting her nerves.

Halting, she turned and looked back up the walk.

Roscoe stood in the archway, one shoulder negligently propped against the stone. Hands in his pockets, he was watching her. Even over the distance, his dark gaze touched her, caressed her.

Awakened her.

Lifting her head, she met that gaze and waited.

The moonlight lit his face; she saw his lips curve, wry,

almost resigned, then he pushed away from the stone, stepped down to the walk, and prowled toward her.

"You shouldn't be out here alone." Halting before her, Roscoe looked down into her wide eyes, watched them smile up at him.

"But, clearly, I'm not alone." She studied his face, then tipped her head in invitation as she turned and resumed her stroll. As he accepted and matched his stride to hers, she said, "I couldn't settle to sleep."

He hadn't been able to either. Certainly not once he'd seen her crossing the lawn. "It's a lovely night."

That comment set the tone for the resulting conversation. Neither he nor she had any agenda other than passing the time, and, perhaps, hearing the other's voice. Certainly their mundane, innocuous exchanges held neither secrets nor ulterior intent. It seemed all either cared about was being in each other's company.

That amused him; he'd never been one for making polite conversation, and, he suspected, she wasn't an exponent of that idle art either, yet here they were, doing just that, in his case contentedly.

He wanted to be with her. Wanted to learn more of her. She enthralled and enticed him, and engaged him at a level different from anyone he'd previously encountered, a connection broader in scope, richer, more intense. He told himself it was only human nature that he sought to understand her . . . and inwardly scoffed. His interest ran much deeper than mere curiosity.

He wanted to explore, to savor, to possess, yet confoundingly it wasn't only the physical effect she had on him that focused him so effortlessly on her.

He'd grown to be a connoisseur of human nature, and in that respect she was unique, at least to him. She wasn't the sort of person who followed, as most women were, yet she wasn't a leader, either. She took her own road, and intriguingly that seemed to be a facet of herself she was only just discovering.

He was a quick study when it came to people, a talent he'd always had, a talent that as Roscoe, London's gambling king, he exercised daily. While at first she'd been a conundrum, he was starting, at last, to unravel her complexities. For much of her life she'd set aside her own nature, suppressing it, making it subservient to her need to protect Roderick. That, he understood, none better. Ironic, then, that it was her very devotion to protecting Roderick that had led her to where she now was.

To the realization that, as Roderick had matured and stepped beyond her protection, she needed to reassess and redefine what, going forward, would drive her, what would be her lodestone, the principle that would guide her.

She hadn't found it yet, and he had no clue as to how she would evolve, but watching her slough off her past and seek her path forward was fascinating, engrossing, and strangely moving.

As he couldn't predict her direction, all he could be sure about was her in that moment. Her and him in the moonlit night.

They walked, talked, and with a simplicity that itself held a staggering power, drew pleasure from the unstructured communion.

Eventually, she sighed. "I think I'm ready to go in."

With a wave, he led her back to the house and around to the front hall.

Side by side, they started up the stairs.

He was intensely aware that since he'd left her bed that morning they hadn't touched. Not a brush of the hand, not a touch on his sleeve, not him grasping her elbow. They'd avoided any contact, any accidental, incidental touch; for both, he suspected, that had been a defensive necessity while they'd dealt with the demands of the day.

But now night had closed around them, and with every step up the long staircase their mutual tension ratcheted higher.

An unfamiliar vice had locked about his chest; with no other woman had he felt so out of his depth.

Their liaison was destined to be a short affair; that had been implicit from the start, underscored by her "just one night." Having to travel alone with him had handed her an opportunity, one she'd elected to grasp, one he'd been willing to grant.

But after that first night, he'd been left feeling like a ship without a rudder. He'd had no idea whether she would wish to extend their one night of passion into a liaison, given fate had landed them in a situation where the possibility existed. So last night he'd held back—had forced himself to read a novel in his room rather than seek her out—in the hope that she would make up her mind and declare her decision. Her position. So that then he would know.

Instead, Fate, abetted by Nurse, had conspired to place him in her room, with her, sleep-tousled, on her bed . . . and she'd drawn him to her again, but had that been deliberate decision on her part, or her simply responding to the moment? He didn't know, couldn't tell.

Which, as side by side they reached the top of the stairs and stepped into the gallery, left him still uncertain. Unsure what she wanted. Unclear as to what was possible, what she would allow.

He did know that he wanted her. Wanted to spend this night, and as many others as she would countenance, with her in his arms.

He halted. When she halted, too, and faced him, brows lightly arching, he said, "My room's in the other wing."

Her eyes, luminescent in the moonlight pouring through the ornate skylight above, widened. "Oh." Those eyes searched his, trying to see, to read . . .

He drew a breath so fraught it almost shook, felt the tension binding him cinch tight. "Invite me to your bed."

She didn't blink but studied his face, his expression. The moment stretched, fragile as spun glass, then she stepped closer, raised one hand and framed his cheek, stretched up and brushed her lips over his in an achingly delicate kiss.

He felt the fingers of her other hand twine with his and grip, then she drew back.

She held his gaze for a heartbeat, then turned and led him to her room.

He stepped inside, held onto her hand as he closed the door, then leaned back against it. He drew her to him and she came. Spreading her hands over his chest, she stretched up as he bent his head.

Lips touched, firmed. Within seconds their mouths had melded.

Tongues tangled as fingers slid apart and they reached for each other. Gathered each other close. Closer. Pressed nearer.

And as had happened on both previous occasions when he'd stepped into this place, this sensual space with her, plans and intentions melted away and each kiss, each touch, each stroke and caress became their eclipsing reality.

Nothing else mattered beyond the next revelation.

The next moment of passionate exploration, of desirous and desirable knowing.

Familiar, yet different. That conclusion sank into him with every heated breath, with every tracing stroke of her fingers on his skin.

They shed their clothes, his, hers, without rush, without haste. With steady determination.

With a shared purpose that, uncounted heartbeats later, brought them together in a rush of fire and need in the depths of her bed.

That had them clinging to sanity as passion raged and desire raced molten through their veins.

Beneath him, Miranda gasped and held tight, lids falling as sensation swept over and through her. Carrying her up, buoying her higher, ever higher.

Amazed again. Stunned again.

She'd thought she'd known, but he'd surprised her again.

She'd surprised herself again.

The sharing, the lack of screens or veils, the undiluted intimacy stole her breath.

The feelings that cascaded through her, searing in intensity, had only grown stronger. More potent, more powerful. More overwhelming.

She didn't understand it, but she knew it was real. Knew in the moment that, panting and desperate, her body engulfed by him, filled by him, her mind and senses awash with him, she reached up and caught his face between her palms, raised her head and pressed her lips to his, that this was beyond price.

He accepted her offering, plunged into her mouth, plunged with her into the fire and glory, then he thrust deep and she shattered, came apart on a cry he drank from her lips. His hips pumped as he sent her flying up, further, and on.

Then he groaned, stiffened in her arms, and she felt the heat of him deep inside.

Ecstasy spilled through her in a scintillating tide.

He slumped in her arms, heavy and hot, damp skin to damp skin, as passion-wracked as she.

Bliss rolled over them in a heavy wave laden with satiation, impossibly deep, impossible to deny.

Chapter Eleven

Miranda walked into the breakfast parlor the following morning to discover a family discussion in progress.

Roscoe—Julian—was shaking his head at Millicent and Cassie, seated opposite him. "You can't simply tell your husbands not to come home."

"Of course not!" Millicent mock-frowned at him. "We don't propose to do anything of the sort."

"Naturally not," Cassie said. "They'll quit Scotland and head home with our blessing—we'll simply send word to be delivered once they reach there that we've decided to spend a few extra days at Ridgware."

Even without looking, he'd known Miranda was there; as she approached the table, Roscoe rose and drew out the chair between him and Henry.

Sitting, she murmured a thank-you. His eyes briefly met hers, then he looked back at his sisters. Resuming his seat, he said, "I warn you I won't be around to entertain you. Henry and I have a lot of ground to cover, and my staff from London will arrive shortly, and then I'll be thoroughly absorbed."

The announcement did not noticeably dim Millicent's or Cassie's enthusiasm. "We quite understand," Millicent assured him. "But you'll be present at dinner, so we'll see you then, and at some breakfasts, and possibly some luncheons as well."

He eyed the pair, then heaved a massive sigh and raised his knife and fork. "I don't like the idea of you disrupting your households—and your marriages—merely to spend a few more hours in my company."

"Yes, dear Julian," Millicent replied, "but it's our choice to make, and we clearly place a higher value on spending time with you than you do."

He merely humphed; in truth, what could he say to that?

Miranda noted that, further along the table, Lucasta, Caroline, and Edwina had been listening to the exchange with affectionate smiles. She glanced at Henry and saw he was grinning, too.

"Besides," Cassie said, smiling as, across the table, she caught Miranda's eye, "a few extra days will allow us to get to know Miranda better."

Roscoe glanced sharply at his sisters, but they were exchanging comments on the bright morning with Miranda. No more than he could order them home could he keep them away from her. Looking down at his plate, hiding his equivocation behind his usual impassivity, he continued eating.

By early afternoon, Miranda was forced to accept that Roderick's continuing recovery did not require her constant attendance in the sickroom. Nurse was better able than she to keep him supplied with barley water and to bring up his meals—and make sure he ate them—and in the matter of keeping him amused, Sarah was significantly better qualified.

As Sarah appeared perfectly amenable to spending hours sitting by his bedside reading or chatting, and as he remained brighter and more engaged in her company, Miranda found herself largely redundant.

Finally accepting that, she rose from the chair by the bed. Roderick and Sarah broke off their discussion and looked up. She smiled. "I'm going to take a turn in the gardens."

Both smiled easily back. "If you haven't yet seen it," Sarah said, "there's a very pretty fountain court at the end of the west wing."

"Thank you—I'll look for it." Miranda turned to the door. A light rap fell upon it, then it opened and Roscoe walked in.

His gaze found her, then moved on to Roderick. "How are you feeling?"

Although still pale, and with lingering pain etched in his face, Roderick grinned. "Nurse insists on feeding me up, and Sarah and Miranda are working diligently to keep me entertained."

"It appears you're in excellent hands." Roscoe glanced at Miranda. "I came to ask if you'd like to go for a walk."

"I was just setting out, as it happens. Sarah suggested the fountain court was worth a visit."

He nodded, then looked at Roderick. "I don't expect to hear from London or even Birmingham today, but I'll let you know when I do."

"Thank you."

Roscoe saluted, then followed Miranda from the room. Shutting the door, he caught her gaze. "The fountain court should provide a pleasant stroll if you truly would like to see it."

"I would." As they strolled down the corridor, she glanced at his face. "But I thought you were going to be busy with Henry."

"Too busy to entertain my sisters. You"—he met her gaze—"fall into a different category."

Which category? The question burned her tongue, but she smothered it. Now they were lovers—were, she supposed, having an affair—did he mean he saw spending time with her outside the bedroom as part of that? Not having previously indulged in an affair, she had no idea. Regardless, she was perfectly happy spending her afternoon strolling by his side.

They left the house through the doors to the rear terrace and paced along in the weak sunshine, in the mild warmth reflected by the house's walls. The terrace stretched along the west wing and around its end. There, shallow steps led down into an Italianate garden court, with, at its center, a white marble fountain with a cupid pouring water into a wide basin.

Halting at the top of the steps, she surveyed the court, bounded to right and left by twin double rows of narrow cypresses that led the eye to the rural vista that lay beyond the end of the court. The space between the cypresses hosted white gravel paths and geometrically arranged beds outlined by low hedges. Elsewhere, encroaching winter had started to strip the leaves from the trees, yet this garden remained a palette of deep greens accentuated by the white of the gravel and the marble fountain; she could imagine the area under snow, when white would dominate over the dark green. "Sarah was right." She started down the steps. "This is the perfect place to stroll."

Roscoe descended the steps beside her. "It was created by the fourth duke for his wife so she would have a place to walk year-around. Apparently she was rigid in adhering to her constitutional regardless of the season or inclement weather."

"You must get nearly as much snow here as we get at Oak-grove."

"So I would think." A smile curved his lips. "In younger days, I sledded a lot." He pointed to where the ground beyond the court sloped down, away from the house. "That was the perfect spot—the best for miles around. It was a favorite pastime for all of us in winter." He glanced at her. "As children, did you and Roderick sled?"

Eyes forward, she shook her head. "No, although I assure you we would have liked to."

"Why didn't you?"

She hesitated, then, her gaze on the view ahead, said, "My aunts considered it an activity beneath our station."

He let a moment pass, then reached out, caught her hand, twined his fingers with hers briefly, then, stepping nearer, wound her arm with his. "Tell me about your aunts. The eldest died, and the younger is the one living with you and Roderick—is that correct?"

"Yes." She found herself being quizzed, but gently, about her and Roderick's earlier life. At first, she wondered if he was asking simply to fill the moments, or because it might shed light on Roderick's character given her brother was now a member of the Philanthropy Guild, but gradually she came to accept that it was she he was interested in learning about.

She hadn't imagined a man involved in a liaison would be interested in the lady's childhood, but the longer they walked and talked—almost inconsequentially, yet guided by an underlying quest to learn more—given he made no effort to disguise his true interest, it became increasingly clear that that true interest was her.

Deciding that two could play that game, she took his questions and turned them on him. An hour and more passed, filled with exchanges, yet as they walked back toward the house, she still felt she'd barely scratched his surface. His childhood, however, seemed to have been filled with the customary hedonistic pursuits considered typical of a noble youth.

They were nearing the house when footsteps crunching on gravel drew their gazes to the opening of a path cutting across the court in line with the fountain, embracing it before continuing on, linking the lawns on one side of the court with the woodland on the other side.

His sisters, all three of them, emerged into the courtyard. Seeing Roscoe and her, they smiled and waved.

Roscoe raised a hand in reply. Miranda did, too. She expected him to halt, but he drew her on, his stride steady. She glanced at his face, then looked at his sisters. The three had their heads together; they continued along the cross-path showing no signs of wishing to join their brother and her.

She refocused on his face. "I thought they would pounce."

He met her gaze briefly, then looked ahead, a subtle curve edging his lips. "I daresay they recognized that attempting to claim my attention at this time would be against their best interests."

The following afternoon, Roscoe found himself seated in a garden chair under the nearly bare branches of one of the old oaks bordering the south lawn, having afternoon tea with the ladies of his family, Henry, and Miranda.

By a consensus of opinion, Roderick and Sarah had remained indoors. Roderick had moved as far as the armchair by the bed, but given Entwhistle's warning that trying to walk too early would prolong his healing, everyone had agreed, even Roderick, that moving any further would be tempting fate.

So the gathering beneath the trees was a predominantly female affair, with only Henry and him representing their gender.

Setting her cup on its saucer, Miranda, seated in the chair next to his, selected a tiny cucumber sandwich from the plate Caroline was passing around. Having never understood why ladies deemed wafer-thin sandwiches to be so superior to those of more substantial construction, he shook his head when Caroline offered the plate to him.

Henry, seated on his other side, took three thin sandwiches and pressed them together to take a bite, grinning at his mother's resigned expression.

Finished daintily consuming her sandwich, Miranda glanced at the other ladies. "I know Caroline is involved in supporting a local school, and that Cassie is on the board of an orphanage. Do you all involve yourselves in such work?"

All the heads around the circle nodded.

"It seems the least we should do," Lucasta said, "and as, thanks to Julian, we are in a position to assist, we do, but, speaking for myself, once I became involved I found the charity work I engage in to be richly satisfying." Lucasta's lips quirked. "There are many within the ton who would be thoroughly unsurprised to hear that I find organizing old soldiers' lives to my liking. It gives one a sense of achievement, I find."

"Yes, that's it." Millicent nodded. "It might have been *noblesse oblige* that nudged us in that direction initially, but, again speaking for myself, it's very much the sense of accomplishing something worthwhile that draws one in and keeps one engaged."

Roscoe sat back and listened as Miranda questioned, and the others, Henry included, described their experiences and the benefits they saw in their involvement with a spectrum of charitable works. His family's views he already knew, although it had taken some years before he'd realized exactly what drove them, each and every one, to immerse themselves in charitable works to a degree significantly greater than the norm for those of their station. Most of the aristocracy who engaged in such works did so at a distance, usually providing money and the rather nebulous cachet of their patronage, and nothing else.

His mother, his sisters, his sister-in-law, and nephew gave money, lent their name and all intangible support, but in addition each had become actively involved in at least one charity to an extent greater than even he practiced with his projects via the Philanthropy Guild.

They'd done it—had seized on that route—as a way to pay him back. Prevented from thanking him in any other way, they'd seen his interest in such projects and had determined to use their time and energy to achieve more and more widely, quietly, without fanfare, yet in their minds it was all in his name.

Not that they'd ever told him they'd done it to thank him, but as they invariably told him of their successes whenever they saw him or wrote to him, eventually the penny had dropped. He'd asked Lucasta in an oblique way; her response had been to wonder that it had taken him so long to realize.

Yet over the years, he'd come to see that, regardless of their initial reasons, for each of them their charities gave them a focus, a purpose, and, as Lucasta had said, a sense of achievement they wouldn't otherwise have had.

So while he listened to them explaining their charities to Miranda, listened to the tenor of her questions, he could see what it was in the activity that appealed to her.

From his research into Roderick's family, he knew she was well dowered. As she hadn't married and was twenty-nine years old, that money was presumably in her hands. Protecting and caring for Roderick had been the principal motivation in her life to date, but that was at an end. And, he suspected, even more than the females of his family, she was the sort of woman who needed a purpose. A reason for living, a goal to work toward.

He sat, sipped, and listened, deftly rerouting the occasional queries directed his way back to one of the others, keeping Miranda's attention on them; he had no wish to engage more directly with her, not in this company. He was frankly unsettled by how quickly his mother, his sisters, and even Caroline had detected his interest in Miranda. Almost as if they saw it more clearly than he did, as if they had a greater understanding of his fascination with her than he. Which was disconcerting, to say the least.

Especially given the limitation on how far said fascination could evolve. They knew as well as he did, as well as, he assumed, she did, that there never could be any question of anything more than a short-lived liaison between them.

Even though his family could not have his insights into her underlying, driven, devotion to respectability, they all knew in their minds, if not their hearts, that he could never marry. Not now. Not since he'd made the decision to become Roscoe.

No eligible, even halfway respectable lady would ever stoop to marry him, nor, to his mind, should they. Aside from all else he would never ask it of any gently-bred woman, would never make an offer that, no matter the lady's standing, no matter his real identity, could only lead to social ignominy.

In becoming Roscoe, he'd cut himself off from ever marrying any lady of his own class, from ever having a family of his own. He'd known what he was sacrificing at the time and had never regretted the choice he'd made. He might not be able to have a family, but Millicent, Cassie, and Edwina could; Henry could. And Caroline and Lucasta could live out their lives as they deserved, with their children and grandchildren around them.

So he sat in the shade, largely silent, and listened to the on-going discussion, one that left him feeling content. One that, in many ways, was the outcome of his own achievement. Hearing the very real enthusiasm in Edwina's voice as she described her plans for taking the concept of philanthropic projects out into the unexplored wilds with Frobisher—did the man have any idea what he was marrying into?—he felt deeply pleased.

Closing his eyes, he let Miranda's focused intensity as she asked how charities were customarily established wash over and through him, and felt pleasure spark somewhere inside.

Even with his eyes closed, she effortlessly riveted, not just his senses but his mind, and something even deeper, as well. Relaxed in the chair, in the shade, he warily circled that something deeper; he had a strong suspicion he knew what it was, but he wasn't about to look too closely, much less give it a name.

With respect to him, she was a master musician, one who expertly played on his strings. On his emotions.

That conclusion resonated in his brain as, on the evening of the following day, he walked beside Miranda in the rose garden. He'd spent the day riding the estate with Henry, while she'd spent her time with his sisters; they'd already shared a comfortable exchange of the highlights of their respective days while walking through the mild night to the sunken garden.

The fact that such a simple, normal, ordinary exchange between him and a lady could occur, could be, remained with him, a lingering pleasure, a novel aspect of their unexpected interaction as they walked side by side down the central path and he turned his mind and his senses to savoring the silence that now claimed them. Not the silence of awkwardness, or of disinterest or disregard, but the silence of a companionship that had deepened to the point where words, the constant exchange of them, was no longer necessary.

He was at ease with her and she with him. At ease in the peace and quiet of the garden. Only their footfalls and the soft shushing of her skirts broke the stillness.

Pacing alongside her, feeling his emotions—those strings she tugged so effortlessly—stir, he felt forced to remind himself that this wasn't permanent, that there was no way he, not even he, London's powerful gambling king, could hold this precious, nebulous connection forever.

Much as he might wish to.

How much he might wish to he refused to consider. There was no point; their interaction would cease when they returned to London. This, their time at Ridgware, was an unexpected, unlooked-for moment in a world outside the one in which they lived. Things could happen, could exist here that never would exist, could not exist, in their normal world.

He glanced at her, at her shadowed face, at the moonlight gilding her hair. Regardless of the bittersweet realization that what was now between them would perforce be so fleeting, he was unwilling—even sensing the danger—to draw back from it, from her, from this unforeseen interlude.

As if feeling his gaze, she glanced at him, met his gaze. Her lips curved lightly. Facing forward, she said, "I have to admit to feeling as if I've suddenly stumbled on some secret, on some path for which I've been searching without even realizing I was." She glanced his way. "Your mother, your sisters, your sister-in-law are all admirable ladies. They're wealthy enough to live a life of ease without lifting a finger to help anyone else, but they don't. They have a different view of themselves, of their roles, of what their lives should be—they accept some significant degree of responsibility for all those around them. That makes them a part of the greater whole, rather than distant observers."

She drew breath. "And being a distant observer, being in large part isolated from the wider world, is a lonely and unrewarding existence. I know because I've been living that way for most of my life, kept apart, held back by what I believed were . . . restrictions. Limitations. But I'm no longer sure they—my perceived limitations—are real."

"If by perceived limitations you mean that the source of your family's fortune renders you ineligible in certain spheres, then as someone who has lived on both sides of the social divide, I can assure you that any such perception is, indeed, wide of the mark." Deciding she deserved even plainer speaking, he went on, "If you were a mill owner's daughter, raised outside society, matters would be different, but you aren't. Your lineage might not be as pure as that of my sisters, but your mother's family has been gentry for generations, and you were raised within society's pale. By anyone's gauge, you and Roderick bear no stigma."

Reaching the reflecting pool at the end of the rose walk, they halted. She looked at him; the shifting shadows hid her expression as she searched his face, then she inclined her head. "Thank you." Lowering her gaze to the pool, after a moment she continued, "I can't tell you how much I value the insights I've gained through your family, through having a chance to talk with them. It's almost as if, in doing what I knew was right and insisting on coming with you to rescue Roderick regardless of any social risk, some kind fate has given me this—my time here at Ridgware with your family—as my reward. They've opened doors for me that I never knew were there, and shown me a way forward with a problem I was only just realizing I had." She looked up and caught his gaze. "So again, thank you for bringing me, us, here. I recognize the trust you've placed in us in allowing us to see this side of your life. Rest assured neither Roderick nor I will ever give you cause to regret it."

He held her gaze and inclined his head, accepting her declaration, not that he'd needed to hear it; he trusted her implicitly. He now knew her well enough to be absolutely certain that he could, that his and his family's secret was safe with her and Roderick.

Looking down at the pool at their feet, after a moment, he said, "When we were children, we called this our wishing pool. We'd come down here at night, stare into its black depths, think of what we most wanted in life, and make our wish."

Unbidden, what the man he now was wished for most leapt into his mind; it wasn't what he'd thought it would be. The reality shook him; he rushed to bury it, to smother the need before it could spread through his conscious mind and take hold. That way lay madness.

Drawing in a deep breath, blinking back to the rose garden and the woman by his side, he was grateful for the shadows that cloaked his face. "So . . . what would you wish for?"

She, too, had been staring down at the pool; for a moment she didn't respond, then she raised her head and met his eyes. "Everyone knows you can't tell someone what you wish for, not if you want your wish to come true."

About them the night lay like a dark blanket; perhaps it was the lack of light that made what flared between them seem more real. More tangible.

More compulsively desirable.

"Let's go back to the house." *To your room, to your bed.* He left the words unsaid, yet they hung in the air between them.

Through the shadows, she held his gaze, then she reached out, took his hand, twined her fingers with his and turned toward the house, her smile as mysterious as the night. "Yes, let's."

* * *

The next morning Miranda told herself she was content with their relationship as it was. That her thought in the moonlight—the wish that had crowded into her mind—was simply that, a moonstruck thought. Nothing to take seriously.

It had been the atmosphere, the intimacy of the moment. The richly hued closeness.

About her, the breakfast parlor was abuzz with chatter as Millicent and Cassie prepared, finally, to depart. The warmth that existed between the members of Roscoe's—Julian's—family was so potent, so strong, that she sensed there had to be some reason, some event that had forged them into such a cohesive, devoted whole. Despite—or was it because of?—the mysterious conversion of Julian to Roscoe.

Watching him interact with his sisters as, fasts satisfactorily broken, the company all rose and went with Millicent and Cassie into the front hall to bestow last hugs and farewells, she wondered again at that transformation. Hanging back a little with Sarah, both of them grinning, touched by the rush of emotions as Millicent and Cassie hugged and kissed their way around the others, she watched and saw.

He'd told her he was Roscoe, and to her he was. She couldn't think of him by any other name; he certainly wasn't the idle hedonist depicted in the portrait of Lord Julian Delbraith.

And while society would be shocked and would deplore the change, seeing him now, knowing him now, she had to wonder if, regardless of what had caused it, the transformation hadn't been the making of him. Hadn't been the fire that had forged him into such a complex, fascinating, enthralling character.

Such a strong character, although, considering Lucasta, perhaps that inner strength had always been there, latent, hidden beneath the rake's sophistication, waiting to be tempered in the forge of experience.

Regardless, the man he was now was, in her eyes, infinitely more attractive than the man he had almost certainly been. Understandable, therefore, that her wish in the night had been all about keeping him in her life. About a way to prolong their liaison, to convert the illicit to licit. A dream.

In more realistic vein, she wondered how long their relationship—their affair, their liaison—might last. For weeks, or for very much longer?

Years?

It would, she thought, take years and years for her to learn all about him, to explore and absorb all the facets he possessed. How long she might have with him she didn't know, but she was determined to make the most of every minute.

Millicent looked around, spotted her, and came bustling over. "Miranda." Millicent took her hands and, smiling warmly, stretched up and touched cheeks. "My dear, when next you're in Northamptonshire you must, positively *must,* stop by."

"And"—Cassie nudged Millicent aside, taking her place to squeeze fingers and touch cheeks with Miranda—"the same applies to Hampshire. Regardless of what the future holds, we don't want to lose touch."

"We'll always have things to talk about," Millicent assured her. "We'll be pleased to show you our local efforts. Whether it's you and Roderick, or just you, if you want to spend a few weeks away from London, just write."

"And we will write." Cassie grinned. "You can be sure of that—we have your direction."

"Girls!" Lucasta called. "Your carriages are waiting and the horses are literally champing at their bits—and you know coachmen never like that."

"Yes, Mama!" Millicent and Cassie chorused.

With laughter and smiles, on another rush of potent emotion the pair swept out of the huge double doors.

Miranda stood with the others at the top of the front steps and waved the two coaches away.

Lucasta and Caroline heaved identical sighs; both turned with similiar smiles on their faces. As they started back into the house, Miranda went to step aside to allow the pair to pass, but Caroline reached out and slid an arm around her waist and, still smiling, drew her with them.

Miranda acquiesced and joined the duchess and the dowager, with Edwina and Sarah bringing up the rear. Roscoe and Henry had dallied on the steps; she heard them debating whether to walk to the stables or check on the hounds.

Beside her, Caroline spoke pensively. "It's going to be quieter without those two here."

"True." Smiling fondly, Lucasta glanced at Edwina. "But now perhaps those less forthright might be able to get a word in edgewise about their own wedding."

Edwina chuckled. "You know that in the end I'll do precisely as I wish."

"Yes, dear." Lucasta led the way to the morning room. "*I* know, but at some point you really will need to let your elder sisters into that secret, too."

Two hours later, Miranda, Roscoe, and Henry followed Caroline into the schoolhouse that stood at the edge of the tiny hamlet of Mill Green.

Pausing in the small foyer just inside the outer doors, Caroline peeked through the glass in the inner double doors, then whispered, "It was originally an old meeting hall." She glanced at Miranda. "We—the board—took it over and refurbished it, and found Mr. McAllister and Miss Trimble to teach here. Both live nearby. Miss Trimble used to teach at a girls' school in Bath, while Mr. McAllister was tutor to Lord Tewkesbury's sons until they grew too old."

Straightening, squaring her shoulders, Caroline pushed the door open and led the way in. Miranda followed, with Roscoe and Henry in her wake.

Mr. McAllister and Miss Trimble were delighted to receive them. Their classes, defined by age and separated by a movable partition erected across the hall, were sufficiently well behaved for the teachers to give their attention to their primary benefactor, diligently answering Caroline's questions on their progress with the agreed syllabus, and reporting on the amenities and facilities of the building, discussing what was presently in place and what ideally should be budgeted for in the coming year.

Miranda listened but also looked. She was impressed by the numbers of children attending—fifteen in the older group, all busy with arithmetic, and twelve in the younger group, their noses buried in well-worn readers. Miss Trimble had been reading to the latter group but had instructed them to read by themselves while she spoke with the visitors.

One towheaded boy, about seven years old, sat at the end of one bench. Miranda noticed he was staring at a page, his finger on it, but not moving. His face was set in a scowl.

Leaving the others, she went to stand beside the boy's bench, then bent so her face was level with his.

His eyes swung her way and he blinked, wary.

She smiled and nodded at the tattered reader. "Is it too hard?"

The boy regarded her gravely, then whispered back, "Not so much hard as . . . it's just this word here, miss." He pointed.

She looked. "*Easy*. The word is *easy*."

The boy frowned distractedly. "I would've thought *easy* would have a *z* in it."

"It doesn't. Just *s* and *y*." Miranda straightened and saw a girl two places down, waving.

"Miss, can you help me with this one?"

Miranda slowly circled the class, helping with this word, then that, smiling, sometimes at the children's comments, but mostly simply smiling to herself.

Despite paying attention to McAllister's and Miss Trimble's reports, Roscoe found a part of his awareness tracking Miranda, taking in her interaction with the children, their responses to her and hers to them.

When it came to bridging the social divide, she was, it seemed, a natural. Possibly because she had never developed the overwhelming arrogance of the nobility, the aristocracy, those of the upper ten thousand families known as the ton. Even committed as they were, all his family, and even he, had to work to set people at ease, but she achieved that effortlessly.

He wondered if she had any idea how truly useful such a talent was.

If he'd needed any proof of the genuineness of her commitment to learning more about charitable projects, her patience with the children left the matter beyond doubt. She'd decided that the path suited her and was intent on learning all she could . . . before setting out to establish and manage her own project?

That was something he could assist her with—something that would give him an excuse to continue to see her after they returned to London.

A connection that could easily last for years.

He couldn't remember when philanthropy had become an intrinsic part of his life, but he knew himself well enough to admit that it fulfilled a certain need he'd always had, a facet of the same drive that had compelled him to become Roscoe in the first place. Once he'd discovered what a drug helping others was to him, he'd grown addicted, but it was an addiction neither he nor anyone else saw any reason he should fight.

Watching Miranda as she straightened from helping another little girl, he suspected that she and he shared the same driving need. He wasn't at all surprised by her rapidly developing focus on charitable works. In his case, his family needed him still, but Roderick's need of her was over; she needed something to fill the void, the hole in her life. That need was something he understood not just with his mind but with his heart, with his soul.

As she stepped away from the benches and drifted back up the room, he stirred and strolled to join her.

Miranda saw the children's attention rise from their readers and fix on Roscoe; until he'd come forward he'd been hidden from them by the partition. Now boys and girls alike stared. Gawped. Visually devoured with the intensity only the young could get away with.

Amused, she glanced at him, and in that moment saw him as they must. As a god, tall, physically powerful, superbly proportioned, his every movement invested with predatory grace, his features bearing the stamp of a warrior-prince, his arrogant assurance a cloak he'd never lose.

He was all and everything they would aspire to, the boys to emulate, the girls to possess.

That was no bad thing. Having high aspirations never hurt.

Reaching her, he halted. "Have you seen all you need?"

All, and a bit more. She smiled. "Yes."

He offered his arm and she took it, and let him lead her to where Caroline waited with Mr. McAllister and Miss Trimble.

Taking their leave of the teachers, both of whom were delighted and encouraged by the visit, they walked out into weak sunshine.

Miranda allowed Roscoe to hand her into the gig. Henry helped Caroline to the seat beside her.

Taking the reins, Caroline asked, "Well, what did you think?"

She waited while Caroline turned the horse and set it pacing back up the lane. Roscoe and Henry, mounted on heavy hunters, fell in behind. "I think," Miranda said, "that you have every cause to feel proud of your achievement. I take it Henry is involved with the school, too?"

"I've insisted that he learn enough to, once he comes of age, sit on the board." Caroline negotiated a turn, then said, "I want the school to grow and continue after I'm too old to oversee it. I want Henry to be there to take over and, bless him, he seems very amenable to accommodating me."

The men riding behind couldn't hear them, not over the rattle of the gig's wheels. "From what I've seen, Henry's had an excellent male mentor in that regard."

"Indeed." Caroline dipped her head in acknowledgment, a smile of a sort Miranda couldn't quite place softening her face. "Twelve years ago when my husband died, I never would have dreamed I'd ever say such a thing, but Julian's been a rock. Literally a rock. He's as immovable and as un-flappable as granite, and while there are times none of us appreciate that, he was the one to hold us all together and get us through . . . what we had to weather."

Miranda held her tongue and hoped for more about what they'd had to weather, about what Julian—now Roscoe—had done to hold them together through what she inferred had been a turbulent time.

Caroline glanced at her, then her lips curved wryly and she looked ahead. "There was a time when I despised Julian to the heels of his well-shod feet. In that, I was mistaken, but it took a disaster for me to see him clearly. For him to show himself to me clearly."

The wheels rattled on, a repetitive, soothing sound.

Caroline said nothing more, but she didn't have to; Miranda could see the parallels well enough. Through disaster Julian had been revealed to Caroline as the white knight he truly was. Now, through Roderick's kidnap and rescue, she, too, had been given a chance to see past the shield Roscoe—like the Julian he'd previously been—hid his shining light behind.

He was a white knight to his soul, but like the best of that breed he saw no reason to flaunt what many would term his goodness. He wasn't a philanthropist on a grand scale in order to garner public accolades or social recognition. He was as he was because that was the sort of man he was—under the glamour of the idle hedonist Lord Julian Delbraith had been, and now behind the more dangerous persona of Neville Roscoe, London's gambling king.

As Caroline turned the gig between the massive twin pil-lars that guarded the entrance to Ridgware's drive, Miranda felt like giving thanks to the deity, to fate, to whatever it was that had arranged for her to fall in with such a deeply fascinating man.

Chapter Twelve

After luncheon, Roscoe and Henry left the dining parlor to pursue estate business. Having visited Roderick and been assured by him and Nurse that all was under control and her presence unnecessary, Miranda left Sarah reading the latest news sheets to Roderick and joined Lucasta and Caroline in the family sitting room. Edwina had retreated elsewhere to write letters.

A pleasant room on the ground floor, the sitting room looked out over rolling lawns and woodland to the rise of the hills beyond. Both other ladies had settled with embroidery hoops in their laps. Sinking onto the end of the sofa on which Lucasta sat, Miranda offered to untangle the silks Lucasta was attempting to tease apart.

"Thank you, dear." Lucasta handed over the mess with alacrity. "My eyes, sadly, are not what they were."

Miranda smiled and set to work.

Heads bent over their tasks, they sat in quiet companionship. She was very conscious of the inclusive, soothing atmosphere; it wasn't something she'd previously experienced. Her aunts had always been too tense, too reserved, too much on guard, watching like hawks for any potential social gaffe, no matter how tiny.

Here, all was calm, serene, and no one was overcritical. Here . . . she suspected the difference lay in this being a true home, inhabited by a real family, not, as her and Roderick's "home" had been, a household forced together by circumstance, with less affection than might have been.

That prevailing sense of acceptance gave her the courage to voice a concern that had gradually grown. Passing the untangled silks back to Lucasta, Miranda sat back and regarded the other women, who were still focused on the works in their respective hands. "We, Roderick and I, have been here for five days." When both ladies glanced up, Miranda caught Caroline's gaze. "We'll need to remain for another five. You've all been very kind—you've included me in your gatherings as if I was family, and Sarah has been so helpful with Roderick. I'm more grateful than I can say, but I fear we're becoming a very real imposition on your household and your time—and I hope you would tell me if that were the case. I wouldn't wish to repay your many kindnesses with obtuseness as to your true needs."

Caroline regarded her for a moment, then gently smiled. "I could retreat to being the haughty duchess and remind you that this is a ducal household, and as such more than up to the task of catering for a mere two unexpected guests, which is nothing more than the truth. However, if we are speaking of truth, then, to deal first with Sarah, I'm very pleased to see her so engaged in being useful—more, in happily putting herself out to entertain someone else, rather than, as she previously has, expecting the world to revolve around her. I cannot stress how much good having your brother here, injured and in need, is doing her, so enough said on that score.

"As to us putting ourselves out to entertain you, dear Miranda, quite aside from you being the most easily entertained guest I've ever had, you must accept that we"—with a wave Caroline included Lucasta—"will do all in our power to make staying at Ridgware pleasant for the guest whose presence ensures Julian remains as well."

Lucasta nodded. "We simply don't see enough of him otherwise, so naturally we're beyond grateful to anyone or anything that results in us having his company. Having him arrive with you and Roderick was a gift to us all. But you not only brought him here without there having to be some estate disaster to claim his complete attention, you, my dear, have kept him here. Kept him here because he wants to be here, which for us, for Henry and Edwina especially, is a special treat." Looking up, Lucasta met her eyes. "And so, my dear Miranda, we can sincerely assure you that to us, having you and your brother to stay, even for ten or more days, is no imposition at all."

Miranda studied Lucasta's eyes, like her son's so dark a blue they were never easy to read. "I know he—Julian— has many and constant claims on his time in London. I had thought he was staying because of estate business, because of Henry."

Caroline shook her head. "He's taking advantage of remaining here to spend time about the estate with Henry, but that's because he's too much the gentleman to monopolize your entire day."

Lucasta snorted. "Not so much the gentleman as the shrewd tactician. If he spent every minute by your side, you'd find him too much, too irritating. He's too wise for that."

Miranda inwardly blinked. Lucasta and Caroline refocused on their embroideries, and a pleasant silence fell over the room. Miranda had to wonder whether they knew she and Roscoe were lovers . . . perhaps they did. Relaxing into her corner of the sofa, she sent her mind circling to her hostesses' perspective, their view of why Julian—Roscoe—was remaining at Ridgware. To Lucasta's assertion that he would spend every minute of the day by her side if such behavior were acceptable. Acceptable to her.

She found it hard to believe that desire for her and her

company was sufficiently powerful to keep him, of all men, there, away from his London concerns. Then again, their liaison and her fascination with it and him was certainly sufficient to rivet her interest.

She'd assumed said fascination was a result of her being a novice in that sphere, and that therefore he, being beyond experienced, wouldn't feel anything comparable, wouldn't be subject to the same enthrallment.

If Lucasta and Caroline were right, then she was wrong.

But . . . what did that mean? What might it mean?

What might he decide it meant?

She wished she knew more about men, specifically about their views on liaisons. As it was, she had no idea what he might think or do, none at all.

Which left her with only one way forward.

Late in the afternoon, Roscoe tapped on Roderick's door and heard Miranda's voice, a trifle strained, bid him enter. Opening the door, he scanned the room. Stifling a curse, leaving the door swinging, he strode in and, dislodging Sarah, looped his arms about Roderick's waist and hauled his weight off Miranda, staggering as she strove to support her teetering brother from his other side.

"Thank you," Roderick gasped. "Entwhistle suggested I try a few short walks—he didn't mention that my balance might be shot."

"It'll come back soon enough, but you'll be staggering for the first little while." Across Roderick, Roscoe looked at Miranda.

With Roderick's good arm over her shoulders, still catching her breath, she nodded. "Thank you."

He sent her an acerbic look. "You can thank me by letting me take that side."

Her eyes widened a fraction, then she eased out from under Roderick's arm. Holding Roderick up, he shifted to take her place. Roderick's right foot had been broken, but it was his left collarbone that had cracked, his left arm that was immobilized in a sling strapped across his chest. He was wearing a thick dressing robe; a crude slipper fashioned from strips of leather and bandages covered his injured foot.

Roscoe was a few inches taller than Roderick. Once he'd settled Roderick's arm around him and Roderick had caught his balance, Roscoe nodded toward the door. "The corridor's a good place to practice—the gallery with its rail will be even better."

Roderick nodded, and they moved slowly forward.

Roscoe saw Sarah hovering. "Find Mrs. Viner and ask for the crutches George used when he broke his leg. She'll have them stored somewhere."

Sarah nodded and slipped past. "I'll get them."

Having heard from Caroline the full story of why Sarah was presently at Ridgware and not with her parents in London, he was favorably impressed with the young woman's continued willingness to help.

Guiding Roderick's uncertain steps, Roscoe steered him out of the door. Once they were in the long corridor and making steady progress down the runner, Roderick gradually grew more assured.

"One thing to remember—you'll have to walk back. The instant you feel your strength fading, turn back."

Roderick nodded. "I can make it to the gallery. After that, we'll see."

With Miranda hovering, Roscoe supported Roderick into the gallery, then let Roderick grasp the wooden balustrade circling the stairwell. Roderick limped along, step by slow step.

Capturing Miranda's hand, drawing her with him, Roscoe stepped back to the nearest window.

Halting beside him, her gaze on Roderick, Miranda blew out a breath and let herself collapse onto the window seat. Eyes on her brother, she felt Roscoe glance down at her. "I had no idea he was so heavy." She'd had no real appreciation of the effort *he* must have exerted in carrying Roderick's dead weight from the cottage and lifting him into the curricle; now she did.

He snorted. "He's not exactly your *little* brother anymore."

"True." And in so many ways.

After a moment of studying Roderick, he stirred, then sat beside her. "Watch his lips. When the line becomes too grim, it'll be time for him to head back."

"Thank you. I seem to be saying that a lot these days."

He reached for her hand, twined his fingers with hers. "A situation with which I have no complaint."

She managed not to blush as an all-too-vivid memory of her thanking him—effusively—in the dark watches of the previous night flared to life.

He'd come to her bed every night, and every night she'd welcomed him with open arms and a thrill shivering down her spine. And every night he'd lived up to her expectations, and more. He'd been assiduous in his attentions; he'd taught her so much over those dark hours, had revealed to her so much of herself, and allowed her to explore both her own responses and reactions, and his.

He was a generous lover, attentive, often frighteningly intuitive, and at times almost reverent, yet beneath his smooth sophistication ran a demand so strong, so raw . . . every time it rose to his surface, as it inevitably and invariably did, his every touch made her shiver with unadulterated delight, shudder with consuming need, and wantonly glory in their passion.

So she sat and watched Roderick take his first difficult steps toward renewed health, with her hand openly clasped in Roscoe's, felt his thumb idly cruising the back of her hand, felt heat spread from the simple contact. Felt her skin come alive, awakened by his nearness, by the expectation of pleasure having him near evoked.

She watched Roderick halt, turn, then make his way slowly back along the gallery. Hearing a clatter on the stairs, she looked to their head and saw Sarah arrive, triumphantly bearing a pair of wooden crutches.

Roderick halted and smiled.

Beaming, Sarah carried the crutches to him.

Roscoe let out a small sigh, released Miranda's hand and rose, then went to show Roderick how to properly use the supports.

With only a modicum of instruction, Roderick mastered the long pegs and managed to get himself back to his room without incident.

Miranda halted by the door, watched as Roscoe stood ready to catch Roderick if he fell, but with Sarah deftly removing the crutches as Roderick let them go, he managed to get himself back into his chair without drama. Settling, the smile he sent her reassured her as no words could have.

With an answering smile, she drew back from the doorway as, after a last word and a nod, Roscoe came striding out. Stepping through the door, shutting it behind him, his gaze locked with hers.

He read her eyes, then his lips curved. "You don't need to say it."

Instead, her own lips curving, she stepped close, stretched up and brushed her lips over his. Murmured against them, "So I'll say it without words," and kissed him.

Lightly—that was her intent, but his hands caught her waist and he drew her in, angled his head and drank her thanks from her lips, her mouth. Claimed his reward and set her senses whirling.

Purring.

Wanting.

Eventually, he raised his head and broke the kiss. The calculation burgeoning in her head was mirrored in his dark sapphire eyes, but then he laughed softly, wryly regretful. "The dinner gong will sound too soon."

She sighed and stepped back; reluctantly, his hands slid from her waist. "In that case, you'll have to wait to savor your reward." She was inwardly amazed that the sultriness in her voice and expression came so easily. Turning, she held his gaze until the last second. "Until later."

Roscoe watched her walk away, hips seductively sway-
ing . . . then he smiled appreciatively, in anticipation, and,
turning, forced himself to walk in the opposite direction.

The next morning Miranda seized the opportunity created
by Caroline being closeted with Mrs. Viner, and Lucasta and
Edwina becoming embroiled in a discussion of the family
members to be invited to Edwina's wedding, to stroll in the
gardens and focus on something she rarely did—herself, her
own life. What was important, what would remain so in the
future—what her future should be like.

Her life was changing, on multiple planes. And on many
of those planes she stood at a crossroads with more than
one avenue, more than one path she might take. And decision time was nearing, but how could she make the correct
choice without knowing the pertinent facts?

Strolling down the path that circled the south lawn, between the drifts of autumn leaves the gardeners had raked
to either side of the gravel, she attempted to bring order to
her thoughts. She had so many questions to which she'd yet
to learn the answers, and every day, every night, only added
to the list.

Last night, for instance . . . when Roscoe had joined her
in her room, she'd insisted that the purpose of their engagement, the tenor of it, should be driven by her wish to thank
him. She'd pressed her claim and, indulgent, he'd granted
it—allowed her to explore and seek and learn what most
pleasured him, and then to wantonly deliver that, fo fulfill
his every wish and press on him his every carnal desire,
raining pleasure and delight upon him, and yet . . . and yet
. . . at the shattering end, long after he'd taken over, seized
their reins and taken command, she'd been left with the
conviction, absolute, ringing true, that his greatest pleasure
derived not from anything she could do to him, but in her
surrender, in her allowing him to pleasure her.

He delighted in her passion, gloried in having her beneath him. In having her with him as together they raced

through the fire and up and over the peak. As exhausted, wrung out, they slumped, deliriously ecstatic, in each other's arms.

Joy, pleasure, and delight—and the greatest gift she could give him, it seemed, was to show him how much those were shared.

She had, and the intimacy, the closeness of the moment when he'd settled her in his arms, her head pillowed on his chest, and he'd raised her hand, pressed a kiss to her palm, then settled her hand, palm down, over his heart, had been shattering.

Acute, intense, soul-deep.

What they shared . . . she thought, sensed, that it was something special. She'd had no other lover, no other affair with which to compare, so the fact that it felt special to her didn't mean that it would feel special to him, yet . . . perhaps there was something in Lucasta and Caroline's view. Perhaps being with her was at least part of what was holding him at Ridgware.

But what would that mean in terms of what came later? After?

She'd taken him as her lover initially purely as a means to an end, as a way to learn something, to experience something she'd needed to experience at least once in her life.

Once had extended effortlessly into many more times; their liaison, their affair, had come to exist without any huge effort from either of them, more as a natural extrapolation of a connection that had suited them both.

How long would it suit them? How far could it go?

She halted, unsettled, unnerved by the strength of her reaction to the prospect those questions evoked—a vision of a time when their liaison was no more and he was no longer in her life.

Looking inward, she recognized and admitted that she didn't want their liaison to end. That she would rather go forward and see what they might make of it. That she'd already gone too far, become too enthralled with him, with them together, to be unaffected by their connection ending. Severing.

Yet once they returned to London, to their lives there, how could such a connection survive? If as Lord Julian Delbraith he was, if not out of, then certainly at the limit of Miranda Clifford's reach, when he was Neville Roscoe she was absolutely definitely out of his.

The only way their liaison could continue was illicitly, as a carefully guarded secret.

Still, perhaps that would do. Would suit them both.

Would allow them to continue—

"Miranda!"

She blinked back to her surroundings and saw Henry striding over the lawn.

"Are you strolling alone?" He halted before her, a smile wreathing his face. "I'm sure it says somewhere that we can't have that."

She smiled. "Your mother, your grandmother, and your aunt were busy, so I took myself for a stroll." She started to walk on. "Where's your uncle?"

Henry fell in beside her. "We just rode in, but the family solicitors were waiting, so he's gone off to deal with them. We've all agreed that I'm not yet up to wrestling with the legal stuff, so I'm excused." He glanced ahead, then at her. "Were you wanting to explore some particular area? It looked like you were lost—or perhaps didn't know which way to go?"

An accurate observation, but . . . she shook her head. "I was just woolgathering."

"Oh." He paused, then more diffidently said, "Would you rather continue alone?"

"No." There was no point pondering unanswerable questions. She smiled at him encouragingly. "Actually, I would welcome your company."

"Well, then." Relaxing, he looked around. "The rose garden is over there—have you seen it?"

Several times, mostly in moonlight. "Yes, but . . ." The

rose garden now held a lingering presence, one that would only distract her. "I'd thought to wander through the shrubbery—I haven't been there, yet."

"Right-ho." With an elegance he had to have copied from his uncle, he gestured ahead. "We can go this way."

She walked on, and he paced beside her. "Tell me, how does your uncle manage with you? I know he's your guardian. Do you meet with him often?"

Henry waggled his head. "Yes and no. If all is going well, I only see him in summer and at Christmas here, when he visits Ridgware. Until recently I was at school, of course, so wasn't here during his occasional other visits."

"If all is going well . . . but what if you have a problem? Do you send word and he comes to you, or do you go to him?" She knew Roscoe well enough to know it would be one or the other.

"Both. Sometimes he would come and stay near the school, and send for me—the headmaster hated that, but given the family, they couldn't argue. And at other times, when he couldn't leave London, he'd send for me and I'd go to his house there."

"In Chichester Street?"

"Yes." Henry glanced at her. "Do you know it?"

"We live close by."

"Oh. Then you know . . ."

"Roderick and I know your uncle as Roscoe."

Henry nodded. "I keep tripping over his name when I'm there . . . but, oh! I say—you must be sure never to mention that I go there to Mama, or Grandmama, or—heaven help us all—the aunts."

When she turned questioning eyes on him, Henry pulled a face. "He doesn't allow them to visit him there, and I don't think—in fact, I'm perfectly certain—he's never let on that he allows me to visit."

She could understand that. "Consider my lips sealed."

"Good. I wouldn't want him to have to face the lot of them, all pining to come and visit him." Henry shuddered feelingly. "They'll pour on the histrionics, and then get angry when he refuses to budge."

She glanced at him. "You're sure he won't budge?"

"Never." The conviction in Henry's tone was absolute. "If he decides something's necessary for your own good, nothing short of the apocalypse will shift him."

From the mouth of babes . . . in this case, an experienced babe. She had little doubt that Henry was correct, at least in general, yet she had managed to get Roscoe to at least bend, several times; she felt rather chuffed about that. "So what's next for you? I take it you've finished school?"

"Yes. I'll be going up to Oxford next year—all the males of the family go there."

She listened with half an ear, throwing out another question whenever he ran down. Henry reminded her of Roderick at that age; despite the difference in class, the similarities were marked. But by the time they'd ambled through the shrubbery and were heading back toward the house, Henry's words had reminded her of a highly pertinent question that had been buried beneath the avalanche of recent revelations.

Why had Lord Julian Delbraith become Neville Roscoe? Why had he dropped one identity and created another? A very powerful other?

Reentering the house with Henry, she felt increasingly sure that the primary motivation behind Julian's transformation to Roscoe would be something to do with protecting his family. How, she couldn't imagine, but if their liaison was to have much of a future, that was one of his secrets she might need to know.

"Julian, dear"—Lucasta caught his eye as they rose from the luncheon table—"if you would, I would like a few minutes of your time."

"Yes, of course." Drawing back Miranda's chair, he watched as she rose, smiled at him, then went to join Edwina and Caroline as they headed for the door, already engrossed in a discussion of wedding bouquets. He turned as Lucasta joined him. "Where?"

She twined her arm with his, patted his hand. "The gardens, I think. It's pleasant enough, and no doubt the weather will soon turn. We should take advantage of clear skies while we may."

He made no reply, simply steered Lucasta through the corridors and out onto the terrace. As they descended the steps to the path circling the lawn, the voices of the three ladies in the morning room reached them, the pleasant, gentrified sound fading as they walked further from the house. He waited for Lucasta to broach the subject she wished to discuss; she wouldn't until they were well away from any chance of being overheard or overseen. She'd wanted privacy, so the matter would, indeed, be sensitive, but he had no idea what it might be; these days, between him and her, there were few topics that would qualify for such discretion.

She waited until they reached the far side of the lawn before saying, "No one knows better than I why you became Roscoe. Why you let Julian vanish into some unspecified limbo."

He managed not to tense; that was a direction he hadn't foreseen. Noncommittally, he inclined his head. "Indeed."

She glanced at his face, trying to read it—something not even she was all that good at. "That said, I wondered if, given the current state of the dukedom, given our collective financial health, whether you'd considered the prospect of stepping back, as it were, and becoming Julian again."

"I can honestly say the thought had not entered my head."

"Yes, well—I did wonder if you'd realized that the prospect was now a *possibility,* or so I judge. You would know better than I, of course, but my understanding is that, courtesy of you being Roscoe for the past twelve years, we are all in excellent financial shape, and, indeed, our continued financial well-being is no longer dependent on the activities of your alter ego." Her gaze remained on his face. "Is that assessment correct, or have I got it wrong?"

"No. You're correct." After a moment, he admitted, "If Roscoe ceased his activities tomorrow, none of you would be materially affected."

He, however, would be, albeit not financially. For some years now, all the profits from his gambling enterprises had gone back into the businesses, or to the people running them, or to charity.

They walked slowly on. Again, he felt his mother's gaze touch his face.

"The reason I wondered if you'd considered the reversal, as it were, is . . . well, you missed giving Millicent away, and Cassie, too, and Edwina is the last. I know it would mean a lot to you, and to her, indeed, to us all, to have you, as yourself, walk her down the aisle."

The emotional tide the prospect conjured damned near swamped his heart, but . . . he was too wise in the ways of his mama to let his reaction blind him. Instead, he looked past it, beneath it, for the real reason Lucasta, of all women, had chosen to prick him with such a potent blade.

Only if she was envisaging something even more powerful . . .

When he didn't immediately respond, she glanced idly around, and as they continued slowly strolling, went on, "If Roscoe were to disappear one day—sell his businesses and simply go, set sail for America, perhaps—and a few weeks later Lord Julian Delbraith returned from wherever his fancy had taken him twelve years ago, repentant, of course, but as charming as ever . . . can you see how that might play out?" She patted his arm. "And, of course, wherever you were, whatever it was you were doing, you've made a spectacular fortune, so, my dear, you'd be beyond eligible, too."

And there it was.

Did she know? As perspicacious as she'd always been about anyone but George, he had to wonder whether she'd guessed what his dearest, deepest, most personal wish—the one he'd set aside, the one he'd knowingly sacrificed to his family's need—was. The wish that, when he'd stood over the old wishing pool, had sprung fully formed, undimmed by the years, back into his mind.

"I hadn't thought of reverting"—he heard his clipped accents, didn't try to soften them—"so if you're asking whether I will, or might, I can't answer." He met her eyes, so like his own. "It's not a simple matter—there's a great deal I would need to consider, with many aspects to be weighed on each side of the scale."

She searched his eyes, then nodded and looked ahead. "Yes, I daresay. And I suspect I cannot even guess at most of those aspects. However, if only to please me, do, I beg you, consider the possibility."

After a moment, he inclined his head. "I will."

Now she'd put it into his head, of course he would.

Now she'd raised the prospect of a way in which he might, just might, be able to pursue the dream he'd refused even to allow himself to dream.

Being Lucasta, she patted his arm and said not a word more.

Leaving him wrestling with a raft of questions he hadn't, until then, thought he'd ever have to answer.

She wasn't going to dwell on what the future might bring. When she heard Roscoe open her door that night, Miranda, waiting by the uncurtained window, reminded herself of her decision to simply make the most of every minute.

On their return to London, what would be would be, but for now . . . the door closed, and, turning, she watched him walk through the moonlight and shadows toward her.

To her.

Halting before her, he drew her into his arms, and she went, raising hers to drape them over his shoulders, hands clasping his nape as he bent his head and kissed her. Lightly.

Raising his head, he looked down at her. She couldn't read his expression, couldn't see his eyes well enough to gauge his mood, but she thought it was serious. "Have you heard something about Kirkwell?"

The question seemed to surprise him.

Shifting his mind from the track, courtesy of his mother's suggestion, it had started down, Roscoe took a few seconds to refocus. "No." After a moment, he added, "Not about Kirkwell." Roderick's abduction was a much safer topic.

Miranda widened her eyes. "About Kempsey and Dole?"

He nodded. "I told you I had men checking in Birmingham. Given the Kempsey and Dole families' state of alert, my men have had to be exceedingly careful, but so far no one's sighted either Kempsey or Dole in the city. And they're not at the cottage any longer—it's deserted."

She studied his face. "I take it I shouldn't assume they've gone back to London."

"They've been sighted near various inns, along certain roads—the sorts of places you'd expect to see them if they were searching for Roderick." For him and her, too. "But you don't need to worry." Stepping back, he shrugged out of his coat, then moved to toss it over a chair. "We're safe here. There are eyes and ears all around the estate—if, or perhaps when, Kempsey and Dole start sniffing around here, I'll know, and we'll be ready. And no, don't ask, 'Ready how?'—I haven't yet decided."

She'd followed him deeper into the room. "About Kirkwell—when do you expect to hear from London?"

"Within the next day or two. Mudd and Rawlins are coordinating the efforts there—they'll come and report as soon as they learn anything definite." Cuffs unlaced, he undid his waistcoat, shrugged the garment off, and tossed it on top of his coat.

Reached for her again and she came, placing her palms on his chest and running them upward, over the upper slope of his chest to curve about his shoulders. He bent his head and she stretched up; cupping his nape in a caress he now associated with her, she offered her mouth and he took. Lips merging, tongues stroking, then tangling, in instinctive harmony they started down their now-familiar road into passion's embrace.

His hands shaped her body, the lush curves of her breasts, the indentation of her waist, the flare of her hips, reimprinting her on him, him on her, stoking their flames. His fingers found her laces; hers slipped the pin from his cravat, deftly reanchoring the diamond in the folds, then unraveling them.

Their lips didn't part but supped, then, hungering, he pressed deeper and devoured, and tasted her growing urgency, her burgeoning desire, the tempo of her escalating arousal, something she wantonly—innocently—allowed on full display.

As always, she captured him; with her open and honest ardor, with her enthusiastic embrace of this, of him, of them, she snared him and held him captive, his mind and senses entirely focused on the simple act of having her. Loving her.

This time he fought against her tide, her siren's lure. The question in his mind, flaring insistently from the moment he'd touched her, was, What is this? Was it what he thought it was? Could it become what he hoped it might?

Most importantly, was she and this the route to his dream? That dream.

Or was it just a more intense liaison—an affair between two people who had somehow connected in a more intimate way, on a somewhat different plane than the norm? Different, but not special.

He kissed her and wondered, then drew a deeper breath and plunged into her mouth, claimed and sought, and she kissed him back with building urgency until between them the flames ignited and rose.

Heat spread, insidiously urgent, beneath their skins. Desire rode, hungry and needy, in its wake.

So many questions and the answers . . . some of the answers, surely, lay here, between them. In what flared between them.

They stood pressed together, pressing close and closer, mouths communing hungrily in the dark, hands searching out the places most sensitive to caress, to pressure. To the evocation of pleasure.

Arousing, yes, but possessive as well, and it wasn't only he whose touch carried that telltale stamp.

But this time he needed more, more than mere surrender, more than possession. He needed revelation.

How to gain that he didn't know. He stood in the whirl-pool of their needs, feeling the maelstrom tug at him, and fought to find the path to enlightenment through the swirl-ing, beckoning enticements.

The first time they'd come together, in the hotel room in the aftermath of danger, her wish to taste passion—a wish she'd already had, but that had been sharpened to need by the threat and their escape—had combined with his own re-sponse to that danger and swept them both into the fire.

The second time, here in this bed, she'd reached for him, wanted him, and he'd been driven to simply be with her, to soothe and comfort and share the triumph of having suc-cessfully rescued Roderick and brought him to safety.

The third time . . . he'd needed her to declare she wanted him, and she had. Since then, indulging in their mutual pas-sion, exercising their complementary desires, feeding the other's hunger, had become an uncomplicated progression.

But tonight . . . tonight he wrested control of his senses from the all-consuming act, held tight to his wits and dove into the engagement wanting to see, to uncover and learn . . . more. To see what lay beneath their passion. To learn what gave it such unprecedented strength, what lent their mutual desire such irresistible power.

With her laces dangling, he slid her gown off her shoul-ders, bared the delicate curves—had to bend his head and taste. She shivered, and pushed the halves of his shirt wide, spread her hands on his chest and, devoured by touch, greed-ily explored and claimed.

He drew the gown down; his hands occupied, he caught the ribbon ties of her chemise in his teeth, tugged them free, then followed the downward slide of the fine silk with his lips.

Heard her gasp. The evocative sound was all encouragement and delight. Her fingers tangled in his hair and held him to her as he cruised his lips over the firm mounds of her breasts, circled, then settled his mouth over one furled nipple, licked, slowly laved, then drew the tight bud into his mouth and suckled.

Her head tipped back and she clung, gasped again.

He immersed himself in the moment, devoted himself to drawing a moan of surrender—sweet and low—from her throat. She was so vibrantly alive, supple and giving under his hands, flagrantly urging him on, a full partner in their game.

He wanted to strip her bare, not just her body, but her heart—if he could, her soul. Wanted to see what it was that brought her so passionately to his arms. Wanted to reach deeper within himself and answer the complementary question.

Instead . . . under his hands, her gown and chemise slid to the floor. Her hands pushed his shirt from his shoulders; he surrendered to her insistent tugs and released her long enough to strip his arms from the sleeves.

While he did, she reached for the placket of his trousers, slid the buttons free, slipped her hand inside and found him.

Caressed and adored that painfully rigid part of him.

He gritted his teeth, hissed in a breath, but it was too late.

Despite his intentions, despite his determination, his senses slipped their leash and his wits sank, subsumed beneath a wave of explicit, unadulterated sensation, while between them passion's fires raged and cindered his every thought.

She stepped free of her crumpled gown, leaving her slippers behind; without thought, without conscious direction, he toed off his shoes, stepped out of his trousers, and their bodies met.

Both felt the jolt, that scintillating senses-stopping moment of contact, of skin meeting naked skin with nerves so aroused and so close to the surface they sizzled.

Miranda drew in a tight breath; wits flown, senses reeling,

she yet marveled—could not do otherwise. This was still so new, so utterly compelling—this moment when he, and this, became her everything.

She wrapped her arms about him, surrendered her mouth to him, pressed naked against him, and let the flames have them.

She'd never defined the man of her dreams, but he was with her now, conjured in the flesh—in the heavy muscles of his chest and the crinkly dark hair that pressed against her breasts and abraded the sensitive tips, sending heat and sensation lancing through her. The powerful muscles of his thighs, his narrow hips and waist, the ridges of his abdomen, surrounded and impressed, male to her female, hardness to her softness, angles to her curves. Above all he was power and strength, dark beauty, and virile masculinity.

He was everything she'd never known enough about to dream.

And he was hers, tonight. Hers to welcome in the moonlight. Hers to draw to her bed, to enfold in her arms and take into her body.

And suddenly—suddenly—there was no more time.

He lifted her, hoisted her against him; instinctively she wrapped her legs around his waist.

Felt his erection nudge into her slick softness; hauling in a breath, she eased down and he pushed up.

Slowly, he slid inside her; slowly, she engulfed him in her heat.

Took him in.

When he was fully seated within her, she could only cling and tremble, all but overwhelmed by the feel of him there, somehow so much clearer to her senses this way.

Then he grasped her hips and lifted her, drew her up until she almost lost the fullness of him, but then he reversed and drew her down, thrust up, and glorious sensation surged through her.

Tipping her head back on a half gasp, half sob, from under heavy lids she met his eyes, burning and sure behind the screen of his lashes. She looked for only a second, needed only that to see, to sense that the fury of the fire within him was every bit the equal of that inside her . . . then she offered him her mouth and he angled his head and took.

And lifted her again.

And again, filling her to a slow, then escalating rhythm; filling her mouth to an echoing beat, he waltzed her into the glorious fire, kept her there, whirling ever faster, ever more desperately burning in the flames until ecstasy fractured her tension and reality split and she shattered.

Sensation poured through her, down every nerve, glory sliding, heavy and golden, down every vein.

Lips parting from his, she hauled in a huge breath; barely sentient, she registered him still hard, rigid and heavy within her.

She felt him carry her the few paces to the bed. Supporting her with one arm, he hauled back the covers, then knelt on the bed and laid her down.

Followed her down, the connection between them unbroken. Settling his hips between her thighs, with one hand keeping her legs curled about his waist he thrust harder and deeper, sinking fully into her.

Then he rode her to glory.

Into the all-consuming heart of passion's fire.

Within seconds, she rose again, rode with him again. The landscape of desire, of passion and need, flashed past, given reality in their panting breaths, in the greedy grasp of their fingers.

Hearts thundering they raced to the lip of oblivion—seconds later they soared, bodies locked, hearts entwined, into a universe of scintillating ecstasy.

Into the mind-shattering pleasure of completion.

Then they fell.

Satiation caught them, buoyed them, carried them away on its golden tide.

Eventually it receded, and left them, hearts barely slow-ing, pulses still pounding, wracked and tangled in each other's arms, on that blissful, peaceful shore.

How long it was before he found his wits again he had no clue. When he could think again, could sort the impulses from his senses into coherent form again, he still lingered—in her embrace, clinging to the moment for just an instant more . . .

Which, he supposed, answered his question.

Did he want this—more of this? Yes.

Would he hold on to it if he could?

Yes.

For how long, if he had the choice?

Forever.

The word resonated in his brain, powerful and sure. Certain.

Easing their slick bodies apart, lifting from her, he reached down to snag the covers and flick them over them both, then he settled alongside her and drew her into his arms.

She made a soft, richly sated sound, one that sank to his marrow and soothed. As his arms closed around her and he let himself sink into the waiting sea, he acknowledged the revelation he'd gained.

That much he'd learned. That much he knew.

What he might do with the knowledge was another matter.

Chapter Thirteen

The next morning, Miranda stepped out of Roderick's room and found Roscoe lounging in the corridor.

As she closed the door, he pushed away from the wall. "I wondered . . . do you ride? Edwina, Henry, and I are heading out for an hour or two." Eyes on her face, he cocked his head. "Would you like to join us?"

She beamed. "I'd love to—and my maid remembered to pack my riding habit." A trunk of her clothes and another of Roderick's had arrived the day before.

He stepped aside, then followed as she headed for her room next door. "I'll help."

He undid her laces, then watched her don the lacey blouse that went beneath her brown velvet jacket. The skirt was of more serviceable twill, but the rich color suited her.

Finally straightening from rummaging in the trunk for her riding gloves, she turned to join him by the door and saw his gaze riveted on her hips. She waited until he raised his eyes, slowly, to her face, then arched a brow.

He held her gaze for a moment, then stepped back, holding the door. As she passed him, he murmured, "Later."

She smiled and led the way down the corridor.

Edwina and Henry were waiting, already mounted, in the stable yard. A strong black gelding she'd seen Roscoe riding snorted and stamped, while a neat chestnut mare sidled alongside. She walked confidently up to the mare, stroked her nose, smiled at the lad holding her reins. "What's her name?"

"Pippin, ma'am. 'Cause she loves 'em."

"Thank you." Meeting the horse's dark eye, Miranda stroked her long nose one last time. "Well, Pippin, we'd better get on, or that nasty brute alongside will be in an even worse temper."

She turned to find Roscoe waiting to lift her to her saddle. She'd always used a mounting block, had never been lifted by a man before. Another new experience courtesy of him; she stepped closer, felt his hands grip her waist, then he hoisted her up . . . and set her gently down atop the mare.

Stifling a giddy impulse to gasp, she managed a breathless "Thank you," then busied herself slipping her boots into the stirrups, rearranging her skirt, then, senses subsiding, picked up the reins.

By then Roscoe had swung up to the restless black's back. His gaze swept her, assessing her posture, her seat, her hands on the reins, then, apparently satisfied, he tipped his head to the stable arch and led the way out.

The ride was an hour of simple pleasures, of unfettered freedom thundering over the fields, galloping down rides and paths, over hill and dale, with no agenda other than enjoyment. They reined in a few times to take stock, to admire their surroundings, exchange grins and comments.

At one such pause atop a small hill, Henry, beside Roscoe, pointed to a farm nestled in the valley below. "Croft has asked if he can extend his fields under plough to include the wild meadow there."

Roscoe looked. "There aren't any other farms in that valley, so"—he glanced at Henry—"why not?"

Henry nodded. "That's what I thought. Croft's young, and

he and his wife have just had their first child. And he's been an excellent tenant so far—he took over the place from his uncle just before the old man died."

"Always a good idea to encourage good tenants." Roscoe gathered his reins. "Why don't you take it up—make the decision, see it through the process, the amendment to the tenant agreement, and so on?"

"Can I?"

"If I say you can, you can—I'll have a word to old Draper. Now you've finished school, you should start picking up the estate reins. Legally you still have to operate under my aegis, but that doesn't mean you can't start cutting your teeth."

Henry looked nothing short of thrilled.

As they cantered on, Miranda, riding with Edwina a little way behind the two males, had time to dwell on the responsibility Roscoe shouldered with respect to his nephew's estate. All who lived on it, who were dependent on it, were dependent on him—on his making the right, proper, and fair decisions.

While he'd been establishing himself as London's gambling king, he'd simultaneously carried that burden, and from all she'd seen, all she'd gleaned, he'd been effective and successful. Quietly, without fuss.

The same way he worked as Roscoe, the same way he worked through the Philanthropy Guild. That was his hallmark, it seemed—that quiet, self-effacing giving.

Encouraged by Roscoe's suggestion, throughout the rest of the ride Henry kept his gelding alongside Roscoe's and raised several other estate matters he'd clearly been mulling over. Roscoe was surprised only in that he hadn't realized how absorbed with the estate Henry already was. That was, in fact, a relief; from his questions, it was clear Henry was eager to engage and, even at a minor level, start to manage his birthright.

George, Roscoe reflected, had never been that anchored.

While part of him felt a swelling satisfaction over Henry's direction, another part noted that, with respect to Ridgware, this heralded the beginning of the end for himself. Over the next ten years, he would increasingly surrender the reins into Henry's hands, until, at twenty-five, Henry would take on full responsibility. Roscoe might remain in the background, but he wouldn't be the one making the decisions; the responsibility would no longer rest on his shoulders.

But he was no longer the hedonistic Lord Julian Delbraith; the man he now was would need something to take Ridgware's place.

Some other responsibility to fill his private life.

As they cantered into the stable yard, he glanced at Miranda—at the light in her eyes, the color in her cheeks, the wisps of hair the wind had teased loose. And sensed, yet again, that his life was changing, shifting.

The grooms came running to take the horses. Cribbs, the oldest, caught the black's reins. "Yer men from Lunnon are here, m'lord. Asked us to tell you."

"Thank you." He swung down from the saddle and walked to where the chestnut mare stood waiting; reaching up, he lifted Miranda down. Keeping his hands about her waist, he looked into her wide eyes. "With luck, they might have news of Kirkwell."

Miranda halted in the front hall and looked down at her skirts. "I need to change."

Roscoe nodded. "We'll be in the library—join us when you have."

Rushing up the stairs, she debated telling Roderick, but he hadn't yet attempted the stairs, and Entwhistle had advised against it for at least another day . . . she raced into her room. "We can tell him later."

Shutting the door, she struggled out of her habit.

Five minutes later, in a day gown of fine, amber-colored wool with embroidered ribbon about the neckline and hem, her hair neat again, she walked into the library.

The four men present, not about the desk but seated on the twin sofas before the fireplace, all rose. Going forward, she recognized Jordan Draper, Mudd, and Rawlins; she inclined her head and the three politely bowed.

Roscoe waved her to the sofa beside him. "We've been discussing other matters, but now you're here . . ." She sat and the men resumed their seats. Roscoe looked at Mudd and Rawlins. "What have we learned about Kempsey, Dole, and Kirkwell?"

Rawlins looked grimly disgusted. "Kirkwell's proving to be a mystery man. We asked all around the Hood and Gable again—the tavern where he hired Kempsey and Dole. We thought perhaps we'd catch him visiting, waiting for word, but no. And no one there or anywhere around could tell us any more about him."

"Fact is," Mudd put in, "that other than when he was there hiring Kempsey and Dole, no one in the neighborhood has seen or heard of him, not even heard his name—he's not a local nor a regular in the area."

Roscoe's lips thinned. "More and more I suspect that Kirkwell won't be his real name."

The other men nodded.

Mudd stirred. "As for Kempsey and Dole, they haven't re-appeared in London, so we called in at Birmingham as we came past and got the latest, but they haven't been sighted there, not since they left with Mr. Clifford. Some of their male relatives did come puffing back—that would've been after you'd rescued Mr. Clifford. Lots of grumbling and growling, but seems they've left Kempsey and Dole to sort things out for themselves."

"So unless Kempsey and Dole summon help, they'll be on their own?" Roscoe asked.

"Seems like they generally operate on their own," Rawlins said. "The rest of the family will hide them or warn them, but otherwise don't get involved in their schemes—at least not this sort."

"Good." After a moment of thought, Roscoe refocused on Mudd and Rawlins. "Anything else I need to hear about?"

Rawlins reported, "Mrs. Selwidge sent word that they

hadn't seen Lord Treloar, so everyone there's relieved, and there's nothing else that's come up since you left town."

"In the matter of Lord Treloar," Jordan said, "I checked at the other clubs. He tried to gain entry, to slide in with a group of his cronies, at two other clubs in Mayfair, but after being turned away—just him, not his friends—he hasn't darkened any of your doors."

"We can hope he's learned his lesson." Roscoe looked at Mudd and Rawlins. "While we're here, you can assist Mr. Clifford should he need any assistance getting about, but otherwise I want you on guard, keeping watch. You know the people here, you know the place. You know its weaknesses."

Mudd and Rawlins nodded, to Miranda's eyes rather eagerly.

Roscoe waved a dismissal. "Wander around, talk to Cater and the staff, re-familiarize yourselves with the house and grounds, and the position of Clifford's room. I'll speak with you later."

Mudd and Rawlins got to their feet.

Given Kempsey and Dole were very likely scouring the countryside for Roderick, Miranda was relieved to know that Mudd and Rawlins, both large and capable, would be rambling around. She rose. "I'll show you my brother's room." She met Roscoe's eyes as he and Jordan politely stood. "I'll tell Roderick the latest, and that he can ask Mudd and Rawlins for assistance—especially if he wants to come downstairs tomorrow."

Roscoe nodded. "Do."

She noticed him exchange a glance—one carrying some indefinable meaning—with Mudd and Rawlins as she turned away, but the two large men dutifully fell in at her heels as she led the way from the room.

"Do you really think Kempsey and Dole will track Roderick—and you and me—here?"

Finishing unlacing Miranda's evening gown, Roscoe

turned aside. "I have no real notion what they might do." Withdrawing the pin from his cravat, he laid it on the dresser. "But as they haven't yet returned to their London haunts, then either they're out there trying to hunt Roderick down, or they've slunk away to avoid Kirkwell's displeasure. Which option they've chosen depends on Kirkwell and the details of the deal they struck with him."

Given Kempsey and Dole's reputation, he knew which option he was wagering on, which was why Mudd and Rawlins were presently patrolling the woods around the house.

"Hmm." Miranda shook out the gown and reached for a hanger. "After a week of calm, the kidnapping is starting to feel like a distant dream—fading like a nightmare."

Having already dispensed with his coat and waistcoat, he looked down to unbutton his cuffs. Dinner was long over, and the house had settled into the comfortable quiet of a usual night; it was too large a house to ever be completely silent, and owls and foxes hunted in the woods, occasionally hooting or barking, but even though, these days, he spent only a handful of nights there each year, the place had changed little since it had been his home—he recognized every creak, every sound.

It was soothing to be there, and, strangely, in some way he didn't understand, it was even more soothing to be there with her, undressing and getting ready for bed.

He'd never indulged in this degree of domesticity with any previous lover. As it was . . . he found the moments a subtle pleasure. The interlude wasn't dispassionate, but rather passion was held in abeyance, the promise of it inherent in the situation, yet with it held back, restrained . . . but only temporarily. Only until they consented to let it off the leash.

His lips curved in anticipation. That was one of the aspects that made the moment so oddly delectable—the sure and certain knowledge of what was to come.

"Edwina told me you usually only visit here for a few days each year. Don't you find it difficult to manage the estate—

all the decisions you have to make in Henry's name—from London?"

He glanced at her—and his mouth went dry. His mind blanked. His tongue stilled, wouldn't move, as he watched her draw her chemise off over her head, then, letting the delicate shimmering silk slip from her fingers to drape over the dressing stool, she glided, graceful and naked in the moonlight, to the bed. She lifted the covers and slid beneath.

Only as she settled and sent a shadowed, questioning glance his way was he able to draw breath and think again. What had she asked?

Peeling off his shirt, he dropped it on a chair. "I grew up here—as a boy I spent a lot of time out and about the estate." Toeing off his shoes, he unbuttoned his trousers. "I wasn't groomed to be duke, as George was, but in some ways my knowledge of the farms was more practical, more in-depth, than his." Looking down, he stripped off his trousers and stockings. "And after George's death, I was blessed with excellent help—Jordan's father was and still is the estate's man of business. He was and continues to be a godsend."

Finally naked, he walked toward the bed.

She watched him approach, her gaze tracking down his body. Her lips curved as she asked, her tone increasingly distant, "Is that why you hired Jordan—in recognition of his father's sterling service?"

"No. I hired Jordan because he's even better than his father." He raised the covers, paused to look down at her, studying her face, her bare shoulders and arms, the cascading bounty of her hair.

Miranda looked up at him, gloriously naked in the night, allowed her eyes to swiftly devour, then she let her smile speak for her and held up her arms, fingers boldly beckoning.

He got into bed, shifted gracefully into her arms, and covered her lips with his.

And in perfect accord they let passion loose, set it free to ravage them. Savage them. And gloried.

They came together without shields or screens, in an open

communication they had, from their first night together, instinctively reached for and now compulsively sought, giving and taking without reservation.

Their delight was there in her smothered gasp as his hand closed over her breast, strong fingers kneading while his thumb cruised her nipple. There in his harsher breaths as her hands splayed over his chest, then swept down to caress.

Mutual pleasure resonated in the shivery sound she exhaled, one filled with anticipation and delight, as he slid into her and made them whole.

They rode to completion, through the fire and the glory to where ecstasy shattered them, glory blinded them, and sensation ruled both body and mind, while freed, their souls soared.

Later, much later, drifting in the haze of aftermath, she recognized and acknowledged how happy and content she was in that moment. How the joy and the closeness of being in his arms, of joining with him and then savoring this glowing consequence, filled her to the exclusion of all else.

There, in that moment, nothing else mattered. Through the heated minutes, skin to damp skin, through the gasps, the soft cries, the groans—through the desperation, through the unbounded, unrestrained togetherness—she knew him and he knew her in ways far deeper and more all-encompassing than the mere biblical meaning.

She might not yet know how he'd come to be him—how and why Julian had transformed to Roscoe—but it was Roscoe in whose arms she lay, whose heart thudded solidly beneath her ear, and she trusted him implicitly. Trusted that if she needed to know, he would tell her.

This may be temporary—theirs only for a few weeks, perhaps only for a few more days—but for however long they had, she would embrace this, would embrace him.

And hold their reality to her heart.

Chapter Fourteen

The following evening, Roderick finally came downstairs to join the company for dinner. Lucasta and Caroline made much of him, and Edwina and Henry were curious, leaving Sarah, Roscoe, and Miranda to watch indulgently as Roderick strove to polish his manners and reply appropriately to a dowager, a duchess, a duke, and a duke's daughter.

They were halfway through dinner before Roderick truly accepted that no one expected to stand on any ceremony; thereafter he relaxed and the conversation flowed more freely.

At the conclusion of the meal, Roscoe suggested that rather than join the ladies in the drawing room the three males should retire to the billiards room. While Henry eagerly seconded the motion and Roderick looked grateful, neither Miranda nor Sarah was keen to allow Roderick out of their sight for too long. In the end, the three younger ladies followed the gentlemen down the long corridor to the billiards room at the end of the west wing.

Roscoe glanced at the windows, uncurtained to the night, then looked at Roderick. His left arm was still in a sling, but he was right-handed; although his progress down the stairs had been slow and heavily assisted by Rawlins, Roderick had otherwise been managing well enough on the single crutch he could properly wield. Roscoe arched his brows. "Are you up for a game?"

Roderick considered, then lightly shrugged. "I'm not sure—let's try it and see."

At first, Miranda sat on a bench flanked by Sarah and Edwina; all three watched the play while simultaneously discussing the various forms of gilt invitations. But after one game, when it was clear that by leaning against the table, Roderick could manage creditably well, Henry suggested they join in, making a three-way game of paired partners.

The three ladies exchanged glances, then as one rose to meet the challenge. Edwina paired with Henry, and Sarah with Roderick, leaving Miranda to partner Roscoe.

The resulting game contained more laughter, more jokes and good-natured teasing than any serious intention to win. A delightful and oftimes hilarious hour passed, culminating in the realization that no one had remembered to keep proper score.

While they were all claiming victory, the clocks throughout the house started chiming.

"Eleven o'clock." Miranda looked at Roderick; so, too, did Sarah. "I'm sure Entwhistle would say you should have retired long since."

Roderick grinned. "Doubtless he would, but don't worry." He reclaimed his crutch. "Mudd and Rawlins will help me upstairs." He paused, then said, "It would probably be best if you ladies went up first."

Roscoe crossed to the bellpull. He caught Miranda's eye as he tugged. "Indeed—you three go up. Henry and I will supervise."

Realizing that if Roderick's progress back up the stairs caused him pain he might not want Sarah to see, and that if she didn't retire, Sarah wouldn't either, Miranda inclined her head. "Very well." She glanced at Sarah; Edwina had already moved to the door. "Let's leave them to it." Glancing back at the men, she raised a hand in benediction. "Good night."

They chorused their good nights, and the ladies left. Climbing the stairs with Edwina and Sarah, Miranda wondered how long Roderick's ascent would take, and how long it would be before Roscoe joined her.

Deftly loading a pistol at the table in the gun room, Roscoe aimed an interrogatory glance at Mudd and Rawlins. "You're sure they didn't see you?"

Rawlins shook his head. "Nah—they're down in that hollow, sitting tight." He tipped his head to Roderick. "They could see their target large as life, moving around the billiard table. Seems they've taken the bait."

Mudd and Rawlins had picked up Kempsey and Dole's trail early that morning, when the pair had slunk onto Ridgware lands. Despite their size, Roscoe's bodyguards were expert trackers, used to slipping through shadows in the lanes and alleys of the capital, yet equally at home in woods or fields. They'd tracked Kempsey and Dole into the woods bordering the gardens on the west side of the mansion, then reported to him, and he'd devised their plan.

"Right, then." Satisfied with the pistol he'd primed, he handed it to Henry. "*You* have only one goal—to keep Edwina, your mother, and your grandmother safe. I doubt you'll need to use that"—he glanced at the pistol Henry was checking—"but carry it just in case. The most important thing is to keep your aunt, your mother, and your grandmother confined to the family wing. If by some chance Kempsey and Dole get free in the house, we don't want them running into any stray females they might think to use as hostages."

Henry nodded, grimly determined. "Once they're in their beds, I'll sit in the corridor just up from their rooms."

"Good." Roscoe looked at Mudd and Rawlins; they were expertly loading the pistols he'd given them earlier. "You know your positions."

Mudd nodded. "We'll let them get past us, then close in from behind. Cater's got the footmen on alert to cordon off the sides of the house once they hear the ruckus, and the stable lads and grooms will do the same, closing in behind us once we move in."

Roscoe smiled intently. "Once Kempsey and Dole come out of the woods, one way or another, we'll have them."

Roderick pocketed the pistol Roscoe had handed him, then grasped his crutch. "I'd better get upstairs and let them see me at the window."

Roscoe pushed away from the table. "You might need to go out on the balcony, just to make sure." He opened the door, waited for everyone to file out, then followed.

Henry glanced at him. "Aren't you going to take a pistol yourself?"

Roscoe's lips curved predatorially. "Like Kempsey and Dole, I prefer knives."

Mudd muttered something. Rawlins snorted.

Unperturbed, Roscoe waved Henry on and followed.

Miranda jerked awake to a resounding crash.

She'd leapt from the bed before she realized she'd been alone in it; Roscoe was nowhere to be seen.

Sounds of an altercation echoed through the house—from the direction of Roderick's room next door.

Hauling her nightgown over her head, she swiped up her robe, flung it on and belted it, grabbed the poker from the fireplace, and rushed to the door. Flinging it open, she raced into the corridor.

The door of Roderick's room stood open. She dashed in, raising the poker—and came face-to-white-face with Sarah.

"Oh!" Sarah swallowed, then waved at the bed. "He's not here!"

Lowering the poker, Miranda stared at the bed—pristine, unrumpled.

A muffled thud and a rough oath reached them; she and Sarah looked at each other. "Next room along." Miranda whirled, but Sarah was faster and shot out of the door first.

On a muttered curse, she followed the younger woman. Sarah had thrown a knitted shawl over her nightgown; the gown flapped like a white flag as Sarah raced down the corridor toward the increasing din, then flung open the next door and ran into the room.

"*Aaah!*"

The short scream halted Miranda as she reached the doorway. Standing in the shadows, she stared into the room.

Into a scene of pandemonium. She took it all in in a single glance. Ahead and to the left, Roscoe had been fighting with Kempsey, both men brandishing wicked-looking knives. Roderick wasn't in the bed but sitting on its left side, across the covers holding a menacing Dole at bay with a pistol and one crutch wedged awkwardly under his other arm.

The right side of this room opened onto a balcony, and the French door stood open; that was how Kempsey and Dole had got in. But there was barely any light. There should have been moonlight streaming through the wide windows, but the night had turned cloudy. All the figures in the nightmare scene were nothing more than dense shadows in the dimness.

And Sarah had rushed straight into the fray.

Kempsey had grabbed Sarah and was now using her as a shield. Even as all she'd seen crashed into Miranda's mind, Kempsey raised his knife's edge to a panicked Sarah's throat and growled at Roscoe, "Stand down! Or I'll cut her."

Roscoe cursed and eased back.

Kempsey shifted, effortlessly dragging Sarah with him. He looked at the bed. "Put down the pistol."

Kempsey's back was to the door.

Miranda raised the poker and rushed in.

Kempsey sensed her coming. He whirled and flung Sarah at her.

Miranda gasped and jerked the poker higher, away from Sarah. The younger woman crashed into her and they fell in a tangle of nightgowns, robe, shawl, and flailing limbs.

Curses, both clipped and guttural, fell on her ears, then Kempsey loomed close. One huge, hamlike hand reached for her arm—

Roscoe flung himself at Kempsey, sending the man staggering back from Miranda and Sarah. Regaining his balance, he planted himself between Kempsey and the women, then smiled.

Kempsey roared and rushed him—and at last it was on.

Roscoe was distantly aware of Miranda moving, of her and Sarah scrambling into the corner where he'd been hiding. Good. That left him free to give his full attention to the matter before him. He set out to beat Kempsey, but to keep the man alive.

Kempsey, on the other hand, wanted him dead.

They feinted and clashed, knives slicing, thrusting. In full light, it would have been a deadly game; in the unexpected darkness, even with his eyes fully adjusted, the engagement was lethal madness.

Kempsey wasn't bad. He was better, but he wanted a certain outcome, was prepared to wait, to sustain the odd nick or slash to get it.

Her heart in her throat, Miranda watched them fight, but then Dole stirred. He eased back, edging not toward Roderick but around the bed toward the knife fight.

"Stay where you are!" Roderick hoarsely ordered.

Dole, his eyes on Roderick, continued to stealthily drift down the bed.

Roderick's pistol roared.

Clapping a hand to his arm, Dole swore, then he focused on Roderick, snarled, and started toward him.

"No!" Sarah sprang to her feet beside Roderick.

Grimly Roderick switched the pistol into his less useful left hand, and, with his right raised the crutch, jabbing the end at Dole, making him weave.

Putting a hand on the ground to push herself up, Miranda found the second crutch. "Here!" She lifted it.

Sarah grabbed it, then holding the crutch firmly in both

hands, she leapt onto the bed alongside Roderick and started raining blows on Dole's head.

Miranda left her to it. Rising, gripping the poker tightly, she clung to the deep shadows by the wall. Watching Roscoe and Kempsey, she circled, waiting for an opening.

Roscoe seemed intent on drawing Kempsey closer, but the big man fought wary of the wicked-looking knife Roscoe held in his right hand. Then Kempsey abruptly charged, trying to overwhelm Roscoe by sheer weight.

Miranda stepped in, swinging the poker in a sideways slash—just as Kempsey, denied by Roscoe, sprang back. The poker connected with Kempsey's skull, but in a glancing blow. The big man started to turn toward her.

Stepping closer, Roscoe dropped his knife, grabbed Kempsey's knife hand, and plowed his fist into Kempsey's jaw.

Kempsey blinked, dazedly shook his head.

Roscoe hit him again. And finally Kempsey's eyes rolled back, and he crumpled and went down.

Satisfied, Roscoe shot a look at Miranda, but she was standing, both hands still gripping the lowered poker, staring down at Kempsey—as if daring him to try to rise again.

Two burly figures rushed in through the balcony door. They hesitated for only an instant, taking in the scene, then they fell on Dole, still trying to push past the flailing crutches; within seconds the pair had subdued him.

Roscoe looked at the bed, saw Sarah, still balancing on it, lower her impromptu weapon. Inwardly shaking his head, he bent and undid Kempsey's belt, then heaved the man over and used the belt to cinch his hands.

He glanced over to where Rawlins, watched by Mudd, was performing the same office for Dole. "What the devil took you so long?"

It was Mudd who, after a moment's hesitation, replied, "You know that trellis we were supposed to climb up?"

"What of it?"

"It broke. Must've been weakened by these two scram-

bling up it. Came down on our heads the instant we tried it.
We had to fetch ropes and grapples."

Roscoe straightened. "The best-laid plans . . . but at least
we've got them both, and, I think, no harm taken?"

Sarah had collapsed beside Roderick, her head down on
her raised knees. Roderick had his arms around her. He quietly asked her if she was all right. She didn't look up, but her
pale head nodded. Roderick looked at Roscoe. "My arm's
sore, but I didn't take a scratch. You?"

Roscoe checked the sleeve on his left forearm. "My coat
took the worst of it. Maybe a scratch or two, nothing of any
significance." He looked at Miranda.

She met his gaze. "Like Sarah. Nothing more than a
bruise from when we fell." Even through the dimness, he
saw her frown. "We should clean those scratches."

He looked down at the figure laid out on the floor between
them and felt his face harden. "Later."

Later, once he'd got the roiling—whatever it was evoked
by seeing Kempsey go after her—under some semblance of
control.

"Let's get these two into appropriate accommodations."
Going to the door, he opened it and looked out. "Cater?"

"Here, my lord." Apprised of their plan, the butler had
remained on duty throughout.

"Did His Grace have any trouble?"

"Not as such, my lord. The dowager's and duchess's
apartments were too distant from the noise. They weren't
disturbed. Lady Edwina did come out, but His Grace persuaded her that you had the matter in hand and would not
appreciate her interference. She subsequently retreated."

"Excellent. Please tell His Grace that the excitement is
over, and that he may now retire in good order."

"Yes, my lord. Do you wish the miscreants to be locked
in the cellar?"

"No." Roscoe turned to see Rawlins forcibly steering Dole
to the door. Mudd bent and hoisted Kempsey, still unconscious, over one shoulder. "The storeroom off the stable has

been prepared to receive them—they can cool their heels in there."

"Very good, my lord. I will convey your message to His Grace." Cater bowed and withdrew.

Roscoe held the door for Rawlins and Dole to pass through, followed by Mudd lugging Kempsey's unconscious form.

Roscoe glanced at Roderick and Sarah. Both were on their feet, although who was supporting whom he couldn't have said. Miranda was watching the pair, too. She hesitated, but didn't cross to help her brother.

Reaching out, Roscoe caught her hand, drew her to him, then steered her out of the door.

She sighed. Poker swinging by her side, her other hand locked in his, she walked beside him back along the corridor, past the open door of Roderick's room and on to the door of hers.

Behind them, they heard Sarah and Roderick go into Roderick's room. The door didn't close, but Roscoe had other things on his mind than helping Roderick into bed. Sarah would manage that well enough.

The tension inside him had subsided somewhat, yet it was still there, simmering beneath his surface. It wasn't going to simply fade away, not anytime soon, not while he could remember that moment when, poker raised, Miranda had rushed into the dim room. The image was indelibly imprinted on his brain, along with the impossibly sharp spike of raw fear it had evoked.

Lips tightening, he set her door swinging open, followed her through, pushed the door closed behind him, then with his grip on her hand, he pulled her back, swinging around so that she landed with a soft "oof" with her back to the door and him directly before her. Holding her there. Trapping her there.

The poker clattered to the floor.

Her hands rising to his chest, she blinked at him, eyes wide, but calm assurance and clearheaded certainty were paramount in her expression.

He trapped and held her gaze, for a long moment let the tension thrum between them, then quietly said, "Don't *ever* rush into a fight like that again."

His tone was flat, unequivocal, an order—a warning—laced with command.

Her brows faintly arched. Her gaze didn't shift from his. "Don't get into a fight like that again, and I promise you I won't."

He narrowed his eyes, but her resolution didn't waver; if anything, her chin firmed. "Idiotic woman." His gaze lowered, fastened on her lips.

"Irritating man."

A heartbeat passed.

They moved.

His head swooped, she stretched up and their lips clashed in a kiss so ferocious, so greedy, so demanding and ravenous that it stole his breath.

Passion ignited. It didn't burn—it blazed.

His hands raced over her, sculpting, shaping, caressing.

He found the tie of her robe, yanked it free. She shrugged the garment off and flung herself at him.

His fingers brushed buttons, fumbled as, driven by desperation, he undid them. He heard something rip.

She didn't seem to care. She wriggled free of the nightgown, wrapped bare arms around his neck and kissed him as if she would devour him.

Then she fell on his clothes with the frantic ardor of a dervish.

Shedding garments, they swept across the room to the bed.

Naked at last, he took her down to the mattress. They sank together, bodies molding, melding. She wrapped her arms around him, arching to press her breasts against his chest, her legs wantonly tangling with his.

He took her mouth, plunged them both back into the wild kiss, and let passion and desire reign.

Her hands spread and seared him, stroked and drove him.

He drew her close, with a single thrust joined with her, and together, tongues tangling, fingers twining, they dropped the reins.

And let the flames have them.

Bodies desperately merging to an escalating beat, they let passion catch them, infuse them, and whip them ever on.

Celebrating the victory.

Exorcising the fear.

Glorying in their mad triumph over both.

The end, when it came—when it rose up and crashed over them—was cataclysmic. It shook him to his soul.

Shook him to see, to register and note how tightly she held him.

How compulsively, desperately, and unrelentingly he held on to her.

"Attempting to kill someone in a ducal house is a sure path to the gallows." Placing a chair with its back to Kempsey and Dole, who were perched on milking stools in the storeroom off the stable with their hands tied behind their backs, Roscoe straddled the chair and, folding his arms over the chair's back, regarded his prisoners with nothing more enervating than mild curiosity.

Mudd stood behind Kempsey, Rawlins behind Dole. Behind Roscoe, Roderick leaned on one crutch, his weight off his broken foot, his arm still in a sling due to his broken collarbone, and looked down with passable dispassion at the men who had injured him.

Flanking Roderick, and looking a lot less dispassionate, were Miranda, her arms crossed, her expression severe, and Sarah, one hand tucked in the crook of Roderick's arm.

Roscoe was pleased with his stage setting. The implication wasn't lost on Kempsey and Dole. Kempsey in particular eyed the three behind Roscoe with wary understanding before finally transferring his gaze to Roscoe's face.

Kempsey didn't say anything, just waited. Dole kept his eyes down, his gaze on the straw-strewn floor.

Inwardly smiling, Roscoe tipped his head to Kempsey. "A hanging offense, but one I'm in a position to see converted to transportation should you tell me all I wish to know."

Kempsey and Dole exchanged a glance, then Kempsey looked back at him. "What do you want to know?"

"Everything, every last little detail, you can tell me about Kirkwell."

The pair exchanged another glance, then Kempsey said, "If we tell you all we know, you'll guarantee we'll be transported, not hanged?"

Roscoe nodded.

"How do we know you'll keep your word?"

"You don't. However, there's really no reason for me to do otherwise. For all your talents, you are nothing more than tools. I want the man who hired you and have only a passing interest in you."

Kempsey and Dole appeared to have a wordless discussion, then Kempsey looked at him. "All right, but we don't know much."

Roscoe was wagering they knew more than they thought. "Describe Kirkwell."

The description Kempsey, with additional comments from Dole, gave was clearly of the same man Gallagher had described.

"Once you'd seized me, you sent word to him," Roderick said. "Where?"

"To the Hood and Gable—same place he hired us," Kempsey replied. "Cagey bastard, he was—we didn't have any other way to get in touch, but he wanted us to meet him there the next day to tell him we'd done the deed. Confirmation, and then he said he'd pay us the rest of the fee."

Roscoe let a moment go by, then smoothly asked, "Kirkwell paid you to seize and murder Mr. Clifford—do you have any notion, did you get any hints, as to why he wanted Mr. Clifford dead?"

Both men shook their heads. "We don't ask," Kempsey said. "It's bad for business, and dangerous, too."

"Indeed. Did Kirkwell specifically ask you to take Mr. Clifford out of London before you murdered him?"

"Nah—that was us covering our arses." Kempsey nodded at Roderick. "Kirkwell told us where he lived. He wanted us to kill him and leave his body somewhere near, where it was sure to be found."

"He specifically said he wanted the body found?" Roscoe asked.

Both men nodded. "Part of the instructions," Dole said.

Roscoe filed the information away. "So why didn't you follow Kirkwell's instructions and leave Mr. Clifford dead in Chichester Street?"

" 'Cause we were fairly sure Kirkwell didn't have the rest of the fee," Kempsey said. "Or if he did, he'd welch on the deal and not pay us anyway, just disappear. He could've been watching from that dark park for all we knew, or he could watch the tavern and see if we turned up the next day as arranged. If we did, chances were the deed was done—he could just leave and not pay us and we wouldn't know where to find him. It weren't like he was a local—someone others 'round about knew."

They did, indeed, know more than they thought. "Why," Roscoe asked, "did you think Kirkwell didn't have the money?"

Kempsey frowned. "A feeling. His coat was old, worn, shabby at the sleeves, but he behaved like he didn't notice—as if it were new out of Bond Street, if you know what I mean."

"He was a toff." Dole glanced at Roscoe. "Not a toff like you, but still a toff." Dole's dark eyes tracked to Roderick. "More like him, now I think of it."

Kempsey, also looking at Roderick, nodded. "Aye—we thought Kirkwell was a gentry-toff down on his luck. That's what he seemed like."

"All right." Roscoe reclaimed their attention. They might have been thugs, but they were thugs who'd lived to a decent age; he respected their instincts. They'd picked up the difference in station between him and Roderick quick enough. "How did you intend to ensure you got the rest of your fee?"

Kempsey shifted. "We figured that if Kirkwell wanted Clifford dead, then if Kirkwell didn't pay we could ransom Clifford back to his family and get the rest of our fee that way. So we kidnapped him"—Kempsey nodded at Roderick—"and took him out of London, then sent word with my uncle. He was to go to the Hood and Gable the next day, meet Kirkwell and tell him we had Clifford and would kill him and leave his body in Pimlico once Kirkwell paid the rest of the fee."

Roscoe nodded. "A reasonable plan. So what happened?"

"Don't know, do we? If Kirkwell paid up, my uncle was to send word to my brother in Birmingham and he'd come to the cottage and tell us, but after you found us and took Clifford, we've been searching all over, so we haven't heard a thing."

"Howsoever," Dole said, "if Kirkwell *had* paid up promptly, like an honest man, we'd've heard the day before you got to the cottage, and we'd've been on the road back to London with the body before you found us."

Kempsey, head down, was nodding. "Aye—if I were a betting man, I'd say Kirkwell didn't pay up."

"Was your uncle going to tell Kirkwell where you'd taken his prize?"

"Nah—we're not daft. He wasn't even going to let on we'd gone out of London—that was just us being cautious and setting things up so we could ransom Clifford more easily."

They'd been convinced Kirkwell didn't have their money. Roscoe considered, then asked, "Where can I find your uncle?"

Kempsey grew wary.

Roscoe sighed. "I have no interest in your uncle, only in what he can tell me. Whether Kirkwell got your message, and if so, what he said. Perhaps your uncle managed to follow him back to his lodgings—who knows?"

Kempsey looked down and said nothing.

After a moment, Roscoe softly said, "Our deal was for *all* I wished to know."

Kempsey's lips compressed, but after a moment, he mumbled, "Goodman's Yard, not far from the Tower."

"His name?"

Kempsey gave it.

There was little more to be had from the pair. Roscoe rose. "The constables will be here later today to take you off. If you give us, or them, any further trouble, our deal will evaporate and the gallows will be your fate."

Picking up the chair, he turned and, waving Roderick, Sarah, and Miranda before him, walked out.

Ten minutes later, they were all in the library, with Henry at the big desk penning a missive to the local magistrate, Lord Bramwell.

Standing before the fireplace, Roscoe spoke to Mudd and Rawlins. "You two start for London immediately. Find out what happened with Kempsey's uncle—see what he knows."

Mudd and Rawlins nodded.

Rawlins asked, "Will you be returning, too?"

"We'll set out tomorrow. Jordan's visiting his family today, but he'll be heading to town from Derby tomorrow, too."

"We'll tell Rundle." Mudd saluted and left with Rawlins.

Roderick caught Roscoe's eye. "Back to town?"

Roscoe nodded. "Entwhistle said you should be up to it." Walking to the sofa on which Miranda sat, facing the one on which Sarah and Roderick were seated, he sat and fixed his gaze on Roderick. "Consider this. Kirkwell hires Kempsey and Dole to kill you and leave your body where it's sure to be found. He wants you dead, and pronounced dead immediately, but he pays them only half their fee. Everything they and we now know suggests that Kirkwell didn't have the cash to pay the second half of the fee—I think Kempsey and Dole were correct in suspecting that. So Kirkwell is almost certainly still in London, and he's short of cash. So what was his most likely motive in arranging for your murder?"

Roderick frowned.

"Money," Roscoe supplied. "His most likely motive is money. And that's only made more likely by his stipulation that he wanted your body found. The only way anyone can profit from your death is for your estate to be passed to your heirs, and that will only happen with reasonable speed if your body is found and you are declared officially dead."

"But . . ." Roderick glanced at Miranda.

"But I'm his heir." Miranda looked at Roscoe. "We've been through this before."

"I know," he said. "But clearly we're missing some pertinent point. Regardless"—he met her gaze—"we've learned all we can here. The answers to the questions of who Kirkwell really is, and why he thinks he'll profit from Roderick's death, lie in London."

She searched his eyes, then nodded. "You're right." She looked at Roderick. "So tomorrow we set out."

To hunt down Kirkwell and make sure her not-so-little brother remained safe.

Chapter Fifteen

Later that morning, having consulted with Nurse on the various means they might employ to make traveling to London easier on Roderick, Miranda stepped out onto the terrace and drew in a long breath of crisp country air.

"Are you storing it up for when you return to London?"

She turned to see Lucasta step out of the door behind her, and smiled. "Yes. The country air smells so much nicer. Sweeter and richer."

"Indeed. I find the London air somewhat bitter." Joining Miranda, Lucasta waved down the steps. "Walk with me. We have half an hour before the luncheon gong sounds, and I understand we'll be losing your company tomorrow morning."

"Now Roderick is sufficiently recovered, we should get back." At the bottom of the steps, they set out, slowly strolling down the gravel path circling the wide lawn. "I must thank you again for your hospitality. Being able to take refuge here has been a godsend. Without the support of you and Caroline, and the household, Roderick's recovery would not have been so swift."

"As to that, my dear, it's truly been our pleasure." Lucasta smiled at her. "But if you wish to repay me, you may do so by indulging me. Are you and your aunt—and Roderick, too—fixed permanently in town?"

"At present, yes. Our intention is to remain until Roderick marries. Once he's settled, my aunt and I . . . well, we always assumed we'd move back to Oakgrove."

"And has your brother met any particular young lady in the capital?"

"No. Not yet." Sarah might be more than a friend in Roderick's eyes, but Miranda didn't know how their acquaintance might evolve.

"And what of yourself?" Lucasta cast her a curious look. "Oh, I know you will tell me that you're twenty-nine and growing quite dusty on your shelf, but I have eyes enough to see that for a certain type of more mature gentleman you would make an excellent wife."

She was tempted to obfuscate but . . . "I have had suitors—indeed, have a potential suitor at present—but we're both still considering if there's any point in him making me an offer." She was thinking of Wraxby, but as she said the words, she realized they might apply even more aptly to . . . Lucasta's son.

"Is that so?" After a moment, Lucasta added, as if in real puzzlement, "How strange. I would have thought that situated as you are, with, if I understood matters correctly, a comfortable portion and no other restriction to hinder you, that you, at least, would allow passion and regard to guide you . . . but forgive me." Lucasta placed a hand lightly on her arm. "I'm being insufferably nosy, a prerogative ladies of my age frequently exercise."

Unperturbed, Miranda smiled back. Nosy she could deal with; dictatorial dictating such as her aunt was wont to offer was another matter entirely.

"This, my dear, is a conversation I've had with each of my daughters—I hope you won't consider me overstepping the mark if I give you the same advice." Without waiting for any permission, Lucasta went on, "To secure happiness in her life, it is imperative for a lady to know her own mind, to define clearly what she wants—what will make her content—and then to go forward and wrest from life all she wants and needs." Lucasta waved dismissively. "Any notion that life will provide without you taking an active part is grossly misguided. You must decide what you want and set out to obtain it—only through that act do any of us find true happiness."

They walked on for several paces, then Miranda murmured, "That's very profound."

"Indeed. It's also immutable." Lucasta removed her hand from Miranda's sleeve. "As it happens, I was speaking with Julian on a related subject. Obviously you know him in his other guise, but you've also seen him here, where he is my son, Henry's uncle, Edwina's brother, Caroline's brother-in-law. It's not my story as to why he made the change, but as I pointed out to him, as matters now stand it may be possible for him to reverse what he did years ago and become Lord Julian Delbraith again."

Miranda frowned. "Is that possible?"

Lucasta nodded, lips and chin firm. "I believe so. And if he could be persuaded to that course, it would make *such* a difference to his future—to the rest of his life."

Why was Lucasta telling her that? The dowager wasn't a garrulous woman who gossiped to no purpose.

The answer seemed obvious; if Roscoe reverted to being Lord Julian Delbraith . . . Miranda glanced at the dowager. Was his mother matchmaking? Or did Lucasta have some other purpose in mind—perhaps hoping she would encourage him to consider the option?

"Mama."

They both swung to see the man himself approaching across the lawn.

Miranda glanced at the dowager and saw a smile of the utmost innocence wreathe Lucasta's face.

"My dear, how delightful. We were just discussing your

return to the capital—you'll take the traveling carriage for poor Roderick, will you not?"

"Yes." Roscoe's—Julian's—gaze shifted from his mother's face to Miranda's, then back again. "I was coming to ask if that would disrupt any plans you have. I'll send it straight back, but it would help Roderick to keep his foot elevated."

"Of course, dear." The dowager patted his arm. "And no, I'm fixed here for the foreseeable future—until Christmas at least—so you may let the coachman take a short break in the capital before you send him back."

"Thank you."

From the house came the deep *bong* of the luncheon gong.

Roscoe offered the dowager his arm.

"Thank you, dear." Lucasta took it, and with Miranda strolling on Roscoe's other side, they returned to the house.

Over the luncheon table, one drawback of their departure was borne in on Miranda with painful clarity.

Roderick and Sarah did not want to part.

Given Sarah's courage in flying to Roderick's defense, and Roderick's subsequent acceptance of her help, Miranda had wondered how far matters between the pair had gone, how deep the affection that had flowered.

Now both were clearly cast down by the prospect of no longer having the other near. Of no longer being able to enjoy each other's company. Not that they protested, or pouted, or, indeed, said or did anything overt, yet it was patently obvious to all about the table that both were subdued.

Sarah had lost her appetite.

Roderick looked wan.

Both made the effort to respond to comments addressed to them politely and fully, but when they spoke to each other the closeness between them shone, and the look in their eyes . . . the distinct impression Miranda received was that both had determined to be brave.

Perhaps irrationally, for any definite connection between Roderick and Sarah would spell the final end to her role in

Roderick's life, she nevertheless found herself searching for ways to allow them to further their romance.

She wasn't a romantic—indeed she'd had a surfeit of romance courtesy of her debilitating long-ago betrothal—but if there was a chance, she wanted that happiness for Roderick.

Beside Miranda, Roscoe watched the interplay on the other side of the table where Roderick and Sarah sat side by side. Lucasta, Caroline, Edwina, and Henry kept the conversation rolling, drawing Miranda and himself in with easy comments and lighthearted banter, but another emotion held sway on the other side of the table.

An emotion with which, for once, he could empathize. He would feel subdued, too, if he faced being separated from Miranda.

As soon he would be.

Yet Roderick and Sarah's prospects were straightforward; if they wished to pursue something deeper than friendship, they could. They simply had to make up their minds, and then make it happen.

He glanced at the woman alongside him, then looked at his plate. Would that his and Miranda's way forward could be reduced to a similarly neat equation. As it was, when it came to him and her, he didn't think any solution could be found.

Of course, in Roderick and Sarah's case, it was Sarah whose reputation was less than favorable, but her family had protected her, and her potential fall from grace had never quite occurred. His case was quite different.

His descent into non-respectability was, at least in his view, irretrievable. Impossible to reverse, let alone erase.

Late that afternoon, packed and ready for their departure the following morning, Miranda walked to the rose garden to take a last stroll in that magical place and seize a quiet moment to think. To dwell on all she'd learned while at Ridgware.

Pacing along the central walk, eyes down, she stopped reining in her thoughts and let them fly where they would; Lucasta's quite intentional words had set several hares running in her brain. The dowager's admonition that the only route to happiness lay in defining what mattered most had rung so true that she'd felt the concept resonate like a tolling bell inside her.

It was up to her to make of her life what she would. She had choices, options, and with the ladies' clarification of her social status, it seemed she had significantly more options than she'd thought.

One point was clear—her role as Roderick's keeper had ended. Whether he chose Sarah or another as his wife, he was already standing on his own feet, making his own life-determining decisions. He'd stepped past her in that; she could now see and admit that because of her familiar and, to her, dominant role as his keeper, she'd put off making any such decisions of her own. She'd flirted with them, but she'd never accorded her life, her future, the same attention she'd given Roderick's.

So she was now twenty-nine, wealthy enough to do as she pleased, with no duty to any other to claim her. The slate of her life was presently empty; according to Lucasta, it was up to her to fill it in, to define what her life would be.

Her feet reached the pool and she halted, her gaze fixing on the still surface. What did she want her life to be like?

She had to reach back through many years to remember her dreams, her untarnished hopes.

If she allowed herself to choose with complete freedom, entertaining no preconceived restrictions, then despite all the ifs, buts, and maybes, marrying and having a family of her own still reigned as her most dearly held aspiration. But marrying and having a family of her own were ultimate goals; in order to secure them, she had first to find an acceptable suitor and—if she allowed her dreams full sway—love.

She stood by the pool's edge and stared into the water, hearing in her mind all the usual arguments, many in her aunt's voice, that she, with her background, simply couldn't hope for such things, that love was a foolish and unnecessary complication, one only indulged in by the reckless, the feckless, the weak-minded . . . she heard all the old strictures one more time, then firmly shut a mental door on them and listened instead to Lucasta's dictate.

It was up to *her* to decide, to choose the details and make them happen, to forge the life she wanted, to fight for it if need be. To choose a husband, to choose to love . . .

Drawing in a shallow breath, she set her imagination free, let it paint as it would . . . as her heart desired.

Eventually, she blinked and refocused on the water at her feet. Roscoe's wishing pool. It wasn't night, yet . . . she closed her eyes, saw again in her mind the future her reckless heart desired, and wished . . .

"Miranda?"

Opening her eyes, she turned to see Caroline walking toward her.

Caroline smiled. "I hoped to have a chance to speak with you before you left."

"And I you." Habit, Miranda discovered, was hard to break, and she suspected she knew what subject Caroline wished to broach. "I wanted to ask for your thoughts about Sarah and Roderick, whether in your estimation encouraging further acquaintance would be wise."

Joining her by the pool, Caroline looked puzzled.

Miranda drew breath and raised her head. "In short, from your knowledge of Sarah's family, would an offer from Roderick sometime in the future be likely to be entertained?"

"Speaking with utter frankness," Caroline said, "I know the family would welcome the connection—and yes, like you, I see the potential for it already there. They seem quite amazingly suited."

Gathering her shawl more tightly about her, Caroline went on, "I should make something clear—about Sarah." She glanced around, then waved. "Let's walk." A narrower path circled the walled garden; they set off along it, leaving the wishing pool behind. "The reason Sarah is here, staying with me in the country, far from London and all associated diversions, is because over the past two years—ever since her come-out—she's been . . . well, wild. Her behavior has flirted on the knife-edge of disaster, so much so that her poor mother was literally turning gray. Sarah's second season earlier this year left her parents shaken—her behavior was frivolous, flighty, verging on fast. Not that any disaster actually occurred—and yes, I'm speaking of social disaster, of behavior unacceptable in a young unmarried ton lady, but underneath it all, there's nothing at all wrong with Sarah's heart. I think that's what has made this so hard for everyone to deal with—it was as if she believed she had to behave that way rather than be the sweet young thing she had been until her come-out. It was as if, on stepping into society, she had no anchor but was just swept into, irresistibly drawn into, the most reckless circles."

Caroline sighed. "It's been very hard on her mother, but, all that said, since she's been here, she's been much quieter, although I still had reservations as to her direction. Yet from the moment Roderick arrived, she's been transformed. Or rather she's reverted to the good-hearted, sweet-natured young lady we've always known her to be." Caroline drew breath. "It's as if Roderick gives her focus. As if he acts as her anchor and encourages her real self, so she lets the false façade fall."

Miranda nodded. "I wasn't sure about her at first, but I've seen more than enough to feel convinced that she would be good for him, and there's no doubt in my mind that he wants to continue the acquaintance. I can't give any assurances as to how deeply he feels about her, but I can say that I have never known him to take such interest in any young lady before."

Caroline nodded. "We're in agreement, then—the connection should be encouraged. I'll write to her parents and older sisters." Caroline glanced at Miranda. "We'll have to see what we can organize."

"I was thinking that once we're back in London, Roderick will quickly grow bored. He has to stay largely off his feet for several more weeks. I wondered, if Sarah were back in London, if she might come and spend the days with him in Claverton Street, much as she has been doing here."

"I'll suggest it to her parents. At this time of year, with London so quiet, I can't see anything against that plan."

Miranda looked down. "I know you've reassured me on this point before, but I still have to ask—and know the answer before this goes any further." Glancing up, she met Caroline's eyes. "Are you sure Sarah's family will consider Roderick's birth good enough?"

Caroline's smile was swift and sure. "I can absolutely assure you the family will be more concerned that the shoe may be on the other foot—that Roderick's family might consider Sarah's recent near indiscretions as an indication of underlying social irresponsibility too great to overlook."

Miranda smiled back. "As Roderick's family is, in this context, primarily me, you may reassure them that that is not the case."

In pleased accord, they walked on, then Caroline looked down. "I didn't come to speak about Roderick and Sarah but about something—someone—else."

"Oh?"

Glancing sideways, Caroline caught her gaze. "Julian hasn't told you why he became Roscoe, has he?"

Curiosity and more leaping, Miranda shook her head.

"He won't." Caroline returned her gaze to the path before them. "Because it affects so many of us—Lucasta, his sisters, me, Henry, indeed, everyone who lives here—he deems it not his story, his secret to tell." Caroline looked up at the house, visible above the garden wall. "What he fails to see is that now all of us and everyone here owe him a huge debt, and we would love to repay it if only we could. We can't, not directly, but perhaps . . ." Caroline drew in a breath, then, still not looking at Miranda, walked slowly on. "I decided I should tell you because I know he won't and I think you need to know."

Miranda hesitated, then quietly said, "I would like to know."

Caroline nodded. "It started when they were children—George, my late husband, and Julian, three years younger—and came to a head twelve years ago."

Miranda listened while Caroline described the Delbraith curse, explained the difference between how George had reacted and how Julian had responded to the same challenge. Explained how, unknown to anyone in the family, her husband, the late duke, had bankrupted the estate, reduced his family to penury, and then had taken the coward's way out, leaving his younger brother to step in, pick up the pieces, and set all right.

"The long and the short of it is that Julian sacrificed his life—the comfortable life he otherwise would have lived as a wealthy aristocrat, one of old and honored lineage—so that we, all of us, could live the lives we'd expected to live." Caroline paused, then, her voice lower still, said, "I never imagined any man, especially the man I at that time thought he was, would behave with such . . . unrelenting selflessness. But he did. He rescued us all."

Caroline glanced at her. "I know Lucasta is nurturing the hope that he might, now the battle is won, reverse the process and reappear as Julian, as her son, and while I might wish that for her, his sisters, for Henry, and Julian himself, too, I will never again make the mistake of thinking I know his mind. Whatever decision he makes on that score will be the right one—he's that sort of man. I will not presume to push one way or the other."

They strolled on. Miranda's mind whirled, reviewing, revising; she'd assumed that the reason behind Julian's transformation had been some major upheaval involving money, but she hadn't imagined a situation as fraught as what Caroline had described—the layers of betrayal, the helplessness of those affected. But she could imagine, and fully comprehended, the compulsion that had driven the man who had become Roscoe; to rescue his family . . . she had no difficulty understanding why he'd done as he had.

Eventually, she reached the point of considering Caroline's last words. The entrance to the rose garden lay not far ahead when, puzzled, she asked, "If you don't want to push one way or the other . . ."

"Why am I telling you the family secret?" Caroline's lips lifted wryly. "Because I'm not blind and, as I said, I want to repay him and will take any route to that that offers." Halting, she faced Miranda as she, too, halted. "More than anyone, Julian deserves to be happy. If there's any justice in this world, then he of all of us should find peace and happiness, contentment and joy." Caroline held Miranda's gaze. "If there should come a time, an opportunity, a situation in which you might have it in your power to grant him any degree of happiness, should you do so, then I, his entire family, and all those here will be forever in your debt."

Looking into Caroline's eyes, Miranda couldn't pretend not to understand, but . . . "Between us . . . it's complicated."

"He's a complex man."

A minute ticked past, then Miranda drew in a tight breath. "*If* an opportunity presents, I'll . . . try. But I don't know what's in his mind."

"Nor do I—nor does anyone. But that's all I could ask of you—that you will try." Caroline laid a hand on Miranda's arm, gently squeezed. "Thank you." Releasing her, she turned to the archway. "Come—we should get back to the house or Lucasta will be wondering where we are."

As, alongside Caroline, Miranda walked briskly back along the path, she reflected that she'd gone to the rose garden to think her way through things. While she'd resolved her direction on some issues, she was leaving the garden, leaving Ridgware, with even more complex matters weighing on her mind.

While scandalously riveting in itself, the story of why Lord Julian Delbraith had become Neville Roscoe, London's gambling king, had come as no real shock. It had underscored what she'd already learned on so many levels, in so many ways, that learning of Roscoe's past had merely rendered his present into a cohesive, comprehensible whole.

Standing before the window in her room, gazing at the shadows playing over the woodland and lawns as heavy clouds scudded across the waning moon, she now saw the reality of him clearly and felt no great surprise.

Complex, yes, but also, in some ways, predictable.

Caroline's revelations had emphasized the similarities between what had, to date, driven him and herself, which perhaps accounted for the attraction between them, on one level at least. In living their lives, they'd both put their families, those they'd deemed in their care and under their protection, first, and to their different respective ends they'd both succeed in their aims. Yet for both of them their families' need was waning. Fading. Their roles were changing.

For them both.

That was something she hadn't known and could never have seen or learned in London. It was an insight their stay at Ridgware had afforded her, and she was grateful for it. Knowing that he, too, was trying to find his way through a similar maze and into a fulfilling future was comforting. Reassuring.

They'd worked as partners in rescuing Roderick. Perhaps they could work as partners in defining their respective futures, too . . . they would have to in order to divine whether or not those futures might be mutual. Coinciding.

Could he revert to being Lord Julian and so be eligible as a husband, as Roscoe could never be? More importantly, if he could, would he marry her? Which, she conceded as she turned from the window, were two separate, albeit sequential, questions.

He didn't tap on the door but simply opened it; she had, she realized, heard and recognized his footsteps in the corridor an instant before. She watched as he entered, shut the door, considered her for a moment, then walked toward her.

Roscoe had one and only one thought in his mind: to make the most of this night. Tomorrow they would start their journey back to London and their normal lives, and this interlude—an unforeseen time in a protected place—would end. He drank her in as he closed the distance, let his gaze trace the svelte lines of her figure, the lush curves of breasts and hips, the sleek lines of her thighs alluringly framed by the amber silk of her gown.

Halting before her, he didn't give her a chance to speak but raised his hands and cradled her face. Tipping it to his, he met her eyes for an instant, then bent his head and kissed her.

Long, slow, inexpressibly sweet, the kiss drew out, spun on without intention or will; she yielded her mouth, one hand rising to cup the back of one of his, lips parting further, tongue stroking, inviting him deeper. She tasted like the elixir of life to him; he couldn't get enough of her bounty, but . . . realizing just how revealing his fascination with just a kiss was, he forced himself to draw back, to at least make some attempt at savoir faire, at being the sophisticated lover that, were she any other woman, he would have been.

With her, he was a different man. He knew it even as he let their lips part, as he raised his head and, like a man starved of tactile stimulation, sent his fingers sliding into the thick mass of her hair, coiled tonight in a loose chignon.

Her hands had risen to rest on his shoulders; now they drifted to his cravat and she drew out the pin, slid the haft back into the material, then, setting her palms to his chest, she slid them down and to his sides, spreading his coat wide.

He drew his hands from her hair only long enough to shrug out of his coat and toss it toward a chair, then returned his attention to unraveling the wonder of her silken locks.

Fingers freeing the buttons of his waistcoat, she studied his face through the shadows.

He didn't want her thinking so hard, or focusing too intently on him. "I saw you walking with Caroline this afternoon."

"Hmm." She pushed his waistcoat open. Spread her hands over the fine linen covering his chest, lightly gripped. "We talked about how to arrange for Sarah to visit Roderick in London."

"A wise idea." Her hair came loose and spilled in luxuriant splendor over her shoulders and down her back. Drawing his hands from the clinging tresses, he stripped off his waistcoat, flicked his cuffs undone, then reached around her and set his fingers to her laces. Drew her closer. "Better than leaving them to mope and grow desperate before trying to arrange some meeting on their own."

Busy untying the complex knot of his cravat, from beneath her lashes she looked up, caught his eyes. Hesitated, then, lids lowering, murmured, "This is our last night here."

He didn't want to talk about that. About them. "Yes." Raising one hand, he slid his fingers past her delicate jaw, gently cupped her nape. Tipping her lips to his, he bent his head. "So let's take everything from it we can."

He kissed her and this time didn't stop. He didn't want to speak of the looming end of their liaison, didn't want to voice the words and make it real. That was for the day after tomorrow; for tonight, and with any luck tomorrow night, he could still have her in his arms.

Drawing her more firmly to him once she was fully engaged with the kiss, he eased his fingers from her nape, let them cruise down the length of her throat. Felt her quiver.

He let his fingertips drift over her collarbone, lightly tracing to the point of her shoulder, and drank in her response. Tonight he was determined to take his time and savor. Every last moment, every gasp, every shivering instant of anticipatory tension, every last fulfilling second of the consequent pleasure. Every scintillating heartbeat of passion, desire, building tension, and release.

Her laces came free; without breaking the kiss, fingers stroking, tracing, lingering over the graceful curves of her arms and shoulders, the alluring swells of her breasts, palms caressing, he drew the gown down to her hips, then let the heavy silk fall of its own volition to the floor.

Through the gossamer silk of her chemise, he closed one

hand about her breast, gloried in the swollen firmness, the perfect fit, the evocative weight. Without conscious direction his fingers found her nipple and squeezed, teased . . . she gasped into the kiss, then pressed closer.

Stepped boldly nearer, her hands spreading, fingers splayed, over his chest, then sliding down and around, slipping beneath the shirt she tugged free of his waistband to slide around and up, over the planes of his back. To claim.

He quelled a shudder at the flagrant, loverlike possession in her touch. Something he wanted, something he delighted in—something he craved.

The melding of their mouths grew hotter, hungrier, demand escalating by steady degrees. And there was no need to mute it, to restrain it in any way. Tonight was all for her, and therefore him. With her as with no other woman before, her pleasure was his delight.

And tonight—all night—was theirs.

They moved in perfect harmony, in instinctive accord. Clothes fell, shed and discarded; hands touched, stroked, caressed, and possessed.

Claimed anew, with a confidence that was shattering in its directness, its unshielded desire.

If he was an expert in this sphere, she'd learned quickly. Learned to respond to him, to his caresses, to appreciate the thousand tiny pleasures that built and built as together they waltzed down their road to paradise.

Miranda followed his lead without hesitation. Without thought or reservation. They didn't rush, didn't hurry; even when they both stood naked, cloaked only in insubstantial shadow but otherwise blazing to each other's senses, they yet seized the moment to absorb. To touch, caress, and wonder. To take joy in the other's delight, and find pleasure in the other's sensual exploration.

Breaking from the kiss on a shuddering gasp, she let her head tip back, eyes closed the better to draw in and hold the sensation of his hard palms tracing from her shoulders, over her breasts, down over the indentation of her waist, over her stomach, then sweeping wide to possessively sculpt the flaring curve of her hips, before gliding down over her bare thighs.

He bent his head and his lips found hers again as his wicked fingers reversed direction and trailed slowly, delicately yet deliberately, up the inner face of her thighs. One hand continued its trailing rise to close about her hip, while the fingers of the other lingered, lightly brushing the curls at the apex of her thighs.

Then the hand at her hip gripped, anchoring her. Nudging her thighs apart, he slid his fingers past the screening curls and stroked.

Slowly exploring, testing and tracing. Learning anew. Impressing her, her so sensitive intimate flesh, with his touch anew.

His mouth supped from hers as his fingers played, on her senses, her nerves, as they stoked her desire. She fed from him, and fed him back the steadily rising heat of their passions, the surging, swelling desires, the burgeoning need. He took all she had to give and returned it in full measure, but . . . she wanted more.

Drawing one hand from the taut, steely muscles of his back, she slid her palm over his side, reached between their bodies and found the hard column of his erection, curled her fingers about the hot rigid length and boldly stroked.

His concentration fractured. She slid her fingers up, then sent them lightly skating over the engorged head. His chest swelled as he drew in a breath, but he didn't stop her. Instead, he resumed his stroking between her thighs, refocusing on their kiss, on the increasingly intimate melding of their mouths, the probing plunder of his tongue mimicking the increasingly probing pressure of his fingers . . . and left her to her own play.

To her own delight in pleasuring him.

She threw herself into the game, one that quickly became a sensual tit-for-tat, where she repaid his increasingly intimate forays with provocative caresses of her own . . . even though she knew it couldn't last, not for long, not with the swelling beat of passion thrumming ever more compulsively in their veins, she clung to the exchange, to the give and take.

The musk of their arousal, his and hers, wreathed around them.

Their skins burned, grew damp; their breathing grew harried.

She could take no more; pulling back from the kiss, her nerves afire, eyes closed, she gasped, "Now." She licked her lips, then murmured, sultry and low, "How?"

He chuckled, the sound a gravelly rasp, then stooped, swung her up and into his arms, and carried her to the bed.

Stripping back the covers, he laid her down upon the sheets, straightened, and, a naked god in the darkness, looked down at her. His gaze slowly swept from her face to her toes, then back, then she saw his teeth gleam fleetingly in the dimness. He knelt on the bed, caught one of her calves in each hand, spread her legs, let himself down between, and put his mouth where his fingers had been.

She bucked, only just managed to hold back a shriek as the wave of sensation evoked by the touch of his lips and the rough rasp of his tongue crashed through her.

He swept her away.

Swept her from this world and into another where sensation ruled. Where the fires of passion burned and desire was a scalding whip driving her on.

Into a cataclysm of delicious pleasures that grew and built, swelled and rose, then imploded.

She saw stars, touched their sensual sun, but even as she crested and sensed the void waiting, she felt him move and forced her lids up. Watched as he rose, wedged his hips between her thighs, braced his body above hers, for one instant hung over her, then he thrust deep and sure, and joined them.

Closed his eyes and softly groaned.

She closed around him, clamped tight, and held him.

Raised her arms, reached up, and embraced him.

He drew a huge breath and withdrew, then pressed in again, slowly. He kept the pace slow, achingly intent, eyes closed, concentration and focus etched in his face as he thrust, deliberate and controlled, within her.

As he pleasured her, and himself.

Lids falling, her parted lips lightly curving, she gave herself up to following his lead, to meeting each invasion, taking him in, rising beneath him as they rode on.

And on.

Roscoe was determined to string the moments out, to extend the pleasure to the ultimate and beyond. To wring every last ounce of pleasure and passion from her, and himself.

To indulge as he never had before, not with any woman.

Only with her.

Why he had no idea; as he hung his head and, his breathing harsh with the need to hold back, to hold on and stretch the moments, he gave himself wholly to the sensual devotion, he only knew that it was unquestionably, irretrievably, and immutably so.

She was all firm, sleek flesh and heated skin, supple and giving; the scalding slickness of her sheath was a sensual wonder, the subtle clamping of her inner muscles an intimate embrace he felt to the depths of his soul.

That she was with him, openly, joyously, as immersed as he in the senses-stealing act was a fact imprinted on his skin, on his muscles, deep in his bones—utterly irrefutable. There was no surrender here, only a meeting, a mating, of equals.

In an exchange of pleasure so deep it scored his soul.

And ripped away any veil.

She came to the exchange with unstinting honesty; he could do nothing less than match her, so there was no shield, no screen, not even a veil behind which he could hide his feelings. Or hide from them. Feelings so powerful he refused to name them, let alone acknowledge them and give them greater purchase, yet as he thrust deep within her and felt her rise to meet him, those feelings swamped him and overwhelmed his mind.

Miranda heard his breath hitch. Glancing up from beneath her weighted lids she saw the rippling clenching of muscles already rock-hard as he strove to prolong their mutual delight. Clinging to his rhythm, urging him on with her body and her hands, urgent and desperate yet willing to remain with him even at the excruciatingly slow pace, willing to brave the ravaging flames of their need as through his very slowness he whipped them to a raging inferno, breathless, gasping, she raised a hand and laid her palm against one lean cheek.

He turned his head and blindly pressed a hot, open-mouthed kiss to her palm.

The intimate, evocative caress made her heart leap.

Made her fingers curl.

Before she could focus on it, on her response, he hauled in a huge breath—and increased the tempo. Set them and their passions on the rising, spiraling path to completion.

And drove them into the furnace of their ravening need. Into flames of desire that seared her skin, that flashed along her nerves and left her wits, her thoughts, all external awareness cindered. That seized her, body and mind, in a vise of sensation so demanding she knew nothing beyond the striving driving of his body into hers, the abrasive rasp of his hair over her burning skin, the sheer power that rocked her with every thrust—then he bent his head, captured her lips, filled her mouth, and raced her into the heart of their sensual sun.

Sensation imploded.

Her scream smothered by their kiss, her being, her reality, shattered into shards of brilliantly hued perception that flashed down her nerves, raced through her veins, and consumed her from the inside out . . . until there was nothing left but scintillating ecstasy, and the emotion that waited beyond.

The emotion that caught her, that embraced and enfolded her, that was not of her, not of him, but of them both . . .

Wracked and shuddering, he joined her in the glory, and they clung . . . held tight.

Wrapped in that powerful, potent joy, locked together, *feeling* together, they fell and spiraled back to earth.

To the tangled sheets, to each other's arms, and the glow of aftermath that claimed them both.

He wasn't going to think about it.

Later, much later, when he stirred enough to lift from Miranda and settle them both beneath the covers, with her sleeping, deeply sated, her head pillowed on his shoulder, he lay back and closed his eyes.

And rather less successfully tried to close his mind against the treadmill of unfruitful speculation his mother's well-meant suggestion had raised and given life.

He didn't need to revisit the prospect; he'd already thought it through, in depth, and had seen the flaw in his mother's view. And even if he could revert to being Julian, it would be for naught—it wouldn't get him what he wanted.

What he now knew he wanted most—the one element crucial to the future he would choose if he could. Yet nothing he could do would yield him the prize the last days had revealed as his holy grail.

Nothing he could do would turn back the clock and wipe out the last twelve years. The years he'd spent being Roscoe, slowly, steadily, purely by virtue of his wits and his innate talents becoming London's gambling king.

He'd done it to save his family, but that didn't make Roscoe any more respectable. Didn't remake, and would not allow the man who had been Roscoe for twelve long years to be reformed into a suitable husband for any lady, let alone into the sort of husband a lady with a deep-seated belief that her future was contingent on her adherence to rigid respectability would accept.

He understood—none better—that respectability was a malleable thing, a concept governed by perspective. He didn't need to ask to know that in Miranda's view becoming his lover and indulging in a short liaison while away from her home, away from society, away from all who knew her, was quite a different matter to consorting openly with him in London.

Let alone marrying him.

More, one aspect he valued in all that had passed between them was her directness, her openness, her unguarded honesty. And if one tiny yearning part of him fantasized about finding some way in which they could continue their liaison and still keep that clear, open, and so wonderfully refreshing connection, the cynical and sophisticated majority of his mind knew there was no hope.

Knew that if he pushed to hold on to what they had, he would damage it, irretrievably tarnish it.

Tonight had been their last at Ridgware. If they were lucky enough to find the right inn, tomorrow night would be the very last of their liaison.

They would reach London the following afternoon, and he'd go back to his house in Chichester Street, and she would return to Claverton Street, and . . . it was perfectly possible he would never see her again.

The thought filled him with a leaden sense of loss, but he was too much of a realist to pretend; for them, for this, for what had grown between them, the end was impossible to deny.

Chapter Sixteen

Late the next morning, Miranda sat on the box seat of Roscoe's curricle, determined to make the most of every moment she had left with him.

The day was overcast, the air carrying the crisp brashness of an autumn that had finally trumped summer. Luckily, there was no rain and little wind to cut through their coats as they rolled along, making it a decent day to travel.

They'd left Ridgware shortly after breakfast; Lucasta, Caroline, Henry, and Sarah had stood on the porch and waved them away. With his leg propped up in the comfortable traveling coach, already drained by the rush of their departure, Roderick had slumped back against the seat and fixed her with an unreadable gaze. "You should ride with Roscoe. I'll be no good company."

She'd studied him briefly, then agreed. Roscoe had handed her into the curricle without question. Once they'd started on their way, driving through the estate to the rear entrance, with the curricle rolling steadily in front of the slower coach, Roscoe had said, "Kempsey and Dole worked on their own, but given we're so near Birmingham and their families, and have to pass through Lichfield, it would be wise to keep your eyes peeled for any sign of recognition or pursuit."

She'd nodded and done just that, but they'd encountered no villains or danger of any stripe. Once safely through Lichfield, they'd given Birmingham a wide berth and taken the road through Coventry, then turned south along the Banbury road toward Oxford. While the route through Banbury was a few miles longer, they'd agreed it was safer to go that way rather than via the route through Leamington Spa, a retreat favored by some of Roderick and Miranda's country neighbors and by local gentry from near Ridgware.

If they hadn't had Roderick to consider, they might have headed even further east before turning south for the capital, but given how difficult each hour of traveling was going to be for him, they'd elected to return via Oxford. As Roscoe had pointed out, "At least we know the Oxford to London road is in reasonably sound condition."

They'd left Coventry behind and were bowling along a well-surfaced stretch, the coach wheels rumbling in their wake. With the likelihood of danger well past, and Roscoe intent on managing his team, on discouraging the powerful blacks from surging too far ahead of the coach, she grasped the opportunity to sit back, fix her eyes on the road ahead, and consider just where he and she stood. Vis-à-vis each other, now, tomorrow, and the day after.

He hadn't said anything, but the prospect his mother had alluded to was not one she felt she could raise. Between Lucasta and Caroline, she now understood his past sufficiently well to comprehend his present, but neither his mother nor his sister-in-law seemed all that cognizant of the man he now was—of who and what Roscoe, as distinct from Julian, was.

To her mind that was crystal clear—Roscoe was the man who had from the first fascinated her, the man to whom she'd grown so attracted, the man she'd taken as her lover. It wasn't Julian who sat beside her but Roscoe, and that distinction became only more definite with every mile they got closer to London.

Lucasta's and Caroline's insights were centered on Julian, but the man she had to deal with was Roscoe. And no matter how she analyzed all he'd said and done—all she'd sensed through the passionate interludes they'd shared over the last eleven nights, through the evolution of the closeness she could all but feel growing between them—she still had no idea what was in his mind, what direction he'd decided on regarding their liaison. Their affair.

She'd initiated it and had continued it at first solely because she'd wanted to know, because she'd been desperate not to have to live out her life as a spinster without ever knowing what it was that passed between a man and a woman in that sphere, and he'd been the only man with whom she'd ever felt she might learn those lessons. He'd been a willing and expert teacher, a devoted instructor, and she'd learned a great deal; indeed, she'd learned all she'd initially set out to discover in just a few nights.

But that hadn't been enough, and still wasn't enough. She now wanted more. More of him. Much more time with him.

To explore, with him, the nebulous but infinitely alluring potential she sensed now lay within their grasp . . . if they wished to reach for it.

And therein lay the rub. They both had to wish to go forward; it wasn't just her decision, and it wasn't a decision she could make for him, or even steer him toward. He had to want it—want her, want to continue their liaison—of his own accord.

As the blacks' hooves drummed on the macadam and the curricle's wheels rattled on, she spent uncounted minutes considering that and evaluating her options, only to reluctantly conclude that in the absence of any sign from him that he wished to shift their relationship to some more permanent arrangement, all she could do was to go along, to let their connection evolve as it would—as he permitted—and see what happened. See where their road led. She would acquiesce and encourage, but she couldn't push.

The realization that she could do little to influence his decision even though said decision would significantly affect her wasn't easy to accept.

"A penny for your thoughts."

She realized she'd been frowning. Wiping the expression from her eyes and face, she looked at him; he'd glanced at her, but his horses had reclaimed his attention. For an instant, she let her gaze linger on his profile, then she looked ahead. "That would be a waste of money. I was just . . . mentally rambling."

After a moment, he nodded down the road to where a conglomeration of roofs was drawing steadily closer. "That's Southam. I suggest we stop for lunch there." He glanced briefly her way. "Roderick could no doubt use the break, and Banbury's still some way on."

She nodded. "A halt for a little while would be sensible."

They found an inn by the bank of a small river. A private parlor looked out over a grassy slope to the rippling water; weak sunlight flashed off the surface, lightening the room and giving the illusion of a more summery day.

After arranging for the parlor, Roscoe left Miranda, once more bedecked in her widow's weeds and veil, to select suitable dishes for their meal, then returned to the coach to help Roderick down.

Accepting the assistance, Roderick swung his injured foot to the ground, then hobbled slowly along using one crutch. His balance had improved, and, Roscoe judged, he was no longer in quite so much pain.

"I managed to nod off." Roderick limped through the parlor door Roscoe held open. "That helped. I don't feel so wrung out anymore."

"Excellent." Miranda drew out a chair by the table. "I hope you have an appetite—the food here sounds quite good."

So it proved. They spent a pleasant hour and a half over the meal, chatting about this and that. Seeing an opportunity, Roscoe grasped it, turning the conversation to the life brother and sister led at Oakgrove. From there, it was a small step to comparing likes and dislikes of life, to learning that neither sibling had ever seen the sea, nor had any experience of barge, boat, or ship.

When, after clearing the main course, the innkeeper's wife asked if they wished for a platter of cheeses and fruits, and Miranda glanced his way, he nodded. "We've plenty of time—no need to rush."

Miranda smiled and resumed her description of the gardens at Oakgrove, telling him which trees, plants, and flowers were her favorites. His next question was whether she was drawn to scented flowers, and if so, which.

Where the compulsion to use the minutes to learn all he could of her sprang from he didn't know, but he felt it, along with the weight of knowing that time was running out, that too soon these moments of easy rapport would be past.

When they left the inn, Roderick smothered a yawn and waved Miranda to the curricle. "I'm going to nap, so you may as well ride with Roscoe."

She acquiesced and allowed him to hand her up, and then they were off again, relaxed and comfortable. Having informed the coachman which Oxford hotel he'd decided to put up at for the night, Roscoe no longer needed to hold back his blacks, yet still he didn't let them range ahead. Wouldn't let them go faster and cut short the time he had to spend with her by his side.

"Tell me," he said, "do you ride in town at all?"

She sighed. "No. I used to almost every day in the country, but in town . . . well, Aunt Gladys never was keen. Too much potential for disaster."

"So what sort of horse do you prefer? Do you hunt?"

He kept the questions rolling, easily extrapolating from one to the next, and she slipped in several in return, yet the sense of this being a last hurrah, that the magical, unexpected interlude in Ridgware was over and, regardless of what he might wish, their personal association was therefore on the cusp of ending, hung in the air.

When the spires of Oxford rose ahead, the thought of simply driving on—driving off somewhere else and leaving both their lives behind—flared in his mind. After a second, he shook aside the silly notion.

He was who he was, and she who she was; changing their physical destination wouldn't alter that.

He'd decided to stay at the very best hotel in Oxford. It wasn't one of the large hotels that anyone in the ton might visit but a smaller and commensurately more exclusive, exceedingly private hotel run by a family who had multiple reasons for wishing him and his well.

"We'll be safe here." Dropping his driving gloves on a sofa table in the sitting room of a well-appointed, quietly luxurious suite, Roscoe studied Roderick. Seated on the sofa, the younger man was massaging the muscles of his calf above his broken foot.

Feeling his gaze, Roderick looked up and grimaced. "Just stiff. Nothing serious."

Miranda strolled out of the bedroom she'd chosen. "What's not serious?"

"The reason I'm rubbing my leg," Roderick replied. "No need to get worried."

Roscoe watched her teeter on the brink of doing just that, but then she drew breath and nodded. "All right."

He inwardly smiled; she was trying to let go. "I have the room beyond yours, but I don't imagine we'll have any nighttime visitors here."

"The staff seem very attentive—not like at the hotel in Birmingham."

"Indeed." Roscoe looked at Roderick. "I suggest we have an early dinner served up here, and then we should get as much rest as we can. If we start at a decent hour tomorrow, we'll have you in Claverton Street by midafternoon."

Roderick nodded. "Good plan."

Miranda didn't look quite so eager, but she crossed to the

bellpull and tugged it, then met his gaze. "Do you want to order, or shall I?"

"You can—I'll go and check that they've brought up my bags."

The rest of the evening passed comfortably. Roderick grew tired soon after dinner. He bade them a weary good night and, assuring them both he needed no assistance, limped into his room and shut the door.

Worry in her eyes, Miranda shifted her gaze from the closed door and arched her brows at Roscoe.

He hesitated, then offered, "It's most likely the low-level but constant pain that's dragging him down, rather than anything being wrong."

She pressed her lips together but said nothing.

He cast his eyes over the local news sheet; she picked up a ladies' magazine and idly flicked through it.

A maid arrived with the tea tray. They sat and sipped, neither, it seemed, inclined to conversation. For himself, he was content enough simply being in her company, able to glance at her whenever he wished, and he saw no reason to precipitately embark on what would be their last night sharing a bed. He could sleep any night; tonight he wanted to stretch each stage, each moment, to the fullest, to extract the maximum he could from each. To *not* let go.

Eventually, she balanced her cup on its saucer, then set both on the low table before the sofa. Sitting upright and raising her head, she looked at him, met his gaze.

He'd already deposited his cup and saucer on the tray, and had been sitting simply watching her for some time.

Holding his gaze, she rose.

Uncrossing his legs, he got to his feet.

She said nothing, simply held out her hand.

He read her eyes, then reached out and closed his fingers around hers, and let her lead him into her room.

Closing the door, he caught her gaze as she turned to face him. Raising the hand he held, fingers twined, he pressed a long, lingering kiss on her knuckles.

She smiled an innocently seductive smile and stepped into his arms. He closed them around her, bent his head as she raised hers. Their lips met, and desire flowed. That simply, that easily. That responsive to their call.

It was so easy, so effortlessly straightforward to step into the flames with her. To let the heat rise, to let passion lick over their skins and sink into them, to let desire set its spark and ignite their need.

For him, tonight, his goal was clear. This night was for laying up memories, for creating moments of quivering awareness and imprinting each second of her response, and his, on his mind.

Memories. Of the soft susurration of silks sliding to the floor. Of silken skin glowing pearlescent in weak moonlight. Of the contrast of his darker, hair-dusted limbs twining with her smooth, slender paleness.

Their bodies came together in heat and in passion, but again neither rushed. Both drew the moments out, not just savoring but examining and absorbing every individual scintilla of delight, every fractured second of pleasure, every moan, every gasp, each tensing grip.

The steady coiling of the inevitable tension, the swelling promise of its release.

He reached for each moment, enshrined each in his mind—every brush of her lips, parted and swollen from their kisses, every seductive caress, every grasp of hands, lingering yet urgent, every desperate pant, each harsh and ragged exhalation.

Every breath, every touch, every nuance of their loving.

He gathered them all in, assumed she was doing the same. This was, after all, the end—the extent of their forever. They'd reached the limit of what, for them, could be. These were their last hours, the last time they would savor the shattering moment when he slid into her body, the senses-stealing intimacy as, joined, they moved together, every last iota of their senses and wits focused on the link, on the giving and the taking, on the transcendent joy.

Eyes closed, senses and wits whirling, Miranda clung and rode their tide, seeking and recognizing, reiterating and re-affirming that this—this glory—was what they could have. Now and forever.

This wasn't some passing connection. This power and glory wasn't something that would simply fade and die—not if they didn't kill it. Not if they fed it and kept it alive.

Through the overriding, all but overwhelming demands of their passions, she yet searched and tried to see, to look through and past the intimacy to what in him lay beneath, to what he thought, what he felt, what emotion drove him.

She looked, summoned the last vestige of her awareness and through the cascading delight and scintillating sensation sought, yet all she saw, all she could discern, was his absolute and unwavering immersion in the moment, his devotion to each heartbeat of pleasure.

They'd reached some other plane. Had together breached some higher level of physical and mental communion, one where touch and intent, will and desire, passion and need fused into one entity. Into one swelling, swirling, rising tide.

Driven by a need whose power she didn't comprehend, desperate to learn—here, now—what might be, she held tight, hauled in a ragged, shallow breath, and reached deeper, not with her senses but with her soul.

And he did the same. He bent his head and their lips met, despite their breathless state melded and clung.

And together they raced on, up, higher, their bodies mere vessels for their joyously desperate souls.

He couldn't hold back from her, not here, not in this.

Not this time.

He'd always kept a wall between his actions and his feelings, a screen that no other had ever stripped away; with all his previous lovers he'd had no difficulty holding emotionally aloof because his emotions had never truly been engaged, not as they were with her.

Regardless, he'd instinctively tried to maintain that wall,

that last bastion of emotional safety, but with her, night by night, day by day, that wall had steadily eroded.

Now, tonight, there was no reason to fight to retain that separation, that screen, his shield, his inner safety. Tonight was the moment beyond which nothing else lay; for them, tonight was their all, their end.

Her body tightened about his, beneath him, around him, her arms tensing, hands clutching, the cradle of her hips embracing, her thighs clamped to his flanks, the evocative clutch of her sheath strengthening as together they rocked and raced up ecstasy's peak.

She was with him, her mouth a cornucopia of passion, the taste of her an elixir that wreathed his brain and beckoned and lured with the promise of a togetherness powerful enough to succor his soul.

He let go. Dropped all restraint and let the unruly, intractable feelings that had been growing since he'd first set eyes on her free, let them surge and swell and reach for her, for the bounty she offered.

He wanted, clear and simple, and let his need show, let the maelstrom of it manifest and infuse him, flow to her and bind them—let it blend with her much more openly declared passion to create . . . something more.

Something wild and untamed, rich and glorious.

He gave himself up to it, sensed, felt, and knew she did the same.

What followed was beyond his experience, beyond his comprehension, barely within his ability to sustain.

They reached the peak in a cataclysm of sensation, the elemental moment heightened, given color and potency by flaring emotion—his, hers, theirs—transforming their desperately urgent climax into a spectacular conflagration that seared them, wracked them, shattered and fragmented them.

That flung them to drift, for one fleeting second, like empty husks in the void, hollowed out and yearning.

Then glory surged—brighter, more brilliant, more powerful and potent—and filled them. Remade them.

Into something finer, better, more complete, forged in passion's fire.

They sank together into the soothing sea, buoyed on the golden waves of aftermath. Clinging, trying to catch their breaths, trading gentle kisses and wonder-filled touches.

Simply being.

He clung to the fragile, delicate moment, didn't want it to pass.

In that moment of clarity, of crystal-clear vision, he saw—could all but touch—the emotion that bound him.

So powerful, so true.

So unexpected.

He'd never thought he would find it, not in him.

He hadn't understood that uncovering it wasn't up to him, wasn't a decision within his power to make, but that the power to evoke that most potent of emotions rested instead with someone else—with her.

He hadn't realized, but now he knew.

Slumped on his back with her stretched alongside him, her head on his shoulder, her legs tangled with his, his arm holding her close, he closed his eyes.

Now, at last, he understood, and tomorrow they would part.

Miranda woke the following morning to find herself alone in the bed. The sheets beside her were already cool. Beyond the window the skies were leaden, a soft drizzle already falling.

She focused on the clock on the mantelpiece. "Blast!" Tossing back the covers, she rose and quickly washed and dressed.

Once more garbed in her widow's weeds, she swiftly packed the few items she'd unpacked the night before, then carried her bag, her cloak, and her bonnet and veil into the sitting room next door.

Roderick was there, applying himself to a reassuringly well-supplied breakfast plate. He waved a fork. "Good morning. I was wondering if I would have to come and wake you."

She'd slept like one dead, deeply and dreamlessly. "I must have been more tired than I'd thought." More deeply sated.

The table had been set with three places. Drawing out the chair before the last setting left untouched, she considered the other, already used plate. "Where's Roscoe?"

"Out seeing to the horses. We just need to ring when we're ready to leave, and the footmen will come up for the bags." Roderick sighed. "And they'll tell Roscoe, and he'll come up and help me down."

She grimaced in sympathy. "We'll make up one of the downstairs rooms at Claverton Street so you won't need to negotiate the stairs."

He shook his head. "No—I need to keep at it. The stairs don't hurt so much as they're awkward, and m'foot's aching less and less with every day."

She hesitated but didn't argue.

After she'd finished her breakfast, they departed the suite. She went down first, leaving Roderick negotiating the stairs with Roscoe. Veil once more in place, she watched as a footman stored her bag in the coach's boot, then Roderick arrived, hobbling on his own again, Roscoe walking by his side.

Roscoe glanced at her, met her eyes; somewhat to her surprise, he didn't smile, and once again she could read nothing in his expression.

He nodded to the coach. "It might be best if you get in first." *In case Roderick needs help once he's inside.*

She heard the rest of the statement. After a moment's mental dithering, she nodded and turned to the carriage door. Lengthening his stride, Roscoe reached for the handle, opened the door, waited for the footman to fold down the steps, then offered her his hand.

She gripped his fingers, felt his grip hers, sensed the connection still there, still strong. Steadied indeed, more assured, she climbed the steps and crossed to sit in the far corner of the coach.

Roscoe drew back. A minute later, with his assistance, Roderick climbed awkwardly into the carriage. With her help, he managed his crutch, his strapped shoulder, and his splinted foot, eventually turning to sink carefully down on the opposite seat.

Roderick blew out a breath, then shot her a weak smile. "Done."

She smiled encouragingly. From the corner of her eye, she saw Roscoe shut the carriage door.

He strode away; an instant later she heard him giving orders to the coachman. Half a minute later, she heard the lighter rattle of the curricle's wheels on the forecourt as Roscoe turned his horses out into the street.

Ponderously, the coach eased into motion and followed.

Which was how she came to be whiling away the miles settled in one corner of the traveling coach while Roderick dozed on the opposite seat.

The situation afforded her an extravagance of time to think and consider, to ponder, weigh, and clarify her thoughts. Her wishes, her wants, her intentions. Her possible ways forward.

She couldn't help but contrast her current view of the latter with her expectations when she'd traveled the same road in the opposite direction, heading out of London alongside Roscoe, rescuing Roderick uppermost in her mind.

Now . . . for a start, she accepted, absolutely and without quibble, that her time as Roderick's protector had ended. He was his own man now and no longer needed her; more, any further interference on her part would infringe on his right to make his own decisions, to live his own life.

She'd always known the time would come, the moment when she set aside that role completely and turned fully to the scripting, as it were, of her own future. Until she'd left London and driven north, her assumption had been that that future could follow one of only two paths. She could remain a spinster and die an old maid, or she could marry some suitably respectable man, like Wraxby. Some man who consid-

·ered her suitable and sufficient to fill the role of his wife—a role he, rather than she, would define.

Courtesy of this journey, her eyes had been opened. There were other paths—more interesting and potentially more fulfilling paths—that she might take. They were there, perfectly real and acceptable; all she needed to do was make up her mind and take whichever she chose.

She could immerse herself in charitable works at a more involved level than she'd previously thought possible; there were multiple avenues she could take in that direction. She could be an adventurer, a traveler, a student of history and civilizations, if she felt so moved. She could be so many things.

If she chose . . .

But what did she want most?

There was one unarticulated lesson she'd learned at Ridgware—that she should choose as her path her most strongly held passion. She'd seen passion for the local school—the local children—transform Caroline, had seen passion for her family still burning strongly in Lucasta. Even Edwina was following her passion albeit alongside her husband.

If she accepted passion as her lodestone, then which path was hers? Which did she feel most strongly called to?

As the coach rumbled on and the miles slid past, she sought to clarify that critical point, only to conclude that she couldn't do so until she'd defined what possibilities might exist between her and Roscoe.

Last night had answered, thoroughly and absolutely, every question she'd had to that point, bar one. The link between them was powerful, not solely physical, and fascinating and potent enough to hold them both enthralled, but what emotion gave it life she still didn't know. She'd felt the strength of it, had sensed it in him, and accepted that for both of them it was the same thing, but he was her first and only lover; she was too inexperienced to feel any certainty in putting a name to that force.

Regardless, that aspect aside, the more immediate question thrown up by the night was: What next? What lay ahead for them on their return to London? What avenues were open to them there?

She was eager to pursue the connection, to see how and what they might make of it. She didn't know what options they might have, but he would.

After last night, she didn't doubt that he was as deeply ensnared as she by what had flared and now existed between them. Sadly, since last night, they hadn't had a chance for any private conversation; even over luncheon, taken at a small inn, Roderick had been present, and Roscoe had been . . . tilting her head, she considered what she'd sensed . . . not distant so much as reserved.

Careful to keep whatever he felt hidden behind an impenetrable screen.

Indeed, now she thought of it, his impassive mask, which had softened over their time at Ridgware, had grown steadily harder and more impenetrable the closer they got to London. Presumably that mask was part of his armor as Roscoe; it would be interesting to discover whether, when only she was near, it would soften again, whether he would again let her see past it.

Lips curved, she was imagining testing that when the coach slowed, then, rocking heavily, turned into an inn yard.

Shouts and orders rang out, muted by the carriage's closed windows and doors. On the seat opposite, Roderick, arms folded, head bowed, slept on. From the maneuvering of the coach, she gathered they were changing horses. Leaning forward, she peered out of the window. Other than a stable and several ostlers rushing about, there was little to be seen, then Roscoe came striding from the front of the carriage.

He saw her at the window, glanced at Roderick through the other pane, then gestured for her to let her window down. She fiddled with the catch and eased the panel down. Roderick, they both noted, didn't stir.

Roscoe nodded briskly. "This is Uxbridge—our last

change before town." He glanced toward the horses, then looked at her. "I've given orders for you to be driven straight to Claverton Street. The coachman will let you off there, then drive on to my stables." His expression was utterly impassive, his dark eyes unreadable. They switched briefly to Roderick, still asleep, then returned to her. "Tell Roderick I'll send word when I learn more about Kirkwell, but for the moment he'll be safe if he remains at home."

She blinked. "Thank you." She felt disoriented. They were parting here? She drew in a breath. "I must thank you for all your help. Without it—"

"No need." His gaze roved her face. Before she could think of anything to say, he nodded curtly and stepped back.

The coach rocked as its shafts settled back into the harness and the ostlers backed it from the changing area. She gripped the window ledge to steady herself; when she peered out again, Roscoe was walking away.

She stared, then Roderick stirred and she looked at him. He blinked owlishly, then yawned. "Where are we?"

"Just leaving Uxbridge. We'll be in London soon."

He closed his eyes again. "Good."

Miranda glanced out but couldn't see Roscoe or his curricle. Inwardly frowning, she wrestled the window back into place. She hadn't expected to part so abruptly, but Roderick had been there, and doubtless she would see Roscoe once they were home again.

She settled back as the carriage turned out of the yard and picked up speed.

From the shadows of the inn's porch, Roscoe watched the coach roll away. He'd spent most of the hours driving down from Oxford trying to decide on the right words to say. Deciding was one thing; saying quite another. He'd wanted to make a clean break, quick, straightforward, and clear, an acknowledgment of their inevitable reality. Instead, he hadn't even managed a simple "good-bye." Just the thought of speaking the word had made his throat constrict.

Spending last night with her had been a mistake. If he'd

known . . . he would have made do with the memories he'd already garnered rather than learn, as he had, exactly what he might have had had he not become Roscoe. Exactly what he most truly, almost desperately wanted from life, what he wanted in his life for the rest of his days.

No need.

His words had been honest enough. No need to extend the exchange. Certainly no need for any thanks. And no need to say anything else because there wasn't anything he or she could say or do that would alter the situation.

For the first time in his life, he'd woken resenting the choices he'd made, actually regretting the long-ago decisions that meant he now had to let her go, had to accept that their time together was over.

Had to let her walk away . . .

Pulling on his driving gloves, he frowned. *He* couldn't walk away, not yet; they still had Roderick's would-be killer to catch. Kirkwell was still out there somewhere. Until Kirkwell was no longer a threat to Roderick or his sister, he would continue to watch over them and wait.

He'd already given orders to have the Claverton Street house kept under surveillance at all times. Given Kirkwell's apparent lack of funds, it was possible he would make a try for Roderick himself. If Kirkwell did, the villain would walk into Roscoe's net. Regardless, directly or indirectly he would find Kirkwell, but while he did, he would keep his distance from Miranda.

Stepping down to the yard, with a curt nod accepting the reins from the ostler who'd readied his curricle, he stepped up to the box seat, sat, flicked the reins, and set the pair of freshly harnessed grays pacing neatly out onto the highway.

For his sake as well as hers, keeping all contact between them to a minimum would unquestionably be the wisest course.

Chapter Seventeen

"I still can barely believe it." Gladys crunched her morning toast, liberally slathered with marmalade, and stared down the breakfast table at Miranda, then at Roderick, seated at the table's end. "The Duke of Ridgware's house, and the family treated the pair of you as if you were guests."

"Hmm." Miranda didn't look up from her lists.

Roderick remained immersed in today's news sheets.

They'd arrived in Claverton Street at four o'clock the previous afternoon, and every minute of the rest of the evening had gone in answering Gladys's myriad questions and relating all that had happened at Ridgware, leaving Miranda no time to pick up the reins of the household and deal with its various demands.

During the fortnight and more she'd been away, Gladys had dealt only with issues too urgent to wait, so she had two weeks' worth of accounts, wages, and details to resolve, as well as the usual mundane decisions required to keep the household functioning. She was determined to catch up with as much as she could that day, so she would be free to turn her mind to the personal issues that, somewhat to her surprise, had kept her wide awake and wondering far into the night.

"It just seems strange," Gladys mused. "I would have expected great ladies like the dowager duchess and the duchess to hold to a much more reserved and superior line."

Miranda's memory supplied visions of Lucasta and Caroline. She glanced at Roderick, determinedly buried in the news sheets, then looked back at her lists. "Despite their station, they're human. They have much the same concerns as ladies everywhere."

Gladys frowned, then snorted and fell mercifully silent. Despite accepting all they'd told her as true, Gladys continued to exclaim and wonder over their stay at Ridgware, rubbing shoulders freely with the ducal family.

Miranda had explained that the friend of Roderick's who'd helped her locate and rescue him from the kidnappers had been a close connection of the Delbraiths', a fact that had instantly rendered said friend entirely above reproach in Gladys's eyes. When Gladys had asked reluctantly, trepidatiously—clearly not truly wishing to hear the answer but unable not to ask—whether she had avoided any scandal while traveling with a gentleman who was not a relative, Miranda had pointed to the weeds she'd still been wearing and had flourished her bonnet and veil. No one, she'd assured her aunt, had known who she was, and with their tale of a gentleman escorting her, a widow, to a country estate, not even a whisper of scandal had been provoked, nor was any likely.

Eyes on her lists, she reflected that that was another thing the journey had taught her; as long as her actions did not become widely known, scandal would never be an issue.

Setting down her pencil, she picked up her teacup and sipped as she scanned the list of tasks she simply had to do. She wanted to stop and think about Roscoe, about her and him and what might be, but first she had to meet with Mrs. Flannery and then talk to Hughes.

Roderick tossed the news sheets on the table. She glanced his way, saw him grimace as he shifted his leg.

Sensing her gaze, he looked up and met it. His lips twisted. "M'leg's still too weak to risk even a turn about the garden." Disappointed disgust laced his voice. Grabbing the crutch propped against his chair, he used it to haul himself to his feet. "I'm going to go and sit in the drawing room."

"Yes. Of course." Miranda watched him make his way from the room. He'd insisted on making his own way up and down the stairs, but the effort had cost him. Once he was out of sight, she murmured, "Hughes?"

The butler was hovering by the sideboard. "Yes, miss?"

"Perhaps, once Mr. Roderick has had time to settle in the drawing room, you might check to see if he wants anything brought to him."

"Indeed, miss."

And she would make time to write a letter to Caroline, and another to the address Caroline had given her. While Roderick might no longer be her primary concern, keeping him amused while he convalesced was nevertheless one of the items on her list.

After so many days once again free of the distracting presence of Miss Miranda Clifford, Roscoe devoted his morning to catching up with his various businesses. An hours-long meeting with Jordan dealt with all urgent financial matters, then he settled at the desk in his study to review the accumulated weekly reports from the forty-three hells and gaming clubs he owned and operated throughout the capital.

Rundle looked in. "Will you be lunching in the dining room, sir?"

Tipped back in his admiral's chair, Roscoe glanced up, then shook his head. "No—back to normal. Just bring me a plate here."

Returning his gaze to the report he was perusing, he was aware that Rundle hesitated—presumably debating whether to press the issue—before wisely bowing and retreating.

He remembered very clearly the luncheons he'd shared with Miranda downstairs, but prior to those instances he'd always eaten at his desk while continuing to work. As she was no longer in his life, it would be wise to reestablish his routine.

Her presence had been . . . a fleeting ripple across the mill pond of his life. And, God knew, those waters ran deep.

Amused by his lapse into poetic vein, he refocused on the report; such weekly reports were his proven method of keeping abreast of all that happened in his now extensive empire.

There had been a time when he, flanked by Mudd and Rawlins, had visited every club and hell each week, a time when the threat of his personal involvement had been the only effective way to keep a rein on the vices and ingrained criminal leanings of those then engaged in running his businesses. But over the years he'd learned how to draw a line in the sand and hold to it; the line he'd chosen was that all activities undertaken on premises he owned, and by those in his employ, had to pass legal scrutiny.

Solicitors would be, and often were, impressed by how acute the sensibilities of the underworld were when it came to what was legal and what was not. Those reared in the slums or the shadows of less respectable neighborhoods had a fine appreciation of the nuances of the law. But even beyond the moral and legal implications of his stance, simply having a line and sticking to it had been critically important in and of itself. It had given him a platform from which to operate, one that distinguished him from his peers.

One that had allowed him metaphorically to stand above them.

And in many ways that had been to his advantage.

The second thing he'd learned, or rather had extended his innate abilities in, was how to judge others. As a successful inveterate gambler, he'd always had a knack for knowing who was truthful and open, and who was not. Who was guileful and who was guileless. He'd focused that ability on his employees, rewarding those he could trust, discarding those he could not.

With a string of businesses as large as his, oversight was a continual, never-ending task, yet it was one in which success bred success; these days he rarely needed to intervene in the day-to-day running of any of his enterprises.

At least not with respect to his employees.

He'd finished the plate of cold meats, bread, and cheese, had drained the mug of ale Rundle had supplied, and had laid aside the last of the reports from his gambling hells and was reaching for the first from the more sophisticated clubs when Rundle tapped on the door and entered.

Seeing the empty plate and mug, Rundle came to fetch them. "Mrs. Keller and Mr. Masters are downstairs, sir. If you have a moment, they'd like to consult you about one of their regulars."

Keller and Masters jointly managed one of his quieter, more exclusive, and long-established clubs, one that catered to the older, more conservative gentlemen of the ton. He nodded. "Show them up."

He glanced at the report in his hand; it was for another of his clubs. Setting it aside, he leafed through the pile until he found Keller and Masters's latest report. He swiftly scanned it, but there was no mention of any looming difficulty; leaving it atop the pile, he sat back and waited.

When Mrs. Keller, a statuesque blond, and Masters, her brother, entered, he waved them to the chairs facing the desk. "What's the name of our problem?"

Masters winced as he settled, otherwise relaxed and at ease.

Sitting very upright, Joyce Keller faintly smiled. "Lord Cathcart."

He took a moment to place the aging peer. His gaze on Keller and Masters, he nodded. "A vicious old bastard who believes he and his ilk are the sort the rest of the world should bow down to, and quick to turn violent at any perceived slight."

Joyce and Masters were the illegitimate offspring of just such a man, in their case an earl. In company with most of the world, the pair thought his background was similar to theirs, an assumption he'd never sought to correct; it conveniently explained so much about him.

Roscoe glanced from Joyce to Masters. They'd worked for him for over five years; they knew the business and also knew his ways. "So what's happened?"

Joyce sighed. "Lisette—the young Flemish woman you sent to us. She's proved every bit as excellent at piquet as you told us she was."

"And as you also suggested," Masters put in, "most of our stodgy old souls like playing with her, even if they lose." He huffed out a short laugh. "In fact, she's so good, the rest of them seem quite happy to lose to her, and truth be told she gives them a damned good education in the game."

"Indeed. She's been a huge success all around, until Cathcart heard about her." Joyce grimaced.

"Let me guess," Roscoe said. "Cathcart fancies himself a past-master at piquet, and Lisette trumped him."

Masters nodded. "Comprehensively. That would have been bad enough, but the idiot—Cathcart—had insisted on a thousand a point. Lisette asked for permission, of course, and fool that I was I didn't think—well, I did, but only about how much we were going to take Cathcart for. And fleece him she did."

"And then?"

"Cathcart paid up, but he was quivering with rage," Masters said.

"Not just rage," Joyce said. "He was incandescent with fury that she'd shown him up for the windbag he was."

"I should mention this took place on Thursday evening—our busiest." Masters's face hardened. "Cathcart organized that deliberately—he'd wanted to have the biggest audience for his match, to show the others that he could prevail against the little foreign woman who had so easily beaten all of them."

"Instead . . ." Joyce held up her palms in a helpless gesture. "And, of course, it being one of your establishments, Cathcart doesn't dare claim she was cheating."

"Not when none of the others have so much as suggested it," Masters said, "and, of course, everyone knows your rules."

Joyce sighed. "You've warned us that there are times it pays not to win, and this might have been one of them, but it's done now and we can't undo it. And, unfortunately, Cathcart's not the sort to let it go." She met Roscoe's eyes. "Cathcart was waiting for Lisette when she left the club. He raised his cane and would have beaten her, but we'd sent Hugo, one of our men, out with her. He caught Cathcart's cane before it connected."

Roscoe moved not a muscle. "But Cathcart actually tried to strike her?"

Joyce nodded. "And that wasn't the end of it. He returned the next day and offered Lisette a very large bribe to play with him again, for five thousand a point, and allow him to win."

His gaze on Joyce, Roscoe let a moment pass, then murmured, "Please tell me she didn't take it."

Joyce smiled tightly. "She didn't."

He let his lips ease. "Excellent. So why are you here?"

"Because Cathcart then made a lot of noise about losing to the house, but the house being unwilling to give him the chance to win his losses back." Joyce met his gaze. "So we've come for advice."

"And help," Masters added, "if you have any you feel inclined to give."

Roscoe leaned back in his chair and let his gaze grow distant while he considered his options; dealing with Cathcart needed a different approach than dealing with hotheads like Lord Treloar. Eventually, he refocused on Joyce, then glanced at Masters. "Lisette pricked Cathcart's pride, clearly a vulnerability, so we'll use his pride against him to shut him up. To make him take his losses like a man."

Sitting up, he reached for a fresh sheet of paper, then his pen. "I'm going to offer to meet Lord Cathcart's challenge and allow him to win back his losses. Against me. I, after all, am the 'house' in question." He wrote while he spoke. "I will allow him to set the wager anywhere between five and ten thousand pounds a point, as he wishes. As with any challenge, should he accept it, it will be entered into the wagers' book. The game will be played at the club, and he may bring two observers of his choice to ensure that all is aboveboard. The offer will remain open for . . . a month, shall we say?" He paused to read what he'd written, then, lips curving, he signed the missive and added a note. "And in case this letter of offer should go astray, I'll leave a notarized copy with you at the club and retain one in my files."

Masters laughed. Joyce grinned. Both knew that Cathcart would never dare accept the counter-challenge. No gambler in his right mind went up against Roscoe and expected to win.

Roscoe blotted the missive, then handed it to Masters. "Take it to Jordan when you leave—he'll get the copies made and have the original delivered to Cathcart." He held up a finger to keep both his visitors in their chairs. "However, as you're both here"—he picked up the latest report from the club—"who the devil has been losing so heavily at your hazard table?"

Half an hour later, the siblings departed, and he settled down to wade through the other clubs' reports, marking any point he wished to question, such as the unexpectedly large takings at the Keller Club's hazard table. He'd long made it a point to know who was going to the dogs before they got too deeply indebted. Sometimes a quiet word in the right ear kept everyone healthy.

He'd just finished reviewing the clubs when Jordan entered with a sheaf of documents and a reminder that Roscoe was due at a meeting of the board of Argyle Investments, a charitable foundation in which he held a sizeable stake.

It was late afternoon before he returned. Leaving his greatcoat with Rundle, he strolled into the library. Crossing to the tantalus, he poured a glass of brandy, then sprawled in his favorite armchair. Raising the glass, he sipped, then held up the glass to observe the burnished amber liquor within . . . and finally allowed himself to focus on the question that had lurked at the back of his mind all day. The question his mother's suggestion had raised.

He'd dismissed her notion on the grounds it wasn't feasible and wouldn't get him what he most wanted, yet the prospect had lingered, a seductive *Why not?* murmuring deep in his mind.

If he'd needed the reasons enumerated, the activities of the day—just this one day—had covered enough of them to make the answer crystal clear. He couldn't go back to being Lord Julian Delbraith, because to do that he would have to cease being Neville Roscoe.

And too many people, *far* too many people, depended on Roscoe, regardless of whether they knew it or not.

Not just his employees, although they were now legion and reason enough on their own. There were no other gambling czars likely to follow his, to them peculiar and irrational, ways, such as protecting his employees from all external intimidation, employing so many women, especially in more responsible positions, and paying all his workers fairly and regularly, let alone insisting that no crime of any kind be committed on his premises.

If Neville Roscoe disappeared, there were many who would breathe a sigh of relief and instantly revert to the laws of the jungle. While he remained, his establishments set a standard that other houses had been forced to match and maintain. If he took himself out of the equation . . . there was no self-aggrandizement in admitting the obvious.

And while his family's fortunes were now secure, and his personal fortune was nothing short of immense, the funds he currently poured into charities via the Philanthropy Guild, Argyle Investments, and various other funding bodies far exceeded the income he could raise from his private wealth.

He'd made the decision long ago that as so many of the ton were addicted to playing for high stakes, then it was entirely appropriate for him to accommodate them, take their money, and redirect it to those most in need. He'd come to terms with the likelihood that that stance had its genesis in his guilt over exploiting so many other gamblers' addictions while rescuing his own family; he'd decided he and his conscience could live with that.

Raising the cut-crystal tumbler to his lips, he sipped the fiery old cognac and let his conclusion wash over and through him.

Lips twisting, he lowered the glass and leaned back in the chair. "Sorry, Mama, but Lord Julian Roscoe Neville Delbraith isn't coming back. For all intents and purposes, Lord Julian is dead."

"Good evening, Rundle." Standing on Roscoe's front step, Miranda raised a questioning brow. "Is your master in?"

"Indeed, miss." Rundle stepped back, bowing her inside.

Walking into the hall, she halted by the central table and drew off her gloves, then let Rundle remove her cloak. Beneath it she wore an amber silk gown with a topaz silk shawl draped over her shoulders. "Is he in the library?"

"Yes, miss. If you'll follow me?"

Inclining her head graciously, she followed Rundle down the corridor, strolling in his wake as if her visiting a gentleman in his house after ten o'clock at night was an unremarkable occurrence. She needed to speak with Roscoe, to learn what he felt and what was possible, and, she hoped, to continue their liaison. As he couldn't come to her in Claverton Street, she had come to him.

Last night had fallen too soon, the evening too full of Gladys's questions and the fuss of settling back into their home. She'd been tired after their two days on the road, yet she hadn't slept well, restless and agitated in an unsettling way. She'd woken several times, her senses reaching for his warmth, only to encounter cold sheets and empty space.

While she felt certain a liaison of less than two weeks' duration could not possibly cause an addiction, she'd still missed him, apparently at a level deeper than her conscious mind.

Reaching the end of the long corridor, Rundle opened the library door, announced, "Miss Clifford to see you, sir," then held the door for her.

Crossing the threshold, it occurred to her that Rundle should have inquired if his master was willing to see her before admitting her to the library. Wondering why Rundle hadn't, she nevertheless grasped the opportunity to assess Roscoe's unprepared response to her arrival; walking deeper into the room, she smiled at him.

He sat in the armchair he'd occupied all those nights ago, when she'd come to plead for his help in finding Roderick. As then, he'd been reading a book; it lay open in his hands, forgotten as he watched her walk toward him.

Heat flared in the midnight depths of his eyes; she felt the lick of flame as his gaze swept over her, then returned to her face, her eyes. Without looking down, he shut the book and rose. "Miss Clifford." His gaze went past her to Rundle, and impassivity reclaimed his expression. "That will be all, Rundle."

"Indeed, sir."

A *snick* told her Rundle had retreated and closed the door.

Roscoe's gaze switched to her face, raced again over her features, then settled on her eyes. He hesitated, then asked, "What is it?"

"I wanted to ask whether you've heard anything about Kirkwell." She continued to walk toward him. Smile deepening, she halted only when her bodice brushed the front of his coat. "And I wanted to do this." Placing a hand on his chest, she stretched up and pressed her lips to his.

He held back for an instant—a moment, she sensed, not of hesitation but calculation—then his lips moved on hers and he took control of the kiss, closed his arms about her and waltzed them into the familiar flames, held them there and let them burn.

For uncounted minutes, for long-drawn-out moments of

simple pleasure, of shared warmth and delight. He let the caress spin out, but then he reined them in, both her and him.

When he raised his head, she was caught hard against him, eyes wide, senses fully engaged, wholly aware of the thrum of sensual, sexual attraction that held them both, trapped them both. Linked them both.

He looked into her eyes, then raising a hand brushed back an errant lock of hair from her cheek. "Why did you come?"

"To ask about Kirkwell, and . . ." With one finger, she traced the line of his lower lip. "Because of this."

He caught the tip of her finger between his teeth, lightly nipped, then released it. "As to Kirkwell"—his voice was a gravelly rumble—"there's little to tell. Mudd and Rawlins spoke to Kempsey's uncle. The uncle had gone to the Hood and Gable to meet with Kirkwell as arranged, but Kirkwell never appeared. Mudd and Rawlins returned to the tavern and asked around again in case someone had seen him nearby, or knew anything more of him, but no."

She studied his face. "So we've no way of tracking him?"

"Not directly. But if you recall, all the descriptions we've had of him mention a scar everyone's taken to be a sword slash. These days that's a common enough scar for most people to recognize correctly, so if Kirkwell is this man's real name, I might be able to make inquiries via the army."

She widened her eyes. "You can do that?"

"Let's just say I have several acquaintances who owe me favors."

"How long will that take?"

"Several days at least. But as long as Roderick remains at home, he'll be safe enough, and with his broken foot . . ."

"For the moment, he's stuck at home and therefore safe."

She studied his face, and he studied hers. She waited.

After a long moment, his lips twisted; his gaze fell to her lips. "As for this . . ." He mirrored her earlier caress, drawing the pad of his thumb over the curve of her lower lip, sending a slow shiver of delicious anticipation slithering down her spine. He sensed it; his lips curved and she felt the spiraling tension in him. He drew a tighter breath. "What about it?"

She waited until his eyes rose and his gaze met hers. "I want to know what's possible. What you want, what we might have should we both wish it." She was quietly amazed at herself, that she'd had the courage to come there, to speak as she was and make a bid to seize what she wanted, yet if there was one thing the ladies of his family had taught her it was that she, too, could reach for her dreams, that regardless of her mother's and sister's experiences, such an act wouldn't necessarily end in tragedy.

"Ah." His eyes held hers, but she couldn't read them.

Some emotion shifted behind the sapphire blue, but she couldn't make it out. "I don't know our options, but I presume you do."

He hesitated. His arms still around her, he studied her eyes; he seemed to be having no greater success divining her thoughts than she was his. "I take it you wish to continue our liaison. Here, in town."

"Yes." She held his gaze. "Can we?"

No. Roscoe knew that was the correct answer, but he couldn't get the word past his lips. The reason he'd never allowed any other to be his mistress applied even more to her. He drew breath into lungs suddenly constricted. "Miranda—"

She silenced him by laying a finger across his lips. "This might be the right time, but"—her gaze swept the chairs and hearth before returning to his face—"this definitely isn't the right place."

He hardened his resolve. "Mir—"

"We can discuss the details later." Gripping his lapels, she stretched up on her toes. "For now, just kiss me."

She pressed her lips to his, then parted hers, enticing and demanding and utterly irresistible. Before his mind had made any decision, his arms had tightened around her, he'd lowered his head, and he was doing exactly as she wished and kissing her. Voraciously.

He was hungry for her, and she was offering succor. He took, and she gave unstintingly. Her hands slid into his hair, clutched his skull, and held him to the kiss, held him so she could return the pleasure.

Tenfold. A hundredfold.

Effortlessly, they spun into desire's dance.

He knew he had to tell her that this couldn't be, that their liaison couldn't go on, not in London, not in safety. But he'd assumed that she would keep her distance, knowing that here in London he was Roscoe and not a man remotely eligible for her to even dally with . . . but she hadn't.

In coming to him tonight, in walking so confidently into his library and making her wish to continue their liaison so blatantly clear, she'd thrown him off-balance. Utterly and comprehensively. She'd reopened a debate he'd thought already resolved; she'd made him question the possibilities anew . . . yet even as he sank into the wonder of her mouth, as he felt her body cleave to his, felt her supple and vibrant in his arms, he knew in his soul that nothing had changed. She simply didn't know enough to see matters as clearly as he.

He would have to explain, but even as he summoned wits and will enough to break the kiss and speak, she pressed provocatively against him, drew her lips from his and purred, sultry and low, "Take me to your bed."

The words shattered his resolve, sent any thoughts he might have gathered winging—any thoughts beyond the image of her lying, sated and boneless, sprawled on his silk sheets.

Heat rose and engulfed him, desire a searing edge to the flames.

He didn't answer, couldn't get his throat to function, didn't trust his voice. Instead, he stepped back; eyes locked with hers, he took her hand, then together they turned to the door. He remembered little of their trek up the stairs; she paused in the gallery and he took the lead. His hand wrapped around hers, he drew her on down the corridor to the double doors to his room.

Opening one, he drew her through, whirled her into his arms as he kicked the door shut. Bent his head and kissed her, and backed her toward the bed.

Last night. Last time. Never again.

His mind was no longer capable of forming words, yet he absorbed the meaning, and that understanding infused his touch, set a honed edge to his desire.

A desire she matched in every way. Halting at the foot of the bed, breaking the kiss, he nudged her head with his jaw and pressed his lips to the long arching line of her throat, and felt her shudder. She was particularly sensitive there; with his lips he traced hot kisses along the fine tendons, following them down to the hollow where throat met shoulder, while his hands uncoiled her hair, raining pins upon the floor until the silken mass descended, then he set his roving palms to her body, to her firm curves, tracing, assimilating, possessing anew. Laying claim to her bounty.

One hand clasping his nape, the other gripping his shoulder, she clung. Lashes low, lips parted, she tipped her head back, giving him better access to the fine skin exposed by the scooped neckline of her gown. With his lips he traced the tempting upper swells of her breasts, then straightened and captured her lips with his while his fingers sought and found the laces at her side, and swiftly undid them.

She didn't seem inclined to rush, allowing him to slowly ease the gown down, savoring the firm mounds of her breasts as he released them from the tight confines of her bodice, as he took them in his hands and, with his lips still on hers, drank in her pleasure as he weighed, caressed, then kneaded. The fine film of her chemise, the last insubstantial barrier between his palms and her skin, added another layer of tactile delight, shifting and sliding, tantalizing.

He pushed the folds of her gown lower, past the sculpted indentation of her waist, over the evocative flare of her hips. From the tops of her thighs, the gown fell with a soft sigh to puddle on the floor.

Drawing back from the kiss, she stepped free of the gown's

folds, kicked the silk aside, then, clad only in her translucent chemise, silk stockings gartered above her knees, and her heeled evening shoes, she stepped boldly closer; eyes locking with his, she lifted her hands to his cravat.

Her turn. She said nothing, but he understood and let her have her way. There was no reason not to draw each moment out, to savor each in turn, to hold back the inevitable desperate race for as long as they could. No reason they shouldn't take as long as they wished for this, their very last time.

So he worked to keep their caresses slow, to string out each moment to the ultimate degree. She noticed, cast him a speculative glance, but he wasn't surprised when she matched her sensual heartbeat to his, and together they moved forward into the slowest, most exquisite dance.

He hadn't expected it to be so enthralling. So overwhelming.

Their previous engagements had opened his eyes, so now he could see and absorb the wonder. And fall hostage to the simple joy.

To the soul-shattering reality of what lay between them.

She held nothing back. As button by button, garment by garment, she stripped his clothes away, she let all she felt color her expression, flow through her touch; she put all she felt for him on display.

He couldn't not honor her openness. Couldn't do anything other than reciprocate. Dropping every screen, every shield, he let them come together in love and blazing passion.

Naked on his knees before her, he carefully removed her garters and shoes, rolled down her stockings, then rose and slowly drew away her chemise to reveal her fully, a goddess of pearlescent curves and seductive shadows.

Even as he let the fine silk slip from his fingers to the floor, she took the crucial step to set body to body, skin to naked skin.

The searing moment rocked them both.

With all sophistication set aside and only instinct to guide him, he bent his head as she stretched up, and their lips met and locked, and passion burned.

The conflagration built slowly, layer upon layer of wicked heat, of hungry flames. They both fought to hold it to a slow, steady cadence, to a rhythm slow enough that they could fully taste and savor each moment.

Could thrill, each of them, to the other's intimate touch, to each evocative caress that he pressed on her, that she returned to him in full measure. Fingers splayed, played, wickedly intent. Their mouths fused, then parted; lips cruised, teeth nipped, tongues laved. Rasped, lasciviously licked.

He worshipped her breasts, then moved on.

She caressed the rigid column of his erection, then spread her hands and devoured his chest, his back, his flanks, his thighs. All of him she could reach.

Fiery tension thrummed through them, forceful and so real, yet they clung to the fraught moments, to the silvery glory, and reverently drank this, the truth of them, in.

But, eventually, need raked too desperately to ignore. He lifted her and she wrapped her long legs about his hips, and slid down as he thrust slowly upward and filled her. A shivering, shuddering sigh fell from her lips, then she wound her arms about his neck and drew his lips to hers.

The kiss was all heat and smoldering latent passion, bucking molten beneath their now tenuous control.

She pulled back, tipped her head, hoarsely whispered, "The bed."

He walked to it. Holding her to him, he kneeled on the silk covers, then shifted forward on his knees and tipped her back until she lay on the dark blue silk, and followed her down.

Let her draw him down fully atop her.

Let her embrace him and hold him as he let the reins slide and let all he felt for her take over and drive him.

Into a dance to end all dances, into the heat of their raging fire.

And she was with him, gasping and clinging, riding and

racing as, bodies plunging, they let passion whip them up the last peak.

To where ecstasy waited, brighter, more brilliant, than ever before.

To where their hearts collided, shattered, and re-formed, transformed and became one as they fell through the glory.

Joy caught them, buoyed them. A sense of peace so pervasive it utterly overwhelmed them, flooded them, enfolded them, and dragged them down.

Despite all, this still had to be their end.

Uncounted minutes later, he stirred, reluctantly drawing his mind from the soothing soporific embrace of satiation. He lay slumped more or less on his stomach. She lay beside him, her eyes closed, her expression blank, as sated and boneless as his imagination had earlier painted her. Her hair was spread in a rippling brown wave of shimmering silk across his pillows.

Easing up on his elbows, he took moments—several—to drink in the sight, to let it sink into his mind, engrave itself on his memory. Then, moving slowly, he turned and shifted up in the bed until he could sit with his back against the pillows piled against the carved headboard. Raising one arm, he set that hand behind his head and gave his mind to finding the words—the right words—he knew he had to say.

Eventually, she stirred. He glanced at her face and saw her lashes flutter. Decided he was as prepared as he was ever going to be to have this discussion he didn't want to have.

When her lids rose, he was waiting to capture her shadowed gaze. "We can't continue to see each other. Not like this—indeed, not at all."

She blinked, then beneath the covers he'd drawn over them, she turned onto her stomach; propped on her elbows, she faced him. Slowly frowned. "Why?" Her voice was husky, still low. "I . . ." A lock of hair fell over her face; she put up a hand to push it back, then froze. Even in the faint light, he saw her blush. "Oh." Abruptly she looked down, her hair, released, curtaining her face.

His jaw clenched. "No. It's not that." He waited, but when she didn't look up, he reached out and caught her chin on the edge of his hand and tipped up her face, then gently brushed back the silk screen of her hair. Only when he could see her face clearly did he finally meet her eyes. "You are the first—the only—woman I've ever brought to this room, to this bed."

She tilted her head, searching his eyes. "Then . . . why? If it's not that you've tired of me"—she raised her shoulders, gestured with one hand—"why call a halt to something we both enjoy?"

"Because I'm not the sort of man you can even be seen with, much less acknowledge as your lover—and ultimately someone will see, will talk. It's too dangerous."

Miranda tipped her head further, her eyes on his. "Isn't that for me to decide?"

He held her gaze for a moment, then his features hardened. Tossing back the covers, he reached for his trousers, rose and hauled them on, then stalked to where a decanter and glasses sat on a tray atop a dresser.

She watched him pour a glass of what she assumed was brandy. About to replace the stopper, he glanced at her. She shook her head. Restoppering the decanter, he picked up his glass, sipped, then prowled back to the bed.

He halted by its side, sipped again as, a frown in his eyes if not on his face, he looked down at her. After a moment, he said, his voice dark and low, "I'm Neville Roscoe, London's gambling king, and as such I am utterly and immutably ineligible to consort with any lady, other than illicitly. Quite aside from the danger of blackmail or abduction, an illicit relationship won't do for you. I might be as rich as Croesus, but the one thing I can't buy is respectability, the sort you need any man in your life to have. And no matter how much I might wish it, I can't change that. No amount of philanthropy will ever alter that." His dark gaze locked on her face, he sipped again, then went on, his voice quieter, "Tell me, did my mother mention her notion of me reverting to being Julian?"

She considered carefully before saying, "Caroline told me of the events that prompted you to become Roscoe. Lucasta mentioned that she thought that, with that earlier situation being fully resolved, you might now feel free to reverse the change."

His lips twisted; he raised the glass to disguise the expression, but his gaze never left her face. A moment ticked by before, his voice still quiet, he said, "I considered it. Because of you, I thought of it."

When he didn't continue, her heart, her flesh, growing colder by the second, her tone flat, she prompted, "But . . . ?"

He held her gaze for several heartbeats, then swung away, picked up a straight-backed chair from by the wall, set it down facing the bed, then sat. Leaning forward, forearms on his thighs, cradling the glass between his hands, his face now more or less level with hers, he met her gaze. "I can't."

It felt strange to be discussing such an emotionally fraught subject in such a calm and detached fashion, but . . . she dragged in a breath and clung to the same quiet, even tone he'd used; she had to understand. "Can't? Or won't?"

He thought, sipped, then grimaced. "Both. I can't because too many people in the ton and elsewhere would recognize me as Roscoe, which would effectively ruin everything I've spent the last twelve years achieving for my family. And I won't—wouldn't—even were that not the case, because . . ." He let an instant go by, then met her gaze. "As London's gambling king, I have over one thousand people on my collective staffs. The vast majority have families. Given their talents, most would have difficulty finding alternative gainful employment." He paused, then lowered his gaze to the dregs in his glass. "I became Roscoe to protect six people—my mother, my sisters, Henry, and Caroline. Admittedly, they were my family and had no one else to help them, but . . ." He refocused on her face. "Roscoe's family numbers in the thousands, and if he vanished—simply wasn't there—or even sold his holdings to someone else, none of those people would be safe, not as safe as they are while I, as Roscoe, am here.

"Those thousand and more people are the responsibility I accepted as a means to protect my family. I can't—won't—simply turn my back on them now that the Delbraiths are safe and it would be convenient to return to the ton."

Convenient. He was speaking of—

"I won't discard them"—his gaze locked with hers—"even if doing so might allow us to continue our liaison." His gaze was uncompromising. "But believe me, you deserve better than an affair with a wastrel lordling, and that's all Lord Julian Delbraith will ever be."

What about something more than an affair . . . an icy sensation locked around her heart. To hold back the realization of what his words implied—to not let the impact shatter her—she forced herself to focus on a point she'd yet to grasp. "I might understand your decision better if I knew why it was necessary for you to become Roscoe in the first place—why that specifically was required to save your family."

The frown returned to his eyes. "I would have thought that would be obvious to someone rigidly set on respectability."

"I understand all about respectability in the gentry," she replied tartly, "but the aristocracy has somewhat different, more fluid, rules, as I've recently learned. You set out to use gambling to pay your family's debts. Dozens of peers gamble outrageously, as your brother did in creating that debt, so why did you, gambling with a higher purpose, need to hide your identity?"

"Ah." His lips twisted in a cynical smile. "The ton has always been two-faced and is frequently flagrantly hypocritical. The reason is . . . multifaceted, as so many situations involving ton mores are. First, the amount of money that was needed to satisfy creditors and refill the family coffers was immense—there was no chance of covering it with a few spectacular wins here and there. And if I'd gone out to amass such a massively obvious amount via the gaming tables, it would have instantly signaled to all and sundry that the Delbraiths were penniless, and that would have spelled ruin for the very six people I wanted to protect. On top of that, society would have been scandalized that in order to rescue the Delbraiths I was, albeit legally, draining vast amounts from the coffers of other ton families. And lastly, I wouldn't have been able to do so anyway, because I would have had to win very large amounts frequently, and within a week every gentleman with money in London would have taken to avoiding me. I wouldn't have been able to find anyone to gamble with, and the gaming houses and clubs wouldn't have let me in their doors, having realized that my intention was to break their banks and that I had the skills to do just that." He met her gaze, his expression beyond cynical. "So while as Lord Julian Delbraith I had the skills to do what I needed to do, as Lord Julian Delbraith I couldn't do it."

"But how did becoming Roscoe allow you to do what you couldn't as Lord Julian?" She clung to her curiosity, using it as a shield to hold her thoughts, her reactions, at bay.

Through the shadows, he simply looked at her and said nothing.

She held his gaze and didn't retreat. After a moment, her voice quiet, she said, "You've just told me that our association is at an end—that I won't be seeing you, spending time with you, again. So humor me, just this once, and tell me." *Trust me, even if this is good-bye.*

He remained silent for a moment more, then raised his glass and swiftly drained it. Lowering the glass, he turned it in his hands. "I needed to give all the inveterate gamblers and the owners of the gaming houses in London time to forget Lord Julian, but the family needed money, large amounts of it, quickly. I went to the Continent. I traveled to every town where wealthy young men rashly wagered their blunt. I won. Because I won, I had to keep moving constantly—no more than a week in one place. Often only two nights if I won a spectacularly large amount." Briefly he met her gaze. "I'd realized, almost from the nursery, certainly by the time I went to school, that for someone with my particular talents it never pays to win too much, or too frequently. By the time I went on the town I'd learned to lose, and did, deliberately, to disguise my winnings. I often walked out of a club ten thousand pounds richer and no one who'd played with me would have had any notion that I'd won more than once or twice, and that only modestly." His lips twisted. "I was very good at what I did." He sighed and glanced down at the glass. "But that wasn't what my family needed, so on the Continent I'd win as much as I could, and then leave town and never go back. I, and the small crew I gradually gathered around me, lived like that for two years.

"Then we came back to England. I'd changed enough that none of the owners or staff of the gambling clubs recognized me, and at first I steered clear of any of the haunts of the haut ton. I'd learned a lot on my travels, and I'd realized that the most certain yet covert way to make lots of money through gambling was to own the club, so I bought one. The Pall Mall." His expression hardened. "After that, I never looked back."

She frowned. "Caroline said gambling was the family addiction, yet I've never seen you gamble."

He shrugged. "I run forty-three businesses, all based on gambling. I feel no need to sit down at a table to add to that." He paused, then said, "It's not the gambling per se that we're addicted to, it's the thrill of success."

A piece of the puzzle of him slid into place. "That's why you push Henry to try all sorts of novel things on the estate—why you insist he takes an active role in running almost everything."

He glanced at her as if surprised she'd seen it, then nodded. "There are challenges in life other than those found over gaming tables that can give us the same satisfaction. We just have to find them."

And he'd found his in becoming Roscoe.

His refusal to revert to Lord Julian did, indeed, now make

sense. Much better sense than it had before. He was Roscoe, and for many many reasons, that was who he needed to be.

The moon was waning. Through the deepening darkness, she met his gaze. "Thank you for telling me."

Now to get out of there and home to her room without allowing herself to think about this being the last time she would see him. She turned away and pushed back the covers. "And now it's time for me to leave."

They dressed in silence, then he fetched her cloak and they left the house and walked through the rear garden to the alley beyond. The night was cold; the moon had set, leaving the alley drenched in darkness. They walked side by side without touching, without speaking, leaving her concentrating on not thinking, on not allowing her mind to dwell on what had happened, what was happening, and what it meant—not yet.

From the instant he'd told her their liaison was at an end, she'd felt compelled to keep her emotions, her feelings, in check, compelled to project a cool, composed façade—to behave as she assumed a sophisticated lady of the ton would in such a situation.

But inside, behind that façade, something was tearing, ripping, but she couldn't look to see what, or how badly. Not yet.

It wasn't far to the garden gate of the Claverton Street house. He reached for the latch but didn't immediately open it. He looked at her. Raising her head, shoulders back, spine straight, she forced herself to meet his gaze without letting any of her inner tumult show. Liaisons by their very nature were short-lived. They ended. She had to accept that theirs just had.

The shadows were too dense for her to see his face, to make out his expression. His eyes were pools of impenetrable darkness. "If I learn anything more about Kirkwell, I'll send word." He hesitated, then somewhat diffidently added, "If you should ever need the sort of help I can give, I hope you won't hesitate to ask."

It was all she could do to dip her head in acknowledgment.

He hesitated a moment more, then the latch clicked and he sent the gate swinging wide. "Good-bye, Miranda."

It was her turn to hesitate, caught by a wild and desperate urge to throw caution to the wind, to throw herself into his arms and demand . . .

She drew in a tight breath and, head high, stepped through the gate. "Good night, Roscoe."

Reaching out, she shut the gate behind her. And waited. Waited, all thought ruthlessly suppressed, suspended, until several long moments later she heard his footsteps moving slowly away from the gate and down the alley.

Once the sound had faded, she dropped her head back, closed her eyes, forced herself to draw a long, deep breath.

And let her thoughts free. Let her emotions and feelings erupt and roil through her, clashing, straining, raking, scouring.

The torrent was so turbulent that she could find no firm ground, no certainty, only confusion.

Only a nebulous all-encompassing hurt, an amorphous, deadening pain.

For which there was no one to blame. She'd instigated the liaison and had never planned for it to last beyond one night, then a few, then beyond the convenient opportunity provided by their sojourn at Ridgware.

Yes, Lucasta's suggestion that he might revert to being Lord Julian had raised possibilities in her mind, but he wasn't able to take that road, and after all she'd learned of his life as Roscoe . . .

So she'd asked for one more night, and he'd granted it, and they'd indulged for one last time, but clearly he'd been right to draw a line and say *No more*. There was nothing in his stance that she could argue with. *She* might know him as an honorable and worthy man—and that he wouldn't turn his back on all those who now depended on him underscored that—but society wouldn't see him in the same light, and ultimately society and its expectations still ruled her life.

The cold penetrated her cloak and she shivered. Gathering the folds more tightly about her, she looked down and started toward the house.

Why was she so emotionally wracked? She had no right that she could see to feel so.

Frowning, she climbed the steps to the terrace and let herself in through the morning room door.

She didn't know what to think. Worse, she didn't know what she felt. Or why. Could it be that what she felt for him was love? Was that why this hurt so much—so very very much?

Regardless, what had grown between her and him—the connection, the closeness, the violently passionate glory—was over. Ended. No more.

Chapter Eighteen

Two mornings later, Miranda sat alone in the morning room mending the hem of one of her gowns and ruthlessly keeping her mind on the simple task.

The previous day had vanished in a miasma of doubts, stunned helplessness, and utterly useless, senseless maunderings; this morning she'd woken firmly resolved to put her liaison with Roscoe behind her and get on.

Get on with living her life, with working out what she most wanted her life henceforth to be, and making the right decisions to secure precisely that. Courtesy of her time at Ridgware, she now knew what was possible and what she had to do; she just had to do it.

The household, however, hadn't ceased to be. Even though it was obvious that sometime soon Roderick would marry and thereafter this house would be his wife's to run, at present that task fell to her; she was still catching up with the myriad decisions her absence had left unresolved.

On top of that, Roderick was finding his convalescence every bit as difficult to bear as she'd guessed he would. She'd left him slouched in an armchair in the drawing room, supplied with the day's news sheets and with Gladys watching over him; although he hadn't made any complaint, the set of his lips, the darkness in his eyes, had spoken loudly enough. She fervently hoped the appeal she'd sent to Sarah's family would solicit a favorable response, and soon; she couldn't think of anything else she might do to alleviate her brother's endurance vile.

She'd just tied off her thread and was reaching for her shears when the knocker on the front door was plied in a rigidly precise cadence, one she recognized. Hughes's footsteps marched to the front door; quickly folding her sewing away, she set the basket aside, rose, and smoothed down her skirts.

Glancing at the mirror on the wall beside the door, she tucked several loose strands of hair back into her chignon, then drew in a breath, plastered on an appropriately welcoming smile, and sallied forth to learn what possibilities Mr. Wraxby might hold vis-à-vis her future life.

She entered the drawing room to see Wraxby bowing over Gladys's hand. He turned and smiled at her, a cool gesture.

"Sir." She gave him her hand, watching critically as he bowed over it. He really was a very *stiff* sort of person. Retrieving her fingers, she waved him to the sofa. He'd been away in the country, she recalled. "Have you just returned to the capital?"

"I returned two days ago." Wraxby waited until she sat, then flipped up his coattails and sat rigidly upright on the sofa's other end. "Business claims my time, but as I had a few hours free I thought to see how you all are faring." He looked at Roderick's foot. "How did you come by that, Clifford?"

Roderick smiled tightly. "Dashed inconvenient. I fell down the stairs."

Because he was drunk? She all but heard Wraxby's thought.

A glance showed Gladys had sensed the same unvoiced reaction. Her aunt hurriedly said, "I've told him time and again that a gentleman shouldn't go rushing up and down as if he were still a boy. But . . ." Gladys spread her hands in a what-would-you gesture.

Wraxby gravely inclined his head. "High spirits and an overabundance of energy. I face the same issues with my sons."

Miranda shot a warning glance at Roderick. Wraxby's sons were children; by the comparison he'd reduced Roderick to the same status. Turning to Wraxby, she asked, "How has the weather been in Suffolk, sir?"

For the next several minutes, Wraxby, Gladys, and she engaged in a stilted conversation revolving about the unseasonable warmth. Other than a pointed comment or two, Roderick contributed little, but she noted the deepening lines bracketing his mouth, his increasing tension.

So when Wraxby asked if she would care to accompany him on a walk around the square, she was perfectly ready to smile and accept, and get him out of the house.

Allowing him to help her into her coat, she reflected that, aside from all else, she needed to evaluate his still-pending offer, and decide whether the position of his wife might align with her newly evolving requirements of life.

Now the uncertainty and distraction of Roscoe was behind her, she would go forward and evaluate the chances fate consented to send her way.

Of course, in reaching the square they had to pass within sight of the big white house on Chichester Street. She fought to keep her gaze averted and her mind from dwelling on any of the occupants.

"Miss Clifford, I wonder if you have given the subject of our previous conversation any further thought?"

By which Wraxby meant his still-pending offer, the offer he was waiting for her to agree to accept before he made it. Strolling by his side, her hand on his sleeve, she inclined her head. "Indeed, sir, I have, but as I'm sure you will appreciate, Roderick's accident has been something of a distraction."

"Of course."

"However," she continued, "I'm glad to have this opportunity to further clarify matters between us. If I understood you correctly . . ." She led Wraxby through the elements of his proposal, encouraging him to further elaborate. He confirmed that his need for a wife was driven by practical considerations rather than any true desire on his part for even a partner, much less a lover.

In the end, she baldly asked, "Sir, I feel I must inquire as to why you believe we might suit."

They'd reached the river and were strolling along the towpath. Wraxby frowned at the path ahead, then opened his mouth and reiterated all the unemotional assessments of her character he'd previously advanced, apparently not realizing that she'd given him a last chance to speak of any finer feelings.

Clearly finer feelings were not in Wraxby's repertoire, at least not with respect to her. While that made his proposal somewhat depressing, at least he was honest.

She accepted his answer with a nod. "I have one final question, sir. What are your thoughts on philanthropy—meaning charitable projects of significant scope, such as the patronage of schools, orphanages, and the like?"

Wraxby didn't immediately reply. They'd turned once more up Claverton Street and were pacing back toward the house when he finally said, "I have heard of such projects, of course. I understand there are several foundations actively engaged in such work. However, I myself see no reason to expend effort and money on matters I deem more correctly the authorities' domain. If improvements to such institutions are truly necessary, they will doubtless be provided. I prefer to keep charity closer to home." He glanced at her, a faint frown on his face. "I sincerely hope you have not become infected with any of this latest fashionable nonsense, my dear Miss Clifford. But then I'm certain your aunt would have guided you more carefully."

Miranda managed a thin smile. "Indeed, sir. I wished for your opinion and must thank you for your candor."

They'd reached the front gate of Roderick's house. Wraxby halted. Drawing her hand from his sleeve, she faced him.

Wraxby studied her expression. "I feel I must ask, Miss Clifford, whether you have reached any conclusion with regard to your willingness to entertain an offer from me."

"I appreciate your patience, sir." She paused, then raised her head. "While I'm almost certain of my decision, I would like a few more days to consider further." She met his gaze. "I believe I will be able to give you an answer shortly."

Wraxby inclined his head; from his self-satisfied expression, she suspected he assumed she would decide in his favor. "In that case, I will, if you're agreeable, call on you in two days' time. I have business to attend to until then, but will be free to visit in the afternoon. I will call on you then."

Smiling politely, she gave him her hand, then watched as he walked to where a boy held his horse. After handing the lad a coin, Wraxby mounted. He raised a hand in farewell, then rode up the street.

She watched him go, eyes on his rigid, unbending back. She tried to imagine him as her husband, and failed. But she had to consider every option.

Turning, she went through the gate, shut it behind her, then walked slowly down the path. Would life as a glorified nursemaid with no compensating chance of enriching her life through philanthropic endeavors or any similar enterprises be enough to satisfy her?

The answer seemed obvious, yet given she had to make a new life for herself, she would do the sensible thing and sleep on her thoughts before she rejected Wraxby.

"No problems of any kind in the Fleet or the Strand. Covent Garden's had its usual ructions, but nothing Kane or Higgens couldn't handle."

Seated behind the desk in his study, Roscoe nodded to Rawlins to continue. Together with Mudd, Rawlins had recently returned from accompanying Jordan on his weekly round reconciling the funds at a selection of the clubs. While

Jordan counted the money, Rawlins and Mudd spoke with the staff. Although their conversations were passed off as idle chatting, the pair often picked up early signs of trouble on the floors of the clubs.

"We stopped at Holborn. My instincts shivered, so to speak, but I didn't hear anything specific." Rawlins glanced at the door. "Might do to ask Mudd when he gets back."

Mudd had been called out by Rundle to receive a report from one of the watchers stationed nearby. As since Roderick's kidnapping there'd been several groups positioned about the neighborhood, until Mudd returned, Roscoe couldn't tell which area, or whose safety, the report concerned. Reining in his impatience, Roscoe asked, "Did you call at Bermondsey?"

"Not this time—Jordan said it's on next week's list. That's where you've got that new gent running things?"

"Yes—Titchester." Roscoe considered, then said, "Let's send one of the other men around, someone Titchester won't recognize. Just to make sure all's continuing smoothly there."

"I'll send Stackpole. He hasn't been out in the clubs for a while."

Roscoe nodded and jotted a note.

The door opened and Mudd came in. For a very large man, Mudd moved silently, light on his very large feet.

Roscoe leaned back and arched a brow.

Mudd halted beside the chair he'd occupied earlier. "That was Coogan from the group watching the Clifford house. 'Parently a gent, tall, forty-ish, graying hair, well-dressed, riding a brown nag, arrived a little while ago, went inside, but about ten minutes later came walking out with Miss Clifford. They strolled through the square. Coogan passed them on to Wilkins there, and Wilkins followed them down to the river, then back up Claverton Street. According to Wilkins, Miss Clifford and the gent were talking the whole way, but not jolly-like—more like they were discussing something serious. Only smile he saw was at the end, when Miss Clifford saw the gent off at the front gate, then, looking like she was thinking hard, she went indoors."

Roscoe nodded and waved Mudd to sit again. "Very well. To return to Holborn." He looked at Mudd. "Rawlins says something's off—did you pick up anything specific?"

Mudd blinked at him, then looked at Rawlins. The pair exchanged a glance, then both looked at Roscoe again.

Rawlins leaned forward. "Don't you want us to find out who this gent who called in Claverton Street is?"

Roscoe met Rawlins's gaze, then looked at Mudd. "Did Coogan or Wilkins see anything to suggest that Miss Clifford is in any danger from this gentleman, or that she fears him?"

Mudd hesitated, then shook his head. "No. Wilkins said they were just walking and discussing."

"Well, then, there's no reason for us to interfere, is there?"

The silence that ensued told Roscoe more clearly than if they'd spoken that neither of his bodyguards agreed.

He fixed Mudd with a pointed glance. "Holborn?"

Mudd shifted, frowned. "Not off, exactly, but . . ."

After Mudd and Rawlins left, Roscoe debated for a full minute, then sighed, reached for a fresh sheet of paper, and picked up his pen.

Five minutes later, he rang for Rundle. When his butler materialized, he handed him the folded missive. "Have this delivered to Mr. Clifford immediately. Tell the footman to wait for an answer."

Rundle bowed. "Yes, sir."

An hour later, Roscoe made his way to Jordan's office. As usual, the door stood open. Propping a shoulder against the frame, he studied the man, no longer as young as he'd been when Lord Julian Delbraith had first tapped him on the shoulder to become his man of business more than thirteen years ago, yet there were still three pencils stuck behind Jordan's ears, he'd taken off his jacket and was working in his shirtsleeves, and his fingers were grimy from handling dozens of sovereigns.

The scritch of pen on paper and the clink of coins was familiar music in the room. Through association with him, Jordan had become a very wealthy man, yet he still loved counting money.

Hiding a smile, Roscoe pushed away from the door and strolled into the room. Aside from all aspects of managing money, there was one other skill at which Jordan excelled.

Finally realizing he was no longer alone, Jordan glanced up and grinned. "You should be pleased with the good weather—people have stayed in town longer, and we're reaping the rewards."

"Excellent." Roscoe halted, fingers tapping lightly on the desk. "I have another job for you. Knowing you, it won't take long."

Instantly diverted, Jordan arched his brows.

"Wraxby—a gentleman from Hill's End in Suffolk. I want to know everything about him."

Jordan whipped a pencil from behind his right ear and jotted on a scrap of paper. "When do you need the information by?" Jordan looked up.

"As soon as you can get it."

Jordan nodded, rose, and pulled his coat off the back of his chair. Shrugging into it, he glanced at the clock on the wall opposite his desk. "Let's see what I can turn up this evening."

With a dip of his head, Roscoe led the way out; in the corridor, he stood back as Jordan locked the door—a strong-room door masquerading as a normal door. Straightening, Jordan flicked him a salute and strode off.

Roscoe followed more slowly, doing everything he could *not* to think about why he'd done what he just had.

He couldn't fault his men for doing as he'd asked.

The following afternoon, having been informed by a blank-faced Mudd that the same gent from yesterday had called at the Clifford residence again, and had this time taken Miss Clifford out driving, and having also received a detailed report from Jordan earlier in the day, Roscoe found himself lurking in the alley alongside the Clifford garden, close to Claverton Street.

He'd sent the men he'd had on watch back to his house for a break; no sense them watching as well, and better still if they weren't about to see how Miranda Clifford reacted. He had no idea how she would take the news of what he'd uncovered about her gentleman caller.

Lounging against the alley wall, he looked out along the street to where a plain gig stood, the horse somnolent between the shafts, the reins held by one of the local urchins always ready to earn a copper or two. Wraxby and Miranda had returned more than twenty minutes ago; if Wraxby and Miranda's aunt adhered strictly to society's rules, then Wraxby would be leaving soon.

All in all, he wasn't best pleased to discover himself there, but the thought of *not* being there—of not ensuring that Miranda knew the truth before she made any irrevocable decision—was inconceivable. Wraxby might not pose any danger in the physical sense, at least not directly, and at least not yet, not before she'd married him, but there was more than one sort of danger that could threaten a vulnerable not-so-young lady.

The sun was low in the sky, the shafts of weak light striking almost horizontally, when he heard voices, then the front gate opened. Straightening, he stepped across the alley, putting his back to the Cliffords' garden wall.

The chill breeze carried the voices of the two people who emerged from the gate and halted on the pavement to him— Miranda and her gentleman caller. He listened, and was honest enough to own to relief when he detected no loverlike tones in the strictly conventional exchanges. Wraxby might have offered, but she hadn't yet accepted him.

He waited until he heard the jingle of harness and the clop of hooves, then looked around the corner.

Turning back to the gate, Miranda saw him. Beyond her, Wraxby was driving away up the street. She paused, frowned, then walked briskly to the front gate, went through, and shut it. He heard the latch fall home.

Now what?

Drawing back into the alley, he debated waiting until Wraxby was out of sight, then walking up to the front gate and approaching the house like any normal caller—

The side gate, further along the alley, the one she used to come and go unseen, opened. She stepped out of the gate, looked at him, and waited.

Pushing away from the wall, he walked down the alley.

"Have you learned something about Kirkwell?"

He halted before her. "No."

She frowned more definitely. "Then what are you doing here?"

"Watching out for you." Her frown just grew more puzzled. He glanced around, then waved her back into the garden. "No sense taking chances."

She looked around, then retreated over the stone step and into the shade of the trees beyond. He followed, closing the gate behind him.

She was studying his face. "Your men are supposed to be watching for any sign of Kirkwell or his hirelings. There's no reason to, as you put it, watch out for me."

He felt his jaw tighten. "Yes, there is, as it appears you're incapable of distinguishing a coldhearted exploiter from an eligible gentleman."

She stiffened. Her head rose. "*If* you recall, our liaison is at an end—there's no reason, no justification, for you to be acting like some sort of guard."

"*If* you recall, my association with your brother continues. I consider him a friend, and therefore his family's welfare is of at least passing concern to me. If I see danger threatening a member of his family, as his friend I would of course warn him—that's what friends do. Furthermore, anyone seeking to kill him and lay hands on his fortune could most easily accomplish the latter via you. In this case . . . I thought you would rather I spoke directly to you."

Her eyes narrowed; lips compressed, she held his gaze for several moments, then very evenly said, "I assume you're talking about Wraxby."

He nodded.

Without taking her eyes from his, she drew in a long breath, then asked, "What have you learned?"

"Wraxby's vices are not those of commission but omission. He's devoted to his three sons, but in his eyes they can do no wrong, and his neighbors openly state that the three boys literally drove their mother to an early grave. Wraxby's principal motive in taking a second wife is to find someone to nurture his sons—of whom devils, fiends, and demonspawn were the most repeatable descriptions given by those who know them. Wraxby is also ambitious, both monetarily and socially, and is rigidly conservative. He believes his wife should devote herself utterly to supporting him in his aspirations, running his household and social affairs as he dictates, with blatant respectability and glowing success. At the same time, he's incapable of believing any ill of his sons, much less acting to rein in their behavior, nor yet allowing anyone else to do so. The household has not kept a governess or tutor longer than a month, and the rest of the staff are in constant flux, and now have to be hired from London as no locals will work in that house." He paused, holding her wide eyes. "For any woman, that's a recipe for disaster. For you . . . you would be foolish beyond permission to accept Wraxby's suit."

Miranda bit her tongue against a near-overwhelming urge to crisply inform him that she did not need him to tell her what she should and should not do. For several moments she stood with lips pressed tight while she fought the words back, then she nodded haughtily. "That matches my own observations."

More, it gave her a context, a framework to make sense of said observations and of all she'd learned from Wraxby.

He wasn't a bad man, but the position he was offering, especially as it came with not a shred of even the mildest affection, was simply and definitely not for her.

If not for the irritation bubbling up inside her, she might have felt grateful for his succinct summary of Wraxby's situation. Instead . . . irritation was compounded by aggravation; simply being within two feet of him was, apparently, enough for her senses to vividly recall what it felt like to be enfolded in his arms, to lean into the solid warmth of him and feel his arms close around her, to yearn to feel that again, only to remember that, thanks to his decision to end their liaison, that wasn't going to happen ever again.

Raising her head, she dismissively stated, "I didn't need you to elucidate Wraxby's shortcomings—I'd already seen them. I'm hardly a ninnyhammer." No—she was the woman who, when she rejected Wraxby, was going to have to bear with Gladys's moaning while simultaneously coping with her own disappointment and still confused feelings over the end of her relationship with . . . the very man who thought it appropriate to lecture her about Wraxby. Tipping her chin higher, she all but snapped, "In future I would appreciate it if you refrained from taking any interest in my life—I'm perfectly capable of dealing with my potential suitors myself."

Something flashed in the dark sapphire of his eyes. "Really? In that case it might help you to know that by and large gentlemen do not appreciate being strung along. If you intend dismissing Wraxby, then do it—don't go walking alone with him, don't go driving with him, and don't continue smiling at him." He clamped his lips shut. His jaw clenched, then he all but growled, "*He* won't appreciate *that*."

I won't appreciate that.

She blinked. He might have said one thing, but his real meaning resonated with bell-like clarity. Her confusion deepened.

He searched her eyes, her face. His features were set, even more implacably unreadable than usual. "Never mind." He ground out the words, turned, and jerked open the gate. About to stride out, he paused; the look he cast her was all heated darkness. "Just get rid of Wraxby—he's not for you."

Before she could respond, he stepped into the alley and rather forcefully shut the gate.

She hauled in a huge breath—then glared at the gate. With a frustrated growl of her own, she swung around and marched toward the house.

What the devil did he think he was doing, extrapolating his friendship with Roderick, presuming upon it to pass judgment on her behavior? On how she chose to live her life? To telling her what she should do?

Damn him! How *dare* he?

As for the nonsense of Roderick's would-be killer seeking to gain Roderick's fortune through marrying her . . . "Rubbish!" The would-be murderer would have to show himself to do that. "As if I wouldn't notice!"

Muttering imprecations fueled by a roiling mix of emotions, she stalked onto the terrace and through the morning room. She was halfway up the stairs before her whirling emotions flung up an alternative scenario. Pausing on the landing, she considered it. "*He* was the one who ended our liaison."

True, but given the sort of man he was, given they had been *that* close, perhaps his attitude was simply an expression of lingering protectiveness.

Minutes ticked by as she stood on the landing, wondering . . . abruptly, she shook her head, mentally shook free of the haunting memories, the now never-to-be-realized hopes, drew in a deep, fortifying breath, and continued up the stairs.

The following morning brought good news and relief in the person of Sarah, who arrived accompanied by her eldest sister, Lady Mickleham, a tall, rather large, fashionably handsome matron considerably older than Sarah.

Gladys, predictably, was flustered, but after consorting

with the dowager and duchess, Miranda confidently greeted her ladyship, smiled and warmly embraced Sarah, then escorted the two ladies to where Roderick had hauled himself out of the armchair and to his feet the better to make his bow.

They sat, and Lady Mickleham consented to take tea. While she poured and passed around the cups and the plate of delicate tea cakes Cook had provided, Miranda was pleased to see Sarah and Roderick with their heads already together, exchanging news of the days they'd spent apart.

Sarah had pulled up a straight-backed chair and placed it beside the armchair Roderick perforce occupied, his bandaged foot propped on a footstool, his crutch leaning against the back of the chair. Gladys remained in the other armchair, while Miranda and her ladyship sat on the sofa opposite. The arrangement allowed the three of them to chat freely while Sarah and Roderick talked quietly of other things.

Taking in Roderick's smile and the alertness and absorption now lighting his expression, Miranda turned to Lady Mickleham. "Dare I hope you can spare Sarah to us for the day? We would be happy to send her home in the carriage at whatever time you wish to specify."

Lady Mickleham, too, had been viewing the young couple with something approaching august approval. Her gaze on them, she nodded, then looked at Miranda. "I must thank you for your invitation. Caroline wrote and told me of the occurrence that left your brother injured and at Ridgware. I and the rest of the family were happy to learn that Sarah had proved so useful. As, clearly, she wishes to remain, and as you are agreeable, I see no reason she shouldn't. If you could send her home by five o'clock?"

The arrangements were made. Fifteen minutes later, tea and cakes consumed, Lady Mickleham rose and took leave of Roderick and a still nervous Gladys, then Miranda escorted her ladyship out of the house.

On the path leading to the front gate, Lady Mickleham halted and swung to face Miranda.

Halting too, Miranda waited, her expression encouraging.

"Forgive me for speaking bluntly, Miss Clifford"—Lady Mickleham held her gaze—"but from what I've already seen, Caroline's suggestion that there could well be a tendre forming between Sarah and your brother appears well founded. Consequently, I feel I must ask if you and your aunt foresee any difficulty should that tendre develop further?"

Miranda wished Gladys had been there to hear her ladyship's question, to understand that it was Sarah's tonnish family who felt that the Cliffords might have reservations as to any prospective match. However . . . she arched her brows. "As we are speaking bluntly, if it should transpire that Roderick and Sarah wish to marry, my aunt and I would be happy to welcome Sarah as Roderick's bride."

Lady Mickleham hesitated. "I understand that Caroline explained the . . . ah, difficulties with Sarah over the last season."

"Indeed, but with regard to that, in the time I've known Sarah I've seen no evidence of any flightiness or inconstancy of character." Miranda paused, then went on, "She and Roderick seemed to develop a bond, almost from the first. She has been nothing but devoted in her care and support. In fact, when Roderick was attacked—albeit as part of a staged trap, but neither Sarah nor I knew that—she flew to his defense without hesitation." She met her ladyship's eyes. "I know because I was there, too."

Lady Mickleham nodded. "From our family's perspective, Sarah's reaction to and continuing interest in your brother had been both a blessing and a relief. That her interest is reciprocated is even more reassuring. When Caroline first wrote of it, I was skeptical, but from all I've seen of Sarah since her return to town, and"—she tipped her head toward the house—"just now, it does indeed seem that my sister has finally found her backbone."

Miranda smiled and together with her ladyship walked on toward the gate.

"That, to my mind," Lady Mickleham continued, "was

what she always lacked. Backbone, and a defined purpose, something she could strive for, with which she could align her will." Her ladyship flicked a smiling glance Miranda's way. "I'm known as something of a plain-speaker, Miss Clifford, but in my experience, to make her way in life, every lady needs to develop backbone, and to exercise it, too."

Opening the gate, Miranda inclined her head in acknowledgment and followed her ladyship through.

After seeing Lady Mickleham into her carriage and confirming that Sarah would be delivered to her ladyship's house in Berkeley Square by five o'clock, Miranda waved the carriage off, then turned and walked back through the gate. Shutting it, she strolled toward the house, her ladyship's words circling in her mind.

"To make her way in life, every lady needs to develop backbone, and to exercise it."

As Miranda now viewed things, that was sound advice.

Wraxby had said he would call that afternoon, and she had, more or less, agreed to give him his answer. Or at least indicate her willingness or otherwise to agree to his offer when he made it.

Shaking her head at such convolution, she sat in the morning room finishing the last of the mending while rehearsing the best words in which to couch her rejection. She'd been surprised when he'd called the previous day to take her driving in the park in a curricle he'd hired expressly for the outing. From her reading of him, combined with Roscoe's revelations, Wraxby's unexpected attention had strengthened her suspicion that, despite what had appeared to be his caution and diffidence over offering for her hand, Wraxby was, in fact, quite keen to have her agree to be his wife.

Given the weeks over which he'd dragged out his peculiar courtship, his sudden attentiveness was, in her eyes, simply confirmation of her reasons to refuse him; there was an element of duplicity in his entire approach, and that was something she had no time for.

She was reaching for the last piece of mending, one of Roderick's shirts with a ripped seam, when the knocker on the front door rapped imperiously.

Not Wraxby's usual, rigid *rat-tat*, but perhaps he was nervous. Inwardly sighing, she set aside the mending basket, rose, settled her gown, neatened her hair, and went out to depress Wraxby and Gladys both.

Hughes had already opened the front door and conducted their visitor to the drawing room. She met the butler as he returned toward the rear of the house. Hughes smiled. "Ah—there you are, miss. Gentleman asking to see you and Mr. Roderick. He's in the drawing room with Mr. Roderick now."

"Thank you, Hughes." Wraxby, of course, would want to ask Roderick's permission before formally offering for her hand. Composing her features, mentally girding her loins, she walked to the drawing room, opened the door, and went in.

She halted with her hand on the doorknob. The gentleman bowing over Gladys's hand wasn't Wraxby.

Straightening, he turned to her. The smile on his face deepened as he met her gaze.

She blinked, stared, then blinked again. "*Lucius*?"

His smile dissolved into a grin, one she remembered. Releasing Gladys's hand, with a nod and a soft laugh he came toward her. "I wondered if you would remember me, cuz."

Amazed, she returned his smile and held out both hands. "Of course."

Taking one hand in each of his, he squeezed gently, then raised one, briefly brushing his lips over her knuckles in an easy, nonchalant fashion.

Distracted, confused, she let her gaze roam his face, the familiar features, his cropped dark hair, then looked past him to Roderick, sitting in his armchair and grinning delightedly with Sarah, standing alongside, smiling sweetly. Hauling in a breath, she swung her gaze back to Lucius. "But . . . we'd heard you were dead. That you died at Waterloo years ago."

His lips quirked in a rueful grimace. "I know." Releasing her, he reached past her and closed the door, then waved to the sofa. "Come and sit down, and I'll tell you all my sad tale."

Still stunned, she subsided onto the end of the sofa closer to Roderick, swiveling to face Lucius as he sat at the other end.

"Obviously," he said, "the reports of my death were in error. During the battle, my troop was in the thick of things and I took a hellish knock to my head. I remember nothing of the battle after that. I didn't come to my senses until days later. I was being cared for by an old farmer and his wife, well away from the battlefield. One of my legs was broken, one of my arms, and I had a raging fever. It was literally weeks before I was strong enough even to think straight. And then, when I could, I discovered I couldn't remember who I was."

"Oh," Sarah breathed. "I've heard about that—about soldiers not remembering who they are."

His expression sober, Lucius nodded. "Indeed. I knew from what little remained of my uniform that I was English, but I didn't have any insignia left, and the troops were long gone by then. I didn't know what to do. I had no idea even what part of England I hailed from, and with my injuries it was months more before I was able to move around on my own, let alone travel.

"Once I'd recovered enough to consider returning to England to learn who I was, it was winter. That winter was very hard in the areas south of the battlefield. I felt I owed a debt to the old couple who had taken me in and cared for me for all those months, so I stayed and helped them through the winter, and then to sow their fields the next spring, and then there was the harvest . . ." Lips twisting wryly, he met Miranda's gaze, then Roderick's. "Whenever I thought of leaving and making my way back to England, well, as I had no idea where to start to discover who I was, I also had no idea if I had any family, or . . . as the years rolled on there seemed less and less point."

"So you stayed in France?" Miranda asked.

Lucius nodded. "I helped on the farm and there was a school nearby—I taught there to make ends meet. I daresay I would still be working on the farm and teaching children their letters except that I got hit on the head again—not as badly as the first time, but enough to jar my memory back into place."

"And you remembered who you were?" Roderick looked fascinated.

Lucius gestured expansively. "It was as if some connection hadn't been there, then suddenly it was and I remembered everything. Well, I still can't remember much of the battle itself, but I remember everything up to that morning." He glanced at Gladys and smiled. "Most importantly, of course, I remembered my name." He looked at Miranda. "I remembered about the family, and knew I had to come home." He spread his hands. "So here I am."

"Have you been to Macclesfield already?" she asked.

"No—I only arrived in London a few days ago. You're the first of the family I've tracked down." Lucius looked from her to Roderick. "I contacted the old man's solicitor in Grey's Inn. I knew he'd have the latest news and directions for the family. He suggested, what with everyone thinking me long dead, that me appearing out of the blue might be too great a shock, and that he should write first, and I agreed. So he's busy doing that—warning them—then once he's heard back, I'll head north. But he knew you two were here in town, and"—Lucius glanced at Miranda—"as I felt fairly certain you at least would remember who used to pull your pigtails, I thought I'd chance my hand and call on you directly." His smile deepened. "I have to say, it's good to be back."

"That's a rousing story," Gladys said. "Mark my words, some angel was watching over you on that battlefield. But now you're back safe and sound after all these years, we should have a celebration—you must stay to dine."

"Indeed!" Beaming, Miranda rose. "I'll tell Cook. You will stay, won't you?"

Lucius returned her smile. "Thank you. I'd be delighted."

She rang and spoke with Hughes, then returned to her seat and the animated conversation. Settling on the sofa, she listened to Lucius describe the farm where he'd lived, then Roderick told him of the changes within the family. Although they called each other cousin, the connection was distant; Lucius was the son of one of their grandfather's brother's sons, so a cousin of sorts, several times removed. But as children they'd met often enough for her, at least, to be certain of his identity; his face still held the same shape, although age had sharpened the angles, and his eyes, the color and set of them, and their wicked gleam, were exactly as she recalled.

Then Roderick was recounting the deaths of the older generation, and Lucius's expression grew somber. Only then did Miranda notice the scar marring his left cheek; when he smiled, it vanished into the lines of his face.

As if sensing her gaze, Lucius turned his head and grinned at her. "Do you remember that time we all went to that house with the huge pond?"

She pulled a laughing face. "And you pushed me in."

He nodded, but she saw the sudden sobering in his gaze as he recalled he'd also pushed her sister Rosalind in. Rosalind who was no more. His eyes met hers, and he tipped his head slightly, then glibly turned the talk to a silly memory of Roderick as a baby.

The front door knocker fell in a rigidly precise *rat-tat*. She heard it over the conversation and very nearly swore. She'd forgotten about Wraxby. "Excuse me." She rose and went to greet him.

Hughes opened the drawing room door before she reached it. "Mr. Wraxby, miss."

Wraxby walked past Hughes, his gaze raking the room.

She inwardly sighed. "Thank you, Hughes. Sir." She offered Wraxby her hand.

With a swift assessing glance down the room, Wraxby bowed over her fingers. "Your servant, Miss Clifford. I hope I'm not intruding."

She smiled politely; he'd told her he would call, so he knew he'd been expected. "An unexpected visit from a long-thought-lost relative." An evil impulse prompted her to add, "But it's an amazing tale, sir—you must come and hear it." To Hughes, hovering by the door, she said, "Perhaps we might have the tea tray now."

"Of course, miss." Hughes bowed and departed.

Turning, she led Wraxby to the gathering before the fireplace. Lucius rose as they neared. Even as she performed the introductions, she sensed Wraxby's suspicions, his immediate disapproval, nay dislike, of Lucius.

They shook hands, Lucius pleasantly urbane, Wraxby stiffly civil.

"Waterloo was eight years ago." Wraxby's eyes had narrowed. "That's a long time to simply not remember."

Smiling amiably, Lucius inclined his head. "Indeed. I assure you it was exceedingly wearying not knowing even my first name."

The courtesies exchanged, they resumed their seats. Wraxby drew up a chair and set it by her elbow. He sat, all but hovering over her, and commenced a less than subtle interrogation. "What brigade were you in, sir?"

Lucius smiled easily and answered, that and all Wraxby's questions.

Miranda's temper simmered, then boiled. From his pointed comments in defense of Lucius, it was clear that Roderick's temper was even further advanced. She shot her brother a warning glance and gave thanks when Hughes appeared with the tea tray and she could distract everyone with the cups and cakes.

She gulped her tea, waited only until Wraxby set his cup and saucer down to lay a hand on his sleeve. "If you would care for a turn in the garden, sir?"

Wraxby blinked; she got the distinct impression he'd only just remembered why he'd called. Once he had, however, his attention was all hers; inclining his head, he rose and nodded to the company. "If you'll excuse us?"

That should have been her line, but she conjured a smile, swept it over the others, and, taking Wraxby's arm, steered him out of the door, out of the house via the front door, and into the garden to one side of the front path.

As soon as they were sufficiently distant from the house to ensure privacy, she drew her hand from his sleeve and turned to face him. He halted, and waited, looking down at her.

"Mr. Wraxby, I have thought long and hard about all we've discussed." She drew herself up, pressed her hands, palms together, before her. "I have weighed the pros and cons, sir, and have concluded that I cannot agree to accept your proposal."

Wraxby blinked again. He looked as blankly stunned as she'd ever seen him. "But . . . you're twenty-nine and unwed."

"Indeed. But I am in control of my life and may pursue whatever path I wish." She shut her lips and calmly held his gaze.

Incredulity flashed through his eyes, but was rapidly superseded by chagrin, and then by an emotion rather uglier. "I see it now." He swung to look back at the house. "Your handsome relative appears and you imagine—"

"Mr. Wraxby!" Somewhat to her own surprise, her voice cracked like a whip and cut him off most effectively. Feeling increasingly belligerent, she trapped his gaze. "My cousin literally arrived back from the dead two hours ago. With respect to your proposal, proposition, however you wish to style it, my mind was largely made up days ago. I extended you the courtesy of giving your suggestion further consideration, but I found nothing, no reason, to alter my decision. In short, sir, the particulars of the position you are offering will not meet my requirements. By any definition we simply would not suit, and that has nothing whatever to do with my cousin's reappearance."

Wraxby had paled; his lips were tightly compressed. After a moment, he nodded stiffly. "My apologies, Miss Clifford. You are correct—this has nothing to do with your cousin. If what we have discussed does not satisfy you, then I would not wish to further press my suit." He nodded curtly.

She expected him to step back and walk away, but although poised to do so, he hesitated, his gaze on her face.

Again his lips tightened, then he said, "Despite your decision I feel compelled to sound a warning before I depart." He tipped his head toward the house. "About your cousin. Waterloo was eight years ago, yet despite miraculously remembering who he is, your cousin hasn't, as I understand it, sought to return home to his immediate family but has instead called on you and your brother. 'Ware, Miss Clifford. I've dealt with enough shady characters to recognize one when I meet him, but in deference to your loyalty toward your cousin, I will say no more."

With that, Wraxby swept her a stiff, rigidly correct bow, straightened, turned on his heel, and strode down the path to the front gate.

Miranda stayed where she was and watched him go. Watched the gate close behind him.

Thought of what he'd said.

Now that she was no longer in Lucius's charming presence—and, yes, he'd always been charming—she could view his arrival and the details of his story with greater distance, greater detachment.

Wraxby might be many things, but he wasn't stupid.

Yet the man in the drawing room, chatting so easily with Roderick and Gladys, revisiting tales of their mutual past, was definitely Lucius Clifford. He'd given them an explanation for his sudden reappearance—an amazing and miraculous tale maybe, yet possible. Even, the way he'd told it, plausible.

Turning, she walked slowly back to the house. As children, she and Lucius hadn't been particularly close. Indeed, as young girls, she and Rosalind had generally viewed him with suspicion; due suspicion—he'd often been up to no good. But many boys were similar and grew out of it, grew up.

Perhaps there was more to Lucius's tale than he'd told

them, perhaps something less savory, but unless and until he gave her cause to suspect him of any less-than-admirable behavior, he was her cousin, if distant, back from the dead, and that was surely a cause for celebration.

Resurrecting her smile, she climbed the front steps and walked briskly back into the house.

Chapter Nineteen

Over the next three days, Miranda wondered more than once whether, on her return to the drawing room after Wraxby had departed, Lucius had somehow divined her equivocation regarding him.

The following day, he'd arrived just after luncheon with three posies—one for her, one for Gladys, and one for Sarah, who had once again been spending the day in Claverton Street. With typically charming flair, Lucius had presented the posies as tokens of his gratitude for their hospitality of the previous evening. He'd spent half an hour talking, joking, and laughing with Roderick and Sarah, with Miranda and Gladys largely silent but appreciative observers, then he'd very correctly taken his leave.

Miranda had walked him out to the street, to the horse he'd had waiting, a good-looking bay gelding. After waving Lucius off and watching him ride away, she'd noticed a strangely intent-looking man lounging against the fence of a house across the street. He'd watched her, had been watching her. With an inward humph, she'd turned and walked back through the front gate.

The day after that—yesterday—had been gloomy and drizzly. Lucius had arrived midmorning with a backgammon board tucked under his arm. Roderick had mentioned he was partial to the game; Lucius had issued a challenge, and the pair had spent the rest of the morning and most of the afternoon engaged in friendly battle, with Miranda and Sarah fondly looking on.

Instead of the dragging grind of a dismal day, the time had passed swiftly and pleasantly. But when she'd walked Lucius out to the street, she'd spied a street-sweeper swathed in a dripping cape leaning on his broom where no street-sweeper had previously bothered to dally.

This morning had dawned brittlely fine, a crisp autumn day with barely any wind, lit by sunshine too weak to warm the already cold ground but bright enough to make everyone eager to take advantage of what might well be the last gasp of fine weather before winter tightened her grip.

Sarah had arrived immediately after breakfast, as was becoming her habit. They'd barely exchanged greetings and had only just broached the notion of taking advantage of the day and allowing Roderick to get some fresh air, when Lucius had arrived with a carriage, his stated intention to inveigle Miranda, Roderick, and Sarah to join him in an excursion to Richmond.

They'd accepted with alacrity. With Lucius's help, Roderick had managed to climb into the open carriage, and they'd set off with Miranda and Sarah rugged up in their pelisses and scarves facing forward, with the two men swathed in their greatcoats sitting with their backs to the driver, Roderick's crutch on the floor between them. The drive had been pleasant, the air fresh and clear, the world washed clean by the previous day's rain. They'd reached the park in good time and had spent an hour ambling down the paths and under the huge oak trees, pausing every now and then to watch the fallow deer and let Roderick rest. Sarah had walked with Roderick, leaving Miranda to stroll on Lucius's arm. She'd been curious as to how he would behave, but while he'd been charming and witty, at no point had he stepped over any line. But then he knew about Rosalind and was clever enough to have guessed her likely stance on propriety; nothing he'd said or done had ruffled her sensibilities in any way.

He'd even been patient and unquestioningly understanding over the slow pace Roderick and Sarah had set.

All in all, Roderick had managed well enough, eventually confiding to her that his leg felt stronger and better for the exercise. They'd been a highly satisfied company when they'd retreated to the Star and Garter for a late lunch, then, after another short walk, they'd turned homeward.

Trailing up the front path in Roderick and Sarah's wake, her hand resting on Lucius's sleeve, Miranda reevaluated the nebulous concern that still lingered regarding him. Thinking back, she could no longer be sure whether it had been there before her last discussion with Wraxby. Was her . . . not exactly *dis*trust but lack of absolute faith in Lucius a lingering echo of past history, a caution shaped by her own assessment, or was it simply a weed grown from the seed Wraxby, her discarded suitor, had sown?

She couldn't be sure, but as she climbed the steps by Lucius's side, she was aware she was still watching him as if expecting to see something in him she hadn't yet glimpsed, as if she'd yet to make up her mind about him.

Regardless, he was family; while she might still harbor some unspecific uncertainty, she didn't imagine him to be any threat, not to her and hers.

Gladys was waiting, eager to hear of their day and prepared to be approving. Although Lucius was a Clifford and, as such, not up to Gladys's social mark, he'd been quick to deploy his native charm to good effect; that had always been his way. Miranda wasn't the least surprised to hear Gladys insist that after Lucius's sterling efforts to keep them all, Roderick especially, amused, he should stay to dine. When

Lucius glanced Miranda's way, she smiled and added her voice to the chorus, and he accepted with easy grace.

It had already been arranged that Sarah would remain in Claverton Street for dinner, so they were five about the table, and a comfortable, relaxed ambience prevailed. With Lucius having spent so much time in their company, it was easy to find topics on which to converse, and his family connection lowered the social barriers further.

Later, once tea had been consumed and it was time for Roderick to see Sarah home, Lucius also rose and took his leave. He bowed over Gladys's hand and murmured something that made her chortle. Gladys tapped him on the arm and waved him away. Waiting to see him out, Miranda watched the byplay; such little touches had always come easily to Lucius.

He joined her and, her hand on his sleeve, she walked with him in Roderick and Sarah's wake down the steps, through the shadows along the path, and out into the street to where the two carriages—Roderick's and Lucius's—stood waiting. Increasingly Roderick was managing, albeit awkwardly, on his own, but everyone was grateful when Lucius stepped up to lend his support as Roderick negotiated the climb into the carriage.

Once he was inside, Miranda and Sarah touched cheeks, then Sarah smiled sweetly at Lucius, who, with an answering smile and a gallant bow, handed her up. After shutting the carriage door, Lucius stood beside Miranda as she waved the pair off, then he turned to her.

She smiled and gave him her hands. "Thank you for the day."

"The pleasure has been all mine, fair cuz." Lucius brushed his lips over the knuckles of one hand, squeezed her fingers lightly, and released them. He stepped toward his carriage, then paused. "I haven't yet heard from the family's solicitor, so I may have another day or so in town. Would it be imposing too much if I call again tomorrow afternoon?"

"No, of course not. You've been a godsend in helping to

keep Roderick amused. If our company entertains you in return, please do call."

He grinned, saluted her, and climbed into the carriage, now with its hood up. She could only see his profile as he spoke with the driver, then the carriage lurched and rumbled off.

She stood on the pavement watching it roll up the street; when it was far enough away that Lucius was unlikely to glance back, she looked around. Drawing her shawl more tightly about her, she scanned the shadows for Roscoe's watchers, but no one was there, at least not that she could see, and thus far his men had been hiding in plain sight.

After searching up and down the street, she humphed and turned back to the house. "At last," she muttered, "he's called off his hounds."

Passing through the gate, she turned and shut it, then swung back toward the house—and walked into a wall.

A solid, warm, muscular wall.

Her heart leapt, but she felt no need to scream. He didn't move, and for a finite instant, she didn't either. She hadn't been walking fast enough to stagger or stumble, so he had no excuse to put his hands on her, yet she sensed the instinctive tensing of his arms, the flexing of his hands as if they wanted to seize her, his arms to close around her, but he held them by his sides.

Sadly, she couldn't simply stay where she was, pressed to him just enough to feel his warmth insidiously sinking into her, to smell the subtle scent of pine soap, leather, and male that burst upon her starving senses.

Drawing in a breath, one tighter, shallower, than she wished, she clung to calm and eased back, breaking the contact. Raising her head, she found his eyes, held his gaze. His expression was its usual implacably impassive mask, yet beneath it she sensed tightly reined aggravation. Slowly, haughtily, still holding his gaze, she arched both brows.

"What happened to Wraxby?"

She inched one brow higher. Considered, then said, "If

you must know, I gave him his congé. Several days ago."

Lips compressing, he seemed to fight to hold words back, but his attempt at rectitude failed. "While I can only applaud your success in coming to the correct decision over Wraxby, who the devil is his replacement?"

She frowned. "What replacement? There is no replacement."

His lips thinned; his jaw clenched. His eyes were dark menace in the night.

"Ah." She realized. "If you're referring to the gentleman who just left, he's Lucius Clifford, a distant cousin recently returned from the dead. He's not a replacement for Wraxby."

He looked at her, faintly nonplussed. "He thinks he is."

Not so, but she wasn't about to argue the point, not with him. "Our thoughts don't run in that direction."

He searched her eyes, her face. They were standing on the path, not under overhanging trees, so the moonlight was sufficient to make out each other's expressions. She got the distinct impression he debated arguing, but then he nodded curtly. "Good to know."

Why? Puzzled, off-balance, and increasingly feeling this was an inappropriate conversation to be having with her ex-lover—he who had ended their liaison—she stepped around him and continued down the path.

Only to sense him swing around and follow, prowling intently at her heels. "What did you mean by 'recently returned from the dead'?"

She could stand on her dignity and tell him it was no business of his, but instinct warned her he would refuse to go, not without learning what he wanted to know. And he was, after all, watching over the household and Roderick. She slowed her pace; the path wasn't that long. "Lucius was reported as having died at Waterloo—the whole family has thought him dead since then. But, clearly, he wasn't dead, only very badly wounded, including a heavy knock to his head, which took away his memories. He didn't know who he was or anything about himself, and had remained on the Continent, until a more recent injury returned his memories to him and he came back to England."

Reaching the porch steps, she halted and swung to face him.

He stopped two feet away and frowned down at her. Again she sensed him debating; again he still asked, "Are you sure he really is your cousin?"

She nodded once, decisively. "Quite sure. We met often enough as children, and although his face has changed with the years, I recognized him before he said who he was. And he knows all the family tales, and things we did—me, him, and Rosalind, and sometimes our other cousins, when we were young. He remembers things about Roderick as a baby. No one else could have those memories. It's definitely him."

Again, she was left wishing she could read his mind, know what he was thinking as he stood looking down at her, but his expression was even more unhelpfully uninformative than usual, and the shadows were too dark to have any hope of reading his eyes.

Eventually, he asked, his tone almost detached, as if the question was merely a final formality, "He doesn't have a scar on his face, does he?"

It was her turn to hesitate while she recalled the description they had had of Kirkwell and realized Lucius matched it well enough. She considered obfuscating, but no good would come of trying to hide the truth, and it was hardly conclusive. "He does, as it happens, but it's not very visible, and as you mentioned yourself, many men—probably most who were on the battlefield at Waterloo—carry scars. It's hardly significant."

His lips twisted. "Perhaps . . . perhaps not." His gaze had grown distant, then he refocused on her face. "Regardless, don't go anywhere with him—you or Roderick—until I've had a chance to verify his bona fides."

Her jaw fell slack. She stared at him. "No." She was so shocked that the word was weak.

He nodded and started to turn away. "Good."

She shook off her stunned stupor. "*No*! I mean 'no, I won't be dictated to,' not 'no, I won't go anywhere with Lucius.'"

He'd halted, stilled; turning back, he narrowed his eyes on hers. After a moment, he growled, "You're not that foolish."

Silence fell, but it was in no way empty.

Slowly, she drew in a breath. For years, she'd managed her temper quite well. No matter how trying Gladys, or even her late but more vituperative aunt Corrine had been, Miranda had not lost her temper. No matter the hurdles fate had strewn in her path, she'd almost always succeeded in restraining her ire, in keeping it leashed . . . but he seemed to have a knack for engaging it, for poking and prodding until it rose up and rode her.

She narrowed her eyes on his. When she spoke, her voice vibrated with suppressed fury. "How *dare* you presume—by what *right* do you presume—to tell me what I, and Roderick, too, can and cannot do? You stood as a good friend to Roderick and helped me rescue him, for which we both owe you due thanks, but your influence ends there. While I and, I'm sure, Roderick, too, appreciate all you and your men are doing with respect to indentifying Kirkwell, you have *no grounds* on which to interfere with our lives, to lay claim to any more personal connection to the point of exercising any control over who we choose to associate with."

The look he cast her was all irritation, with just the hint of a cynical male sneer. "I see this cousin of yours has charmed you to his hand."

"*What*?" Her temper erupted—and suddenly she saw what this was truly about. Her eyes couldn't get any narrower; stepping closer, she jabbed a finger into his coat, into his chest beneath the fine fabric. "*By your own choice* you've stepped back to being just a friend—an acquaintance, no more. That gives you *no right whatever* to order my life, and *absolutely no right* to make insinuations about the men I choose to allow to share it. *You* stepped back—yet here I am having to push you away!"

She glared into his dark eyes; she felt like heat, steam— even sparks—were coming out of her ears. She held his gaze mercilessly and hammered her finger into his chest. "*Stop* being a dog in the manger." She'd lowered her voice—it was just him and her—but the precision of her diction magnified the force behind each word. "You had your chance, and you turned it down. I understand why you did, but you made the choice. You metaphorically made our bed, and we both have to lie in it."

She eased back a fraction. Her eyes still locked with his, she said, "At least Wraxby and, according to you, Lucius, are interested in having a relationship with me. Even if I don't want a relationship with them, at least they're *interested*!"

With that, she spun on her heel, stamped up the steps, and stormed into the house.

She met Gladys in the corridor at the top of the stairs.

Her aunt frowned at her. "I thought I heard you arguing. Who were you arguing with?"

Miranda didn't slow, didn't even cast her aunt a glance. "Someone who should have known better."

Roscoe strode into his front hall in the grip of a fury unlike any he could recall. He shrugged out of his greatcoat and tossed it at Rundle as the butler came hurrying from the rear of the house. "Tell Jordan I need to see him now. In my study. And send Mudd and Rawlins up, too."

Not even waiting to hear Rundle's reply, he took the stairs three at a time, then strode to his study at the end of the wing.

The windows were uncurtained, letting moonlight wash in. He lit a lamp, then fell to pacing—something he almost never did—striding back and forth before his desk as if he could thus rid himself of the tumult of reaction her words had evoked.

His *choice*?

"Huh!"

Did she truly think he wasn't *interested*?

Beneath his breath, he swore—in words and even languages she wouldn't have understood, any more than she had, apparently, understood him.

No matter. He didn't care. What she thought of him wasn't important.

Hell, if he could turn his back on all of society and not give a fig for what it thought, he wouldn't have any real problem ignoring Miss Miranda Clifford's opinions.

Of course, she wouldn't thank him. She'd just demonstrated that, and it shouldn't have surprised him. Disturbed him.

All the more disturbing that it had.

But he didn't care—wouldn't care—about what she thought. About what she felt. He protected those close to him and always had. That was how he was made, and he couldn't be any different, not for her, not for his mother.

He was Roscoe, and this was him. Come within his orbit— let alone become his lover, take him as her lover in the true sense of the word—and this was the inevitable consequence. "She'll just have to live with it."

The reverberations of his growl had barely faded when a sharp rap on the door heralded Rawlins and Mudd.

"You wanted us?"

"Go and arrange a meeting with Gallagher. Tonight. As soon as possible."

Both men stared at him for a second, then nodded and left.

Jordan arrived as the pair departed. Jordan took one look at him, then shut the door. "What's happened?"

Roscoe halted, drew in a breath, and focused. "I need you to learn everything you can about one Lucius Clifford. He's a distant relative of Roderick's—they refer to each other as cousins. I judge the man to be of similar age to Miss Clifford. They were children together."

Jordan had pulled a notebook from his pocket and was scribbling. "What else do you know?"

"Lucius Clifford was in the army . . . no, wait, she didn't

specify army, but he was on the field at Waterloo, so most likely some arm of the army. I'd say infantry, not cavalry—he didn't have the look. After Waterloo his family was notified that he'd died in the battle, but he has just miraculously reappeared in London with a tale of having lost his memory through an injury sustained in the fighting, and having only recently remembered who he is."

"When did he reach England?"

"I'm not sure—the implication was recently. According to our watchers he first called on the Cliffords four days ago. His tale is that he spent the interval since Waterloo on the Continent."

Jordan looked at what he'd written. "On what evidence do the Cliffords believe this man is in fact their long-lost cousin?"

"They recognize him, or at least Miss Clifford does, and she's quite sure of it. In addition, he knows tales from their childhood that she assures me no one else could know."

Jordan paused in his writing and glanced up at him. "But . . . ?"

Roscoe set his teeth. "But my instincts are screaming that it's too coincidental to be accepted at face value. Clifford may be entirely aboveboard, but . . . and aside from all else, he has a scar on his face."

Jordan's hand froze; pencil poised over his notebook, he stared at him. "Scar on face. Distant cousin. Back from the dead. Just now?"

Grim-faced, Roscoe nodded. "Just so."

A tap on the door and Mudd walked in. "I had a chat with Gallagher's man in the square. He says Gallagher's at home, but if you want to meet somewhere else, it won't be tonight. On the other hand, if you're willing to go to Gallagher's, his man's fairly certain the old joker will see you immediately."

Roscoe grunted. He'd made it a habit never to meet with Gallagher or any of the numerous underworld figures with whom he occasionally had reason to consult on their home turf. It was a subtle but telling declaration that he wasn't part of their world and never would be. In this case, however, he needed information urgently—why urgently he didn't know, only that said urgency was pounding through him—and of all the underworld czars, Gallagher already understood to a tee exactly where he stood.

He nodded. "All right." It was time to make an exception—which, sadly, would also tell Gallagher how much he wanted the information, but, again, he didn't truly care. Gallagher hadn't risen to his present preeminence because he pushed his luck in unwise ways. "We'll go and call on Gallagher. Order the carriage, tell Rawlins, and you may as well fetch Gallagher's man, too." He bared his teeth. "He can be our scout."

Mudd rumbled out a dark chuckle and departed.

Jordan had been rereading his notes. He glanced up as Roscoe strode for the door. "Anything more you can tell me?"

"Not that I can remember at the moment."

Jordan frowned. "Why Gallagher, and why the rush?"

"Because I want Gallagher, or more specifically his men, scouring this town for Lucius Clifford as well as Kirkwell, and the sooner the better."

Jordan's expression cleared. "Ah—I see." He waved his notebook. "I'll get on with this and let you know what I find."

With a curt nod, Roscoe left the room and strode for the stairs.

His interview with Gallagher went more or less as he'd anticipated, except that, after searching his face, Gallagher decided to be even more circumspect than he'd expected.

When, after outlining his requirements in crisp, precise tones, he asked Gallagher what he wanted in return, Gallagher stared at him for several long seconds, then harrumphed and stroked his chin. "Well . . . perhaps, as you do have me nevvy under tutelage, so to speak, we could leave the precise terms until later—let's just say that you'll owe me a favor, sometime in the future."

Roscoe considered, then stipulated, "I'll agree to owe you a single favor as long as it's one I can deliver within the scope of the laws applying at the time."

Gallagher grimaced, but his eyes were laughing. "Cautious beggar, you are, but that'll do. So I'm to have m'lads find out everything about this Lucius Clifford, as well as Kirkwell."

Roscoe nodded. "Look especially for any connection—of any kind, no matter how slight or apparently innocuous—between Kirkwell and Clifford. If their paths have crossed in the last year, I want to know."

Gallagher nodded. "If they met in London, m'lads will find out."

"Excellent." Roscoe rose. "One thing—time is of the essence, so send word the instant you learn anything, no matter how insignificant it may seem."

"Aye, I'll do that." Gallagher met his eye and grinned widely. "Hope she's worth all the fuss."

Roscoe met Gallagher's eyes and said nothing.

Gallagher's grin quickly faded.

A heartbeat after the grin vanished altogether, Roscoe slowly inclined his head, then turned and, flanked by Mudd and Rawlins, left Gallagher's study in the heart of Gallagher's empire, deep in the warrens of the slums.

Miranda lay on her back in her bed, the covers to her chin, and stared at the play of moonlight and shadow on the ceiling.

Her temper had finally cooled enough for her to remember why she'd long ago taught herself so comprehensively to rein it in—because no good ever came of letting it out to rage.

"At least they're interested!"

Her words resonated in her head, replaying with the regularity of a tolling bell, and each and every repetition made her squirm. How . . . depressingly revealing. As if she'd ripped off her emotional clothes and danced naked in front of him.

Still, perhaps he wouldn't see, or wouldn't remember, given he'd been angry, too, or perhaps he simply wouldn't guess what had made her—impelled her—to blurt out those words.

She hoped he wouldn't . . . but suspected he would.

"Ugh." If she could have sunk lower, deeper into the bed, she would have. For uncounted minutes, her mind went around and around, fixated on those far-too-revealing words.

But, eventually, her focus shifted to him. To what had brought him to their garden and had driven him to prod her temper. To what had possessed him to imagine a nonexistent connection between herself and Lucius.

She snorted. His intervention had been as misguided as her sneaking into his house that first night, intent on rescuing Roderick from the "orgy" that had proved to be a meeting of the Philanthropy Guild. The similarities were obvious . . .

Her thoughts stuttered to a stop. Then shifted and swung to a new angle, a different perspective. She looked at both incidents from that novel viewpoint, compared them. They were, indeed, very alike—the time she'd gone to the Chichester Street house to rescue Roderick from him, and the time he'd come to Claverton Street to rescue her from Lucius.

She'd been driven by her overwhelming need to protect Roderick—someone she loved. That need, or more specifically the drive behind it, had been strong enough to cloud her judgment to the extent she'd crept into Roscoe's house.

So what had driven him to the point that he'd unwisely tried to take control of her life?

Protectiveness, certainly, but what drove it?

It was tempting to draw the obvious correlation, but he was a complex man, and that might be equally unwise.

The minutes ticked past; night drifted on. Eventually, she yawned, turned on her side, and closed her eyes.

As she'd made the same mistake, and he had oh-so-graciously forgiven her, she supposed she would have to forgive him in return, but there was no denying that the thought of a man like him, London's all-powerful gambling king, caring enough about her welfare to lose his perspective . . .

Lips curving gently, she slid into sleep.

Chapter Twenty

At an unfashionably early hour the following morning, Roscoe's name gained him admittance to Rafe Carstairs's house in Wigmore Street. A minute later, he was shown to Rafe's study.

As the door closed behind him, Roscoe wasn't entirely surprised to find not only Rafe but Rafe's wife, Loretta, waiting to greet him.

"Mr. Roscoe, it's a pleasure to meet you." Coming forward with a smile, Loretta offered her hand. As he bowed over it, she said, "I've long wished to thank you in person for your help with that fiend, Manning, and for being such a stalwart supporter of my aunt Esme and the other directors of Argyle Investments."

"As to the latter," he replied, "it's been an educational experience, one from which I've benefited greatly. Your aunt is a remarkable woman."

Loretta's smile deepened. "I've always wondered what the board meetings must be like."

He tried to return her smile. "Suffice it to say they're never boring."

Rafe joined Loretta and held out his hand; as Roscoe shook it, Rafe's gaze searched his face. "But what brings you our way at such an early hour? Is there something we can help you with?"

Roscoe met Rafe's blue eyes. "As it happens, there is."

Rafe spread his hands. "We're in your debt—you have only to ask."

"Can you check a man's army record?"

Rafe blinked. "Yes, most likely." He tipped his head. "Whose?"

Briefly, Roscoe outlined Lucius Clifford's story.

Rafe shrugged. "That should be straightforward."

"There's another man who might be connected—John Kirkwell. I've no idea if he was in the army, but there's possibly a connection between the two, and it might be there."

"I'll check for Kirkwell, too." Rafe studied Roscoe's face. "I take it this is urgent."

Roscoe hesitated, then admitted, "I'm not sure, but I'm operating on the assumption that there's something seriously nefarious in train, and that the matter is therefore urgent."

The last vestiges of Rafe's easygoing manner vanished. He nodded decisively. "I'll start this morning. I can't say how long it will take, but I'll get it done as soon as I can. Where should I send word?"

"Chichester Street, number eleven." Roscoe bowed to Loretta, then saluted Rafe. "Thank you."

With protestations of their support, both saw him to the door.

He walked down Wigmore Street toward where he'd left his carriage. The need to learn more about Lucius Clifford, to expose the man—although where the conviction that there was something to expose came from he couldn't explain—still rode him, a compelling weight. He'd done everything he could think of, called in every useful favor, thrown all the men at his disposal into action. Was there anything more he could do?

He didn't think so.

Could he—should he—approach Miranda and reiterate his warning?

His lips twisted. If he did, if he tried . . . courtesy of his "dog in the manger" attitude, as she'd perfectly accurately termed it, reinforced by his earlier reaction to Wraxby, he would be lucky if she listened, and regardless of what he said, without proof she wouldn't believe him.

And as yet he had nothing to advance by way of solid evidence that her dear cousin Lucius Clifford wasn't exactly as he purported to be. Family loyalty would trump the warnings of any "secret acquaintance" or however she now viewed him.

Yet his instincts, instincts that had saved his life more than once and had rarely, if ever, proved wrong, were screaming that Lucius Clifford posed a very real threat to Miranda, to her well-being. Unfortunately, given his feelings toward her, even he couldn't be certain that his instincts weren't simply reacting to the fact that Clifford had his eye on her—her, who, despite all his words, decisions, and resolutions to the contrary, his instincts still saw as his.

Not even he knew whether his instincts were detecting anything truly villainous in Clifford.

Halting beside his carriage, he reviewed his options but still came to the same conclusion. He was an expert in evaluating risk, and ignoring his instincts wasn't a risk he was prepared to take.

Reaching for the carriage door, he glanced up at his coachman. "Back to Chichester Street."

"Aye, sir."

Climbing into the carriage, he dropped onto the seat. Given all the inquiries he'd set afoot, he should soon know whether Lucius Clifford was a blameless victim of the war and a perfectly respectable gentleman for Miranda to associate with, even to wed if she chose.

Or whether Clifford was a villain.

If the latter proved true, he knew how he would react. Dogs guarding mangers were expected to be vicious.

"My dear Miranda, can I tempt you to join me for a drive in the park?" Lucius bent an easy smile on Miranda. "I'm trialing a curricle and a pair of bays I'm thinking of purchasing, and I want to see how they perform in such surrounds."

After her contretemps with Roscoe the previous night, she'd been surreptitiously observing Lucius ever since he'd arrived on the dot of three o'clock to charm Gladys and chat with Roderick, Sarah, and her in the drawing room. She might have dismissed outright Roscoe's assertion that Lucius had any matrimonial interest in her, but then she hadn't anticipated any such regard from him; it was possible Roscoe had seen something she hadn't.

And now here was Lucius inviting her on an outing for two. She smiled with the same easy grace as he. "Thank you. The rain's held off and looks set to stay away—a drive would be pleasant."

Ten minutes later, they were bowling north along the road that led past the walls of Buckingham House to the green swathes of Hyde Park beyond. Her bonnet tied beneath her chin against the tugs of the brisk breeze, she held her tongue as Lucius guided the unfamiliar team through the always congested traffic at the crossroads where Piccadilly met Park Lane. They entered the park via the corner gate; once the curricle was bowling smoothly along the less-crowded avenue, outwardly relaxed, she looked around with feigned interest and waited to see what the interlude might bring.

"I spoke with the family's solicitor this morning. Apparently the family are agog to see me, so I expect I'll be heading north in a few days."

She studied Lucius's face. "You must be just as keen to see them."

They spent several minutes discussing the likely reaction

of various family members, then Lucius sobered. After a moment, his gaze on his horses, he said, "I want to go home, yet it's only going to highlight that I've lost the last eight years of my life to my cursed injury." He sighed, glanced briefly at her. "I've got nothing to show for it. I'm no further forward than I was when I left Macclesfield more than eight years ago."

The bitterness in his voice sounded entirely genuine. Before she could formulate any suitable response, he went on, "I'm thirty-one years old. I had hoped by now to have married—all my sisters have, and have families. It's what people in our sort of families do, but"—he shrugged—"I haven't had a chance. Not yet."

She hadn't either. Not yet.

That unvoiced observation lay between them. She seriously doubted Lucius had missed the similarity, but perhaps he hadn't intended to touch on the point and was embarrassed to have done so. Regardless, he promptly changed the subject by pointing out a flotilla of ducks on the Serpentine.

Subsequently, they chatted easily about things they saw and the topics those brought to mind, smiling and occasionally sharing a laugh while Lucius tooled the curricle down the gravel avenues and tried out the paces of the bays. She waited and watched, but not by word or sign did he return to the subject of raising a family, and therefore marriage.

Not until they were back in Pimlico. Nearing Claverton Street, he grew pensive. Finally, he glanced at her.

She met his gaze but could read nothing beyond the mildest glimmer of speculation in his brown eyes.

"I wonder . . ." His lips twisted wryly, and he faced forward. "I know you well enough to be sure you'll tell me to go to the devil if you wish, so . . . as I mentioned, I would like to marry and start my own family. Being in a war brings home how short life truly is—I don't want to wait, but I've yet to find any suitable lady, and, frankly, I doubt

I'm cut out for any wild romance, let alone a love-match. Against that, I know you're twenty-nine, and clearly you, too, haven't had any luck in finding the right gentleman or having him find you." He glanced at her again, met her eyes for a moment longer before returning his gaze to his horses. "We share a history, you and I. I'm fond of you, and although it makes me sound like a coxcomb, I'm inclined to believe you reciprocate the sentiment. I know you want what I do—a home of your own and a family." He didn't look her way again but drew in a deeper breath and let it out with, "So I wondered if perhaps you and I should . . . explore the notion, let us say, of making a go of things together."

Before she could think of her response—what she wanted to say, let alone how to say it—he continued, "Don't say anything now—we're almost back to the house. Just think about it, sleep on the concept, and we can talk tomorrow. I have a few unexpected matters to deal with in town before I head north. We have time to decide if our future paths might coincide."

He smiled at her, his usual easy, charming smile. She met his eyes and found herself nodding. "All right."

When he pulled up outside the house, she invited him in to take tea, but he shook his head. "I have to get these horses back—I'm not convinced they're right for me."

Relieved not to have to wrestle with further conversation immediately, she waved him off, then, head down, mind awhirl, she walked slowly up the path and into the house.

Pausing in the hall, she heard the rumble of Roderick's voice and Sarah's lighter, laughing tones. Hanging up her cloak, she headed for the stairs. She needed time to think, to consider and analyze and see things clearly—to make sure she was seeing things as they truly were.

On the landing, she ran into Gladys on her way down; her aunt would never leave Roderick and Sarah alone for any length of time, but at sight of her, Gladys's features lit and she slowed. "Well, then—how did your drive go? While I thought you unwise to dismiss Wraxby, if you have Mr. Clifford dangling after you . . . well, although he's not as well established as I could wish, he's very personable, and he is connected, after all."

"I pray you, Aunt, don't start speculating about any such thing." Sliding past Gladys, Miranda continued up the next flight.

Behind her, Gladys humphed and raised her voice. "You're not getting any younger, my girl. There's not many men who'd want to take an ape-leader to wife, not when they can get much younger girls who, what's more, know to hang on their every word."

Miranda didn't respond. Reaching the top of the stairs, she went straight to her room. Shutting the door, she felt a certain relief as peace and quiet—and most especially privacy—engulfed her. Untying her bonnet, she laid it aside, then walked to stand before the window. Her room overlooked the stretch of lawn outside the morning room, the same stretch she crossed every time she returned to the house via the alley gate.

She hadn't taken that route since Roscoe had last walked her home. And said good-bye.

Staring down at the trees that hid the gate from view, she couldn't help register the irony of the three men she'd recently had cause to consider as potential husbands. The man she wanted to marry couldn't and wouldn't marry her, while the men she didn't want kept lining up to not propose but to discuss the possibility. Wraxby had been cold and passionless, while Lucius was at best lukewarm, a friend, no true lover.

In contrast, Roscoe burned like a flame in her mind, dominant, passionate, powerful, and, it seemed, unattainable.

She stood looking out and down, refusing to lift her gaze toward the trees to her left that screened his house from sight.

Wallowing. She was, quite simply, wallowing, and she had no time for that.

Backbone. That was what she needed. To focus on her wants and needs, on what was possible, and then exercise her backbone and act to make her life, shape her life, into the life she wanted to live.

Resolve returned to her, an invigorating tide flowing through her veins. Swinging to sit on the window seat, she stared unseeing over her brother's garden and mentally inventoried her position. She was twenty-nine and, despite what Gladys and the late Corinne had taught her, she was *not* overly constrained by society's expectations. Society would accept whatever she did as long as she created no outright scandal. That left her with significant scope to create her future life.

She had money, more than enough to buy a town house of her own, and even a cottage in the country as well, and employ a companion and a small staff. She could live as she chose and do whatever she willed with the rest of her not-inconsiderable funds.

That scenario held a certain appeal, but . . .

Lucasta's wise words rang in her head. *"To secure happiness in her life, it is imperative for a lady to know her own mind."* To know what she wanted, what would make her content, and then to wrest from life what she needed. Lucasta's advice had been echoed by Lady Mickleham, but the dowager had also made it clear that defining the right aim, the right goal—the elements of life a lady *most* wanted—was as crucial as any resolve to achieve them.

Living the rest of her days alone wasn't what she most wanted. It wouldn't make her happy, not even mildly content. It would be an existence, not a life.

What she wanted . . . was a husband and a family of her own. From her youngest days that had always been her aim, her never-changing holy grail. She wanted a home, not a house. She wanted a family, not just a household.

She drew in a breath and refocused again on the three men lately in her life. Roscoe wasn't going to revert to being Julian, the only act that might possibly make him an eligible husband for her. More, he'd made it clear that she shouldn't even think, let alone dream, of him anymore.

Wraxby she'd dismissed, and she had no wish at all to rethink that decision; it had been the right one.

Which left her with Lucius, and the lowering realization that, if she wanted a husband and family, a home rather than a house, then accepting Lucius—assuming he made an offer—might very well be her last chance to secure anything like the life she sought.

But Lucius wasn't offering love, only affection.

What she might have had with Roscoe, extrapolating from what had, over their short liaison, grown between them, might have been love, might have grown to be love, but there was no way she would ever know that now.

Which left her to decide if affection would be enough.

If affection and nothing more *could* yield the closeness, the strength, the relationship with her prospective husband that, she now realized, lay at the core of her needs. Marriage, family, home—none would be what she wanted them to be . . . "Without love."

She sat on the window seat and let the realization sink in.

As to where her new insight into her own needs left her . . . when the gong to change for dinner sounded, she still had no firm idea.

Instead of sitting reading a book by his library fire, as he usually did in the evening, Roscoe paced before the fireplace, restless and impatient. He shot a glance at Mudd, who had brought in reports from various clubs—reports that at that moment he did not wish to read; he'd tossed them on a side table. "Still nothing from Gallagher?"

"No, sir."

Mudd left it at that. Earlier in the day, Mudd had been the bearer of the tidings that Lucius Clifford had called and taken Miss Clifford out for a drive. Roscoe had actually snarled—a fact he was not happy about, although in the same situation he would do it again.

He never lost his temper, at least not in ways anyone could see. Yet since his interview with Miranda the previous night, his temper, along with his patience, had been riding on a fraying rein. He continued to prowl, waiting, waiting, and hating every minute of inactivity. He'd never felt so caged in his life, so impelled to act while simultaneously being so thoroughly stymied. His instincts continued to insist that she was in danger, and that danger emanated from her long-lost cousin, but as yet he had no proof.

And until he had proof, he was helpless to act.

Footsteps in the corridor leading to the library heralded the arrival of Jordan, who took one look at him and waved his notebook to stay his growled question. "I managed to run the solicitor who handles that arm of the Clifford family's affairs to ground. As far as he's aware, the family—all Lucius's nearest relatives—still believe Lucius to be dead. They and the solicitor were told he'd died on the battlefield at Waterloo and have received no information to the contrary."

"Aha!" His fist clenched, but immediately he reined in his enthusiasm; he needed to play devil's advocate with everything he and his people uncovered, because Miranda surely would. "Clifford could explain that by claiming that due to his memory loss he didn't know who to contact—or for whatever reason hasn't yet had the time." He gritted his teeth. "It's not enough." He looked at Jordan. "What of the family itself? Are there any members in London who Clifford would have been expected to contact?"

"No. The entire clan—his part of it anyway—live near Manchester."

He frowned. "What's the exact connection between Lucius Clifford and Roderick and Miranda?"

"That"—Jordan consulted his notebook—"is where things get interesting. The connection is via Roderick's paternal grandfather, Malcolm Clifford. Lucius Clifford is the second and sole surviving son of Morecombe Clifford, deceased, who was himself the son of Malcolm's older brother, Melrose Clifford, also deceased."

Roscoe studied Jordan. "From your delivery I deduce that those gentlemen being deceased is pertinent. Why?"

Jordan flashed him a grin. "Because as far as I can tell—and as I was passing, I stopped in at Montague's and he concurs—if Roderick Clifford were to die, even if his will stipulates that his fortune pass to his sister, Lucius Clifford, as the nearest male in line, could make a very-likely-to-be-successful claim to a portion of the estate. He wouldn't get it all, but Montague believes that, in the circumstances, Lucius could push for half, and depending on the judge presiding, might even be awarded more than that. The critical point is that Roderick's wealth derives solely from his grandfather's fortune. Neither Roderick nor his father have added to the capital but only lived off the income. So depending on the wording of not Roderick's will but that of his grandfather's, Lucius, via his grandfather and father, could make a claim to some of the old man's wealth, now Roderick's wealth. If Roderick had a brother or a son, the claim would be harder to bring, but with only an unmarried spinster to inherit, the courts often take the view that such wealth would be better in what they regard as safer hands."

Roscoe snorted.

"Indeed," Jordan said, "but in the present legal climate, that's a very real scenario."

Rosoce thought, then shook his head. "It'll never go to court. That's not Lucius Clifford's intention—he's thought of a simpler way. If he marries Miranda, and later kills Roderick, he'll end controlling the whole."

He tensed with the compulsion to hurry to Claverton Street and speak with Miranda, to warn her again . . . he clenched his jaw. "That's all conjecture. I need more." He fixed his gaze on Jordan. "I need something unequivocal that connects Lucius Clifford with Kirkwell. Something that cannot be readily explained away, and that at the very least suggests Kirkwell is working with Lucius Clifford to kill Roderick." If he had that, Miranda would believe him. She'd be much quicker to question Lucius Clifford's bona fides if she suspected he was the source of the threat to her brother.

Jordan shifted. "The Cliffords' solicitor didn't recognize Kirkwell's name."

Roscoe looked at Mudd, who had stood silently listening to the exchange. "Still no word from Gallagher?"

On the words, Rawlins arrived. Roscoe repeated his question. Rawlins shook his head. "No more than he sent earlier—that Kirkwell hasn't just scarpered, he's outright vanished."

Mudd rumbled, "If I was this Lucius Clifford and had changed my mind about killing Mr. Roderick, at least for the nonce, I'd have 'vanished' Kirkwell, too."

Grimly, Rawlins nodded.

Roscoe fought not to grind his teeth. His instincts kept insisting he was running out of time. That Miranda was running out of time. But if he went to her with what he had now . . . there was, he estimated, a fifty percent chance she would turn from him even more definitely than she had. She might even refuse to see him again, and that wouldn't help either her or him.

Carstairs had yet to get back to him, and Gallagher was still searching in those ways only Gallagher could. Drawing in a slow, steady breath, he counseled himself to patience.

In gambling, knowing when to exercise patience was a massive advantage, one he generally enjoyed over his opponents. Indeed, patience was a virtue he'd traded on for much of his life, child and man.

And he knew to his bones that his wisest course was to wait—wait for the vital, crucial, critical piece of information that would tip Miranda's scales definitively his way. Away from Lucius Clifford.

So he'd wait.

And hope and pray that was the right decision.

He glanced at Jordan and nodded. "Good work. It's got us significantly further. You'd better get some rest."

Jordan flicked him a salute and headed for the door.

He turned to Rawlins and Mudd, both patiently waiting for whatever orders he chose to give. "Make sure the watch on the Claverton Street house continues unbroken, with at least two men at all times. If Lucius Clifford visits, I want to know immediately, but make sure the men know to always leave someone on point at all times. If anything at all happens there and he's involved, I'll want witnesses."

Mudd and Rawlins grunted, nodded, and left.

Leaving Roscoe to prowl before his fireplace, nursing a glass of cognac and remembering the brush of silk over his bare chest and the sounds of passion in the night.

"I regret, Mr. Clifford, that as matters stand I am unable to advance you any further sums." Abrahams, one of the wealthiest moneylenders in Mile End, folded his hands atop his scarred desk and calmly regarded Lucius Clifford, seated in the rickety chair on the other side of the desk.

Lucius stared back, unable to believe what he was hearing. "But . . . I told you. I'm about to contract an engagement with a lady more than wealthy enough to enable me to pay my debts, all of them. In a few weeks, I'll be able to clear my slate."

"Indeed." Abrahams appeared unimpressed. "I fear I have heard such protestations before, Mr. Clifford. Oh, not from you, but from too many of your peers to be moved by such speeches." Abrahams met Lucius's gaze. "Evidence would be more convincing. Show me the announcement of this so felicitous betrothal in the news sheets, and I will reconsider. I daresay, with such proof before me, that I will be able to extend further monies on credit. Until then, however"—the squat little man raised his hands palms up—"I am unable to fulfill your request."

Lucius sat and stared at Abrahams as the implications of his words sank in. There was no point arguing and, Lucius knew, even less value in approaching another moneylender.

They all knew each other, and such an act would only serve to convince Abrahams, who held all his larger debts, that he was in fact unable to meet them . . . which could prove hazardous. Personally Abrahams might pose no physical threat, but he had bruisers waiting just behind the curtain at the rear of his office, and two more lounged outside.

Yet he was so *close* to laying his hands on old Malcolm's fortune, or at least on Miranda's share, which would be more than sufficient to tide him over until he could arrange the next step and claim it all. But at that moment he had no chance of winkling any more cash out of Abrahams. Swallowing his chagrin, he nodded curtly. "I'll be back with that proof in a few days at most."

He didn't think his bravado was misplaced. He knew he'd played his cards perfectly with Miranda; Sarah and Roderick had let fall enough about the recently dismissed Wraxby to give him a fair idea of how to approach her, and he'd made good use of the intelligence.

Abrahams merely inclined his head, an action that screamed *we'll see* even though he said not a word.

Suppressing his curses, Lucius rose and left the small office.

Stepping out onto the darkened street, he started walking.

He would be back with the proof, and then he'd have enough cash to see him through, but what the devil was he to do until then? He would have a roof over his head tonight, but after that? After his recent expenses—better clothes, hiring the curricle and pair, let alone the ruinous cost of the carriage and driver to take them to Richmond—he had no more coins with which to hire even a donkey, let alone an equipage suitable to be seen in Claverton Street.

"I'll have to get her to agree as soon as possible." Eyes narrowing, he considered the ways. "As soon as she agrees, I can have a notice in the *Gazette* and money in my pocket by the following morning. If necessary, once she agrees I can go to ground for a few days—I can concoct a tale of illness to cover that. They'll feel sympathetic, so that won't hurt."

Which left him with the question of how to get Miranda to accept the proposal he hadn't yet made.

After a moment of assessing, he snorted. "The first step, at least, is obvious."

Chapter Twenty-one

Increasingly restless, increasingly tense, Roscoe forced himself to attend to business; there were too many people on his payroll for him to simply stop paying attention. He'd just settled in his study to review various accounts with Jordan when Mudd tapped on the door and entered.

One glance and Roscoe forgot the accounts. "What have we learned?"

Mudd grinned ferociously. "Gallagher's man just reported. Seems a Mr. Lucius Clifford is deep in debt to Mr. Abrahams in Mile End. Apparently Mr. Clifford called on Abrahams last night, seeking to extend his credit. When Abrahams declined, Clifford told him that he, Clifford, was about to be betrothed to a lady wealthy enough to pay off all his already sizeable debts."

"And?" Roscoe prompted.

"Abrahams still declined but agreed to reconsider if presented with a formal announcement of the engagement. Abrahams said Clifford wasn't best pleased—well, he wouldn't be, would he?—but according to Abrahams, Clifford seemed confident he would be back very soon with the announcement in hand."

"Indeed?" Roscoe looked at Jordan. "Is Miss Clifford's portion large enough for her to qualify as Lucius Clifford's unwitting savior?"

Jordan grimaced. "I couldn't extract such specifics from their solicitor—he's a sound man—but from the funds we know Roderick Clifford commands, then I would say very likely, and as she's twenty-nine years old, then her wealth is almost certainly in her hands, hers to do with as she pleases."

Roscoe frowned. "What happens to the money if she marries?"

Jordan waggled his head. "Difficult to say absolutely—it would depend on how her father's will was written, but the most likely case is that all the wealth she inherited will pass into her husband's hands on her marriage. The only way it wouldn't is if there was a specific clause in her father's will stipulating that it remained in her hands."

"So her wealth will most likely shift to her husband?"

Jordan nodded. "That would be my best guess."

Roscoe slumped back in his chair. Staring unseeing at the papers littering his desk, he reviewed all the information he thus far had, juggling the pieces, putting each in place to create a whole; he forced himself to view the incomplete result dispassionately, with detachment, as Miranda would.

He had proof that Lucius Clifford was in dire need of money, enough to make it plain that her wealth was a major factor driving Lucius's attentions and his pending offer for her hand. But did that prove Clifford was *only* marrying her for her money?

Features hardening, he shook his head. "It's *still* not enough." There were many questions about Lucius Clifford that remained unanswered, such as his surreptitious return from the dead—in such circumstances, what man didn't inform his closest family that he wasn't dead but alive? And the scar on his face . . . could he possibly *be* Kirkwell, or was that simply reaching for straws? Yet if they did find evidence that Clifford was Kirkwell, Miranda would be first in line to hand Clifford, distant cousin or not, to the authorities.

However, as yet, Roscoe had no such evidence.

He exhaled; his lungs felt tight. He'd never felt so torn in his life. On the one hand, his instincts were all but pummeling him to act, and act now, to protect her, to do whatever was needed to keep her safe—even to abduct her and hold her prisoner. Against that, experience cautioned that acting prematurely wouldn't yield the result he sought, and, worse, would carry a real risk of estrangement.

He'd faced fraught situations before, but never had the frustration been this bad.

Never had the stakes been this high.

The words rang in his mind. He was tempted to push them aside, to deny and bury them, but they were true, a truth he hadn't wanted to acknowledge. It had been beyond foolish to imagine he could ever turn away from her and put her out of his mind as if she'd been no more than a passing fancy.

She'd taken up residence in his heart—at times it felt as if she *was* his heart, the way that organ responded to her, especially to her being in danger. Protecting her wasn't a duty, it was a compulsion, one he knew would never leave him.

Keeping her safe wasn't, for him, an option; it was a necessity. And while the more reckless, rebellious part of his mind toyed with the notion of kidnapping her and keeping her there, he reluctantly accepted that, despite being able to, he couldn't simply step in and take over her life.

She wouldn't stand for it, and, in this, he had to play by her rules.

He glanced across the desk at Jordan, then raised his gaze to Mudd. "If what we're thinking is correct, then Clifford now has a looming deadline—he's low on funds and can't get more until he has Miss Clifford's agreement to a betrothal. That also means we're running out of time to expose him, or to at least gather sufficient evidence to demonstrate his true colors, before matters get even more complicated."

Jordan shifted. "If we could find evidence of Clifford

doing something—even something unrelated to Miss Clifford or her brother—that was itself villainous, would that do?"

"Yes. What do you have in mind?"

Jordan grimaced. "I don't know, but that whole 'back from the dead' business—while it might be possible, why has he returned now?"

Roscoe considered, then said, "What I need is some irrefutable evidence that Lucius Clifford and Kirkwell are connected, or that Lucius Clifford has engaged in some illegal or unsavory act."

"Or," Mudd rumbled, "for Clifford to do something nefarious now, so we can catch him in the act."

"True," Roscoe allowed, "but I would prefer to avoid any situation that could put Miss Clifford, or Sarah, or anyone in the Clifford household in danger."

"So what do we do?" Mudd asked.

Roscoe paused, then said, "The watch on the Clifford house?"

"In place—at least two at all times, like you wanted," Mudd replied.

Roscoe sighed. "In that case"—he picked up the document on the top of the pile on his blotter—"we wait."

Patience, patience.

Luck, as he well knew, favored the brave, but favored even more those who waited for the right moment.

Miranda was contemplating the empty patches left after the gardener had cleared the withered summer annuals from the beds bordering the side lawn when she heard the snick of the front gate latch.

It was barely midmorning, rather early for callers. Puzzled, she walked across the lawn to where she could look up the front path, and saw Lucius striding toward the front steps, a bouquet of late blooms in one hand.

"Oh, blast!" She flirted with the notion of sliding back into the shadows, but that would only postpone the inevitable. If Lucius was bringing her flowers . . . assuming, of course, it was her he intended the flowers for, but assuming he did, better she deal with him, with this, now. Privately, between the two of them. Summoning a smile, she raised her voice. "Lucius."

He glanced her way. His expression was deathly serious; if she'd been closer she would have been able to see the scar his smile normally hid.

The memory of Roscoe asking if Lucius had a scar, the implications of that, flashed through her mind, but she quashed the recollection, buried it, and continued to smile.

The instant he'd seen her, Lucius's expression had altered to one of delight. Leaving the path, he crossed the lawn to her. "Miranda." Reaching her, he bowed and presented the bouquet with a flourish. "For you, my dear."

"Thank you." She took the bouquet in both hands, raised the blooms to her face, and sniffed. "How thoughtful. But I'm not aware of having done anything to warrant such a pretty gift." There were roses mixed with lilies and various other blooms. "These must have been difficult to get in this season."

"It was entirely my pleasure to hunt them down, just to see the pleasure on your face." Lucius smiled, transparently satisfied.

She studied his eyes, his expression—not quite besotted but willing to be so. Or as he'd put it the previous afternoon, willing to explore the notion of them making a go of things together.

He'd surprised her yesterday, but today she knew her own mind.

"The others are in the drawing room, but I would be glad of a chance to speak with you privately about the prospect you raised yesterday afternoon." Turning, she waved to the terrace and the door to the morning room. Better she end any speculation on his part now, and preferably without Gladys, Roderick, and Sarah looking on. "We can talk in the morning room."

"Of course." Lucius readily fell into step beside her.

She glanced at him. His features looked a trifle peaked, but his expression looked . . . eager was the word her mind supplied.

Facing forward, she led him to the terrace, cynically wondering at the curse that had afflicted her, condemning her to refuse gentlemen's offers before they'd made them.

By midmorning, Roscoe was fighting an uphill battle to keep his mind focused on the business of being London's gambling king. Jordan was doing his best to assist by insisting he pay proper attention to the structural reports on a house in Mayfair he was considering buying to convert into an even more exclusive club than the Pall Mall when Rundle tapped on the door and entered.

Roscoe looked up, and knew hope shone in his eyes. "Yes?"

"A Mr. Carstairs to see you, sir."

"Thank God!" Roscoe pushed back his chair. "Show him up."

Jordan started gathering the papers. "I'll tell the owner we'll get back to him next week."

Eyes on the door, Roscoe nodded. "Do. The property looks suitable, but given how much we'll have to plow into the refurbishing, the price is too high—but the haggling can wait."

Rundle opened the door and Rafe Carstairs strolled in.

Roscoe came to his feet; Rafe might have been strolling, but his expression was grim. Roscoe held out a hand, shook Rafe's, then waved him to the chair facing the desk.

Jordan had drawn his chair to the desk's side; he stood beside it, hovering, unsure.

Roscoe waved Jordan to sit again. "You might need to hear this."

They all sat. Roscoe noted the restless tension in Rafe—a minor variant of what thrummed insistently through him. "What have you learned?"

"That there's something very strange going on with Lucius Clifford." Rafe met his eyes. "He was listed as dead on the battlefield at Waterloo. His diary and an inscribed pocket-watch were found on a body, and the body was therefore presumed to be his. Both items were returned to his family, who confirmed that said items had indeed belonged to Lucius Clifford."

Roscoe arched his brows. "But, of course, the family never saw the body."

"No. And as it happened, neither did anyone who knew Clifford, but in the aftermath of that hellish day that wasn't unusual. Sadly, however, no one who knew John Kirkwell saw the body either. Clifford and Kirkwell were in the same infantry platoon. They fought alongside each other. Their platoon came under heavy fire relatively early in the day, and took massive casualties. Several men deserted." Rafe shrugged. "It happens, especially in circumstances like that, with their officers gone and panic and mayhem all around. Kirkwell was thought to be one such deserter. The others were all captured within a few days, but Kirkwell never was."

Drumming his fingers on the desk, Roscoe slipped the last pieces of the jigsaw into place. "It wasn't Clifford who died—it was Kirkwell. Clifford put his diary and his watch on Kirkwell's body, then deserted."

Rafe nodded, slow and definite. "That's the way it looks, and if you're sure that Clifford is alive—"

"He's been identified by members of his family who knew him from childhood well enough to recognize him, and he knows all the expected family tales."

Rafe inclined his head. "Then Clifford is, indeed, a deserter." Rafe's lips curved, but not in a smile. "The army will want him."

Roscoe nodded. "I'll bear that in mind." He rose and rounded the desk, extending his hand to grip Rafe's as he, too, came to his feet. "Thank you."

Rafe's lips twisted in a half grimace. "If this ends by

bringing a deserter to justice, believe me, it was entirely my pleasure."

Roscoe glanced at Jordan. "Mr. Draper will see you out. If you'll excuse me, I need to visit someone immediately."

"Of course." Rafe, a veteran of Waterloo as well as a much decorated hero of the Indian campaigns, tipped him a salute and followed Jordan to the door. Reaching it, Rafe glanced back. "Incidentally, depending on how matters play out, you might be interested to know that both Allardyce and Wolverstone are presently in town. I'm dining with them tonight—Wolverstone's place."

It took Roscoe a moment to work through the implications, then he met Rafe's eyes and nodded again. "Thank you—that might be useful."

Rafe and Jordan left. Crossing to the bellpull, Roscoe tugged twice, then turned and strode for the door.

Two minutes later, with Mudd and Rawlins a pace behind, he strode across his rear garden to the back gate and the shortest, most direct route to Miranda.

His instincts' screams had reached fever-pitch—was there anything a deserter like Clifford would balk at?—but at least, at last, he could act.

He was three paces from the gate when the latch lifted and the gate swung open. A man in the cap and cape of a street-sweeper stepped through, and nearly stepped back on seeing the three of them bearing down on him.

Roscoe slowed; Mudd and Rawlins did as well.

The man recognized them; spine stiffening, he raised a hand in salute. "Just coming to report, sir. Mr. Lucius Clifford arrived on foot at Mr. Roderick Clifford's house a few minutes ago."

Roscoe swore and charged through the gate.

Miranda was forced to deal with the flowers first. Given Lucius had gone to such lengths to obtain them, she couldn't simply leave the bouquet to wilt on a side table. So she tugged the bellpull, then waited until Milly, the parlormaid, arrived and took the bouquet away to arrange the flowers in a vase.

Miranda filled the following minutes with the usual pleasantries, relieved when Lucius, elegantly relaxed on the other end of the sofa, did his part to keep the meaningless conversation flowing. Eventually Milly returned with the vase. Miranda directed her to set it atop the wall table that stood beneath a mirror. Vase bestowed, Milly bobbed and retreated, closing the door behind her.

Finally. Drawing breath, Miranda turned to Lucius.

Smiling his most charming smile, leaning forward, he took one of her hands in his. "My dear Miranda. I hope you know that to me you are fairer than any bloom in the land, and are worth far more than a paltry bouquet can express."

She blinked, then cleared her throat. "Yes, well." She tried to ease her fingers free, but tipping his head quizzically, Lucius gripped them more tightly. Jaw firming, she left her digits trapped and forged on, "That's what I wished to discuss with you."

His lips curved, but his eyes . . . his eyes were now watching her with a predator's coolness. A predator's calculation.

Never had she seen the expression so clearly, but she had seen it, sensed it in him years ago. Why had she forgotten? Because she hadn't seen it since. Drawing a determined breath, eyes locked with his, she raised her chin. "I appreciate your consideration in approaching me with the proposition you alluded to yesterday, on our way back from the park."

"Of us marrying to our mutual advantage?" he said. "Now I've thought further, there are so many benefits for us both I'm surprised it took us so long to think of it. We both hail from the same region, and I daresay have similar aspirations, and—"

"Be that as it may"—she was *not* about to be told what she must want—"I've done as you requested and given the matter due thought, but, no doubt as an outcome of my advanced age, I find my true interests are no longer encompassed by matrimony. In short, I am no longer in the market for a husband, not you or any other."

She might be in the market for a lover, a lover who loved her, but that was another matter, one she'd yet to resolve.

Lucius didn't ease his grip on her fingers. His gaze rested on her face, on her eyes, then he softly said, "Do you expect me to believe that you no longer wish for a husband and a family?"

She drew in a tight breath, stiffened her spine. "Lucius, there's no point pursuing this. I am not going to marry you."

For an instant, his expression remained unreadable, then his face contorted and he snarled, "Yes, you are."

Crushing her fingers, he hauled her to him.

She gasped and instinctively pulled back; the ugliness flaring in his eyes stunned her. Appalled her. She fought against his tugging; when he redoubled his effort, she strained away from him.

He let go of her hand.

She went sprawling back against the end of the sofa.

Lucius flung himself on her.

She shrieked, but the sound was cut off as Lucius landed on her and his weight drove the air from her lungs. She struggled, trying to heave him off, but his body pinned hers. Frantically wrestling, she fought to free her arms enough to strike him. He held her down, grappling to control her arms, her hands.

"What are you doing?" she gasped.

"Making sure you marry me," he snarled.

"I *won't*—not after this!"

"You *will*—*especially* after this."

She realized his intention; her mind momentarily froze.

He reached down and grabbed her skirts.

She hauled in a breath and kicked, bucked.

Nothing worked. They were both breathing heavily; she could hear panic in the jerky rhythm of her breaths. No one had come; no one had heard her earlier weak scream. But the longer they wrestled, the weaker she was growing, and there was only one way this would end.

She had to think. Had to find a way.

With his weight crushing her, she couldn't get enough breath for a loud enough scream.

He was tugging up her skirts. Desperate, she twisted her head, searching for inspiration—from the corner of her eye glimpsed the brass statuette Gladys had placed on the table beside the sofa.

Lucius's breathing was a heavy, rasping—increasingly aroused—pant.

Cool air flowed across her thigh above her garter.

Gritting her teeth, she arched up; lifting half of Lucius's weight, as well as her own, she jammed her forearm across his throat, holding him off enough to reach up and back behind her head. Groping blindly, her fingers found the statuette; gripping it, she brought it swinging up and around at Lucius's head.

He saw it coming, reared back, and caught the statuette in one hand.

She didn't fight him for it; her chest freed of his weight, she filled her lungs and screamed. "*Help*! Help me!"

Lucius swore and slapped his other hand across her lips.

She twisted her head away, then quickly back, and bit his hand hard.

He cursed and yanked his hand away. She filled her lungs to scream again, but he grabbed a cushion and shoved it over her face.

Forcing her deeper into the sofa, he wrenched the statuette from her grasp.

She couldn't see; she couldn't breathe. Lucius's weight returned, collapsing her lungs . . .

Something slammed. A heartbeat later, Lucius's weight left her, rolling away. Thuds and grunts reached her. Someone pulled the cushion off her; she blinked up into Sarah's shocked face.

She turned her head. Roderick and Lucius wove on their feet, wrestling in the room's center.

Her chest heaving, she struggled up on one elbow. Gladys stood before the closed door, her eyes on stalks as she took in the scene. Miranda waited for her aunt to try to pretend the obvious hadn't happened—so scandalous, after all—but instead Gladys's old eyes fixed on Lucius and all but blazed. "You *blackguard*!"

Her aunt hobbled forward, hefted her cane, and brought it down on Lucius.

He saw the blow coming and with a roar swung Roderick across as a shield.

Gladys's weak whack was swept aside by Roderick's shoulder, but the unexpected shift in his weight sent Roderick, his balance uncertain because of his bad foot, toppling.

He crashed to the floor.

Gladys staggered back, collapsing into the armchair beside the sofa.

Hauling in a breath, lips set, Miranda swung her legs off the sofa and pushed to her feet.

With a cry, Sarah rushed around the sofa, apparently intending to interpose herself between Roderick and Lucius.

But Lucius had already stepped back several paces. Cursing, he pulled a pistol from his pocket.

Miranda stared at the small but powerful-looking pistol. Lucius's hand shook slightly, but, she judged, more with temper than fear. She didn't doubt he knew how to use the pistol. He held it pointed at Roderick.

They'd all frozen at the sight of the pistol. Sarah recovered first; she dragged in a breath to scream.

Lucius shot her a glance. "Don't." He kept the pistol trained on Roderick, on the floor before Miranda's feet.

Sarah met Lucius's gaze, then shut her lips, pressed them tightly together.

Lucius nodded. "That's right." His gaze flicked to Miranda. "No need for any heroics."

He glanced over his shoulder at the door. No staff had

come to investigate; they must all be below stairs getting ready to serve luncheon, unaware of the unfolding drama.

Lucius backed toward the door. "Everyone remain calm and we'll all come out of this with whole skins."

Miranda tracked his movements, as did Roderick, Sarah, and Gladys.

Without shifting his aim, even for a second, from Roderick, Lucius lifted the straight-backed chair that stood by the wall near the door and wedged its back under the doorknob. "Just so we won't be disturbed." He tested the door; satisfied it wouldn't easily open, he returned to the room's center.

Roderick, his face white and strained, struggled into a sitting position. Knees bent, he laid his arms over them and stared at Lucius. "Why?"

Lucius arched his brows. "I would have thought that was obvious. I need money, I want yours, and you're going to give it to me."

Roderick snorted. "You've lost your mind."

"No, I haven't." Lucius paused, head tipping as if considering how much of his plan to reveal.

Miranda suspected that he'd had a plan, but now it was in disarray and he was having to retrench, to think of new ways.

"I heard," Lucius said, his gaze on Roderick, his voice low and calm, "that you were planning to give the bulk of your fortune—the fortune you inherited from old Malcolm—to charity."

She glanced at Roderick. He kept his gaze on Lucius's face; she could only see his profile, but she sensed he was as surprised as she. How had Lucius learned of that? Not even Gladys knew of Roderick's involvement in the Philanthropy Guild; Miranda only knew because she'd followed him to Roscoe's all those nights ago.

Roderick didn't respond to Lucius's comment, effectively confirming it.

Lucius smiled. "I decided that, given that charity should begin at home, that you should, instead, give that money to me."

Still, Roderick said nothing; she felt proud of him. She wondered if he'd learned the tactic from Roscoe.

"So what you're going to do," Lucius said, still addressing Roderick, "is write me a note of hand. An I.O.U. to the tune of . . . shall we say forty thousand pounds?"

Roderick laughed. "I don't owe you anything. Why would I pay a debt extracted under duress?"

Lucius's nasty smile deepened. "Because of the scandal if you don't." He glanced at Gladys, then at Sarah, and lastly at Miranda, before returning his gaze once more to Roderick. The pistol never wavered; Lucius kept it aimed squarely at Roderick's chest.

"You see," Lucius continued, "I won't be presenting the note to you myself. No—the instant I leave here, I'll sell the note on. Perhaps not for the full amount, but I'm sure I'll be able to raise at least twenty thousand pounds against your good name."

Roderick's features had hardened.

Sarah touched a hand to Roderick's shoulder. "But we"—with her other hand she waved to include Gladys and Miranda—"know the truth. We'll tell."

"Indeed?" Lucius arched a brow. "Three females all of whom have a connection to dear Roderick—the sort of connection that means you'd lie to save his reputation. Who do you think will believe you?" Lucius let that sink in, then sneered. "No—this will work. It's simple and straightforward." He shot a sharp glance at Miranda. "I should have tried it from the start, rather than wasting time with you."

He'd meant the comment to cut, but the barb missed her completely.

But then he shifted the pistol and aimed it at her. He looked at Roderick and snarled, "There's an escritoire over there. Get up and write the damned note."

Miranda looked around, searching for some weapon, for some way to bring this to a better end. But Lucius was out of easy reach of any of them; even if she threw herself out of the current path of his pistol, even had Roderick been hale and whole, he wouldn't be able to reach Lucius before Lucius turned the pistol on him—or re-aimed at her—and fired.

There was no way out but for Roderick to write the note.

Once written, once Lucius left with it in his possession, there'd be no way of stopping him laying his hands on the stipulated small fortune.

Roderick, his gaze locked with Lucius's, appeared to reach the same conclusion. He glanced away, then, lips tight, looked up at Sarah, still standing protectively beside him. "Help me up."

Sarah glanced at him, then at Lucius, then she bent and locked her hands beneath Roderick's good arm and assisted him to his feet.

With Lucius's attention on Roderick and Sarah, Miranda wondered if there was an opening, a chance; she tensed.

Lucius's gaze flicked to her and she froze.

Then Lucius's gaze went past her. He frowned.

A second later, his expression flooded with confusion and alarm.

She realized he was staring at the French door to the terrace. Then she heard a snick. The French door opened; she felt the faint stirring in the air as someone walked in, then the door clicked shut.

Lucius's expression was a study in stunned disbelief. "Who the devil are you?"

She didn't need to look to know who had entered, to know who had come to their aid; she glanced over her shoulder anyway and nearly fainted with giddy relief. Even though Lucius still held the pistol, still held the nasty thing aimed at her heart.

Roscoe came forward with his usual prowling stride. Focused on Lucius, he smiled a distinctly sharklike smile. His gaze deflected to meet hers as he drew level with her. "I'm known as Neville Roscoe." Returning his gaze to Lucius, he kept walking.

Raising the pistol, Lucius backed a step. "Stop! Or I'll shoot."

Roscoe raised a languid hand, a fencer's gesture of surrender, and took one final step—sideways, interposing his body between Miranda and Lucius's pistol—then halted.

Miranda sucked in a breath, fisted her hands against the urge to shove him aside. What was he *doing*? *He* might get shot. *Oh, God!* Her heart surged into her throat and blocked it. What had possessed him?

Facing Lucius, he was calmly saying, "We can't have that. As I recall, it's considered terribly bad form to shoot a pistol in a lady's morning room."

The fashionably drawled words confused Lucius even more. Frowning, he shook his head. "Are you mad?"

Roscoe paused, then, his tone grown cold and made even more chilling by the terrifying precision of his diction, said, "No. But any underworld czar in London will tell you that you are. Pointing a gun at me is generally considered . . . ill-advised."

Lucius attempted a sneer. "I can't see anything ill-advised about it."

"Can't you?" Rosoce let the moment stretch, then said, "That's because you haven't thought further than pulling the trigger. You might be able to put a ball into me, but then what? How do you imagine getting out of this house alive? My men are all around it." He glanced at the windows, then looked back at Lucius and tipped his head toward the terrace. "Take a look."

Lucius looked.

Roscoe pounced.

Springing forward, he caught Lucius's arm and drove the hand gripping the pistol upward as his body slammed into Lucius's. The pistol discharged with a deafening retort. The ball tore into the ceiling; flakes of plaster showered down.

Roscoe pulled back, raised his fist, and smashed it into Lucius's face.

Bone crunched, and Lucius dropped like a felled log.

"Thank *God*!" Stepping closer, her eyes raking Roscoe's face, Miranda gripped his arm. Then she looked down at Lucius and confirmed he was unconscious.

Roscoe dragged his gaze from Miranda's face, then kicked the pistol to Roderick; given what he'd deduced, he didn't trust himself with the weapon. Lucius Clifford had laid hands on her, and even though she appeared physically unharmed, the compulsion to use the pistol to beat the man to death was strong.

Sarah, standing beside Roderick and gripping his arm, stooped, picked up the pistol, and handed it to Roderick.

In the chair nearby, Miranda's aunt wheezed, struggling to take in air. Sarah murmured to Roderick, then patted his arm and went to help the aunt.

Shaking out his hand, massaging the bruised knuckles, Roscoe remained standing over Lucius Clifford. Given how much fury had been behind his blow, he doubted the man would wake any time soon, but he needed the moment to rein in said killing fury.

He glanced at the terrace—just as someone started pounding on the room's main door.

Standing beside Roscoe, Miranda had been staring at him as realization crashed through her, washing away all uncertainty, leaving everything—*everything*—startlingly clear. Following his gaze, she saw Mudd and Rawlins barreling across the lawn from the side gate; they must have been in the alley and heard the pistol discharge . . . Roscoe had bluffed about them being near enough for Lucius to see. She looked at Roscoe. "Shall I let them in?"

He nodded. "Please."

Drawing her hand from his arm, she went to the French door.

Sliding the pistol into his pocket, Roderick had already limped across the room to open the main door and deal with the inevitable staff crisis. After admitting Rawlins and Mudd, leaving them to confer with Roscoe, Miranda went to help Roderick, but after confirming he was successfully reassuring Hughes, Mrs. Flannery, and the rest of the staff, who, brought running by the shot, had crowded into the corridor, she went to help Sarah with Gladys.

While instructing Mudd and Rawlins in how he wished Lucius Clifford restrained, Roscoe tracked Miranda with his eyes; hauling his gaze from her took too much effort, and he'd given up trying.

Her aunt had succumbed to full-blown hysterics. While Sarah and Miranda dealt with her, Roderick, having at Miranda's request dispatched the staff to fetch water, smelling salts, and anything else that might help the hysterical woman, limped across to stand beside Roscoe.

Leaning on the aunt's cane, which he'd appropriated, Roderick looked down at Lucius Clifford, then shook his head. Under cover of his aunt's breathless shrieks, he said, "If he needed money, I would have lent him some—he only had to ask."

Roscoe realized Roderick didn't yet know the truth of Lucius Clifford. "I came to tell you and Miranda what I've discovered about Kirkwell."

Alerted by his tone, Roderick glanced at his face, then looked down at Lucius Clifford with even greater revulsion. "Lucius was Kirkwell?"

"He switched identities with Kirkwell on the battlefield."

Roderick took a moment to work it out. "So . . ." He dragged in a huge breath. "Lucius is a deserter?"

Roscoe nodded grimly. "And that puts an entirely different light on things—especially on what needs to happen with him."

A glass of water and some smelling salts had arrived, along with several burnt feathers, and the aunt's hysterics were gradually abating. Roscoe finally dragged his gaze from Miranda; she was moving without any detectable stiffness and was alert and focused. A weight lifted from his chest. He looked at Roderick. "What did you tell your staff?"

Leaving Lucius Clifford gagged with his own cravat and

with his hands trussed behind him, Mudd and Rawlins stepped back, taking up positions by the wall nearby and doing their best to become invisible. For such large men, they were very good at that; they'd had plenty of practice.

Roderick was still staring at Lucius Clifford. "I told them the pistol going off was an accident—which in some respects it was." With the toe of one boot, he nudged Lucius Clifford's shoulder. "But this . . ." His jaw firmed. "Obviously we'll need to summon the constables—"

"No."

Lifting his head, Roderick blinked at him. "No?" He was incredulous. "But . . ." Roderick glanced at Miranda, then, face flushing with anger, he lowered his voice. "He attacked Miranda."

"Yes. I know." Roscoe glanced again at the evidence of that—at her badly crushed skirts, at the many tendrils of hair that had come loose from her chignon, itself askew. Once again he quashed the lethal urge the sight provoked. "That's precisely why we have to act to ensure that Lucius Clifford does no further harm to her, or to the rest of your family. That he and his machinations pose no further threat to them."

Roderick frowned. "I don't follow—how is he still a threat? How can he hurt us further?"

"Because of the scandal." The other sounds in the room had ceased. Roscoe looked across and saw that the aunt had recovered. She was still breathing shallowly, but together with Miranda and Sarah, she was now listening to his and Roderick's conversation.

And staring uncomprehendingly at him, whom she'd never met.

He inclined his head to her. "Ma'am." He glanced at Miranda, then Roderick, then looked back at their aunt. "If you'll permit me to explain, perhaps we can decide how best to deal with this situation."

The old lady stared at him, then waved weakly. "If you can help us get clear of this without any scandal, then by all means, sir."

He looked down at the man at his feet, who was finally stirring. "From what we've pieced together, Lucius Clifford was in an infantry troop that took heavy casualties on the field at Waterloo. Many were killed. Several deserted. Lucius deserted, too, but before he did he planted his diary and his watch on a fallen comrade and took that man's name—John Kirkwell. So Kirkwell was thought to be the deserter, while Lucius Clifford was pronounced dead. At some point, and we don't think it was recently, Lucius returned to England."

Roscoe glanced at Roderick. "For obvious reasons, he didn't contact his family, all of whom believed him dead. To resume his identity with people who knew him would have risked identifying himself as a deserter, and everyone knows what the army does with deserters. Whenever he wished to, he used Kirkwell's name, but otherwise simply avoided anyone who'd previously known him. However, Lucius presumably took due note of his father's death two years ago. Sometime after that he realized that if inheritance was passed strictly through the male line, then if you died, he, now your nearest male blood relative, stood to inherit at least some of your wealth. While your will would presumably leave most of your fortune to Miranda, any wily solicitor would have informed Lucius that he stood a reasonable chance of being able to claim at least a portion of your estate on the grounds that your wealth stems from your grandfather, and therefore, in the event of you dying without a male heir, your grandfather's brother—Lucius's grandfather—could have pressed for a portion of what was originally your grandfather's estate.

"I'm informed that such a case would be messy, with the outcome depending on the language used in various wills, and even more on the prejudice of the judge rather than on the relative merits of any legal arguments—and strong arguments might be made either way, to grant Lucius a part of your estate, or not. Regardless, to Lucius, penniless as he was, the chance was worth taking. But, of course, before he could mount any legal challenge to your will, you had to die."

Roderick, his gaze again on Lucius, shook his head. "On the chance that he *might* be able to claim a portion of my fortune, he set out to kill me." He made a disgusted sound. "That's why he hired Kempsey and Dole, and sent them to murder me."

Roscoe nodded. "But when that didn't go as planned—"

"When you stepped in and saved me."

"When Miranda and I stepped in and saved you, after that, Lucius pulled back and regrouped. Rethought."

"He said something before," Miranda put in, "about hearing that Roderick was giving the bulk of his fortune to charity."

"What?" Miranda's aunt looked from her to Roderick. "I thought he was touched, but what's this? Giving away your funds?"

"Not that much." Roderick waved the point aside. "But clearly Lucius thought it was more."

"Ah." Roscoe nodded. "That makes sense. He thought you were about to give away a lot of your wealth, so he felt impelled to act—first with Kempsey and Dole, and then, when that scheme went awry, to come at you again, but from a different angle."

"Through me." Miranda looked coldly at Lucius, who was almost certainly conscious now and listening. "And for that I'll never forgive him."

"In deciding how best to deal with your cousin," Roscoe smoothly went on, "it might help to catalog his crimes. Today, he attacked Miranda, but Roderick and the rest of you foiled him in that. Subsequently, he attempted to extort money from Roderick at pistol-point—"

"But you foiled that," Roderick said.

"Yes. And prior to that, he attempted to kill you by hiring Kempsey and Dole to do away with you, but Miranda and I foiled that." Looking down at Lucius, Roscoe observed, "Through all those attempts, beyond Roderick's injuries and Miranda's nerves, his actions haven't caused any real damage. No lasting damage. But that leaves us with his

most serious and heinous crime. Desertion in the face of the
enemy. The authorities view it as one of the greatest crimes,
with good reason. In his case, however, he compounded his
villainy by leaving another man, and that man's family, to
bear the ignominy of his desertion. Although he switched
identities purely to evade capture, in doing so he saved
the Cliffords from the scandal of having a deserter in the
family."

"Oh, my heavens!" Gladys raised a hand to her bosom.

"No palpitations," Miranda warned. "We don't have time
for them."

Gladys blinked, then looked at Roscoe as if expecting him
to rescue her from impending distress.

As if taking up the challenge, he responded, "At this
moment in time, Lucius Clifford is ours to dispose of as we
deem fit. We need to consider what will happen if we hand
him over to the constables, and weigh that against what will
transpire if we hand him over to the army instead."

"Can we do that?" Roderick asked. "Hand him directly
to the army?"

Roscoe nodded. "I can arrange it, yes."

Miranda drew breath, forced her mind to function. "If
we hand him to the constables, we'll have to press charges,
won't we?" She looked at Roscoe.

"Yes. And in order to prosecute the case, you and Roderick will need to appear in public court, and the earlier attempt on Roderick's life will need to be explained, too, and
all the details of how that played out, with Kempsey's and
Dole's testimonies and those of all others involved, and in
the end, because any such case will inevitably attract the
attention of the entire ton, let alone the news sheets, the fact
of Clifford's desertion will come out, along with his use of
Kirkwell's identity, and that will cause a scandal of quite
stunning proportions. It will be the sort of trial that's remembered and talked of for years."

"*No*." Gladys's voice rang with adamantine refusal. "I
will *not* countenance that." Her face set in belligerent lines,

she looked at Miranda, then Roderick. "View it as you may—and Lord knows, *I'm* not a Clifford—but even I will say: *don't do it*. You cannot possibly wish to blacken your family's name." She looked down at Lucius Clifford, immobilized on the ground. "You cannot wish to allow that blackguard to take the entire family down with him."

"I agree." Roscoe inclined his head to Gladys. "To my mind, there's no sense in going down that road. Admittedly, Clifford will be found guilty and hanged, but all that will be achieved by giving him a public trial will be to cause irreparable damage and irretrievable harm to the Clifford family, to all its branches. As we all know, society will not differentiate. You'll all be tarred with his brush."

Miranda and Roderick exchanged a long glance; for the first time, she sensed her own violent sibling protectiveness reflected back at her. But it wasn't just the two of them involved. It wasn't even only Cliffords involved. There was Sarah, and the dowager, the duchess, Henry, and above all Roscoe himself; he hadn't mentioned himself or his family, but in any court hearing he, too, would be called, would have to front the galleries, and put his carefully guarded identity, and therefore his family's name and reputation, at risk.

Which would result in the scandal to end all scandals.

Drawing breath, she looked at Roscoe. "What will happen if we hand him to the army?"

At their feet, Lucius Clifford writhed, futilely testing his bonds.

His gaze on their captive, Roscoe replied, "I know several people in positions of power. I understand the army will be very glad to lay their hands on one of the last deserters to have escaped justice. I believe that, in return for his family surrendering him to them, the army will be perfectly prepared to deal with him through their own courts and in their own ways—all of which can be done out of the public eye." He paused, then said, "The army will inform Kirkwell's family that he was listed as a deserter in error, that instead he died serving his country, and suitable reparation will be made to the Kirkwells to right the wrong done Kirkwell's memory and his family's standing. So that aspect of Lucius Clifford's wrongdoing will be righted as well as it can be. As for Lucius Clifford, once he's in the army's hands, I seriously doubt we'll hear anything more of him."

For several moments, Roscoe, Roderick, and Miranda stood looking down at Lucius Clifford, lying bound, gagged, and helpless at their feet.

Then Miranda drew breath and nodded. "We'll hand him to the army." She sounded like a judge handing down a sentence.

No one demurred.

Roderick shook himself, then asked, "How?"

Roscoe took charge. He gave orders for Lucius to be taken to his house and held in the cellar there until the army had been notified and came to fetch him. Mudd and Rawlins hefted Lucius to his feet; desperate, he tried to kick, so they tied his ankles as well, then between them lugged him out of the morning room, across the terrace, and set off over the lawn toward the side gate.

With Roscoe, Miranda went out onto the terrace. Roderick hobbled after them. They were watching the small procession—the two men Roscoe had had watching the house had been summoned to assist Mudd and Rawlins—when a startled gasp from above, followed by a wail and an exclamation, drew their eyes to an attic window high above.

Three maids—Milly, the housemaid, Ginger, and the scullery maid—were hanging out of the window, pointing and exclaiming. Milly and the scullery maid were doing the exclaiming, while Ginger looked stricken.

Roderick stepped to the edge of the terrace and turned to look up. "Here, you three—what is it?"

Ten minutes and a great deal of reassuring later, and they'd discovered how Lucius had learned about Roderick's plans to "give away his fortune." Lucius had taken to walking out with Ginger over the course of several months. He'd been planning and plotting for at least that long.

Miranda shook her head but patted Ginger's shoulder. "Let this be a lesson to you all—don't trust gentlemen who seem to be too good to be true. They're all but guaranteed to be villains. But how did you learn about Mr. Roderick's plans?"

The maids looked sheepish, but Milly admitted, "We all hear things, miss. Bits and pieces, never all that much—and then there's the things Mr. Roderick asks Hughes for, or about, the pieces in the news sheets that Mr. Roderick likes to read. The philly-stuff. When we put it all together, well, it seemed as plain as pie." Milly looked at Roderick. "We've been expecting to hear you'll be closing up the house any day."

"Yes, well." Looking faintly stunned, Roderick blew out a breath. "I expect we should reassure everyone that I'm not doing anything so daft as giving away my fortune. Just using a bit of it for schools, and that sort of thing. Nothing to get anxious over. I certainly don't plan on shutting up this house."

"Oh." Milly brightened. "Them below stairs will be so pleased to hear that, sir."

With Roderick's blessing, the maids were dispatched to spread the good news.

Roderick exchanged a look with both Miranda and Sarah.

From the armchair, Gladys narrowed her eyes at him. "Remind me to ask Milly next time I want to know what you're about." Gladys tipped up her chin. "Seems the staff know more than I do."

Roderick looked at Gladys; Miranda wondered what he would say. Then he smiled. "It's really of no importance, Aunt. It's just an interest I have."

Gladys humphed. Her gaze shifted to Roscoe. "I'm afraid, sir, that I don't know you, and no one has thought to introduce us."

Roscoe smiled what Miranda imagined was a Lord Julian smile, one of easy, effortless, truly graceful charm. He took Gladys's hand and bowed over it. "I'm Neville Roscoe, ma'am. I live nearby."

Gladys nodded. "Ah, yes—you're the gambling king. You live in the big white house on Chichester Street." When both Miranda and Roderick blinked in surprise, Gladys sniffed. "I do talk to Mrs. Flannery, you know."

Miranda was left wondering what else her aunt had heard.

Gladys, however, nodded with gracious approval at Roscoe. "Regardless, I have to thank you, Mr. Roscoe, for all your help today. And as it's already time for luncheon, and after all that effort and drama I daresay we're all ravenous, I would take it very kindly if you would join us at table."

Roscoe glanced at Miranda, saw her stunned surprise. He looked back at Gladys, then inclined his head. "Thank you, ma'am. I'd be delighted."

He shouldn't accept; there was no hope of any future between him and Miranda, and with Roderick's would-be killer laid by the heels, no longer any reason to continue any degree of association, but he wanted, for the last time, for just a few more hours, to bask in the warmth of Miranda's presence, in the delight of her company, in the joy of her smiles.

Chapter Twenty-two

Roscoe sent word to Wolverstone House. At six o'clock, the Duke of Wolverstone, together with his guests for the evening, Christian Allardyce, Marquess of Dearne, and Rafe Carstairs, arrived in Chichester Street. Rundle conducted them to the library, where Roscoe and Roderick waited.

Roscoe performed the introductions. Once they were all seated and supplied with glasses of the very best cognac, he explained all he and Roderick now knew of Lucius Clifford and his military service. He said nothing about the attempt on Roderick's life, or Lucius's subsequent interest in Miranda.

At the end of his recitation, Wolverstone fixed him with a faintly questioning look. "And how, pray tell, did you stumble on Clifford's secret?"

Roscoe had anticipated the question. "Roderick and I were pursuing Kirkwell on another matter entirely, and through that stumbled on his true identity."

Wolverstone shifted his dark gaze to Roderick. "You're related to the man. Are you here to plead for leniency?"

Roderick shook his head. "No—if anything the opposite."

"Oh?" Wolverstone sipped. "How so?"

Roscoe watched with approval as Roderick paused to order his thoughts, always a sound idea when it was Wolverstone with whom one was conversing.

"I'm here representing the family's interests. Although the relationship isn't close, we—my sister and I—have known Lucius and his immediate family, our cousins, all our lives. Lucius has been dead to us all since Waterloo. There's no more grieving to be done on that score. At present, none of the family other than my sister and I know that Lucius survived, or that he was a deserter. His mother is still alive, and he has three sisters, all married with children." Roderick met Wolverstone's gaze. "The area in which they live, around Macclesfield, is country and very parochial. Any whisper of Lucius's infamy, and his family—totally innocent of any crime though they are—will assuredly suffer." Roderick paused, then glanced at Allardyce and Rafe, before returning his gaze to Wolverstone. "Gentlemen, if there is any way to deal appropriately with Lucius while shielding his unsuspecting family from harm, then if at all possible I would urge that that course be adopted."

"Ah." Wolverstone's lips curved approvingly. "In that case . . ." He cast a glance at Allardyce, who nodded, then cocked a brow at Rafe, who nodded even more definitely. Smiling faintly, Wolverstone looked again at Roderick. "I believe we can arrange to have Lucius Clifford appropriately dealt with in camera." Wolverstone turned to Rafe. "You're acquainted with the current head of the army, aren't you?"

Rafe nodded. "He's an old friend. I'll take a detour via the barracks on the way to your house." Rafe looked at Roscoe. "If you'll lend me a few of your men, I'll take our prisoner with me—best we deliver him to the barracks as soon as possible and set the process in motion."

"Indeed." Wolverstone's expression grew cynical. "And just to be sure there are no sudden impulses to bruit abroad the story of the capture of a lingering deserter in pursuit of some glimmer of political glory, I'll have a word with the minister tomorrow, just to indicate my interest and impress on him the desirability of keeping the entire sorry tale out of the public's gaze."

Christian Allardyce snorted. "Remind him that the war's long over, and people don't like to be reminded of it, not in any way."

"Good idea." Wolverstone drained his glass, as did the other men, then all set the tumblers down and rose.

"I'll do better than just the men, I'll lend you a carriage." Roscoe met Rafe's gaze. "I think it's wise to remove Clifford from my care—I wouldn't want him to meet with an accident before he got to his court-martial."

Rafe grunted. "You never know—he still might. I'm not fond of deserters myself, and as for those at the barracks . . . well, we'll see."

Turning to Wolverstone, Roscoe held out his hand. "Thank you." They all shook hands.

Wolverstone turned to the door. "I have to say that, in aiding us to bring a deserter who deliberately left another man to bear the stigma to face his court-martial, it's I and mine who should thank you."

With a gracious dip of his head, Wolverstone led the other men out of the library.

"So it's all arranged? All taken care of?" Seated on the drawing room sofa, with Sarah alongside her and Gladys in her usual chair, Miranda looked at Roderick as he stood before the fireplace; he'd just finished relating the details of the meeting at Roscoe's house.

Roderick spread his hands. "It was amazingly straightforward. They all know each other, but it was more than that. They think in the same way. It's as if they recognize they're all similar, and that breeds trust, so it was merely a matter of us describing the issue with Lucius, and them seeing our point and agreeing it would be best to proceed as we wished."

"So it's done." She steadfastly put Lucius from her mind;

to her and their wider family, he had died at Waterloo, albeit by his own act. After a moment, she smiled up at Roderick. "No more adventures for you."

"No, thank heaven." Roderick looked down at his injured foot. "I'm still recovering from the last, but at least I no longer have to hobble with a crutch."

"We must remember to return that to Ridgware." Miranda glanced at Sarah. "Whoever next goes to visit should take it back."

Sarah smiled, nodded, and looked at Roderick.

Gladys claimed Miranda's attention, then Hughes came in to announce that dinner was served. They all rose and went in.

Dinner proved a lighthearted, rather joyous gathering. While Roderick and Sarah, with the resilience of youth, had already left the past behind and were looking forward to shaping their future, Miranda judged that for herself and Gladys, their principal emotion was more in the nature of euphoric relief, although in her case her euphoria welled from multiple sources.

The threat to Roderick, and to her, had all stemmed from Lucius, and Lucius was no more.

That left her with issues to face and matters to decide, but although she now saw her direction clearly, the dinner table was not the place to dwell on her next step. Instead, she focused on what was before her—Roderick and Sarah, and the acquaintance that had become friendship, and was now so much more.

A soft smile on her lips, she watched her brother discussing his project for the Philanthropy Guild, something he wished to actively pursue now he was free to move around again. After her time at Ridgware, Sarah understood the concept and was quick to lend her support, discussing the next steps Roderick thought he should take, and the best ways to achieve them. Gladys listened, not entirely sure what Roderick was about, but willing to listen, to learn, to accept.

There was no doubt in Miranda's mind that Roderick would soon ask Sarah to marry him, and that Sarah would accept. No one who saw the two together could fail to see the glowing connection between them, the mutual awareness and regard that shone in their faces and warmed their eyes.

Love. It was there in front of her, demonstrated, given life in a thousand little things.

Now her eyes had been opened, she saw it clearly.

Dessert had come and gone; the others were disposed to linger.

Easing back her chair, she stood. When Roderick and Sarah broke off their animated discussion and looked at her, she waved them to remain seated. "If you'll excuse me, I've some . . . unfinished business to attend to."

Sarah smiled sweetly, but Roderick studied her for a moment, then nodded. "Yes, of course." He hesitated, then added, "If there's anything I can do . . ."

She let her smile deepen. "If there is, I'll let you know."

Quitting the dining room, she turned to the stairs. On gaining her room, she shut the door, then walked to the window seat and sat. She looked down at the side lawn, silvered by the light of a nearly full moon, at the trees whose almost-bare branches nevertheless largely blocked her view of the side gate.

Raising her gaze, she looked to the left, to where, between the various intervening trees, she could glimpse glimmers of white.

He was there, and she was here. How best to bridge that gap?

She sat and pondered, let her mind sweep back over the last weeks, over the days since she'd first met him.

Thought of all she'd learned—of him, and even more of herself.

Thought of what had grown between them, of what she now knew it to be.

Thought of what she most truly wanted of life.

Thought of backbone and the exercising of it.

Her conclusion was there, solid and sure in the center of her soul; she knew what she wanted. The only question remaining was how much she was willing to risk, and possibly to sacrifice, to secure it.

She studied her goal, evaluated her options, then rose and crossed to the bellpull.

Lady Mickleham was right. For a lady, exercising backbone was what life was truly about.

Roscoe sat before the fire in his library. A book lay open on his lap—the same book he'd been reading more than a month ago when Miranda had arrived to ask him to help find Roderick. A glass of brandy sat on the table by his elbow, but both the printed page and the brandy remained ignored as he stared into the fire's golden flames.

And remembered the warmth of different flames, the flames that leapt in Miranda's eyes, that flared and flowed over him whenever they were close, when they touched, when they loved. The flames that had truly warmed him.

That had, for a short time, made his life complete, made him whole.

But it was over, their brief liaison at an end. And for a man as powerful as he, it was galling indeed to be forced to admit that there was nothing he could do to change that, no matter how much he might wish it.

He was who he was—Neville Roscoe—and he couldn't turn back the clock. Couldn't wipe the slate of the past twelve years clean, nor did he wish to. But because of that, there was no hope for them, no way . . .

She was who she was, too, and that meant there was no future for them.

He forced his gaze to the book, tried to focus on the words. Failed.

Tried again; he *had* to put her out of his mind and get on with his life, his earlier life which previously had seemed full to the brim with work and achievement, but somehow now felt like a hollow shell.

Leaving a man on guard watching the Claverton Street house wasn't exactly letting go, but over the next weeks, he would probably get there. When the watchers grew bored and complained.

The front doorbell pealed, the sound faint, muted by distance and the thick walls of the library. Rundle would deal with whoever it was, yet he waited expectantly for several minutes before looking again at the book.

He tried to read but continued to hear sounds drifting from the front hall. Not a commotion, but there was something going on. He wondered if Rafe had encountered some difficulty and had brought Lucius Clifford back for safe-keeping, but a glance at the clock confirmed it was past ten o'clock—too late for that, surely.

Besides, Rundle would have alerted him by now, or shown any visitor to him, but no one had appeared.

Gradually, the distant sounds faded, and silence returned.

He looked back at the book, then, jaw firming, closed it and set it aside, alongside his barely touched drink. Restlessness, curiosity, and an unsettled, distracted feeling combined to push him to his feet.

Footsteps. Straightening, facing the door, he strained his ears and heard the steps increasingly clearly as whoever it was came down the long corridor toward the library doors.

A light swinging stride. A female stride.

One he recognized.

He froze.

He vaguely registered that Rundle's heavier tread was not in evidence, then the footsteps reached the door, it opened, and Miranda walked in.

Miranda saw him, smiled, then turned and shut the door.

He'd looked stunned—as stunned as she'd ever seen him—but when she turned back, he had his impassive expression in place, the impenetrable mask he used to face the world. She didn't allow that to dim her smile as she crossed the room to him.

"What are you doing here?"

The growled, slightly rough question suggested he wasn't happy to see her. She wasn't about to let that turn her from her path either; she knew what she knew. Halting before him, she tipped up her head and met his eyes. "I'm here because . . . well, I suppose you could say I'm taking up residence. Here, in your house."

For a moment, he didn't react, then he blinked. Slowly. "What?"

She waved over her shoulder, toward the rest of the house. "Rundle and the others are taking my trunks upstairs. We decided to put them in the room next to yours. It seemed the most appropriate place."

He dragged in a breath; when he met her eyes again his impassive mask was gone. Completely gone. Raw emotion filled his face. "Miranda . . . no. You can't do this."

She arched her brows. "Can't I?"

"You're not thinking clearly." His eyes searched hers, saw the determination and resolution she made no effort to hide. He raked a hand through his hair and swung away to face the fire. "I can't let you do this."

She closed the distance; from behind him, she slipped her arms around his chest, laid her temple against his collar. "Yes, you can. I want a family, I always have, and I want to create that family with you. I know you want a family of your own as much as I do—I've seen you with your family, and with the family you've built here, but it's not the same, is it? I want a family and a home of my own, and you want one, too." She tightened her arms, hugged him. "All you have to do is say yes."

For a moment he stood within her hold, one hand rising to rest over hers, then he sighed and let his head fall forward. After a moment, he gently pried her hands loose and, holding one, turned to face her. He met her eyes. "I can't stop being Roscoe."

"Yes, I know, and I'm not asking you to." Moving closer, she raised her free hand and laid it on his chest, held his gaze. "I love you as you are, for who you are, not for who you were, or who you might be."

He stilled. His eyes almost desperately searched hers. A heartbeat ticked past. "You love me?"

She fought to keep her smile from wavering, fought back the tears that leapt to her eyes at the utter vulnerability that rang in those simple words. She managed a decisive, almost belligerent nod. "Yes, I do. That's why I'm here—I love you, and I *know* nothing in heaven or earth is strong enough to change that." She looked into his eyes, felt more confident than she'd expected as she continued, "And I know you love me, that you return my sentiment on all levels, to every degree. You tried to let me go, to set me at a distance, and you couldn't do it. Powerful as you are, disciplined as you are, still you couldn't do it. This afternoon you put yourself between a pistol and me, which, as dramatic demonstrations go, was rather emphatic, not only in terms of your feelings but also in terms of clarifying mine. After today, being apart is never going to work, is never going to satisfy either of us, so I'm here to find a way for us to be together—a way for me to be your lover, your helpmate, for as long as our love lasts, which in my estimation will be forever."

His expression was a medley of emotions—disbelief, confusion, stunned shock, and rising hope. "But what about respectability? If you live with me, you'll have none."

Her eyes on his, she paused, then said, "I could simply say that I don't care about respectability anymore, and that would be the truth, but I suspect you won't readily accept that, so I'll explain. All my life I was taught that respectability was the ultimate virtue, to be courted and worshipped above all else. I'm not sure that I ever truly, in my heart, believed that, but I did, indeed, hold rigidly to that code, yet it never brought me happiness. Then through our adventures of recent weeks, I saw and learned, and had demonstrated unequivocally that social respectability is at best a minor virtue. It doesn't hold a candle to the greater virtues, like love, and honor, and devotion. Like loyalty and integrity, and the respect gained through one's actions. Like truly caring about others, and actively protecting those weaker than oneself. Against those virtues, respectability is insubstantial, an ephemeral construct held to by those lacking greater strength.

"So no—I no longer value respectability as I once did. To me, now, it's largely immaterial. What matters to me—what now anchors my world—is love. And you. Because it's you I love."

She'd come there prepared and determined to risk all; that was one thing Wraxby had taught her. Wraxby, and Lucasta. If she wanted to claim love, she couldn't hold back and wait for it to be offered. She had to be willing to risk all to gain it—to risk her heart, to offer her heart to him if she wanted his in return.

He drew in a breath, and it shook. "I . . . don't know what to say—you've blindsided me."

"I would apologize, only once I saw clearly what I wanted, I knew it would be pointless to wait for you to make an offer. Indeed, to wait for you to even come knocking at my door." She arched a brow. "You wouldn't have, would you?"

He held her gaze, eventually said, "I was determined not to."

Her lips curved at the unvoiced admission that he might not have been able to hold to his so-determined line. "On the one hand I would have liked to have seen you falter, but . . ." She drew in a breath and bluntly stated, "I understand that you feel prohibited from offering for my hand, but—"

He laid a finger across her lips and silenced her. He held her gaze for two heartbeats, then lowered his head and leaned his forehead against hers. "I can't." His voice was anguished and low, then it strengthened, "I won't. It would be asking you to make too much of a sacrifice, and that's something I cannot, will not, do." Raising his head, he looked into her eyes, his expression starkly bleak. "I can't ask you to set aside the life of a lady and accept what I can offer you."

She let her lips curve again, raised a hand to frame his cheek. "No, I know. I know you can't ask me. Won't ask me. Which is why I'm here, to ask you."

He blinked.

Before he could speak, she went on, "Did it ever occur to you that you constantly make sacrifices for others, that you are always the one giving, and you never allow others a chance to return the favor? Believe me, your family, and doubtless others, too, feel the imbalance most strongly, but you are very *very* good at keeping the scales tipped in the direction you think right—with you doing the giving and all others the accepting." She paused, tilted her head, kept her eyes locked with his. "In me, however, you've met your match. Because for me, the challenge before me, the challenge I have to meet to get what I most want in life, is to convince you to change your stance—to convince you, just this once, to allow me to be the one to give, to allow me to be the one to make the sacrifice, and for you to accept it, to be the one sacrificed for."

She paused, her eyes on his, then tipped up her chin. "So my question for you, Neville Roscoe, for the man who goes by that name, is whether you are strong enough to, whether you want me as your wife enough to, accept my proposal."

He was silent for a full minute, then said, "Why don't you propose, then we'll find out?"

Her lips kicked up; she wasn't sure he'd realized, but his hands had risen and slid about her waist; he was now holding her gently against him.

"My proposal, my proposition, my offer to you, my lord, is simply this—marry me. Marry me, love me, hold me, and never let me go. Let me fill the place by your side, manage this house and make it into a home, and if God is willing, create a family with you."

He looked into her eyes, and there was no mistaking the terrible yearning, the concomitant exultant joy he yet held back. "Life as my wife won't be the sort of life a lady would expect."

"No, but it will be the life I want—as your lover, your helpmate, your wife, and the mother of your children."

For several seconds, time stood still. Then he drew in a huge breath and lowered his head so his temple rested alongside hers. His voice was low, hoarse, as he said, "I love you—beyond words, beyond adoration. And yes, I'll marry you. You seem to see the challenge that it will be, and I'm more than willing to take the risk with you, as you are so bound and determined to attempt it. Above all else in life, I want you as my wife. You are a remarkable woman, and I don't deserve you."

He shifted his head, brushed his lips over hers.

Surrender.

She smiled. Delight, joy, and sheer exuberance well-ing, overflowing, she pushed her hands over his shoulders, wound her arms about his neck. Brushed her lips over his, left them hovering as she said, "I'm a remarkable lady, and you definitely do."

Then she kissed him. His arms tightened about her and he drew her in, drew her fully against him.

Giddy, with passion, joy, boundless love, and endless de-votion all vying for expression, they pledged their troth in an exchange infused with so much raw emotion it left them both breathless.

They didn't need words.

When they finally drew back long enough to breathe again, long enough to hear, register, and think, the house was quiet again and they had only themselves to please.

Hand in hand they left the library, walked back to the front hall, and climbed the stairs.

He led her to his room, drew her inside. Drew her into his arms.

She'd been in his room before, but she hadn't, then, felt the same sense of coming home, of having reached the end of her journey. Of belonging.

As they came together in joy and in love, in passion and blatantly acknowledged desire, she knew to the deepest depths of her soul that she'd been right.

She tipped her head back, fingers threading through the dark silk of his hair as he pressed a hot, openmouthed kiss to the spot where her pulse thundered. "We'll make this work." A whispered promise. "There'll be hurdles, I know, but together we'll overcome them."

His hands closed about her breasts, evocatively kneaded. "Together we can triumph over anything fate sends us"—he raised his head, met her eyes—"just as long as you love me as I love you."

From beneath her heavy lids, she held his gaze. "Forever and always."

She drew his head down, raised her lips and kissed him— and let their love have its way.

Let it lead them like a beacon, shining and true, through the heated moments, through the passionate fire. Let the flames of desire claim them anew, let ecstasy rive them so the glory, love's benediction, could pour in and forge them anew, into an irrevocable one.

When at last she lay in his arms, sated and blissfully exhausted in his bed, when he settled his head on his pillow and felt her cheek on his breast, her hair spread in silken glory over his chest, he could barely believe that, truly, he had this.

That, despite all, he was going to get a chance at a wife, a home, a family of his own. That he was going to get to roll the dice in a game he'd thought forever denied him.

Desire and hope welled in his chest, swelling so high he closed his eyes against the tide of sudden weakness, the unexpected, unprecedented, soul-shattering joy.

She was giving him her life, her future, in order to create his.

In doing so she brought him, figuratively and in every way

that mattered, to his knees. He would worship her until the day he died.

Lifting one hand, he stroked her hair. "Thank you."

He felt her lips curve against his skin. "I have every intention of making the rest of our lives my pleasure."

Epilogue

"Just a moment." Miranda rose slowly from her chair at the side of Roscoe's desk, waving at both Roscoe and Jordan to remain seated. "I have a report from the school that should clarify those costs. Just wait while I fetch it."

Roscoe forced himself to remain in his chair as, one hand absentmindedly pressed to the small of her back, his very pregnant wife shuffled at her best pace through the door they'd opened up between his study and the room beyond. That room had become her office. Over the past eight months, she'd gradually filched the reins for the various schools and orphanages he funded from his hands; she now managed them and kept a much sharper eye on what went on there than he could ever hope to do.

Once the people involved got over the shock that a lady such as she was indeed his wife—it seemed that figured as an even bigger shock than he himself was—they inevitably ended confiding in her, revealing all sorts of things while answering questions that drew them out, yet also left them feeling engaged and appreciated.

She had a knack; he wasn't sure she'd even been aware of it, not until she'd flung herself so unrestrainedly into his life.

He could hear her shuffling papers in the other room. He and Jordan traded glances; both smiled and waited patiently. At the other end of the room, facing each other on the sofas, Mudd and Rawlins were amusing themselves playing a game of cards.

All in all, he reflected, all was well in his world.

It was a very nice feeling. He couldn't think of anything he would change.

The formalities of their marriage had been something of a hurdle. His solicitors, Roderick's solicitors, and Jordan had spent days working out exactly how to manage the reality of who he was, who Miranda would be on her marriage to him, and how any children would be legally accounted for; in the end, he'd been forced to accept that Lord Julian Roscoe Neville Delbraith would have to reappear at least long enough to front the altar.

So Miranda was now formally Lady Delbraith; everyone in his household and businesses referred to her as "my lady" or "your lady," neatly sidestepping the issue of which lady she actually was.

The wedding itself would have been a massive hurdle, but the arrangements had been taken, firmly, out of his hands. They'd ended being married in a private ceremony in the chapel at Ridgware, with his mother and Caroline weeping copiously, and even his three sisters all teary-eyed. At least his wife hadn't been; she'd been radiant. But most surprising to him had been the number of onlookers who had traveled to the house on the day. The chapel had been packed to the rafters with people from the estate, from the various estate-associated businesses, and a large contingent of his London staff.

Aside from those he saw daily, he hadn't thought they'd be

interested and hadn't invited them, but someone had. And they'd come. The wedding breakfast held in the great ballroom had been a gargantuan affair at which everyone had mingled—even Gladys, which had amazed even him.

In the wake of the wars, little by little society truly was changing.

They'd been married just before Christmas, and this coming Christmas, they would have even more to celebrate.

Miranda waddled back into the room, frowning at the sheet of paper she held in one hand. Her hair, thick and lustrous, had started to escape its chignon, strands tugged free due to the pencils she'd taken to carrying tucked behind her ears, a habit she'd copied from Jordan.

"This is it." Miranda handed the paper to Jordan. "I think you'll find those charges are due to the new drainage system the county introduced."

"Ah, yes." Jordan frowned. "We'll need to make adjustments."

Settling back into her chair, Miranda felt a small limb flex, then stretch; putting her hand on her hugely distended stomach, she waited, and sure enough the baby pressed his—or her—small foot firmly into her palm. She grinned, glanced at Roscoe, and saw him smiling back. They were both so eager to meet their child; just a few more weeks, and he—or she—would be there.

And then they would be a family.

She blinked rapidly.

Roscoe, bless him, noticed, and engaged Jordan with a question about the other costs they were considering incurring as part of their latest project. Her husband had allowed her free rein with such ventures, and he'd also allowed her to learn about his gambling businesses, his clubs, and the hells and dens. She only visited the clubs, and even then only with him and his bodyguards, but she'd quickly seen the possibility of improving the lot of the large number of women who worked in those houses. When she'd suggested a certain merging of interests—the clubs and some new philanthropy projects—Roscoe had blinked, but he'd thought, and then agreed.

Her life, truly, could not be more purposeful. More complete.

There were moments she was so happy she was reduced to tears. Silly, but there it was.

Regaining her composure, she settled the heavy weight of the baby more comfortably, then leaned forward and rejoined the discussion.

Rundle appeared with the tea tray, as he inevitably did at what he considered an appropriate hour. "Where would you like this, my lady?"

Frowning at another receipt, without looking up, she waved down the room. "Thank you, Rundle—just set it down there. Mudd, would you pour?"

"Yes, m'lady."

Roscoe bit his lip and avoided Jordan's eye. Both Mudd and Rawlins had become Miranda's devoted slaves; she only had to ask and they leapt to perform even the most unexpected tasks, like handing around the delicate teacups. But the pair watched over his wife as if she was porcelain, something she bore with from them, but which she frowned at if he tried. For that, he was infinitely grateful. Both Mudd and Rawlins were experienced fathers and had taken to giving him hints on how to manage, some of which had, he had to admit, proved useful. He might have rubbed her back, but he would never have thought to rub her feet, but she had indeed been very appreciative.

Jordan, too, approved of Miranda; he'd confided to him that she had a practical bent that in Jordan's view they both lacked. Jordan considered her a valuable addition to their team and had taken to treating her much like an older sister, a level of connection she in turn relished—it gave her an opening to inquire into Jordan's private life, and to make suggestions.

That interaction had afforded him countless hours of amused entertainment.

Mudd and Rawlins arrived with the teacups, and they all paused to sip.

He glanced around the faces, thought of the others not present—of the family he was now much more involved with on a daily basis.

Edwina's wedding had gone off without a hitch, and Sarah and Roderick had got engaged in April and would marry next year. Henry was at Oxford, getting into all the expected larks, but with a surprising degree of moderation. Even more amazing, Caroline was bearing up well; one of Miranda's suggestions, that whenever Henry felt the urge to gamble he should drop down to London and spend a few days in Chichester Street, playing against Roscoe, had greatly eased Caroline's mind. As Henry inevitably lost, and heavily, the exercise tended to quash any budding dreams that he might ever be able to gamble and win.

Edwina was still overseas with Frobisher, but Millicent and Cassandra had taken to calling at Chichester Street. At their husbands' insistence and his, they did so covertly, yet there'd been several impromptu dinner parties which their husbands had also attended.

At times, the distinction between Roscoe and Lord Julian blurred, but he never lost sight of who he really was—and neither, he knew, did his wife.

And that remained the greatest joy of their marriage— that she knew him, saw him as he really was, and in turn he knew her.

She was the lady who held his heart, who had risked all to claim it, and to thus give him all he'd ever wanted and never thought to have.

He had a wife, a home, and a family.

All the very best in life was his.

See the first appearances of
Lord Julian Roscoe Neville Delbraith
in these scenes from
Stephanie Laurens's

The Edge of Desire

and

The Reckless Bride

From The Edge of Desire

Christian alighted from the hackney he, Dalziel, and Justin had taken from the Bastion Club, joining the other two on the pavement in Chichester Street, Pimlico. As the hackney rattled away, they all stood and surveyed the large white-painted mansion that was Neville Roscoe's residence; overlooking Dolphin Square, it was an imposing sight.

Yet there was nothing overdone about it. The house was a simple statement of solid wealth and permanence, a description that fitted the owner as well.

They trooped up the steps and rang the bell.

The butler was expecting them; he led them through halls and corridors that could very easily have graced any of their houses. Opening a door at the end of one wing, he announced them, then stepped back, allowing them to enter an airy, excellently proportioned room, well-lit by long windows and elegantly furnished as a gentleman's study.

Tall bookcases were built into one wall. Pedestals bearing a set of superb busts stood between the windows. A large mahogany desk, its lines clean and precise, dominated the room. Various furniture polished to a lustrous gleam, green leather upholstery, brass lamps and two spindle-legged side tables completed the decor.

That the gentleman who rose from the chair behind the wide expanse of the desk belonged in such refined surrounds no one could doubt.

Neville Roscoe was an enigma. He was rumored to be the scion of a minor branch of one of the major ton houses, although no one had ever identified which. Roscoe almost certainly wasn't the surname he'd been born with. Tall, with the same aristocratic features that marked all of them as descended from one or another of William's nobles, long limbed and rangy, blessed with an athletic physique and the muscles to match, after a cursory glance at Christian, who he'd met before, and a curious glance for Justin, who he hadn't, Roscoe fixed his dark gaze on Dalziel.

The only obvious difference between the two men was that Roscoe wore his dark hair in a close crop, while Dalziel's sat in elegant waves about his head.

Watching the pair take stock of each other, Christian hid a wry grin. "I believe you haven't previously met. Dalziel. Neville Roscoe."

After an instant's hesitation, both inclined their heads, the action eerily similar.

Roscoe transferred his attention to Justin. "And this, I take it, is Lord Justin Vaux."

Justin politely inclined his head.

Roscoe didn't offer to shake hands; he waved them to the three substantial chairs set before the desk.

Christian knew Roscoe's history. He'd appeared in London about a decade earlier, and had made his fortune much as Randall had, although in Roscoe's case he'd had no truck with secrecy—that wasn't his style. The other difference was that, while Randall had worked to come up in the world, Roscoe had patently, and very deliberately, stepped down from whatever his base within the aristocracy was to run a string of select gambling hells. He was a superb card player, was known to have won fortunes, yet rarely lost more than modest amounts. Even by the ton's jaded standards, he was a gamester extraordinaire. Yet although he was now very wealthy, rather than attempt to rejoin the ton—something he most likely could do with reasonable ease—he continued to eschew society. Indeed, he lived a very private life.

One of the few concessions he made to his true station was his surroundings; he lived in luxury, and the way he moved within the elegance of his house verified beyond doubt that that was, indeed, the milieu to which he'd been born.

He sat as they did, then arched his brows. "And how may I help you, gentlemen?"

"At this stage," Christian replied, "we're interested in information about the proposed sale of the Orient Trading Company. We've been led to believe you were hoping to be the buyer."

Roscoe's eyes were watchful. "And what's your interest in the sale?"

"I'm acting for Lady Letitia Randall née Vaux, Randall's widow." Christian waved at Justin. "Lord Vaux is here as her surrogate."

Roscoe's gaze flicked to Justin. "The one with a warrant sworn against him for Randall's murder?" His gaze shifted to Dalziel. "But of course, you'd know that."

"Indeed," Dalziel replied. "We also know someone else murdered Randall."

Roscoe's brows rose. That was news to him.

"We're currently pursuing the avenue," Christian smoothly went on, "that Randall was murdered because of the proposed sale."

Roscoe met his eyes, then dropped all pretense of nonchalance; leaning his forearms on the desk, eyes narrowing, he was suddenly all business. "If that's the case, obviously the murderer wasn't me."

Christian inclined his head. "Just so. But we need to learn all we can about the proposed sale in order to identify those most affected—at present there's possibilities aplenty as to who might actually have done the deed."

Roscoe's gaze turned inward.

They waited.

"First," he eventually said, his gaze lowering to fix on his hands, clasped on the desk, "I should clarify that, as matters stand, at some point I would, almost certainly, have made an offer for the Orient Trading Company—an offer Randall and his partners wouldn't have been able to refuse." Lifting his gaze, Roscoe met Dalziel's eyes, then looked at Christian. "Randall and the others had worked diligently to establish themselves. They'd come a long way."

"All the way from Hexham," Christian said.

Roscoe smiled; that had indeed been the information he'd been probing for. "You discovered that, did you?"

"Indeed. And you?" Christian asked.

"Only recently." Roscoe met Dalziel's eyes. "I make it a point of learning all I can about those I propose to do business with."

"So you approached Randall?" Dalziel continued the interrogation.

Roscoe shook his head. "I would have eventually—there's many who'll tell you that. But I didn't have to make overtures. Randall came to me—or rather, he let it be known in the right quarters that he and his partners were interested in selling the Orient Trading Company, lock, stock, and barrel."

"There were other potential buyers," Dalziel remarked.

"True, but none with pockets as deep as mine. And I was prepared to pay well—acquiring the company was always a part of my long-term strategy."

Christian could well imagine it. And there were few who would or could effectively stand in Roscoe's way. Although the acquisition and the merging of the company's gaming hells with his own would make him extremely powerful, as Gallagher had intimated, even the underworld czars would nod and let him be. Roscoe was regarded as a stabilizing influence at the interface between legal and illegal activities. He refused to allow any underhanded practices in his establishments, and by and large, all was kept strictly aboveboard.

He held no truck with crime, and with his views so widely known—and so rigidly enforced—even the czars preferred the devil they knew, even if he marched to a beat not their own.

"Apropos of which"—Roscoe's dark eyes turned to Christian—"I'm willing to tell you all I know about Randall's proposed sale in return for an agreement to be presented, at the appropriate time, to the new owner and the other two partners, as Randall's chosen buyer."

Christian held his gaze for a moment, then nodded. "We're prepared to give you an assurance to that effect."

Roscoe inclined his head. "Very well. On that basis . . . in response to Randall's fishing for buyers, I contacted him by letter. He came here . . ." Roscoe paused, then went on, "It was two days before his death. We discussed the sale—he'd had offers from others, Edson, Plummer, and Gammon, that I'm sure of, but none of them would take all the properties. They each wanted only certain ones, and there was overlap, so, quite aside from the price, if Randall went with any of them, things were going to get messy. So he and I sat and talked—we worked out an offer that satisfied us both. I agreed to take the entire company for a price he thought reasonable. Once the others heard I wanted the whole company, they would back off. Any further interest from them would only result in Randall making more, and while there's no love lost between them and me, there was even less goodwill for Randall—essentially because he pretended to be something he wasn't."

"We've heard you had conditions," Christian said, "and that you and he hadn't yet shaken on the deal."

Roscoe nodded. "I had two conditions Randall had to meet before I was prepared to do more than talk. The first is an obvious one—I wanted to see the books from each of the hells. I'm sure that wouldn't have been a problem. The other condition was one peculiar to the situation." Roscoe met Christian's eyes. "As I'm sure you've discovered, Randall was the active partner of the three. Because of that . . ." Roscoe paused as if considering, then continued. ". . . and because of another piece of information which I suspect I was one of the few privy to, I asked Randall to provide a signed written statement from each of his partners to the effect that they were willing to sell their shares at this time."

Trowbridge's written statement. "Why insist on that," Christian asked, "and what was the piece of information?"

Roscoe tapped a finger on his blotter. "I insisted primarily because I don't have partners. I don't have time for them—having any sort of partner would slow me down and generally get in my way. Although the Orient Trading Company is structured so it's supposedly all or none for any sale to proceed, there's ways around that, namely for the buyer—me—to take on one of their partners as my partner in a new company. That wasn't going to happen. I made it clear I was only interested in acquiring the Orient Trading Company if I could buy it outright."

"So it was all the shares in one deal, or no deal?" Dalziel asked.

"Just so." Roscoe paused, then went on, "Obviously I would have asked Randall for those declarations anyway, but the reason I haven't bothered to make any appointment with my bankers regarding the deal is because . . . well, frankly, I had serious doubts it would proceed."

Justin's eyes had narrowed. "You thought one of the other two wouldn't sell?"

Roscoe nodded. "I made my offer for the company primarily to ensure it wasn't sold to anyone else." He paused, then went on, "That piece of information I mentioned came to me in a roundabout way. I was approached about an investment—it sounded an excellent prospect, but instinct reared its head and at the last I didn't buy in. Naturally I kept an eye on what happened. The investment was a swindle, a very sophisticated one but a swindle just the same. Everyone who'd invested lost every penny they'd put in."

"Swithin," Christian guessed.

Roscoe met his gaze. "He was mentioned as one of the principal investors. The gentlemen behind the scheme specifically targeted the knowledgeable investors—they courted us, pandered to our vanity. That was what made me suspicious, but in Swithin's case it apparently played into his hubris. His reputation went to his head, and he risked . . . a very great deal."

"So, he's what?" Justin asked. "Ruined?"

"No, but my sources suggest he's very close to it, and he's taking extreme care to hide the fact. He knows money, how to move it around, how to practice sleight of hand with it to conceal his state. But he's already liquidated most of his other investments, and even his new wife's portion is gone. He still owns two houses, one in London and one in Surrey, but when it comes to cash, he'd be lucky to lay his hands on two pennies to rub together."

"But," Dalziel said, "if he needs money so desperately, wouldn't that make him more likely to sell, rather than less?"

Roscoe shook his head. "You're forgetting what the Orient Trading Company is—it's a cash-generating machine. Swithin has liquidated all the assets he can that don't show. He desperately needs more cash, but he can't sell his houses without people knowing—and if it becomes common knowledge that he—the canny, wily investor—was ruined by some smooth-talking swindlers, his reputation as a man to go to for investment deals will evaporate. His standing in the ton will be gone."

Glancing at their faces, Roscoe went on, "My guess is that Swithin is counting on—banking on, if you will—the steady income from the Orient Trading Company to keep him afloat. If the company is sold and he gets his third share, it won't be enough to cover his debts *and* generate any future income. But the company has always been a gold mine, and with that steady income behind him, he can go to a bank and take out a loan to cover his shortfall—the bank will look at the company's income and happily agree."

Roscoe leaned back in his chair. "What I suspect, gentlemen, is that Swithin is down to his last penny and was preparing to make that trip to the bank when Randall proposed selling the company. My understanding is that the three partners weren't close, so Randall's tack might well have come as a complete shock to Swithin, and given Randall was sitting in my office discussing the sale, it seemed Swithin hadn't shared his situation with his partners. My request for a written statement from Trowbridge and Swithin would, I reasoned, force Swithin to tell Randall and Trowbridge of his difficulties, and that would be the last we'd hear of any sale, at least in the short term."

He met Christian's eyes. "All that said, I have no idea if Swithin killed Randall. I honestly can't see why he would have—Randall and Trowbridge couldn't have forced him to sell. However, I know he had a very good reason for not wanting to sell his share of the Orient Trading Company."

Christian exchanged a glance with Dalziel and Justin, then looked back at Roscoe. "You've been a great help."

They all got to their feet. Christian held out a hand. After a fractional hesitation—one induced by surprise—Roscoe gripped it.

Dalziel's lips quirked; he nodded to Roscoe. Justin opted to shake the man's hand.

Roscoe remained standing behind his desk while they walked to the door. As they reached it, he said, "Dearne, Vaux—you will remember our agreement. When all this is over, I'll still want to buy." His lips lifted slightly. "And I daresay the lady will want to sell."

Justin nodded. Christian raised a hand in salute and followed Dalziel out of the door.

"Mr. Roscoe, my lord. My lady."

Letitia rose from the chaise in the smaller drawing room of Allardyce House, Christian beside her. Her gaze fixed on the doorway as Percival stepped back; she would own to considerable curiosity over Neville Roscoe. Quite aside from the fact that she expected to divest herself of the troublesome business of the Orient Trading Company, everything Christian had told her of the mysterious Roscoe had only whetted her appetite.

Four days had passed since Swithin had tried to push her to her death; somewhat to her surprise, her fear-filled memories had all but immediately been overlaid by feelings of relief, and then happiness.

Christian had been responsible for both.

He'd also contacted Roscoe. She in turn had visited the house in Cheyne Walk, to tell Trowbridge and Honeywell all that had transpired, and to get from Trowbridge his written agreement to sell his share of the company if and when she did.

She'd also sent one of Christian's grooms into Surrey with a letter for Mrs. Swithin confirming the business of the Orient Trading Company and the desirability of a sale, and the consequent need for a written agreement. She had received by reply the requested agreement, along with a declaration from Swithin's solicitor, who had, most fortuitously, been in Surrey dealing with Swithin's affairs.

So all was in readiness to effect the sale.

Roscoe appeared; he literally darkened the doorway. With his close-cropped dark hair, dark clothes, and cynical, dark blue eyes, he looked the epitome of a dangerous character. With an inclination of his head, he moved past Percival and approached them; he walked with the same arrogant, faintly menacing stride Dalziel employed. Not so much an intentional affectation as an expression of what, underneath the sophisticated glamour, they really were.

As he neared, she saw that Roscoe was as tall as Christian, but not quite as large, as heavy, his build more rangy, but in no way less lethal for that.

Christian extended his hand.

Roscoe quirked a brow—apparently at being accorded the courtesy—but gripped and shook nonetheless. "Good evening."

It was after ten o'clock.

Christian inclined his head. "Thank you for coming." He turned to her. "Allow me to present Lady Letitia." He left out the Randall, she was quite sure deliberately.

Letitia gave Roscoe her hand, smiled as she looked into his face . . . and barely felt his fingers close about hers.

Barely heard his proper, "Lady Randall," barely registered the rumble of his deep voice or his perfectly executed bow.

She knew, looking into his eyes, that she'd met him before—long ago, when they'd been in their teens.

She let her smile widen, and sensed his wariness grow. "I believe we've met before, Mr. Roscoe, although I can't at the moment recall where. But then I expect you would rather I didn't recall at all, so perhaps"—retrieving her hand from his suddenly slack grasp, she waved to the armchair opposite the chaise—"we should get down to business before I do."

Roscoe cast Christian a look, then moved to comply.

Still smiling delightedly, Letitia sat and promptly took charge of the negotiations.

Much to Roscoe's disquiet.

Realizing that the threat of her knowledge of his identity, plus the inherent difficulty a man like Roscoe faced in negotiating business with a female of Letitia's class, played heavily into her hands—and that she was supremely well-qualified to capitalize on the fact—Christian sat back and left her to it.

She did well, extracting both a higher price and more favorable payment terms than Roscoe had expected to have to concede; that much was clear from the irritation that briefly shone in his dark eyes.

But he took it well.

When, all the details thrashed out and agreed upon, the written agreements from Trowbridge and Mrs. Swithin tendered and accepted, they all rose and Roscoe shook Letitia's hand, there was a reluctantly admiring glint in his eyes. "I'll have my man of business draw up the contract in conjunction with . . ." Roscoe cocked a brow at Christian. ". . . Montague?"

Christian nodded. "He's under instruction to take over the management of Lady Letitia's affairs."

Roscoe's lips quirked. "Naturally." He looked at Letitia, hesitated, then said, "I understand felicitations are in order." He bowed, inherently graceful. "Please accept mine."

Letitia glowed. "Thank you."

Straightening, Roscoe met her eyes. "And don't try too hard to remember our previous meeting."

She waved airily. "I doubt I'll have time, what with all else that's going on."

"Good." With that dry comment, Roscoe turned to Christian; this time he spontaneously held out his hand. "Dearne."

Christian gripped his hand, entirely content with how the meeting had gone. "Come—I'll walk you out."

Roscoe bowed again to Letitia, then fell into step beside Christian as he headed for the door. While Christian opened it, Roscoe glanced back—at Letitia settling on the chaise to await Christian's return.

Then he turned and went through the door.

As they passed down the corridors and into the front hall, Christian was aware of Roscoe glancing about—not so much taking note as breathing in the ambience. "Do you ever think you'll return to"—he gestured about them—"tonnish life?"

Roscoe didn't immediately reply. When they reached the front door, he turned and faced Christian. "Much as I might envy you the life you now have, I long ago realized it wasn't in the cards for me."

There was a finality in his tone that closed the subject.

Roscoe accepted his cane from Percival, then, when that worthy opened the door, nodded to Christian and went out into the night.

Christian watched him go, saw him disappear into the gloom before Percival shut the door. He stared unseeing at the panels for a minute more, then recalling all that awaited him in the smaller drawing room, he smiled, turned, and strolled back to embrace it.

And her. The love of his life and, God willing, the mother of his children.

From The Reckless Bride

January 5, 1823
City of London

Rafe met Gabriel on the pavement before the building in which Sir Charles Manning maintained a business office. Rafe glanced back at the unmarked black carriage that stood waiting at the curb half a block away. Loretta had accepted that dealing with Manning would be best left to men, but had wanted to be near to hear the results immediately.

Gabriel blew on his hands and glanced about. It was early afternoon, yet even in this season the city pavements were bustling with clerks of all descriptions scurrying hither and yon. "Roscoe should be here soon."

Rafe nodded. Neville Roscoe's involvement in their plan had been a surprise to everyone. Christian had suggested asking Roscoe, who apparently knew a great deal about the shady side of London business dealings, for his opinion on Manning and how best to deal with him. Montague, the highly respected Cynsters' man of business, who also acted for Esme, had supported the suggestion; he, too, knew of Roscoe and patently valued the man's insight.

Royce and Minerva had come down to London as Royce had more yet to do with bringing the charges against the Black Cobra. Rafe was staying with the ducal couple at Wolverstone House while Loretta had returned to her brother's roof. But as soon as Manning was dealt with and Esme's release from captivity assured, Rafe and Loretta would head into the country, first for a visit with Margaret, Loretta's eldest sister, then to stay for a time with Rafe's family, who were, after all these years, eager, even ecstatically so, to embrace him and his betrothed to their collective bosom.

All those involved in dealing with Manning had met the previous evening at Wolverstone House. Royce, Rafe, Loretta, Christian, Gabriel, and Tristan had all been present, as had Montague, and, to everyone's surprise, Roscoe had sent word that he would attend, too.

When he'd arrived, Minerva had blinked, but then she'd smiled, welcomed him, then left them to their deliberations.

Roscoe had exchanged a look with Royce, but then had sat and told them what he'd learned of Manning's business affairs. Montague had confirmed some points, but had been intrigued to hear of others, his attitude leaving little doubt he considered Roscoe's intelligence sound.

Once all their information had been verbally laid on the table, they'd concocted a plan—a reasonably simple one they'd all felt would work.

However, while Roscoe had agreed that their plan would release Esme from any threat from Manning, he'd pointed out that the most likely result was that Manning would sell his shares to someone of similar ilk who would then take up where Manning had left off, and Esme and her fellow shareholders would once again be besieged.

Roscoe's proposal to eliminate that risk had made them all blink, but Montague had seconded the idea, and after a moment's consideration, Royce had given it his imprimatur as well. That had been enough for the rest of them.

Which was why Rafe and Gabriel were waiting for Roscoe to join them before confronting Manning in his lair.

The various bells of London had just started tolling two o'clock when the tall figure of Roscoe, impeccably groomed, turned the corner. He saw them and strode briskly up.

Roscoe exchanged nods, then tipped his head toward the door. "You lead. I'll play the part of silent and enigmatic supporter until we start explaining what will happen next."

Feeling very much like he was leading another charge, Rafe led the way up the narrow stair. They walked into Manning's outer office without knocking, awed the crafty-looking secretary and sent him scurrying into the inner office to announce their presence and convey their desire to speak with Manning on a matter of urgency regarding Argyle Investments.

Less than a minute later, they were shown into Manning's inner sanctum.

The man himself—a gentleman, well-dressed, elegantly turned out, of middle age and just a touch portly—rose from the chair behind a large desk. "Gentlemen." His gaze flicked from Gabriel to Rafe. "I take it you are the Mr. Carstairs who has recently become betrothed to Miss Michelmarsh?"

Their engagement had been announced in the *Gazette* three days before. Rafe nodded. "Indeed." He gestured to Gabriel. "I assume you've heard of Mr. Cynster."

"Ah, yes." Manning's expression suggested he couldn't understand what Gabriel was doing there; the uncertainty took the edge off his arrogant assurance.

Especially when neither Rafe nor Gabriel made any move to offer their hands. Nor did Rafe introduce Roscoe, who had hung back by the wall just inside the door.

An awkward pause ensued, then, considerably more sober, Manning waved to the chairs before the desk. "Please be seated, gentlemen."

They all sat; Roscoe subsided into a straight-backed chair against the wall. Rafe hid a smile. Christian had warned that while Manning wouldn't recognize Roscoe by sight, learning his name would have a definite effect. Apparently

Roscoe ran a number of questionable enterprises with an iron fist, but the code he adhered to was rigid, unbreakable; he was one of the few men in London guaranteed to put the wind up a slippery practitioner like Manning.

Like a jackal coming face-to-face with a full-grown lion.

"Now then, gentlemen." Manning clasped his hands on his blotter and looked from Gabriel to Rafe. "What can I do for you?"

"It's more a matter," Rafe informed him, "of what we can, or will, or might deign to, do for you." In an even tone, he related what he'd learned in Mainz, all the Prussian had told him, and described the sworn document, now in the keeping of a magistrate, that named Manning as the Prussian's employer in the attempted abduction and murder of Lady Congreve.

Manning rushed to open his eyes wide and spread his hands. "I had no notion of any of this. Clearly the Prussian was misinformed—it was not I who hired him."

Gabriel smiled, all teeth. "We thought you might say that. However, we've confirmed that you have acquired a position in Argyle Investments, a company with charitable aims, and are seeking to alter the company's direction against the wishes of the other, original shareholders. Of particular note, you borrowed heavily to purchase the shares, no doubt counting on a windfall should Argyle accept the offer made by Curtis Foundries."

"It's plain," Rafe said, reclaiming Manning's attention, "that were you to be pressed to repay the interest on those loans, let alone the loans themselves, prior to any windfall, you would be run aground—which leaves you with a very real motive to seek to remove Lady Congreve."

"Further to that," Gabriel continued, "we've confirmed that certain parties in the city"—he listed the names; as each was spoken, Manning's face paled a touch more— "now hold notes of hand from you. Each and every one is growing anxious for repayment. However, what you failed to mention when you borrowed from each was that you were simultaneously borrowing from the others." Gabriel shook his head. "Your creditors are not at all happy with you, Manning."

"Indeed," Rafe said, "you might say they're baying for your blood." He tilted his head, his gaze on Manning's now wide and fearful eyes. "Or they would be, except . . ."

To say that Manning was close to panic would be an understatement. He gripped the edge of his desk, in a strangled voice asked, "Except for what?"

"Except for me." The words, in Roscoe's deep voice, floated past Rafe's shoulder.

Manning focused on Roscoe. Frowned. "I don't believe I know you."

From the corner of his eye, Rafe watched Roscoe uncross his long legs and gracefully stand. Roscoe was over six feet tall and, like Wolverstone, exuded a pronounced predatory aura.

"No. You don't." Roscoe walked forward to stand between Gabriel's and Rafe's chairs. "All you need to know is that I now hold all your loans, all your notes of hand."

Manning's eyes grew round. His jaw went slack. "All?"

From beneath hooded lids, Roscoe watched him. "You, Manning, are a minnow swimming in a pool of sharks. You've been splashing in the pool, stirring up mud—the sort of mud that brings me looking, and the sharks don't like that. They'd much rather I stayed focused on my own concerns and didn't look too closely at theirs.

"So." Reaching into his coat pocket, Roscoe drew out a sheaf of papers. He fanned them out, showing Manning, who looked, and lost the last of his color. "I now hold these, but I haven't yet paid for them. If I hand them back to their present owners and tell them what I know of your finances, they'll tear you to shreds. As you know, given the nature of these gentlemen, I am not speaking figuratively."

Manning wasn't stupid. Terrified to his toes, but not stupid. He raised his eyes to Roscoe's. "What do I have to do?"

Roscoe smiled, a chilling sight. "To make this nightmare go away you need to do two things. One—make all your shares in Argyle Investments over to me. And two—retire from the city and never let me hear of you dabbling in investments again."

Manning paused. "If I make over the shares, you'll redeem the notes of hand, the loans?"

Roscoe nodded. "I will." He tipped his head at Gabriel and Rafe. "These two gentlemen can bear witness to my word."

Both nodded.

Manning noted their certainty, then looked up at Roscoe. "As for the second stipulation, I—"

"Let me be frank." Roscoe spoke over him. "I don't like having shady characters like you operating in the same market I do. You may be well born, but you give us all a bad name. Removing you permanently would be no great difficulty—many in the city expect me to effect your disappearance, one way or another, now that I know you've been muddying our waters. I can't be seen to be weak, after all—so one way or another, you will go." Roscoe's thin-lipped smile was the epitome of deadly. "I'm merely being kind enough to allow you to choose the manner in which you disappear."

The trick in uttering threats, Rafe knew, was to believe in them yourself. In Roscoe's case, there was absolutely no doubt that he meant every word.

Manning was outgunned, outclassed. Never taking his eyes from Roscoe's hooded ones, he nodded. "I'll have my secretary draw up the necessary papers."

Roscoe smiled approvingly. "Excellent." He looked at Rafe, then Gabriel. "I believe I can handle matters from this point, gentlemen." He glanced at Manning as Rafe and Gabriel rose. "And I believe you may inform Lady Congreve that Manning here has lost all interest in her continuing health, in light of concerns over his own. Is that correct, Manning?"

"Yes. I mean . . ." Manning dragged in a breath. "I never had any interest in her ladyship's health, and I certainly have none now."

Rafe smiled. "Excellent. I'm sure she'll be delighted to hear that." With a nod to Roscoe, he headed for the door.

Gabriel followed him out of the room, down the stairs, and out of the front door. He halted on the pavement and held out his hand to Rafe. "An excellent outcome all around. I'd heard whispers that Roscoe dabbled in some non-profit-making enterprises, but for all his obvious presence, the man prizes his privacy. Still, you can tell Lady Congreve that Argyle Investments have a new shareholder and a very able protector."

Shaking his hand, Rafe nodded. "Thank you for your help."

Gabriel smiled. "That's what old friends are for."

They grinned, exchanged salutes, then Rafe headed for the carriage while Gabriel strode off in the opposite direction.

Loretta leaned forward as Rafe opened the carriage door and climbed in. "Well? How did it go? What happened?"

Still grinning, Rafe closed the door, dropped onto the seat beside her, pulled her to him and kissed her soundly.

Then he told her all that had happened, ending with the need to send an express letter to Esme in Bingen informing her that it was safe to come home.

"Thank goodness." Loretta leaned against his shoulder, comfortable within the circle of his arms. "She'll be home in a month or so, in good time for our wedding." She met Rafe's eyes. "I wouldn't have wanted to get married without her."

Rafe laughed. "I wouldn't dare."

The carriage turned into Mayfair. He glanced down, and saw a pensive expression on Loretta's face. "What is it?"

She looked up, then smiled. "I was just imagining—trying to imagine—the next meeting of the board of Argyle Investments. What do you think will happen when Esme and Roscoe meet?"

Rafe thought, then said, "I think they'll get on famously."

Loretta nodded. "Esme has little respect for rules. I rather think Roscoe's the same."

Rafe thought of Roscoe, of Esme, and of them both together. He grinned. "I suspect it's the other investors in Argyle who are in for a disconcerting time."

Watch for
the next sweeping
historical romance
from #1 New York Times
bestselling author

STEPHANIE LAURENS

Coming April 2013
From

Avon Books